Lilac City

the end of innocence

KEN BAYSINGER

Lilac City

the end of innocence

Lilac City the end of innocence

ISBN 979-8-218-45714-3

Copyright © 2024 by Ken Baysinger. All Rights Reserved

No part of this publication may be reproduced, stored in a retrieval system or transmitted in any way by any means, electronic, mechanical, photocopy, recording, or otherwise, without the prior permission of the author, except as provided by USA copyright law.

This is a work of fiction. Unless otherwise indicated, all the names, characters, businesses, places, events and incidents in this book are either the product of the author's imagination or used in a fictitious manner. Any resemblance to actual persons, living or dead, or actual events is purely coincidental. Opinions expressed by the author or the characters are not necessarily those of the publisher.

Published by Ken Baysinger

June 2024

Book design copyright © 2024 by Ken Baysinger. All rights reserved.

Cover design copyright © 2024 by Ken Baysinger. All rights reserved.

Cover Images:
Brick Wall Background, *Dmitrich, iStock*
Neon Skyline of Spokane, *Greens87, iStock*

Published in the United States of America

Lilac City
the end of innocence

A Word from the Author

This novel is fiction, intended purely for the entertainment of readers. Connie Pratt, his family members, friends, and associates are all fictious, as are the activities attributed to all of the fictional characters. The "Draper Case" is entirely fictitious, as are the characters associated with it.

However, in creating this novel, I have made use of real events in order to give accurate historical context to my fiction. Specifically, I have included discussions of well-known murder cases in the Pacific Northwest, including the Candy Rogers murder in Spokane, the Peyton-Allan murders in Portland, and the Bogle-Kalitzke murders in Great Falls, as well as the murders known to have been committed by convicted serial killers Hugh Bion Morse and Edward Wayne Edwards.

All of these cases are presented as accurately as possible and are not fictionalized in any way. I lived in Spokane at the time of the Candy Rogers abduction, rape, and murder. Like most of us of that era, I was deeply affected by the tragedy.

Years later, I was a student at Washington State University at the time of the trials in the Peyton-Allan case, and I have some strong opinions about it, which I have attributed to my fictitious character, Connie Pratt.

The Crown Victoria case is loosely based on a real case in Spokane, but all of the names used are fictitious. The Skateland case is based on the real-life arson fire at Cloud's Valley Skateland, but again, all of the names used are fictitious, though I do believe that police at the time knew who set the fire, as did a number of students at Central Valley High School.

I have made extensive use of the on-line archives of the Spokane Daily Chronicle and the Spokesman-Review. With the exception of references to my fictitious Draper case, all of the headlines and articles quoted are real. I do this to portray the events covered, exactly as they were seen at the time.

I have the highest respect for the families of the real crime victims named here, and dedicate this novel to the memories of their lost loved ones.

Ken Baysinger

Prologue

Hallucinations

January 20, 1962

On my hands and knees, I clawed my way through the snowdrift, up the embankment toward the road. It was only ten feet, but it seemed insurmountable. I had to rest. I was bone-weary and so, so cold!

Random thoughts swirled through my mind. The snow had stopped falling, and the nearly full moon had broken through the clouds, illuminating the snow-covered roadway. I pushed myself to my knees and struggled to my feet. *What the hell was I doing here?* I forced my brain to focus.

Oh yeah. I had to get it done. Everyone was depending on me. Back up on the road, I looked around. The only tracks in the snow were my own. Of course. Who else would be out here? *I had to get to the forward radar installation.* My tracks came from the left, so I turned right and shuffled forward.

When I exhaled, the moisture in my breath froze into tiny ice crystals that sparkled in the moonlight, and when I inhaled, the sub-zero air would catch in my throat and lungs, forcing me to breathe in short gasps. I clutched the musty old quilt more tightly around my throat. *Why didn't I have proper winter gear? It was like Bastogne, where our guys had been sent into a winter fight without adequate cold weather gear. Now, six years later, it was the same damn thing, all over again.*

The KORCOMS had warm quilted parkas, but all I had was a blanket that smelled like rat piss. None of that mattered. I still had to get to the forward radar station. I was the only guy in Korea who could calibrate the transmitter, and we needed the radar to warn us of incoming enemy planes. I strained to stay focused on the mission, but it was increasingly difficult to think clearly.

My hands and feet were numb, and I drifted off to sleep. The nearby explosion of a mortar round jarred me awake, and I scrambled forward on my hands and knees looking for a shell crater where I could take cover. I was losing coordination, and crawling was increasingly difficult.

Major Thomas said, "Pratt, I don't care what it takes. You *have to* get that radar fixed, otherwise those damned MiGs will tear us all to pieces."

"Yes Sir! I'll take care of it!"

So, there I was. I became aware of the utter silence. Had the war stopped, or had the soundwaves frozen? Could soundwaves freeze? I forced myself to keep crawling. It would be warm in the radar shack. *Why was I crawling? I should be running—anything to get out of this cold!*

I struggled unsteadily to my frozen feet and tried to run, immediately crashing back into the snow. Gasping to catch my breath, I tried again. *Start forward. Build up momentum before trying to run.* I pushed my right foot forward through the snow. Then the left.

I woke up. I didn't even know I'd fallen asleep. My mind was playing tricks on me. I was still on my feet, but what was I doing? It hurt to breathe. Everything glittered in the frozen moonlight, even the frost that had accumulated on my eyelashes. I tried to brush it away, but my glove felt like a cheese grater against my face.

The road was gone, and I was crawling through a sparse forest of stunted pine trees. It was a perfect place for an ambush. I pushed myself into a sitting position and looked around. The white parkas of the KORCOMS blended in so well that they looked like snowdrifts. They were all around, lying perfectly still. But apparently, they hadn't seen me.

The stinking old quilt had once been white, and maybe that's what kept the enemy from seeing me. *What's good for them is good for me.* But I still had to fix the radar. I had to keep moving. I had to find the radar shack. I slithered through the snow on my belly.

Time passed. I don't know how much. The moon was gone, and the only light came from a blanket of stars overhead. It seemed colder without the moon. *Does moonlight carry heat?* I looked for Polaris, tracing the imaginary line from the outer rim of the big dipper to the tip of the handle on the little dipper—the North Star.

I was going north, toward our forward lines, to the forward-most radar outpost. Follow the North Star, and I'd find it…

…unless I'd already passed it, in which case I was somewhere behind enemy lines, and was colossally screwed. That would explain why the KORCOMS were all sleeping. But I couldn't believe I'd passed the radar station. Surely, I'd have seen the antenna array.

There was something in the distance, off to my right—a dark shape blocking the starlight. I had to rest. My arms and legs ached from the cold and fatigue. Anything that wasn't numb hurt. I dragged myself toward the dark shape. I smelled wood smoke, and it reminded me of summer evenings at Liberty Lake and campfires in the picnic area.

All I wanted was to go home—home to the Lilac City…

Chapter One

Spokane

March 20, 1960

The morning paper told the whole sad story, though it is unlikely that anybody who cared didn't already know that Central Valley had lost the state high school basketball championship game. And they didn't just lose it. They were blown out of the arena. It was an inglorious end to a season that had held such promise.

The Bears had steamrolled through the season with a 17-2 record, and going into the sixteen-team double-elimination state tournament, sportswriters ranked them second only to the 16–1 Ballard Beavers from Seattle. Central Valley had not "gone to state" since 1949, and had *never* made it into the final round of play. In their six prior tournament appearances, they had accumulated a grand total of just two wins. But the Central Valley Bears of 1960 would change all that.

The opening round game, on March 16 pitted Central Valley against the 14-3 Roosevelt "Teds," in a game that, on paper, looked like a cake-walk. The Bears led for most of the night, but never really found their rhythm, hitting only fifteen field goals in the entire game. So, with 3:09 left on the game clock, Roosevelt took its first lead of the game, at 43-41, and when the clock ran out, the game was tied at 48. In overtime, Roosevelt's over-aggressive defense caught up to them, and seven free-throws saved the game for the Bears. Some fingernails were chewed down to the first knuckle.

In the second round, Central Valley looked sluggish when they took the floor against the 15-5 Franklin-Pierce Cardinals from Tacoma. Despite shooting 50% from the floor, the Bears never managed to close the door on the Cardinals, who closed to within 5 points several times. Once again, free-throws made the difference for the Bears, who took the win with a final score of 49-44.

This put Central Valley up against the one team that was favored to beat them, the Ballard Beavers, on March 18. This time, the Bears found their game. Trailing 8-7 at the end of the first quarter, they surged to a 23-17 halftime lead, and were never threatened in the second half. The final score was 54-43.

The Renton Indians were the only other team that was undefeated in the tournament, and would face Central Valley in the Saturday night state championship game. Renton's 6' 4" forward Lowell Scott took the opening tip straight to the basket. Central Valley's star forward, 6' 2" Larry Sloan came right back up the court and tied the game at 2. That was the last time the Bears were in the game. Dominated by the Indian's front line with their 6' 8" center, Clint Peoples, Renton controlled the game on both ends of the court, with a final score of 59-41.

In accepting the second-place trophy, Central Valley head coach Ray Thacker said, "From where I was sitting, it looked like the best team won. If you have to lose, it might as well be to the greatest."

****

My life does not revolve around high school sports. Sure, I never lost my emotional attachment to my alma mater, but it is hardly a focal point of my life. I have bigger fish to fry, like making a living and looking to the future. Still, when Central Valley played for the state championship in 1960, I was among the fans cheering them on, just as I had been eleven years earlier, when the Bears last made an appearance in the state tournament.

Back in 1949, I was in my senior year at Central Valley, and most of the players on that team were my friends. I dearly wished I could've made the trip to Seattle for the tournament, but that just wasn't in the cards. Even if I could've afforded it, I couldn't go, because I had an after-school job, and the boss wouldn't let me have the time off. The boss was my old man. He owned Pratt's Radio and Electronics on Sprague Avenue at Robie Road.

"Someday you're gonna own this place, and then you'll learn what's important," he told me. "And it isn't basketball."

"Taking a couple of days off won't destroy my future," I countered.

"No, but the *idea* that a basketball game is more important than your job most certainly *will*."

"Come on, Dad. It's just a one-time thing!"

He ignored my plea and pointed at a Stromberg-Carlson multi-band console radio that had just been brought in for repair.

"Mrs. Harder says that when she switches it on, it just makes a big loud buzz. What do think might cause that?" The discussion of going to Seattle was over.

"Uh, maybe a bad filter capacitor in the power supply?" I speculated.

"Then you know what to do about it," he said.

I turned the radio around and removed the back. The chassis was mounted on a wooden shelf in the upper quarter of the maple veneer cabinet, with a pull-out phonograph drawer and a massive twelve-inch hi-fi speaker mounted below. It clearly was a top-of-the-line unit. I pulled-off the knobs and removed the screws holding the chassis in place and slid it out of the cabinet.

At the workbench, I identified the suspect component. That was easy, since the power supply filter would always be the largest capacitor in the circuit. I touched a ground wire to it to short out any residual charge that it might be carrying, but didn't get so much as a spark—confirmation of my diagnosis. I unsoldered the capacitor and used an ohmmeter to confirm that the internal insulation had failed and the capacitor was shorted out.

Ten minutes later, I reinstalled the chassis into its cabinet and switched on the radio. After thirty seconds, the rich sound of a big band broadcast from New York City proved that the repair was successful.

"What are you putting on the invoice, Connie?" Dad asked.

"Seventy-nine cents for the capacitor, plus a quarter-hour labor," I said.

"Are you sure about that?"

"Well, yeah. That's what it took to fix it," I said.

"So, $3.29 total," he said.

I nodded, still not seeing where he was going with this.

"You think that'll keep us in business?"

"Not all by itself, but…"

"What do you figure a radio like that cost?"

"I don't know. Maybe around a hundred twenty bucks?"

He nodded. "What do you think it's worth to Mrs. Harder to hear it working again?"

"Uh, I don't know."

"You think it might be worth ten dollars to her?"

"Yeah, probably. But it only took ten minutes to fix it."

"Sure. It was an easy fix. But what *made* it easy?"

"Well, I knew what causes a radio to buzz like that."

"So, it was your knowledge that made it an easy fix."

I nodded.

"Your knowledge has value, doesn't it? Isn't that how you earn your pay?

"Yeah, I guess …

"Here's the deal. A lot of times, the job won't be that easy. Suppose you had to spend two hours discovering an open resistor somewhere in the circuit that *caused* that capacitor to fail, maybe taking along the rectifier tube?"

"Well, then the bill would probably come to more like $35."

"Right. Now suppose that same thing happened to an ordinary Sylvania clock-radio? How much would you charge for that?"

"I guess it'd be the same amount."

"Now, who would pay $35 to repair a radio that he can replace with a new one for $29.95?"

I shrugged stupidly.

"Think about it, Connie. Lots of times, you won't be able to bill for what it actually cost to make the repair. The most you can expect a customer to pay for repairing that Sylvania is maybe fifteen bucks. You have to make that up somewhere else—somewhere where people will gladly pay more, because the end result is worth more."

"So, Mrs. Harder ends up paying for the repair on someone else's clock-radio?"

"You can't look at it that way. Her repair job is worth more, because her radio is worth more. And that's how we stay in business.

"Okay, but…

"And before you go too far down the path, thinking Mrs. Harder is getting cheated, ask yourself what it is worth to *her* for us to be in business. If we're not here, she can't get her radio fixed—not at any price. That leaves her with just two choices: buy a new radio, or go without. Lesson learned?"

So, Mrs. Harder got her radio fixed, we stayed in business, and I didn't go to Seattle in 1949. After graduation, I went to work full-time in the family business. Except for an extended trip to Korea a couple of years later, I've worked there ever since.

* * * * * *

My name is Constantine Roman Pratt. To my knowledge, I did nothing to deserve that. Mom was a Catholic, and was enthralled with Roman Emperor Constantine, who was the first emperor to convert to Christianity. So, she insisted on honoring him by bestowing his name on me, and for that, I was subjected to perpetual ridicule for most of the first eighteen years of my life. The family called me Connie.

How many times did I hear other kids in school taunt me, "*Connie*—isn't that a *girl's* name?"

"It's short for Constantine. He was a great…"

"Hey, *Connie*, wasn't constipation named after that guy—because he was full of shit?"

"Yeah, just like you."

"Hey, *Connie*, are you a girly boy, or what?"

"Or what's that up your *ass*, homo?" I always had a snappy comeback.

It was during my early teen years that I made a serious attempt to get people to call me *Stan*, which seemed like a more acceptable diminutive form of Constantine than *Connie*. For all of my sixth, seventh and eighth grades, I wrote Stan on all of my school work and corrected everyone who called me Connie. But I just couldn't make it stick, so I reconciled myself to being called by a girl's name for the rest of my life.

Ultimately, I was saved by a hockey player named Connie Madigan, who played for the Spokane Spokes. Nobody teased *him* about having a girl's name—at least nobody who was interested in keeping his teeth. By then, I was almost 27 years old, had spent two years in Korea, inherited my old man's TV shop, and become a licensed private detective.

While electronics had been my life, I'd always been interested in criminal behavior, believing that by having a thorough knowledge of why and how crimes are committed, I'd be able to interpret crime scene evidence and get closer to identifying the criminal. People have asked why, in view of my interest in criminal investigation, didn't I go to the police academy and become a *real* cop. The answer to the question is the same as the reason I didn't go to the basketball tournament back in 1949: I had to make a living.

A couple of months after the ceasefire agreement in Korea, I was released from active duty at the Fort Lewis processing center. The army gave me a bus ride to the train station in Tacoma, where I got a ticket for the late-night train to Spokane. I arrived at the Northern Pacific depot in the morning.

Still in uniform, with my G.I. bag on my shoulder, I put out my thumb and hitched a ride out Sprague Avenue to the valley—home. I paused on the sidewalk to look at the three new television sets that were turned-on in the front window. One set was tuned into some kind of puppet show for children, and the other two had a man selling kitchen cookware, the way hawkers try to sell everything from knife-sharpeners to cure-all tonics at county fairs, trade shows, and carnivals.

Disinterested, unshaven and feeling grimy, I turned and backed through the door into our store, dragging my bag in behind me. And that's when I met Dale.

"May I help you find something?" asked a cheerful, but childlike voice.

"Well, no. Actually, this is…"

I turned and found myself looking at the prettiest girl I'd ever seen, and I was completely unnerved by her presence. I forgot what I was trying to say and left the sentence unfinished. But her expectant expression demanded that I say something.

"…uh, I'm Connie. Connie Pratt."

Her eyes widened and she exclaimed, "*Oh!* We didn't expect you until this afternoon. I'm Dale—Jeffries. I've heard so much about you, I feel like I already know you."

I managed to say, "My folks mentioned in letters to me that they'd hired you, but I think they left out some of the details."

She cocked her head and smiled. "Welcome home."

My second shock that morning was when the old man came out from the back room. I was stunned to see how his health had deteriorated. I had long observed his chain smoking, insomnia, and obsessive worrying, but somehow, I never envisioned the consequences. He'd always been there, so it seemed like he always would be. Suddenly it didn't look that way.

"Connie, you're home early!" Mom exclaimed as she came down the stairs from our apartment.

She rushed over and wrapped me up in a bear hug.

"We were going to put up decorations and have a proper welcome-home party!"

"When I called last night, I told you I'd be here this morning," I said.

"Oh. We thought you meant you'd get *on* the train in the morning," Mom said.

Our method of communicating without racking up charges for long-distance phone calls had failed us. I'd called the long-distance operator from a phone booth in the Tacoma train station and placed a person-to-person long-distance call to myself, in Spokane.

When Mom answered the phone, the operator said, "I have a person-to-person call for Connie Pratt."

Mom said, "Connie Pratt is not here right now."

The operator then asked me, "Would you like to speak with anyone else at this number?"

I said, "No, I'll just call again tomorrow morning."

I hung up the phone and retrieved my nickel from the coin return. Mom knew I was on my way home, and I'd just told her that I'd be home in the morning to accept a long-distance phone call, in case one came in. But somehow, she'd interpreted it differently.

In the end, it worked out better this way, because it gave me time to shave and shower before the crowd of relatives and friends showed-up for the afternoon welcome-home party, for which Mom insisted that I wear my uniform and come in the front door at a pre-determined time, as if I'd just gotten home. No one noticed that I had no luggage.

People popped out of hiding, yelling "Surprise" and "Welcome home." I talked with so many people in the next two hours that I never had time to *really* talk with any of them. And throughout all of it, I had to compete with the television sets, which attracted people's attention like nothing I'd ever seen, except possibly the strippers in the bars in Seoul. They could disrupt any quiet conversation, and so could television. Was this *really* our future?

And then there was Dale Jeffries. Sure, she was just a *kid*—probably four or five years younger than me. Actually, it was only three, but… But damn! She sure was cute! I tried to talk with her, but it seemed like every time I said a word, someone else would butt-in and divert the conversation—usually to questions about how it had been in Korea, which was about the *last* thing I wanted to talk about.

But mostly, I was troubled by the old man's coughing fits and general appearance.

* * * * * * *

The old man had been a pioneer in the business that he'd spent his entire adult life building, though he never saw it that way. Straight out of high school, he'd joined the army in a spasm of patriotism, with every intention of going to France to fight the Huns. Instead, he was assigned to signalman's school, where he learned how to send and receive Morse code over the Marconi wireless telegraph sets. During this time, the army was also experimenting with radio transmission of voice, and Corporal Desmond Pratt began a lifelong obsession with radio.

When released from the army, he returned to Spokane valley and tried to find a way to make a living in radio. He ran across a small-time government surplus broker who had access to warehouses full of new and used equipment of all kinds, including electronics, and Dad wrangled himself into a job as salesman.

After a couple of years, he had a corner on the retail market for electrical components in Spokane, and he decided to go into business for himself. He quit his job and soon became his former employer's best customer.

It was about then that he met Mrs. Griffith, who owned the building that still bears her name, on East Sprague in the little town of Opportunity in Spokane valley. Sprague Avenue was, until the recent construction of Interstate 90, the main thoroughfare from downtown Spokane, through Opportunity and all the way to the Idaho state line. The two-story brick "Griffith Building" sits on the corner of Sprague Avenue and Robie Road, with retail space on the ground floor and three residential apartments upstairs, accessible by an outside stairway on the back of the building.

The old man rented a two-room upstairs apartment and a ground floor storefront, and in that little shop, he built radio receivers and sold parts to other radio enthusiasts. By 1925, when Spokane got its first radio station, radio broadcasts were becoming the earliest form of mass entertainment.

Since he was well established in the radio business, the old man was able to secure dealership contracts with Emerson, Crosley, RCA, and Atwater-Kent for retail sale of their products. His business grew, even after the stock market crashed, so when the sewing machine shop next door went out of business, the old man took over their lease and expanded into that space.

One day, a teenage girl came into the store with a couple of friends to listen to a live broadcast from the Palmer House in Chicago. It was common for people to come in just to hear this technological wonder, and the old man let them stay as long as they wished. He even provided some comfortable chairs for them, figuring that eventually every one of them would buy a radio from him.

But the girl with the dark eyes and black hair had bowled him over. And that went both ways. Aletta was just seventeen when they got married, in 1930. I was born exactly nine months later. It was right around this time, as the country slipped into the

Great Depression, that Mrs. Griffith told my parents that she was going to have to sell the building under threat of foreclosure by her bank.

That left my old man with a level of uncertainty that his system couldn't tolerate. He agonized over all of the ways he could be put out of business and evicted from the apartment if the building was taken over by an uncaring bank. It seemed to him like the best way to prevent that from happening was to buy the building.

Not that our family had any money to speak of. But $16,000 in war bonds that represented the life-savings of my grandparents, who'd died in the great influenza epidemic, was enough to buy the building. And to Desmond, it was as much an act of compassion as an investment. Mrs. Griffith, who would have been left destitute and homeless by a foreclosure, was the widow of a soldier who had died in the Great War, and that meant a lot to my old man. Perhaps because he'd never personally experienced combat during his time in the army, he had unlimited admiration and respect for those who did—especially those who had died.

After buying the place, he swapped our tiny apartment in the rear of the building for Mrs. Griffith's larger one in the front, and let her live there rent-free until her death in 1953. For my entire life, except for my two years in the army, I'd lived and worked in that old brick building, which despite multiple renovations, still looks largely as it had in 1905 when the Griffith brothers built it.

* * * * * * *

I got to be pretty good at diagnosing problems with radios and television sets. The old man made sure of that. I built my first radio when I was in fifth grade, using plans from a *Popular Mechanics* magazine and parts salvaged from scrapped radios that were beyond repair. I loved listening to news reports, radio dramas, and play-by-play coverage of baseball games. At night, when radio signals travel greater distances, I'd delicately work the dial to pull-in stations from as far away as Salt Lake City, Denver, San Francisco, and occasionally even Chicago.

Right around the time the Second World War ended, I started to work for the old man, and by then I knew the function of every part in a radio receiver. From the time I learned how to talk, he'd been teaching me about electricity and electronics. When other kids were learning the alphabet, I was learning how to read the color-codes on resistors. I knew about oscillators, rectifiers, amplifiers, and transformers before I was eight years old.

One day in 1946, a Railway Express Agency truck stopped in front of the shop and unloaded a large wooden crate shipped from Chicago. The old man carefully pried the crate open with a claw hammer and crowbar to reveal a second-hand television receiver given to him by the west coast representative for RCA—the Radio Corporation of America.

It was an RCA console built in 1939, which had gone unused since April of 1942, when the government suspended all television broadcasting for the duration of the war. At that time, only about 5,000 television receivers were in use in the whole country, and this was one of them. By the time broadcasting was resumed after the war, the old RCA Model TRK-9 was both outdated in appearance and obsolete in function.

The numeral nine in the model number referred to the diameter of the cathode ray tube—or picture tube, as most people call it. The image was projected on the phosphorous-coated inner surface of the viewing screen by a cathode ray emitted from an electron gun at the back of the tube. So, by the time you allow for the thickness of the glass envelope, the actual image size on the nine-inch tube is barely eight inches.

Our TRK-9 was as big as Mrs. Griffith's old fashioned ice chest, and had a cyclops-like screen centered on the front, near the top. Below the television screen was a multi-band AM radio receiver that operated independently from the television set. The art deco hardwood cabinet prominently identified it as an artifact from the 1930s.

But it worked. The first thing the old man did was plug it in and switch it on. As the tubes warmed up, the screen lit-up in a blizzard-like portrayal of nothing, and from the speaker came the roaring sound of random static.

"This is the future," the old man proclaimed. Twenty-five years from now, everyone will have one of these in their living room."

I asked the obvious question, "Is that all it does?"

I was having a difficult time understanding why anyone would want the thing.

"Well, there are no broadcasting stations around here," he said. "But just you wait. Spokane will get a television station soon enough—maybe even two! Then you'll see. It'll be just like watching a movie in the theater."

Underwhelmed as I was, I could only nod.

"Listen, Connie, the television sets they're building now have twelve and even fifteen-inch pictures. There are television stations in all of the big cities back east—and out west too, in Los Angeles and San Francisco. You know, they're even building a nation-wide coaxial cable network to carry the signal from the studios in New York and Los Angeles to stations all over the country! Television will be one of the biggest consumer products in the economy—second only to the automobile."

"When is Spokane going to get a television station?" I asked.

"Maybe in a year or two. But before that happens, we—you and I—need to get inside this thing and figure out what's in there and how it works. We'll need to know everything about it before someone brings one in for us to fix."

So, after watching the electronic snowstorm for half an hour, we lifted the beast onto a four-wheeled dolly and rolled it into the back room. We pulled off the back, and found schematic wiring diagrams in a brown envelope glued to the inside of the cabinet. The old man unfolded the television schematic and spread it on the bench. He pulled up a stool and started studying the symbols and lines.

I did the same with the schematic for the radio portion of the unit, and I found it to be a high-quality unit, but unremarkable in every other respect. It was a conventional super-heterodyne AM receiver, not much different from a hundred others I'd fooled with in the shop.

Not long after that, the old man's crony from RCA brought in something he called "a monoscope camera," which was housed in a ventilated metal cabinet the size of a large breadbox. When connected to the antenna terminals on our TV set, it acted like a television station, producing a channel-three signal. For the first time, we were able to see an actual image on our TV screen and hear a one-kilocycle audio tone from the speaker. We referred to the device as a "test-pattern generator."

The test-pattern let us experiment with the various adjustments that we could make in the stability, brightness, contrast, size, position, and shape of the image on the screen. But the entertainment value of that wore off pretty quickly, even when the old man would screw-up all of the adjustments, and then challenge me to bring back the picture. And other times, he'd sabotage the circuitry and leave me to figure out what was wrong.

Five years later, Spokane still didn't have a television station, but I'd learned how that old TV set worked, and what purpose was served by every component in it. After I was drafted, while I was in basic training, the army determined that I was some kind of electronic whiz, and that led to my assignment as a radar specialist, operating and maintaining the radar sets used to track the North Korean and Chinese MiG aircraft that swarmed the skies. A radar screen was a cathode-ray tube, and it worked just like television. So, I went to war armed with a voltmeter and oscilloscope instead of hand grenades and a rifle.

I'd been in Korea for nearly a year when the old man wrote to say that Spokane finally had its own television station—and another would be transmitting before the end of the year. He said our old set worked fine, despite its age and all that we'd done to it over the years.

Chapter Two

Back Home from the War

After Mom's big welcome-home party, and after a good night's sleep in my own bed, I started seriously thinking about what lay ahead. It had always been assumed that I would pick up my life as it had been the day I reported for the draft. The only life I'd ever had involved working in the old man's radio shop and living in the family apartment upstairs. As to whether or not that was what I wanted, that was a question never asked—not by anyone else, and certainly not by me.

Rolled up in that presumption of sameness was the belief that everything else would remain unchanged when I returned from Korea. But in reality, nearly everything had changed. The old man was dying. It didn't take a doctor to see that. And in a lot of ways, as he went, so went the business that he created with all of his energy and initiative. The business was his life, and he was the life of the business. How could it survive without him?

There was only one answer to that question. If the business was going to survive, I'd have to become what the old man had always been. In effect, I'd have to become Pratt Radio and Electronics, and it was not a matter of choice.

That is what was on my mind when we sat down for breakfast that morning. It was the middle of the week, but Mom had prepared a Sunday breakfast for us, with eggs, bacon, and pancakes. The conversation was filled with words of gratitude that we were back together again, and would remain so forever. So, when the old man and I walked downstairs into the shop that morning, my future had already been decided—not by me, but by unalterable circumstances.

If I closed my eyes, I could imagine that nothing had changed. The sounds were the same. A radio was playing somewhere. Cars passed by on Sprague Avenue. Our old cash register clicked and clattered with each transaction, its bell ringing whenever the cash drawer opened. And the familiar smells were still there: the freshly waxed floor, the aroma of new hardwood cabinets, the smell of solder smoke, mixed occasionally with the smell of ozone from electrical arcing in a radio that needed repair. It was all comfortably familiar.

But, with eyes open, *everything* had changed. No longer was the display floor dominated by large console radios. Only one remained. The rest of the store was dominated by television. There were tabletop models that were priced as low as $160, console models priced up to twice or even three-times as much, and a seventeen-inch television set with a hi-fi three-speed phonograph, and five-band radio, all built into a wide, credenza style cabinet for $725.

Mom still did the bookkeeping and paid the bills, but she had been largely replaced on the retail floor by Dale—the girl with a boy's name. The irony of that had not escaped me. Had other kids teased her about her name, the way they'd teased me? And that uniquely shared anomaly in our lives did nothing to explain how her presence in the room stirred up in me an unsettling feeling of something left unfinished—a nervous uncertainty that left me feeling off-balance.

An hour later that first morning, when Dale arrived in the shop, she said, "Good morning, Connie. I almost didn't recognize you without your uniform,"

I said, "And I hope I never have to wear it again."

Realizing how negative that sounded, I added, "I mean, it's great to be a civilian again."

I felt the need to say more, but for some reason, nothing came to mind, so I awkwardly excused myself and retreated to the back room, where the old man was starting work on a Silvertone console that featured an AM radio, a 78-rpm phonograph, and a wire recorder. That was a novelty. You could actually record audio—from a microphone, the radio, or the phonograph—on a spool of thread-like magnetic wire. Wire recording had been around for years, mostly used in office dictation, but the Silvertone was designed specifically for home entertainment. It was an anachronism now, after the invention of tape recorders that used acetate magnetic tape instead of wire, but a few of these units were still around.

One was sitting at the back of a drawer on our test bench. It was a miniature wire recorder that had been abandoned by a customer who decided that the repair cost was higher than the value of the device. The big problem with repairing the device was that it was Russian-made, and the electronic components bore none of the familiar markings or color-coding to indicate what they were.

The customer who had brought it in told the old man that he was a former OSS officer, and had taken the device from a Soviet spy after his capture in Washington DC. These concealed wire recorders were the origin of the expression, "wearing a wire." I put it in the drawer, thinking that someday I would try to fix it. But instead, I simply forgot about it.

So, while the old man worked on the Silvertone console, I looked at the repair tags on several radios that were in for repair. Actually, I'd hoped to find a TV set in the shop, but since television in Spokane had been around for barely a year, most sets in use were nearly new.

For conversation's sake, I asked, "When do you think people will start needing repairs on their television sets?"

The old man said, "I'd guess that six months to a year from now, tubes will start getting weak, and people will need repairs. I had one in here last month. Actually, I've had several this year. All were brought in by people who moved here from other cities, where TV stations have been on the air for a few years already."

I quietly closed the door to the showroom and said, "For now, it looks like there isn't much to do here. Do we really need to have Dale working here, now that I'm back?"

It pained me to ask the question, because letting her go was about the *last* thing I wanted to do. What I *really* wanted was to get to know her, but from a business standpoint, she looked like extra overhead. The old man's answer to my question surprised me.

"Yes," he said firmly, "we *do* need her working here. Look at me, Connie. Can't you see what's happening? I'm not going to be here forever. You need to be thinking ahead. I needed help when you were gone, and you're going to need help when I'm gone."

"Dad, I just…" Words failed me.

But he continued, "And Dale Jeffries is family. She stays until *she* decides otherwise."

"Family?" I asked.

"We're the nearest thing she has to a family. If we let her go, she has nobody."

"I didn't know that. Mom's letters said that you'd hired her, but didn't say much else about her."

"Dale came in looking for an after-school job. She had a resumé all typed-up, showing that her work experience consisted of babysitting and a little bit of housekeeping. I had already reached the conclusion that I needed some help in the store, but I wasn't convinced that Dale could do the job.

"Her resumé listed some personal references, so after she left, I made a couple of calls and found out what Dale hadn't told me. Just about the time you were reporting for the draft, when she was only 17 years old, Dale's grandmother in Illinois died unexpectedly. Her parents made arrangements to fly to Chicago for the funeral, leaving Dale with their neighbors, Norm and Carolyn Hanson.

"The Jeffries caught a flight from Spokane to Salt Lake City, where they connected with United Flight 610 for the remainder of the trip to Chicago. Flight 610 crashed into Crystal Mountain, 50 miles north of Denver. There were no survivors.

"Her mom's parents had been killed in London during the blitz, and her remaining grandfather had died about five years ago. Neither of Dale's parents had any siblings, so Dale was left with no family at all."

"So, what did she do?" I asked.

"The county wanted to put her into the foster home system, but Norm and Carolyn offered to let her live with them until she finished high school. They had three kids of their own, all under ten years old, and they could scarcely afford to take-in a teenage girl, but what else could they do?

"At the time of the crash, Dale had just finished her junior year. Her parents' estate went into probate, and nearly everything they had went to pay-off creditors. Dale ended up with her clothes and a couple of boxes filled with photo albums and family papers. She could see what a burden she was to the Hansons, and resolved to get a job and pay for her room and board.

"She came here because we are within walking distance of where the Hansons lived. Her options for employment were limited by how far she could walk, since she didn't have a driver's license and the family car had been repossessed."

"I had no idea," I said.

"I don't think she knows that I'm aware of all this, so it would be best for you to keep it to yourself."

"Is she still living with the Hanson family?"

"No, their house barely had room for their own kids, let alone someone else's. After graduation, she moved into a ten-dollar a week efficiency unit in an apartment house on Pines Road, up near Mission. By then, she'd scraped together enough money to buy a cheap car, so she wouldn't have to walk to work."

"She seems like a real go-getter," I said.

"That's putting it mildly. I hired her based entirely on her attitude, and I've never regretted it. She's a treasure. And you see it too. Don't think for a minute that I haven't noticed how you look at her."

I hadn't realized I'd been so obvious. I poked my face into the back of a big old radio to conceal my embarrassment.

"It looks like the audio output tube is bad," I said, a bit too loudly.

"You know what you really need to do?"

I braced myself for incoming love-life advice from the old man.

"You need to find a panel truck or van that you can convert into a mobile repair shop. Television sets are too big and heavy for people to bring here for repair. If you can get setup to do in-home service, you'll double your repair business."

Relieved that I wasn't getting a lecture, I lied, "I've been thinking the same thing. Do we have money to buy a van?"

"Maybe not a new one, but we can afford a pretty good used one."

"I'll start looking around. It'll take a few days to figure-out what things cost these days," I concluded.

Half an hour later, after replacing the audio output tube and making the radio work, and with nothing else to do in the shop, I went back out front.

"What was it like In Korea? I mean, being in the war, and all that," Dale asked.

I said, "I don't know much about what it was like being in the war. I never saw combat and never fired a rifle. I took care of electronic stuff—not so different from working here. But the food here is a lot better."

"Quite a few people thought it was going to turn into another world war," Dale said. "We had to do duck-and-cover drills in school, in case the Russians dropped an atom bomb."

Wanting to change the subject, I said, "You know, when I left, we didn't have television in the store. There weren't even any TV stations around."

"Yeah. That's how it was when I first started working for Mr. Pratt—I mean, your dad. Then, as soon as Channel 6 came on the air, we started putting TV sets in the front windows and on the display floor. People would stand outside and watch TV through the window. Some still do."

"I knew just about all there was to know about the radios we used to sell. But I'm going to have to learn about television—you know, things like what features one set has that another doesn't, or which one is better and why. Do you know all that stuff?"

"Probably not all of it, but quite a bit. Your dad taught me a lot. Your mom, too."

A man walked in the door, as if on cue, and looked quickly around the room. Dana started toward him, but before she could say anything, he approached me—man to man.

He said, "I've never had television, and I don't know anything about it. What can you tell me?"

I said, "I've been in Korea for the last two years. This is my first day back, and I still haven't even *watched* television. I think Miss Jeffries can tell you a lot more than I can."

I pointed toward Dale and saw the customer's expression, which said, *"She's just a kid. And a girl. What could she know?"*

Without waiting for him to put his thoughts into words, Dale said, "There are three main things to consider. Picture quality, reliability, and of course, price. As a rule, the better picture and overall reliability come at a higher price. But there is no universally right answer as to which is the best set for you. And there's no wrong answer either."

"Well, young lady, I'm not looking to buy the 'Cadillac' model right off. I think a lower-priced unit would be better—at least until I find out if I even like watching television."

"That sounds good. As you'd expect, the table-models will cost less than the consoles. And among them, the ones with metal cabinets usually cost less than the ones with crafted hardwood cabinets."

While she talked, Dale led the customer toward the side of the store where half a dozen table-model sets were on display. She stopped next to the first set and switched it on. It took about a full minute for the tubes to warm up and a picture to appear on the screen.

"The RCA 21T-207 is a high-quality unit in an affordable cabinet. RCA has been a pioneer in the development of television, and this is their lowest priced 21-inch set."

"How much is it?"

"It's $279.95. That includes the swivel base. The stand is $17.50."

"Hmm. What about these other ones?"

"Let's take a look at this Motorola. It's a 17-inch screen, and it's just $179.95. In fact, I have several other brands at the same price: Westinghouse, Crosley, Raytheon. All have 17-inch screens."

"What's your cheapest set?"

"I have a 17-inch Admiral at just $159.95."

"That's your lowest price?"

"It's our lowest price, but I can show you our best deal. It's a 21-inch Sylvania that normally goes for $289.95, but today it is just $199.95."

"Let's see what the picture looks like on that Admiral," the customer said.

I was pretty sure that he'd made up his mind, even before the tubes warmed up. He bought the Admiral, and I helped carry it out to the man's station wagon. When I went back inside, I asked Dale if the set was any good.

"It's okay. Actually, your dad says it's junk. For ten bucks more, he should've bought the Emerson—much better quality, and an all-wood cabinet."

"Okay. What can you tell me about the quality of the circuitry?" I asked.

"I simply repeat what your dad says about the different sets. If a customer really wants the details, I let *him* explain it. But different brands have different features. Sylvania has Halo Light, Zenith has Cine-beam. The manufacturers reps come around whenever a new model comes out. They bring all kinds of literature. That's where I get most of what I say to customers."

By this time, I had been totally distracted by the smoothness of Dale's presentation. She talked like someone much older than her age, which I think was about nineteen.

"It seems like a lot to learn, but I've had two years to do it," she said.

I was contemplating asking her for a date, but I knew that the old man would blow a cork if I "fraternized" with an employee. Besides, I didn't even have a car in running condition.

"Mr. Pratt says that he expects you to take over the repair part of the business."

"He hasn't told me that. But I kind of figured it out on my own."

"Have you ever worked on television sets?"

I laughed. "Only one—a 1938 RCA set that we got in here seven or eight years ago. I've taken it apart and put it back together a dozen times or more."

"You mean that antique in the back room?"

"Yep. Dad and I learned together on that. But I've worked on dozens of radar sets, and they work just like television. I can handle anything that comes in the door."

"I came in the door," she said.

And without waiting for me to figure out what she meant, she turned and walked back to the counter. Did she throw a little extra swing in her step, or was I imagining things?

Chapter Three

My Declaration of Independence

I had to get serious about my life. I would work in the family business, and sooner or later, would take over running it. Of that, there was no question. But I could not simply return to life as it had been before Korea. Everything was different. I was different.

For starters, I had to get my own place. Even before the draft board forced the issue, I was feeling too old to be living with my parents. Two years later, it was more than just a feeling. Too much dependence is unhealthy, no matter how comfortable life with the family is. And I needed a paycheck, not an allowance. That was the kitchen table discussion on my second evening back home.

Mom objected, "But Connie, it's never been a problem. Why do you want to change everything?"

"Mom, everything has already changed. It isn't about whether or not there's a problem. It's about growing up and taking responsibility for myself. I have to do that."

"You can do that here, Connie. You've *already* done it."

The old man said, "No, Aletta, Connie's right. A man has to make his own way in life. He cannot do that if he stays too long with his parents."

"Nonsense! In most of the world, families stay together their whole lives," Mom protested.

"We don't live in most of the world. We live *here*, and here, a man who lives with his parents is not taken seriously. And what kind of girl will be interested in a grown-ass man who still lives with his parents?"

At this point, I felt the need to speak. "What I actually had in mind was moving into Mrs. Griffith's old apartment. I'd still be here, but I'd have my own place."

Mrs. Griffith had died eight months earlier, and her apartment had been vacant ever since, awaiting a long-overdue renovation. The apartment still looked as it had in 1931, when Mrs. Griffith first moved into it, after selling the building to the old man.

Mom said, "Well, what would be the point of that? It'd be just the same as living here."

"The difference is that it would be *mine*, Mom."

The old man came down on my side, and over the next couple of weeks, I updated and repainted the little apartment. Meanwhile I went on a spending binge, buying furniture, appliances, dishes, and all of the other things I needed. By the time I was done, I'd spent most of the money I'd saved-up during my time in the army—money I'd planned to spend on a better car.

Down in the garage behind the shop sat my 1940 Ford coupe, untouched since I parked it in 1951. It had been a good-running old car, but it urgently needed tires and a battery. With some help from an old high school friend, I got the engine running and overhauled the brakes.

The old tires were too rotten to drive on, and the 16-inch wheels were rusted and unsuitable for new tubeless tires, so I got a set of Lincoln 15-inch wheels from the wrecking yard and five new 8.00 x 15 Goodyear tires. The wider, lower tires gave the coupe a cool, aggressive look.

There were lots of other things I could've done to it if I'd had more money, but this was the most I'd spent on the old Ford in the entire time I'd owned it. I bought it during my senior year in high school for $225, which the old man said was too much for a nine-year-old car, but it had only 35,000 miles on it. In the three years I'd driven it, I'd added another 15,000, so it could still be considered a low-mileage car.

While doing all of that work, I hadn't spent much time in the shop. The old man had kept me up to date on all of the things that came in for repair and how he'd fixed them. None were television sets, although there had been an interesting job fixing the two-way radio in a city police car.

The day I finally put the new tires on my car, I took it out for its first drive in over two years, and I was pretty happy with it. After washing and waxing it, I parked it at the curb in front of the store, so that Dale, who'd been pestering me to show her what I'd been spending so much time doing, could take a look at it.

"That's such a cool car!" she exclaimed. "Are you going to give me a ride?"

With no particular destination in mind, I made the left turn onto North Pines and drove up toward Broadway, where I made another left. Broadway was a residential street, where Bing Crosby owned a house.

"That's Bing Crosby's house," she said. "Did you know that?"

"Really? I didn't know that," I lied. Everybody knew that.

I stayed on Broadway all the way to the Playfair horse race track and Ferris Field, where I used to go with the old man, to watch the Spokane Indians play baseball. I went down Havana Street and stopped at a little restaurant that had once been the dining car on a passenger train.

"The old man brought me here after a Sunday afternoon ball game when I was about eight years old. I think it was the first time I'd ever eaten in a restaurant."

"Can I ask you something that's, uh, kind of personal?" Dale asked.

I nodded, so she continued, "Why do you always refer to your dad as 'the old man?'"

I laughed. "I guess you're probably thinking that's pretty disrespectful."

"Actually, yes. That's exactly what I was thinking."

"From as far back as I can remember, he's referred to himself as 'your old man,' so I picked it up. There's never been any disrespect in it. It's kind of like when sailors call the ship's captain the old man."

"If I'd ever called my dad 'old man,' it would've been about the same as swearing in church. He'd have sent me to my room without dinner."

"Order anything you want. I'm buying," I said, as a way to change the subject.

"Are you about finished working on your apartment and car? I mean, are you going to be in the store now?"

"Starting tomorrow. This afternoon, I'm going to go look at a few trucks, to see if I can find something that we can make into a mobile repair shop. The old man and I think that we'll get more business if people don't have to bring their TV sets to us."

When we got back to the store, Dale said, "I really like your car. It's cute."

"No! A guy's car is not supposed to be cute. It should be tough. Or hot. Cute is for girls."

The previous evening, I'd scanned through the "want ads" in the afternoon newspaper, and circled trucks and vans that might make good service vehicles. I made some phone calls and narrowed my choices down to three. So, after letting Dale out, I went out to take a look.

The nearest of the three "finalists" was at McCollum Ford Ranch, just a couple of miles down Sprague. The 1951 Ford panel truck looked like new and had only 28,000 miles on it. Priced at $1,050, it was well within the old man's budget.

Before taking it out for a test drive, I looked at the new 1954 models in the showroom. The one that caught my eye was the Skyliner hardtop, which featured a green-tinted glass roof over the front seat. It had overdrive, and Ford's new Y-Block overhead valve engine. It was really sporty—and also was one of the most expensive cars in the Ford line-up.

"She's a real beauty," said the salesman, who'd sneaked up behind me while I was reading the window sticker.

His tweed jacket had leather patches on the elbows, and didn't match his pleated slacks. His tie was knotted way too short, giving him the look of a kid in prep-school, despite the fact that he was probably twice my age.

I said, "Yeah. I'm just looking."

"I saw you looking at that F-1 out front. Pretty nice little truck, isn't she?"

"Do you know what engine it has?"

"You bet. It's a V-8. A hundred horsepower, but still pretty good economy."

He let me take it for a test drive, and when I got back, he hurried out to meet me. "Well, what do you think of her? Smooth-running rig, ain't she? You notice the new tires? Got new brakes, too."

He was wasting his breath. I'd already decided to buy it. I beat him down a hundred dollars on his price, and then phoned Mom.

"I found our service truck. I'll need a check for $950 to McCollum Ford. And I'll need a ride back here, so I can drive the truck home."

When the old man saw it, he agreed that it would be perfect. It already had metal shelves along both sides, leaving room in between for almost any TV set, in case we had to take one back to the shop. The next day, I went shopping for all of the tools we'd need in the truck, including a portable tube tester, a volt-ohm meter, and a small oscilloscope. My final purchase was a special suitcase to hold an inventory of vacuum tubes, including all of those we figured to be the most commonly needed ones for TV sets.

That shopping trip cost more than the truck, and it took the rest of the week, plus the weekend, to modify the shelves on one side of the truck into a long, narrow workbench. I rigged a drop cord on a spool, so that I could plug-in and have electricity in the mobile workshop. When it was all done, we hired a sign painter to put the store name on the side panels of the truck.

We put an ad in the newspaper, announcing our new in-home TV repair service, and while waiting for the phone to start ringing, I took the radio out of my coupe and did a full renovation, with new tubes and capacitors throughout.

The first call that came in started with a line that we'd hear on about half of all repair calls.

"I think my picture tube burned out. The screen is completely black."

At least nine times out of ten, when I got that complaint, I'd find no problem with the picture tube. Sometimes, I'd find the TV set unplugged. I could hardly charge for simply plugging it in, so before doing that, I'd test all of the chassis tubes. In most cases, there'd be one or two that would test weak or bad, even though they might have still worked to some degree. I'd plug in new tubes, plug in the power cord, and presto—happy customer and enough revenue to make the trip worthwhile.

* * * * * *

While Dale and I were decorating the store for Christmas, I started thinking about giving her some kind of a gift. Like the old man had said, she was almost like family, so it seemed appropriate to include her in our holiday celebration.

"The last couple of years, we've given her a nice turkey," Mom said, when I asked.

"I'd like to give her something more than that. She does so much for us, I think she deserves something special," I said.

"Did you have something in mind?"

"I think she might really like having her own television set."

"Oh, Connie, that's a lot. I mean, even at wholesale, it's going to be over a hundred dollars."

"I know, but where could we ever find a better employee? If anyone is worth an extravagant gift, it's Dale," I said.

"You think a girl her age wants to sit around watching television? She should be going out dancing, meeting boys, and having a good time!"

The idea of Dale out meeting boys and dancing with them hit me like a knitting needle through the eyeball. Nobody else in the store had a social life. Why would Dale have one? I answered my own unspoken question in an instant. But I said nothing.

"So, buy her something nice, not a television set."

I admitted, "You're right, Mom. I'll think of something."

That was easier said than done. For two weeks, I scanned the ads in the evening newspaper, looking for some clue about what might appeal to a nice a young lady. Women's clothing was a complete mystery to me. I tried to sort it out by visiting some shops downtown, but most of what I saw seemed more appropriate for my mom than for a nineteen-year-old girl.

I thought about giving her a bracelet or necklace, but jewelry struck me as suggestive of romance that I could only wish existed. In fact, romance between us existed only in my imagination, so any kind of jewelry might strike Dale as presumptuous and inappropriate.

A nice winter coat seemed like a possibility, but it seemed too "practical," almost like giving her a toaster. I wanted to give her something special, but not *too* special.

About ten days before Christmas, I said to Dale, "I'd like to take you out to dinner—for all of the things you do every day in the store."

She looked surprised, but I didn't see any hint of opposition to the idea.

I continued, "I was thinking, maybe Saturday evening, at the Crystal Room in the Davenport Hotel."

I'd picked that, because it was the classiest place I could think of. It had always been the top choice in Spokane for senior prom night, although I had never been there. It was way too rich for my blood in those days. I held my breath, wondering if I'd overstepped.

"I'd *love* that," Dale said.

"Great! I'll pick you up at 7:00." I didn't particularly try to conceal how happy that made me.

Saturday, when Dale came to the door, I was bowled over. I'd never seen her dressed-up, and it took my breath away. She was dynamite, and I said so.

Dale said, "You're looking pretty good yourself. I haven't seen you wearing a tie since you were in uniform at your welcome home party the first day we met."

When I opened the car door for her, she said, "Oh, wow! New carpet—it makes the car smell brand new."

That was exactly the reaction I'd hoped for. "Yeah. I found it in a mail-order catalog from Chicago. It just got here yesterday. I spent half the night installing it."

With my freshly refurbished radio playing, I set out on the fifteen-minute drive downtown. I'd tuned-in a station that played a Saturday evening rhythm and blues show, only vaguely aware that the announcer was a Negro, and that rhythm and blues music was considered "race music." The record that was playing was something called *Lawdy Miss Clawdy*.

"This song *rocks*," Dale exclaimed. "Lloyd Price, right?"

"If you know that, you must listen to this station, because as far as I know it's the only one in town that plays it."

She said, "Actually, there's a station in San Francisco that comes-in at night, and they play all of the Negro music."

"I like the kind of music you can dance to. When I was a kid, I didn't play sports much, because the old man wanted me to hang around the shop and learn about radios. But somewhere along the way, my mom decided to teach me how to dance. When I got into high school, knowing how to dance saved my social life. I never asked, but I suspect that Mom had foreseen that.

"She had a collection of 78 rpm records, and was a big fan of Glenn Miller. She taught me how to do a ballroom swing to *In the Mood*, and in the store, when something good came on the radio, she'd drag me to the middle of the showroom to dance. I used to be pretty good."

Dale said, "I'll bet you still are."

"Naw. I'd be pretty rusty. But anyway, that's why I like this show. They play the kind of music that just begs you to dance."

Someone called Fats Domino came on, doing *Suwannee River Hop*, a wild piano boogie.

"I've heard this a few times before, and I can't understand why it isn't on the Billboard charts."

Dale said, "Fats Domino must be a Negro, since the record is being played on this program. And of course, most stations just won't play the race music."

"Probably right, but it's all piano. How can it be considered race music?"

She shrugged. "Beats me."

"It'd be fun for dancing," I said, as I pulled to the curb in front of the Davenport Hotel.

The Davenport had been Spokane's swankiest hotel ever since it opened, fifty years before. We were directed to the Crystal Room, where I had 7:30 reservations.

The maître d' said, "It will be just a few minutes. Would you like to wait in the bar?"

I was caught off-guard by the question, and I hesitated for a second, knowing that Dale was a couple of years too young to go into the bar.

Dale came to my rescue. She turned to me and said, "If it's only going to be a few minutes, why don't we just wait here."

Dinner was great. I'm not sure it was worth the twenty bucks I paid for it, but I'd happily pay that much just to sit for an hour and a half looking at Dale. She could quicken my heartbeat with just a smile. When the waiter brought the check, I laid down the twenty, plus a five-dollar tip.

As we were leaving the restaurant, Dale took my hand and pulled me to a stop.

"You know what I'd like to do?" she asked, and then answered herself. "I'd like to go dancing."

Once again, I was caught off-balance. The dinner was a Christmas gift from the store. Going dancing made it into something else, and I hadn't expected it.

Thinking quickly, I suggested, "Are you familiar with the Metronome Dance Hall? They just changed their name to the Hi-Spot. They have a house band, and sometimes feature out of town musicians."

Dale said, "I've never been there, but it sounds like fun."

"We can check it out. It's only a couple of blocks away."

It wasn't snowing, so we left the car where it sat and walked to the Hi-Spot. A small sign on the door said No Minors. Oops. I hadn't thought about that.

"Let's pretend we didn't see it. The worst they can do is make us leave," Dale suggested.

The hostess escorted us to one of the tables that surrounded the dance floor, and as we sat down, she gave me a bar menu.

I whispered to Dale, "I think there's a two-drink minimum."

"Order me a strawberry daiquiri."

I raised my eyebrow.

"Come on, I'm not a *complete* babe in the woods," she said.

I went with rum and Coke, which had been my standard in the bars of Seoul. Fortunately, nobody asked Dale to show I.D. And as I looked at her, I thought about my first impression of her. How had I ever thought she was too young for me?

We danced for two hours, and I found our dancing skills to be well matched, whether that meant mediocre or great. Actually, I think we were individually good, but together, we were electric. On one particularly fast piece, I did my best impression of a Lindy hop, and Dale stayed with me, step for step. A few people even clapped when we left the floor for a rest.

As I drove home, I knew that my life had changed. Dale and I had said a lot to each other that night, but there was far more that was left unspoken. Chief among them was that we were a couple.

For Christmas, a week later, I gave Dale a gold-plated Bulova wristwatch, feeling that it struck a balance somewhere between a toaster and an engagement ring. She surprised me with a sport jacket that was way more stylish that the one I'd worn a week earlier. Maybe she was telling me something.

Chapter Four

Passing the Torch

As we went into 1954, the old man limited himself to working half-days. By 1:00 most days, he'd need to go upstairs and rest. About once a week, our long-time family doctor would stop by to see how he was doing. The news was always bad. The only question was *how* bad.

I tried scheduling my service calls in the mornings, so that I could be in the store in case Dale needed help after the old man went upstairs. Through the spring and into summer, I learned things about television that I'd never previously thought much about. I'd always focused on the technical side of television, and I believed that I knew as much about that as anyone.

But I knew nothing about the programming. Years before, the old man had said that it would be just like going to the theater and watching movies. In reality, it turned out to be nothing at all like that. In the course of repairing customers' TV sets, I was exposed to a broad cross-section of the programming of the era, though it was mostly daytime programming, since I rarely had a need or desire to watch television after the store closed.

Nearly all daytime programming fell into four categories: children's shows, game shows, 15-minute soap operas, and personality shows featuring celebrities like Art Linkletter, Gary Moore, and Arthur Godfrey. Most of this material was banal and boring, so in that respect, even though I remained enthralled with the technology, television was becoming a big disappointment.

One of my first in-home repair calls was from someone who complained that his picture was out of focus. When I took a look at his TV set, the picture was not discernably different from what I was accustomed to seeing on our brand-new sets in the store. I hooked-up my monoscope test-pattern generator, and went through the process of carefully adjusting the controls to optimize the picture on the screen, even though the set had been in nearly perfect working order to begin with.

"I don't understand," the customer said. "Your test-pattern looks great, but when you switch to whatever's being broadcast on either channel, the picture looks all blurry. Is something wrong with the tuner?"

I changed channels, and confirmed that what he was saying was true. But the test-pattern generator also went through the tuner, so I couldn't see a problem there. What's more, in my experience, this was how things had always been.

"What you're seeing here is what's on the film that the networks and stations are playing. Film is never as clear as live telecasting," I explained.

"We never had this problem before we moved here," he said.

"Where did you come from?"

"We lived in New York. Albany. We moved to Spokane a couple of weeks ago, and right away, we started having this problem. I figured something got jiggled loose during the move."

At that moment, I understood.

"Okay, that explains it," I said. "Most TV broadcasts originate in New York City. What goes on the air is the live video feed. And now, with the coaxial cable, the live feed is carried all over the country. But here in the west, the programming has to be delayed three hours. Otherwise, you'd have to turn on TV at 4:00 a.m., to watch the Today Show on NBC."

"Yeah, so?"

"The only way to delay the telecast to compensate for the three-hour time difference is to copy it onto film, using a Kinescope film chain. Essentially, a 16-millimeter movie camera pointed at a special video monitor with an extra bright picture—the Kinescope. In the TV business, it's called 'the Kinny.' Then, after shooting the Kinny film, it has to be developed and dried, and cue marks and leader have to be added—all within three hours. Most of what we see in this time zone is Kinny film. But the process isn't perfect. A little bit of blurriness is inherent in the process, no matter how well the equipment is calibrated."

"Are you putting me on? This is the best we're gonna get?" he asked.

"It is, at least until they figure out how to put video signals on magnetic tape. Engineers are working on that, but it's probably still a few years away."

That wasn't the only technology we were waiting for. Not a day went by on the sales floor without someone asking about color television. Magazine articles had been talking about it for years—even before the second world war. But as of 1954, it hadn't yet become a reality.

"Man, like I'd hate to spend a bunch of dough on a black-and-white set now, and then have color TV come out next month."

I gave Dale my best answer to that objection, "It won't happen that quickly. It'll probably be ten years before there's enough programming being broadcast in color to make purchasing a color set a reasonable choice for most people."

Another common customer complaint was, "I heard that black-and-white TV sets won't work with color broadcasts, and I'll have to buy a new set, even if I don't want color."

This was confusion created jointly by CBS and the Federal Communication Commission. The complete answer was more complex than most people needed to know. CBS had developed a color TV system that was called "field sequential color imaging." In that system, each image frame would be made-up of three separate images, one for each of the primary colors. This required a completely different scan rate inside the picture tube, so the system was fundamentally incompatible with all existing black-and-white TV sets. The FCC licensed the CBS color system in 1950, but then rescinded the license a year later. A total of only 200 TV sets were built for the field sequential color system, and only a handful of programs were ever broadcast for them.

Concurrent with the development of the CBS system, RCA was working on an entirely different concept, which they called "compatible color," because their color broadcasts would be completely backward-compatible with existing black-and-white TV sets. This standard was adopted by the FCC in the middle of 1953, and color TV sets made after that date would be of the RCA design.

The answer I gave to Dale was, "That was true of some early color television system designs, but the newer designs don't have that problem. You'll be able to watch color telecasts in black-and-white as well as color."

Like I said, I love the technology, just as the old man had loved the technology involved in early radio broadcasting. There seems to be no limit to what we can do with electrons. That had always been the motivating force behind the old man's single-minded drive. All of his business decisions had been rooted in his understanding of the state of the technology.

But the thing that the old man never had to consider was crappy programming. For all of its technical promise, television had become a garbage pit of vacuous, mind-suffocating drivel. How long would people continue to buy a product that delivered a perpetual insult to their intelligence? The future of our store, I believed, would be connected to the quality of television programming. I could only hope that the broadcasting industry would grow up, and do it quickly.

In the meantime, our business decisions were based largely on faith, rather than on optimism, of which I had none. And more and more, I was finding myself alone in running the store, as the old man's health continued to deteriorate. By the middle of 1954, he was effectively absent, and I was running the store and making all of the business decisions.

So, what was our reason for existing—our mission statement? The old man never attempted to express a mission. He went into the business simply because he wanted to make a living doing the thing that he loved—and that was building, repairing and selling radios. He never tried to analyze the public or cultural "need" for what he did. He simply acted on the belief that the need existed, or people wouldn't come into the store.

But that was something that I couldn't take for granted. People had *needed* radio. They didn't *need* television. And worse than that, they seemed never to notice what an intrusion television was on their personal lives. People needed me to repair their television sets, but they didn't need television—not as it existed in 1954.

My mission statement was thus self-serving and shallow. I needed to keep the store in business because it provided me an income doing about the only thing I knew how to do—troubleshoot and repair radios and TV sets. The only shred of altruism in my mission was that I also provided income and shelter to my parents, and a paycheck for Dale. And those were important motives—maybe the most important of all.

In October, Spokane got its third television station, when KREM-TV came on the air as the ABC network affiliate. I wish I could say that the broader selection of programming improved the quality of programming. But it looked like simply more of the same.

The old man died in January of 1955, at the time when television was creating Davy Crockett mania across the land. I rated the three-part Walt Disney series as one of the better pieces of TV programming up to that point. Production values were relatively high, and Disney gave us a hero. As for the old man, he never saw the final episode.

It left me feeling unexpectedly empty and overwhelmed. I'd known for a year and a half that this day was coming, but I wasn't prepared for how it would feel.

A man called me out to repair his 24-inch Zenith, which was still under warranty. As I went through the preliminary steps in troubleshooting, it struck me that I no longer had someone to call if I got stumped by a mysterious circuit failure. I was on my own.

Chapter Five

Changing Times

Dale was the one truly bright spot in my life, and she never disappointed me. Two or three times a month, we'd go out for dinner, a movie, or dancing. We talked occasionally about the future, but mostly, we simply had an understanding. Whatever the future held, we would meet it together. That's how it was.

One morning when there were no customers in the store, I called Mom and Dale over to the counter and said, "There's something that we need to talk about."

Mom smiled, winked at Dale, and said, "I was wondering when you were going to say something."

I gave Mom a stern look. "We need to decide if we want to compete with the department stores. They all have TV departments now, and big advertising budgets. And new stores are opening every week."

"Are you suggesting that we consider expanding to become a department store?" Mom asked.

"No. I think we need to stay within our area of expertise, but do it better than the department stores can. Department stores are, as the saying goes, jacks of all trades, but masters of none. The person you talk with in their TV department might have been selling ladies underwear the day before. They can't compete with us when it comes to product knowledge."

"So, what are we talking about, then?"

"First thing is advertising," I said. "We need to do more than our little weekly ad in the Valley Herald. That works for in-home repair service, but it doesn't bring people into the store."

"But the department stores have a ton of money to spend on big newspaper ads. We can't possibly compete with that," Mom said.

"That's quite true. But for a fraction of what that would cost, we can buy radio time. You've heard that a new radio station will be coming on the air in December. The new KZUN studio is only a block away from our store, and their goal is to be the 'voice of the valley.' And they're writing ad contracts right now."

Dale asked, "What would we say on the radio? It takes *a lot* of talking to sell a TV set. I can't imagine how that would work on the radio."

"Good point. I'm not suggesting that we do *product* advertising. I'm proposing *institutional* advertising, with a very limited objective—to make our store the first thing people think of when they need anything related to electronics. Top of mind. That's where we want to be. And we get there by repetition of a short message during their wake-up time news broadcasts on the only station that focuses on our marketing area."

"What's that going to cost," Mom asked.

"If this advertising campaign brings in two additional sales per month, it'll pay for itself."

"Well, if you're sure it's the right thing to do," she said, "then, go ahead."

"There's one other thing that we need to think about, and that's store hours. All of the big stores are open evenings and weekends. We will lose customers to them if our door is locked while theirs is open."

"We've always been open nine-to-five. It's what people expect," Mom said.

"For people with nine-to-five jobs, those hours have always been an inconvenience. They have to rush over during their lunch hour, or take time off work."

"Well, they can always come in on Saturday."

"Or, they can go to North Town Mall at their convenience—including evenings and Sundays," I countered.

"But we can't work twelve-hour days, seven days a week," Dale said.

"No. And I'm not suggesting that. The decision we need to make is whether or not to hire another person—someone to work the sales floor evenings and weekends."

"That's an awfully big step," Mom cautioned.

"I think it is the future of retail—not just in television, but across the board. Stores that aren't open will lose business to those that are."

"But, goodness, how can we find someone we can trust with our store?"

"People do it all the time. I'm not saying it's easy, but it's certainly not impossible."

Dale summed it up. "Wow. This is a lot to take in."

Mom nodded her agreement.

"Think about people you know. Maybe there's someone who'd like to work here," I said.

July 25, 1955

My cousin Penny was a couple of years older than me. The daughter of Mom's older sister, Penelope Ransom had recently moved back to Spokane from Great Falls, following the breakup of her marriage to a truck driver who spent more time on the road than at home. There was a lot more to it than that, but Penny came to Mom because she needed a place to live.

She explained to Mom, "Darrell bankrupted us. He started gambling, and after he'd maxed-out our credit cards, he took out a second mortgage on our house to pay them off. But he kept gambling, and pretty soon, the credit cards were maxed-out again. I didn't know about any of it until creditors started calling.

"He stopped making payments on the car, the refrigerator, the television, and the furniture, so one thing at a time, everything got repossessed. When the power company shut off our electricity, I packed-up and used most of my last twenty dollars to buy a train ticket to Spokane."

She moved in with Mom, taking the room that had once been mine. I hadn't seen Penny for ten years, and I barely knew her. But her arrival just days after our conversation about hiring someone seemed to be the work of an unseen hand. Still, I wasn't about to take that step until I got to know her. And above all, I had to talk to Dale.

I took her out for dinner and, after we placed our order, I asked, "What do you think about becoming our store manager?"

She stared at me. "Isn't that what *you* are? Wait! Are you going away?"

I put my hand over hers. "I'm not going anywhere. I'll officially be the supervising co-owner and, of course, I'll continue doing the repair work. But you'll be in charge of running the store."

"I must be missing something. What's the point?"

"Two things. Mom wants you to take over the bookkeeping and payables. She's having a hard time with her eyesight, and it's becoming difficult for her to do the job. The other thing is my cousin. Mom thinks I should hire her to work in the store."

"I was wondering when that was going to happen," Dale said.

"Right. But before doing it, I want it to be clear to everyone that you're in charge."

"Wow. I'm in shock."

"Am I going to have to render first-aid?" I asked.

"Not here, but maybe later," she said.

The next day, I called the attorney who handled the store's occasional legal matters, and asked him to draw-up a formal contract that outlined Dale's authority and responsibilities. He also gave me some needed advice on how much the store manager should be paid. What it came to was her old paycheck plus half of what the old man had paid himself.

When Dale read it, she said, "Holy cow! Is this for real?"

"Not yet. I'll show it to Mom tomorrow. We'll all sign it, and then it'll be for real."

"Suppose your mom thinks Penny should take precedence—maybe not now, but sometime in the future. After all, she's family, and I'm not."

"We can take care of that before it becomes an issue," I said.

"So, what are you proposing?" she asked.

"Yes. I am."

"You are what?"

"I'm proposing." I showed her the diamond solitaire that was the main reason I was still driving a fifteen-year-old Ford coupe.

"Now I'm *really* going to need some first-aid."

The first of September was Dale's twenty-first birthday. Nine days later, we were married in a very small private ceremony at the Presbyterian church on North Pines Road, thus settling any question about who was family. Our honeymoon consisted of two nights at the Davenport Hotel, stretching the limit on how long we could be away from the store.

Back in the store on Tuesday morning, Mom beckoned Dale and me to come over to the counter, where she handed us an envelope containing a savings bank passbook in my name, showing a balance of over four thousand dollars.

"Mom, this is way too much," I protested.

"You think it's a gift," she said, "but it's not. This money has been yours all along. It was going to pay for college, but then you went to work in the store, and plans changed. So, use it to buy something for yourselves—something nice, with four walls and a roof."

Chapter Six

Dale and Connie

When I called about a new house that I'd found in the classified ads, the answering service took our phone number and names. A real estate agent called back, and we arranged to meet him at the house, which was on 22nd Avenue, just off South Pines Road, only a mile from our store. As Dale and I approached the man with the briefcase, he extended his hand to me.

"You must be Dale Pratt. I'm Ray Olerude," he said.

"I'm Connie Pratt. This is Dale," I said, motioning toward Dale.

Mildly embarrassed, he stammered, "Oh, I'm sorry. Connie. Dale."

This would become a fairly common occurrence, and I waved it off. We shook hands, and then picked our way through construction debris, into the garage of the unfinished house. It was surrounded by tall ponderosa pine trees, and was one of three houses under construction in the recently platted subdivision. The 1,100 square-foot house featured three bedrooms, a two-car garage, and surprisingly, had two bathrooms—a private bathroom off the master bedroom.

"That's the wave of the future," Olerude proclaimed. "New houses everywhere will have a master suite, instead of a simple master bedroom."

That feature alone made the house stand out. And it was built on a sloping lot, so the back of the house was two stories tall. Ray called it a "daylight basement." The lower level was unfinished, but could later be made into a workshop or recreation room.

"If you buy now, you'll get to pick out the paint colors, appliances, countertops, and flooring for the kitchen and bathrooms," Ray said.

It was priced at $17,500, which was way more money than I ever expected to pay for a house, but Dale and I both loved everything else about it. Over the next few days, we applied for financing and were approved with 20% down, leaving us with money for grass seed and some furniture. The house was finished in May, and we moved-in a few days later.

This was a very busy time in the store. We got a new RCA color set and put it on display, but we turned it on only when there was a color program on the air. We posted a TV schedule with the color programs circled, and sometimes a dozen or more people would come in to watch.

We'd hired Penny shortly after our wedding, and at the first of the year, extended our store hours, so we were open evenings and weekends, and immediately our retail sales rose by fifteen percent.

Penny was a good worker, but teaching her all that she needed to know was a long-term project. You never know how much there is to know until you have to teach it to somebody. Most of that fell on Dale, while I focused on the service and repair side of the business.

So, there was a long period of time before Penny was ready to work the store alone. Sometimes, Mom would help out with that, but most of the time, either Dale or I had to be there to back-up Penny. That meant long hours and long weeks for us, and we both started questioning our decision to extend store hours.

January 28, 1956

The big news in entertainment was a singer named Elvis Presley. He hit the pop charts like an atomic bomb in January, and for the rest of the year, he had at least one or two records in the top ten every week. Rock and roll music became so popular that one of Spokane's radio stations changed to a "Top 30" format, and KNEW instantly became Spokane's most popular station.

Rock music hit television with the American Bandstand show on ABC. The 30-minute show came from Philadelphia, and featured one or two singers in the studio lip-syncing their hit songs, while a group of teenagers demonstrated the latest dances. The afternoon broadcast brought kids into the store, by the dozen, to hear the popular music and learn the dances.

Mom grumbled about it, because the kids always turned the volume up, but Dale let the kids have their fun. While a lot of people my age ridiculed the new music—and some of it actually *was* pretty ridiculous—I actually liked a lot of it. A national controversy broke out over the evils of rock and roll music, to the point where preachers were delivering sermons about it, but whenever one of the big stars of rock and roll appeared on television, new audience records were set.

"What do you think about selling records in the store?" Dale asked one morning.

"You think we can make any money selling records?"

"At full retail, we'll clear about half a dollar on every record. With all the kids coming in to watch Bandstand, we have a ready-made customer base. I'll bet we can sell maybe a hundred records a week, once we get established."

"I'm not opposed to making an extra $200 a month, as long as it doesn't become a distraction to the TV business," I said. "But let's look at a different strategy. How about discounting the records to 79 cents? We'll pull customers from all the stores that hold out for full retail. That's a double win."

Dale said, "I like that. A lot of the kids who come in to buy records will also be buying phonographs and radios; and in a few years they'll buy TV sets. We gain a whole new customer base. I think we can afford a little distraction."

She put a record rack behind the counter and posted KNEW's weekly top 30 on the wall. She signed an agreement with a record distributor to keep the rack stocked with the current top hits plus a selection of new releases that showed promise. Once she had it all set up, she put Penny in charge of the record department.

* * * * * *

By the middle of 1957, workload in the store had reached a state of perpetual imbalance, with too much work for the three of us, but not enough to pay for a fourth position. This situation led to some daydreaming and soul-searching on my part. There was something that had been on my mind for half my life, an itch that I couldn't scratch.

I was interested in things other than tubes, resisters, capacitors, and transformers. Even as a kid, some of my favorite radio programs had been the *ABC Mystery Theater*, *Ellery Queen Mysteries*, *True Detective*, and *Gang Busters*. I loved the challenge of trying to figure out the mystery before the guys on the radio did—though I was rarely successful. It was the mental exercise that drew me in.

Crime reports in the news had the same effect. I always wanted to be the one who solved the mystery, and toward that end, I collected whatever I could find about the great mysteries of the era: The Lindberg kidnapping, the Elizabeth Short "Black Dahlia" case, the murder of "Bugsy" Siegel, and many other notorious crimes intrigued me. I will admit that this sounds like a morbid obsession, but crimes need to be solved. The alternative is having criminals walk among us, free to inflict pain and tragedy on any of us.

One morning over breakfast, Dale and I were talking—for about the hundredth time—about the situation in the store. It gave me the opportunity to express the idea that had been forming in my mind for a couple of months, so I laid it on the table.

"We need to get our work hours under control so that we can see each other outside the store from time to time."

Looking perplexed, Dale asked, "Who are you, and why are you in my house?"

"That pretty-well sums it up," I said.

"Either we get someone else onboard, or we cut our store hours. What we're doing now is slow suicide. We'll end up like your dad."

"Do you think we could make it work with a half-time employee?" I asked.

"Maybe, but that comes with its own problems. It takes just as long to train a part-time worker as it does a full-time worker. But part-time workers are much more likely to move on, leaving us to train another."

"So, hire the full-time worker, and I'll be the part-time employee," I suggested.

"What? How would that work?" she asked.

"For half my life, I've wanted to get into investigation. You and I have talked about that. Maybe this is my chance to do it—get a private investigator's license and split my time between that and TV repair."

"Can you make any money doing that?"

"Other people do. There seems to be a lot of demand for investigative services."

"What's it take to get a license?"

"Some reading and a written exam. I probably could get it done in a couple of months," I said.

"So, you'd work half-time as a private detective and half-time as a TV repairman?"

I nodded. "That's about it."

"Can we think about that for a while?" she asked.

While we were thinking about it, I ran across one of those "be your own boss" magazine ads, promoting a correspondence school that promised a private investigator's license upon graduation. The course turned out to be pretty hokey, with cheesy loose-leaf "textbooks" and stupidly simple workbook exams, but I stuck with it, spending an hour or two every day studying and memorizing the laws associated with private investigation. A practice exam was included in the course, but the real exam was administered at the courthouse.

Late in 1957, I had the unpleasant task of evicting the attorney who had occupied the tiny office space in the front corner of our building. He hadn't paid his rent for five months, and we couldn't remember the last time we'd actually seen him.

So, when I got my private investigator's license, I had an office right next to our store, with a separate entrance from the sidewalk. The door on the left was Pratt's TV, and the door on the right was C.R. Pratt, Private Detective. An interconnecting door inside let me move freely from the repair shop in the store to my investigator's office.

With a small ad in the Valley Herald and an even smaller one in the yellow pages, I waited for the phone to ring. My first call came from a divorce attorney representing a woman who wanted me to get the goods on her husband—hardly the kind of investigation I wanted to do, but you have to start somewhere.

I borrowed Mom's 35 mm camera, and waited for my target to come out of the office where he worked. In my inconspicuous old Ford coupe, I followed him to a tavern on Trent Avenue, where he was joined by a lady. I shot some pictures of them through the front window, realizing that I needed to get a camera with a telephoto lens. After a couple of drinks, the couple parted, and the man went home to his unhappy wife.

Around the lunch hour every day for a week, I staked out the parking lot at his office. Twice, he left the office and drove to a house on Grace Avenue in Millwood. I snapped a couple of pictures of my subject going into the house. He stayed in the house for forty minutes, and then returned to his office. I went to the county records office and found that the house was owned by Arthur and Margaret VanBergen, husband and wife.

After 22 hours of surveillance over the course of three weeks, I turned over my photos and notes to the attorney, who got a very favorable settlement for his client.

I took my pay from the case to a pawn shop on West Main downtown, and bought a decent Nikon camera kit. The attorney introduced himself to Arthur VanBergen, just letting him know that if he ever needed representation in a domestic case, he was available.

Over the next few months, I had several similar cases, giving me funds to set up a photo lab in the back room of my office. I also bought a Polaroid camera for cases where I need an instant photo. But building a client base was a difficult and slow process.

Chapter Seven

My First Criminal Investigation

The man who came into my office said, "My name is George Bardon. Your yellow pages ad says you do all kinds of investigations."

"That's right," I answered, "as long as it's legal. What kind of investigation do you have in mind?"

"Last month, my car was stolen, and…"

I interrupted, "May I assume that you reported it to police?"

"Oh, sure. I reported it right away. But they haven't been able to find it, and they say that the chances of getting it back are pretty slim."

"What kind of car is it?"

"It's a Ford—1956 Crown Victoria."

"Nice car. Is it insured?"

"Yes, but the insurance company is holding-off on paying the claim. They won't pay out until it's been gone for ninety days."

"Are you still making payments on it?"

"No, I paid it off last year," George said.

"Okay, so what makes you want to pay for a private detective? I mean, if the police don't find it in the next couple of months, your insurance will pay off."

"Well, the thing is, I think I found it. But I don't know how to prove that it's actually my car. I'd like you to find out if it is."

I said, "That should be a simple matter of checking the serial number. I assume you have a registration certificate with the serial number on it."

"Yeah, of course. I checked it, and it doesn't match. The serial number says it's not my car, but I'm sure that it is. I think someone changed the serial number tag."

"You've shared that with the cops?"

"Yeah, and they sent someone from the Department of Licensing to check it out. They say the serial number is correct for the car."

"Let's go back a little bit," I said. "How did you find the car, and where is it now?"

"Okay, well, I started looking around for a new car—well, actually, a used car. I can't afford a new one. At least not until the insurance pays out. So, anyway, I've been watching the want ads in the newspaper. Last Friday, I saw an ad for a '56 Crown Vickie, and I went to take a look at it."

"Dealer, or private party?"

"It's not a dealer or used car lot. It's a guy who has a car repair shop in his back yard."

"What did he say about the car?"

"He said he bought it cheap because it needed some repairs. He fixed it, and now wants to sell it."

"Did you ask what kind of work he did on the car?"

"He said it was body repair—the car had been damaged in the rear end, and I could see that some of the paint looked fresh."

"So, what's the problem, then?"

"The freshly painted area didn't square with his description of the damage. And here's the thing. My car was all black. This one is black and yellow, and it's the yellow paint that looks fresh."

"Just playing devil's advocate here," I said. "Isn't it possible that the damage was limited to the yellow part of the car?"

"I don't see how that could happen in a collision. I think the yellow was added so that it wouldn't look like my car. But then other things caught my attention."

"Such as?"

"First thing was the sound. As soon as he started the engine, I recognized the sound. My car has the 312 Thunderbird Special engine. This engine *looks* just like mine, except for the valve covers, which say it's the standard 292 V-8, but it looks like the valve covers have recently been off the engine—like maybe they swapped them out."

"Seems like they'd get more money with the larger engine."

"Yeah, and the T-Bird Special engine is pretty rare. About the only fifty-sixes that got it were Thunderbirds and police cruisers."

"You said it was the sound that got your attention. Does the 312 engine sound that much different from the standard 292?" I asked.

"Not really, but here's the deal. A couple of weeks before my car was stolen, I had the mufflers replaced—with a pair of Mitchell glass-packs. They gave it a really sweet sound, ya know. And the car this guy's trying to sell me has the *exact same* sound. I look underneath, and what do I see but a pair of Mitchells, and the paint hasn't even burned off.

"So, then I started looking for other things. Sure enough, there was a little burn spot on the carpet, right where I'd dropped a cigarette. And a rock chip in the windshield, right down by the passenger-side wiper."

I had to admit that all of those things taken together made a pretty good case for it being George's car. Still, if the Department of Licensing had inspected it and concluded that the serial number was correct, the rest of it *had to be* coincidental, didn't it?

"No," I said in answer to my unspoken question. "I think you have good reason for suspicion. I can go take a look at the car. If I can't find evidence to support the seller's story, then I can look into the serial number."

"How much will that cost me?" George asked.

"I charge ten dollars an hour, and I bill in half-hour increments. I think I can determine whether or not it's your car within ten hours. If it turns out that it *is* yours, your insurance should pay my bill."

"Yeah, well just in case it's not mine, I can go up to a hundred dollars—maybe two hundred. I just need to know."

After George left, I called the number in the newspaper ad and asked if the car was still available. The guy said it was, but urged me not to waste time getting out to see it, because he was getting lots of calls. Well, I knew that he'd already had the car for sale for a full week, so it probably wasn't quite as urgent as he wanted me to think.

And before looking at the car, I needed to know what to look for, so I called a friend who owns Stevenson's Auto Body Repair.

"Steve, this is Pratt. Got a minute?"

"Sure, Connie. What do you need?"

"I have a client whose car was stolen. He thinks he's found it, but the serial number doesn't match his. He thinks it has been changed. How hard is it to do that?"

"Depends. What make is it?"

"It's a Ford—a '56 Crown Victoria."

"Fords have a stamped aluminum patent plate, riveted to the A-pillar on the driver's side, below the corner of the windshield. It's almost impossible to change the serial number on the plate. It's three-dimensional, stamped from the back side, so the numbers are raised. You'd have to drill out the rivets, and then try to flatten the old number out before stamping the new number in its place. And then there's the dies.

Regular number and letter dies are in mirror-image, made for front-stamping. But for back-stamping, you need the opposite. I don't know where you'd get something like that. All in all, I don't think you could ever make it look good enough to pass an official inspection. More likely, you'd just replace the whole plate with one from another car—but there's problems with that, too."

"What kind of problems?"

"Well, the plate doesn't have just the serial number. It also tells the body style, type of engine, paint colors, and interior colors. So, you'd have to take the plate from a car just like the one you're trying to falsify. A patent plate for a station wagon would be an obvious fraud on a convertible, ya see what I mean?"

"Sounds like they'd have to get their hands on a new blank patent plate, and fake the whole thing."

"Yeah, except you can't just go out and get blank patent plates—not legitimate ones. In theory, you could counterfeit the blanks, but that would require some tooling. You couldn't afford to do it in small quantities. You'd have to make a thousand of them to absorb the setup cost. Nobody's gonna do that."

"So, you're saying that they'd have to take the plate from a car just like the stolen one. Maybe they could go to a big wrecking yard, like Spalding's, and find a wreck that matches."

"I doubt that you could do that. First off, Spalding's isn't going to turn you loose in the yard to go looking, and even if they did, they wouldn't let you take the patent plate off it."

"I think I'm getting the picture. If I go look at this car, what should I look for—to determine if the serial number is legit?"

"First, get your hands on a data sheet from Ford that'll decode what's stamped on the patent plate. You ought to be able to get that from a Ford dealer. Then compare each thing on the plate with the car. But just because all items don't match, it doesn't mean that it isn't legit. People do change engines and re-paint cars for legitimate reasons.

"You'll need to look very carefully at the rivets holding the patent plate. If there's a hole in the center, it's a pop-rivet. Ford doesn't use pop-rivets, so that's a dead giveaway. A professional thief would use real rivets, but it's really hard to remove the rivets without damaging the plate. If you see little scratches or gouges around the rivets, you'll know that someone's tampered with it."

"This isn't as easy as I'd hoped it would be."

"There's one more thing. The serial number is stamped into the car's frame. Once where it is visible, and then one or two more times where it's hidden. Ford dealer can tell you where to look."

The nearest Ford Dealer was McCollum, where I'd bought my service truck. I drove down there and asked to see the salesman who sold me the truck. He gave me a sheet that told the meaning of every code on the patent plate.

The service manager showed me where to find the serial number stampings on the car's frame. One is visible under the hood. There's another on a rear frame crossmember, where it can be seen only from below, with the car on a lift. The third one can be seen only by removing the front bumper and the left-side bumper mounting bracket.

By the time I left the Ford dealer, it was late in the afternoon, so I wound up in rush-hour traffic as I headed through downtown and up North Division to the seller's auto repair shop.

"Sorry," the man said. "I sold that car about two hours ago."

"You're putting me on," I said, knowing that he wasn't.

He shook his head. "Wish I'd a known you were coming. I'd a held out for my price, instead a letting him beat me down."

When I got back to my office, I called George Bardon and told him the bad news.

"Can you track-down the buyer?" he asked.

"Maybe. I know a lady in the Department of Licensing office in Olympia. She might be able to help, assuming the buyer didn't take the car out of state. I can ask her to keep her eyes open for a title transfer on a '56 Crown Vic."

A week later, my friend called back to say that the paperwork had come through. The title was being transferred from Division Street Auto Salvage to Donald Matson. She gave me Matson's address, which I confirmed in the Spokane phone book.

I called George and gave him an update, and then I called Matson.

After introducing myself, I said, "It is my understanding that you bought a 1956 Ford Crown Victoria from Levine's Auto Repair last week."

"Yes, I did," he replied. "But why is that of any interest to you?"

"My client believes that the car was stolen from him and now has a falsified data plate. He'd like me to do a quick inspection."

"Oh crap. If it really *is* his car, will I be charged with having stolen property?"

"Not a chance. You are protected by your paper trail. If anyone's going to get into trouble, it'll be the guy who sold it to you."

"But I'd still have to give the car back to its real owner. Can I get my money back?"

"You ought to be able to, but you may have to go to court to do it," I said.

When I went over to Matson's place to look at the car, I took along a copy of the data from George Bardon's factory warranty card, which had the serial number and assembly codes. I compared that with what was on Matson's car.

    Bardon's Serial Number: P6RW 112165
    Matson's Serial Number: M6LW 100529

The first character in the serial number designates the engine. The M code on Matson's car indicates that the car should have a 292 4-barrel engine, which is what the car appeared to have. The P in Bardon's serial number indicates the 312 Thunderbird Special engine. Under normal circumstances, nobody would ever disguise the premium engine to look like the smaller, less powerful one.

But the new cork gaskets visible under the valve covers suggested that someone may had done exactly that. As Bardon has speculated, it appeared that the valve covers had been changed to make the engine appear to match the serial number on the patent plate.

    Bardon's Assembly Code: 64A A BN1 29E 1103
    Matson's Assembly Code: 64A AM R 18G 109

On both cars, 64A is the code for Crown Victoria. The next character is the color code. On George Bardon's car, the letter A means Raven Black, Next, Bardon's interior color code is BN1. The numeral 1 means that it is a non-standard amendment to the black and white vinyl, in Bardon's car meaning black and black

Don Matson's car shows color code AM for two-tone Raven Black and Goldenrod Yellow, which was a special-order combination in 1956. The interior code R on Matson's car is actually a 1955 code for Black and Yellow vinyl, which had to have been another special order. Alternatively, since Matson's car was assembled very early in the 1956 production year, it might have actually been ordered from the 1955 specifications.

The car I was looking at was yellow and black, matching the AM code in the production number, but the yellow paint appeared to be fresh. It showed no sign of the wear and tear that you'd expect to see on a two-year-old car. Of course, the seller had said that some collision damage had been repaired, so that might account for the fresh yellow paint, even though it seemed unlikely that only the yellow panels had been damaged. Had the yellow paint been added to Bardon's all-black car to match the code on the patent plate?

A more obvious discrepancy was the interior color code. Matson's car had an all-black interior, as did Bardon's. But Matson's assembly code called for yellow and black. Now, it is always possible that the discrepancy happened on the assembly line. That's not unheard of, and maybe that's what the serial number inspector had concluded. Or more likely, he just didn't notice.

I explained all of this to Matson as we went over the car.

"But I don't see any evidence that the patent plate has been changed," I said. "So, maybe the innocent explanations for the discrepancies are right."

"Is there any way to know for sure?" Matson asked.

"We can look for the serial number on the frame. And we can try to see engine characteristics that tell which engine it is. That will require putting the car on a lift and doing some disassembly."

"You mean we'd have to tear the car apart?"

"No. I think the most we'd have to do is remove the front bumper," I said.

He sighed. "I guess it'll have to be done sooner or later. Might as well get it over with."

With the car on the lift at nearby Maxey's Texaco, we went underneath with a flashlight and a dental mirror. Shining the light up behind the fanbelt pully, I looked for a 5/16-inch dot drilled into the crankshaft flange. Other than the valve covers, that is the only visible external difference between the 292 engine and the 312 engine. We had to rotate the engine in order to find it, but the dot was there, indicating that this was the P code engine, matching Bardon's serial number, not Matson's. But it still wasn't conclusive. Someone could have changed engines, although we could see no evidence that the engine had ever been out of the car.

Next, we looked at the rear frame crossmember, where I located the serial number. It matched the one on the patent plate. But I could see what looked like marks from a disc grinder in the area around the number, and the crossmember appeared to have been recently painted.

Up front, on the right-hand frame rail, we found similar evidence of tampering. However, it wasn't conclusive proof. Maybe the serial number inspector had used a power tool to remove dirt and rust in order to see the serial number stampings. Or maybe the recent collision repair had somehow required sanding and painting those areas—unlikely, but possible.

There was one more place to look. We removed the front bumper and the left-side bumper bracket. As we did so, I could see nothing to indicate that the bolts had ever been touched. And the serial number there was Bardon's, not Matson's.

So, we called the police and went through the whole verification process with a detective, who agreed with our conclusion. Unfortunately for Matson, the car was impounded, and nobody could say if he'd ever get it back. His only recourse seemed to be to demand compensation from the guy who sold him the car. But that guy was occupying a cell in the county jail and facing an extended stay in the state penitentiary in Walla Walla.

The investigation uncovered a major fraud and car theft ring operating out of Division Street Auto Salvage. They ran a legitimate towing and auto-wrecking service, but they kept their eyes open for highly-desired cars that were wrecked beyond repair.

When one came in, they'd carefully remove the patent plate before sending the wreck to be crushed for scrap metal. There was a small network of car thieves who would steal cars to order. Someone at the salvage yard would put out the specifications, and the thieves would go out looking for a matching car.

The stolen car would go to Levine's Auto Repair, where the license plates and patent plate would be swapped-out for those from the wreck. They'd doctor-up any other serial numbers, and make any easy modifications needed to make the car match the scrapped car's patent plate.

After a three-month investigation, a dozen people were arrested and charged with having stolen and re-sold more than a hundred cars over the last three years. George Bardon eventually got his car back, with a certified copy of its original patent plate installed by the Department of Licensing. But by then, he had already bought a new car and had no use for the Crown Victoria. I called Don Matson, but he didn't want to buy it again. It seemed that nobody wanted a car with this car's history.

So, I bought it for myself and returned my old coupe to the garage behind the shop, where I'd stored it while in Korea. Maybe I'll restore it someday.

The Crown Vic looked pretty nice sitting next to Dale's new Impala hardtop in our garage at home.

Chapter Eight

Moving Forward

A reporter for the Chronicle got my name from George Bardon after we turned the investigation over to the police, and when he wrote a feature article about the take-down of the car theft ring, he credited me with breaking the case.

Having my name appear prominently in the news coverage of the case lent a lot of credibility to me as an investigator. And I did make *one* good connection inside the police department. Sergeant Jeff Warden was the plain-clothes detective who responded to my phone call after I found the hidden serial number on Don Matson's car. He was a Korean War vet, and with that in common, we had something to talk about over a beer after his shift was over.

Most of the other police investigators involved in the Crown Victoria case resented me for the news coverage, feeling—quite accurately—that they'd done all of the hard work, while all I did was give them something to investigate. But the big benefit came from having my name in front of all the people who might need a private detective.

"I hope you're not going to become an insufferable snob, now that you're a celebrity," Dale said.

"Do you think my hair style presents well on television?" I asked.

"You *have* no style." She was quick.

Clutching my heart, I said, "Oh, the slings and arrows of outrageous fortune!"

"Okay, *Ham*let. Maybe a bit less Brylcreem, then." I noted her emphasis the *ham* in Hamlet.

"Can you say something nice about the *only* TV repairman detective in the whole county?"

"You have a nice butt," she said.

"So do you, but… Wait. What were we talking about?"

"The store. We were talking about the store. They say we're in a recession, but our sales go up every month. I think it's time to bring-in that new clerk we talked about last year. Especially if this detective thing is going to work out."

It had been nearly three years since my cousin Penny joined us and we extended our store hours. The transition period had been challenging at first, and both Dale and I had worked twelve-hour days for most of six months. But Penny was sharp and a quick study. As soon as we were confident that she could run the store without one of us there to help her, we started allowing ourselves a little bit of leisure time.

Dale opened the store every morning, while I took care of any service calls or in-store repair work that needed to be done. Most days, I'd be finished with that by noon, at which point I'd take off my blue coveralls and go over to my detective's office.

Penny came in at 1:00, her schedule overlapping with Dale's until 5:00, when Dale and I went home—or at least, tried to. People often joke that getting married is the best way to ruin a good love affair. If they really believe that, I feel sorry for them. For me, every day with Dale was an adventure.

We watched the neighborhood grow around us, as more new homes were built up and down Twenty-Second Avenue. Hardly a month passed without a concrete truck pouring another foundation, and the sound of power saws and hammers went on all day. Neighbors moved in on both sides—an older couple to the left and a young couple with a new baby on the right.

A little further down the road, a pair of families moved into two of the other newly-built houses. Both men, I learned, worked at Kaiser Aluminum, which was the biggest employer in Spokane valley. Tom and Myra Evans had two grade-school-aged boys and a big white dog. Bob and Jean Murphy had about ten children—I've never been able to figure out an exact number—ranging from infant to high school age.

On Sundays, they'd all pile into their station wagon and head off to church. On many such occasions, I tried to count the number of kids in the car, but I couldn't get a consistent number.

"He sounds like a drill sergeant," Dale observed one Saturday morning when Bob was loudly excoriating three of the older boys for the way they were preparing their yard for grass seed.

"No, drill sergeants are more friendly," I said. "Either those boys can't do anything right, or else they're all deaf. Funny, though. When I talked to Bob, he seemed nice enough—kind of quiet, actually."

Dale shook her head. "Well, I'm glad they're not right next door. I wouldn't want to listen to that every day."

The oldest of the Murphy boys had an old brown Oldsmobile 4-door that he drove to school every morning at 7:30, just about the time I'd be heading down to the store. We'd always exchange waves, but I didn't learn his name, which was Bob, until I hired him to mow our lawn every week.

The one thing I knew about the younger boys was that they all were obsessed with gravity. Or, maybe it just seemed that way, because we lived on a hillside. As a kid, I'd always lived on flat ground, so gravity didn't offer any particular recreational opportunities.

But the Murphy boys seemed to always be finding some new way to get from the top of the hill to the bottom. Now, our street wasn't paved, so it made for a pretty bumpy ride, but Pines Road was steeper, longer and smoothly paved. When the boys came home on their bicycles, they'd hit the corner at full speed, jamming on the brakes, skidding in the gravel, and somehow avoiding a catastrophic crash.

The younger kids would go down the Pines Road hill in their wagon, on tricycles, scooters, or homemade contraptions built from scrap lumber and wheels scavenged from old lawn mowers and baby buggies. I don't know how any of them lived to adulthood.

Kenny was the third-oldest of the Murphy boys. He showed up in our store one day after school looking for a radio tube that he couldn't find in the tube tester at the drug store. It was an obscure tube for an old radio that his mom had given him. I looked it up and found it in my reference book, but I couldn't locate a new one through any of my normal sources.

"How old is the radio?" I asked.

"I don't know. I think it might be from around 1940. Mom said the radio fell into a sink full of water and hasn't worked since. The tube doesn't light-up, so it must be burned out."

I felt a connection with the kid. When I was his age, radios were the most important thing in my life. But this particular radio was a lost cause. It had been a nice idea in its time—a multifunction pentode tube that would greatly simplify the radio's circuitry. But the tube never caught on, and very few radios were built to use it. Nobody had made that tube since 1941.

After Christmas that year, Kenny showed me the instruction book for a twelve-in-one Knight Kit "electronics lab" that he'd gotten as a gift. It had a basic triode tube circuit and a row of terminal strips, where you could move wires around to make a dozen different devices.

"This is pretty good," I told him. "It doesn't simply tell you how to wire-up each device, it tells you how it works and explains the electronic principles behind it."

"Yeah. I've already made the first two projects. It's working as a radio receiver now, but I have to listen on a headset. I'd like to add an amplifier circuit, so that I can hook-up a speaker."

I dug around and found the schematic for a simple table-top radio, and circled the audio amplification circuit.

"Build that and hook it to the headphone connections. I'll let you figure out where to tap into the power supply circuit in your kit. And if you smell smoke, it probably means you did something wrong," I said.

I let him pick a handful of used parts out of my "things I may need someday" bin, and sent him on his way. A couple of days later, he came back for a few more parts, and the day after that, he came in to say that the radio and its new amplifier were working.

About once or twice a month, he'd come into the shop, and if I had a repair job going, I'd sometimes let him watch how I fixed it, just as I'd watched and learned from the old man.

* * * * * *

"Mrs. Littleton called," Dale said. "She wants you to go back and fix her TV again."

"What's wrong with it now?" I asked.

"She says it's the same thing as before."

A week earlier, she'd called because her picture had gone black. I discovered that the filament in the horizontal output tube had burned out. I replaced the tube, and the picture came back. Two days later, she said she'd lost the picture again. And I found that the filament in the new tube had burned out. Well, sometimes a tube can be damaged in shipping, so figuring it was something like that, I replaced the tube at no charge to Mrs. Littleton. But had it burned out again?

"She seemed kind of unfriendly on the phone," Dale said.

"She's just frustrated."

"Frustrated? Do frustrated women make a habit of calling you?"

"Only when they're frustrated about their television sets, sweetheart."

"Your dad told me about a house-call where the lady came into the room wearing nothing but her high-heeled shoes. I guess she was frustrated, too."

"Yeah, I heard that story. But Mrs. Littleton is old and fat. I wouldn't want to see her do that."

Dale said, "And what would you say if she was twenty-five and beautiful?"

"I'd say she was old and fat. But she really is. And homely, too." I winked.

Chapter Nine

Spokane's Great Unsolved Case

March 6, 1959

The banner headline on the afternoon paper on March 7, 1959 screamed:

'COPTER CRASH IN SEARCH KILLS MAN; TWO MISSING

There were two stories beneath the headline. One told of the search in the Spokane River for the missing airmen. The other told why the helicopter was flying in the first place. They were looking for nine-year-old Candy Rogers.

Candy Rogers was a Bluebird, selling Campfire Girl mints the previous afternoon, in the neighborhood where she lived in an apartment above a small grocery store, near the west end of Mission Avenue. Unopened boxes of mints were found near the Spokane River half a mile from the Rogers home. Early reports said the number of boxes was five, but later reports said six. Candy left home with seven boxes, and was known to have sold two. If six boxes were actually found, there is a discrepancy that has never been resolved.

Over the next two weeks, hundreds of professional and volunteer searchers scoured every inch of ground within a mile of where the mints were found. Candy undoubtedly had been told many times, as all children were, to never talk with strangers. But that rule was always suspended when it came to going door-to-door to sell cookies, candy, magazine subscriptions, garden seeds, or Christmas cards. It was how kids made money for themselves or, as in Candy's case, for clubs or organizations they belonged to.

There was a photo in the newspaper of the happy, blond-haired girl holding her little dog. It still brings tears to my eyes when I see it. Candy's mother, Elaine Rogers, appeared on TV newscasts, begging for the return of her only child. As days passed, desperation set in.

Hoping that perhaps I might see something that all of the searchers had missed, I drove across town and walked down Pettet Drive from Mission Avenue to Fort Wright Road and back. Of course, I found nothing, but I came away with some impressions about what was unquestionably a terrible crime. Candy Rogers did not get lost or have an accident. She was abducted, and probably had been killed.

Those were easy conclusions to reach, and I'm sure the police had reached them as well, even though their daily press releases were still attempting to convey some hope that the girl would be found alive. Early on Palm Sunday, March 22, that hope was dashed, when Candy's body was found northwest of Spokane, along Old Trails Road.

According to newspaper reports the next day, police were led to the scene Saturday evening by two enlisted men from nearby Fairchild Air Force Base, who had found a pair of little girl's shoes while hunting groundhogs earlier in the day. Police showed the blue, single-strap shoes to Candy's mother and grandmother, who identified them as belonging to the missing girl.

The body was discovered just ten feet from where the shoes were found. The fourth-grade girl had been sexually assaulted and strangled with strips of cloth torn form her petticoat. Her body was hidden under a pile of pine boughs and needles, 130 feet from the road. The most direct route from the probable abduction site in her own neighborhood to the place where the body was found involved crossing the Spokane River on the bridge to Fort George Wright, in the area where the boxes of Campfire mints had been found.

I found it intriguing that the mints were left in the open, where they would be found during the earliest hours of the search for Candy Rogers. It appeared that they had been simply tossed from a moving car. That seemed out of character with the killer's careful concealment of the body. Some people speculated that Candy herself had tossed them out the window, hoping to leave a trail for searchers to follow.

I think a more likely explanation is that the mints marked the site where Candy was assaulted after being lured into the car of her killer. Whatever ruse the killer used to get her into his car, he couldn't go very far before she would figure out that he'd lied to her. It would have taken only a minute or two to drive from Candy's neighborhood to the George Wright bridge, an area where there were no homes and not much traffic.

The search for Candy's killer started with a re-canvassing of the area around her home. Dozens of police officers were assigned to knock on every door within a half-mile of 2106 West Mission, looking for anyone who had seen Candy or any suspicious activity on March 6.

On the day after Candy was found, police were called to Downriver Drive. just north of the Downriver Municipal Golf Course, where fifty-year-old Alfred Graves was found in his car, dead from carbon monoxide asphyxiation. A hose ran from the car's exhaust pipe into a front window.

The thing that got my attention was that Graves lived on North Cannon Street, only half a mile from the Rogers apartment. Furthermore, the site of Graves' apparent suicide was only three-quarters of a mile from where the boxes of Campfire mints were found, and he had killed himself on the day Candy's body was discovered.

The one-paragraph article in the newspaper didn't give any other information, so I called Jeff Warden, the police detective I'd met during my Crown Victoria investigation, to ask if anyone in the police department had noted those connections.

"Believe it or not, Connie, you aren't the only person on earth who can read a map," he said.

Ignoring the jab, I said, "I guessed as much, but I wanted to be sure."

"There's a bit more than that. Graves left a suicide note, but nobody around here is talking about what it said. And when they searched his apartment, they found a collection of newspaper clippings about women and children who had been sexually assaulted."

I let out a low whistle.

"There's more. In the trunk of Graves' car, they found bobby pins and some pieces of rope. I heard that at Candy's autopsy they found rope marks around her waist. They're going over the car with a magnifying glass now."

"Do they think he's the guy?" I asked.

"Not *everything* points to him. This part is off the record, okay? We had a call from a woman who may have been the last person to see Candy Rogers alive. She saw her walking near Cannon Park, and she saw a bright green car driving slowly toward her. She didn't see what happened after that, but the slow-moving green car stuck out in her mind after she learned that Candy was missing. The problem with that, as far as Graves is concerned, is that his car is black."

"So…"

"So, we're still looking—at Graves, and at everyone else. And don't go messing around with this thing. A hundred detectives are working on it, and it isn't likely that you'll come up with anything they don't already know."

Weeks later, I got word that among the evidence gathered from the area where Candy's body was found, there was a green seat cover from a car. That might corroborate what the witness said about a bright green car being at the place where Candy was last seen alive.

Police questioned a man who had owned a car that was nicknamed "*the Green Hornet*," but had sold it to a used car dealer shortly after Candy's death. The dealer told police that the suspect told him that he needed some quick cash to pay for a trip to California. But the suspect had not taken any such trip.

Meanwhile, the dealer sold the car to an Oregon man whose suspicion was aroused when he found children's clothing in the car. A careful examination of the car and the clothing failed to find any connection to the Candy Rogers case, so another suspect went into the "pending more evidence" file.

At this point, I dearly wished that I could have gone through the process to become a police detective, because if I had, perhaps I might be among the hundred officers working the case. Like nearly everybody in Spokane, I was shocked, outraged, and saddened. The Lilac City had lost its innocence and would never be the same.

November 7, 1959

In the early morning hours of Saturday, November 7, a 28-year-old woman was brutally beaten in an apartment at 527 South Lincoln Street in Spokane. Mrs. Gloria J. Brie was taken to nearby Deaconess Hospital, where doctors said that her cheekbones were shattered so badly that fragments of bone had to be removed from around her eyes.

The victim's husband said that he left the apartment at 4:05 a.m. to go wake-up a friend with whom he was planning to go hunting that morning. He returned thirty-five minutes later to find his wife barely clinging to life. He told police that upon returning, he heard someone run down the stairway at the rear of the apartment, and he got a glimpse of a man wearing a blue coat.

An official at the hospital said that Mrs. Brie's face was "literally smashed in." and that she may never see again. Other injuries included a compound fracture in her left hand and severe lacerations on her right hand. No weapon was found at the scene.

As I read about it in the newspaper the next day, I had no reason to associate this attack with the Candy Rogers case. My impression was that it was a crime of extreme rage, and such assaults are almost always committed by someone close to the victim. Based on what I knew at the time, the husband seemed like the logical suspect.

Gloria Brie never regained full consciousness. She died on November 17, ten days after the attack. Her husband was never considered by police to be suspect in the attack.

February 3, 1960

On February 3, a man named James Howard Barnett was arrested on suspicion of having committed a sex crime against a child. That made him an automatic suspect in the murder of Candy Rogers. The 49-year-old man lived on West Sinto Avenue, just two blocks from the Rogers apartment.

Four days after his arrest, Barnett hanged himself in his cell at the Spokane County Jail, leaving a message written in his own blood on the wall, saying, "I have sinned against the Lord." When police went to notify Barnett's wife of his death, she was not even aware that he had been in custody.

Mrs. Barnett's first comment was, "That bastard killed Candy Rogers, didn't he?"

It wasn't a question.

Now police had two suspects, both dead by suicide, who might never be cleared unless someone else could be convicted of the crime.

Chapter Ten

The Draper Sisters
March 20, 1960

The Central Valley Bears dominated the Spokane high school basketball league and in March went to the state tournament in Seattle. And that's where the case of two missing girls began, and quickly pushed the unsolved Candy Rogers case from the newspapers.

The day after the Bears lost the championship game to the Renton Indians, the morning newspaper in Spokane was filled with words of consolation for the fans of Central Valley—a very tough opponent, a valiant effort, a fight to the end, and so on. A second-place finish, after all, was nothing to be unhappy about. It was an honor just to have made it to the championship game. Maybe all the platitudes were true, but some people were in tears about it, just the same.

A day later, on March 21, 1960 the headline on the Monday afternoon newspaper abruptly put the loss of the state championship game into perspective.

LOCAL GIRLS VANISH

Suddenly, a basketball game ceased to be important. Two Spokane valley girls had disappeared from a roadside restaurant in Ritzville, 50 miles southwest of Spokane. The girls had been driving home from Seattle after attending the championship game Saturday evening, and had stopped for a sandwich at Hand's Café located at the junction of Highway 10 and Highway 395.

The missing girls were identified as 18-year-old Lisa Draper, a senior at Central Valley High School and her sister, 16-year-old Gail Draper, a sophomore. They had gone to Seattle the previous Wednesday and had stayed with relatives in Bothell. They were reported missing by their parents in Spokane early Monday morning, when they failed to arrive home as expected Sunday evening.

That was all that was known on that beautiful early spring afternoon, and even when the train carrying the Central Valley basketball team arrived in Spokane at 6:30 Monday evening, many of those present to greet them had not yet heard about the missing girls. A rally was held at the school an hour later, but the girls were not mentioned. It was still too soon to sound the alarm.

But the Tuesday morning newspaper left little room for continued optimism in the city where Candy Rogers's fate was fresh in everyone's mind.

KIDNAPPING FEARED

The story beneath the headline added a number of details that hadn't previously been reported, and over the ensuing days, bits and pieces came together to form a confusing and troubling picture.

The Saturday night game had lasted until nearly 11:00, and by the time Lisa and Gail got back to the Bothell home of their aunt and uncle it was well after midnight. They'd slept-in on Sunday, and then had a late breakfast before starting home at around 12:30. In a phone call just before leaving, Lisa had told her parents that she'd get home around 6:00 p.m. Sunset that evening was at 6:05. By 7:00 it was fully dark, and the parents were beginning to worry.

At 9:00, they called the Washington State Patrol to ask if there had been any accidents along the highway between Seattle and Spokane that could account for the delay. None had been reported, they were told, but often such reports took hours to come through. When the girls still hadn't arrived home by midnight, they were formally declared missing.

On Monday, authorities found Lisa Draper's light blue 1960 Ford Falcon, which had been the subject of a statewide all-points bulletin that had been issued late Sunday night. It was parked next to Hand's Café in Ritzville. A waitress at the café recalled serving two girls matching the descriptions of Lisa and Gail late in the afternoon on Sunday.

On the Wednesday following the girls' disappearance, an all-points bulletin was issued calling for authorities to stop all dark green 1949 and 1950 Chevrolet Fleetlines, and write-down registration information and driver's license numbers. Exactly how that related to the Draper case was not revealed.

That was all that was known after the first week, but it was more than enough to strike dread into the hearts of everyone in Spokane. I hadn't known the Draper girls, but I knew their family through the TV repair business. I'd been to their home two or three times over the years to service their 19-inch Zenith console, which was too big to easily transport to the shop. I'd have been interested in the case even without that connection, but knowing the family made it intensely personal to me.

March 30, 1960

The morning newspaper published an article that added more detail and summarized the status of the investigation at that point. The story was presented in timeline sequence, beginning with events surrounding the state championship game on Saturday, March 19th.

Justine Sorenson was the sister of Earl Draper, father of Lisa and Gail. The girls had stayed with the Sorenson family in Bothell, just north of Seattle and only a few miles from the Hec Edmonson Pavilion on the University of Washington campus, where the state basketball tournament took place.

According to Mrs. Sorenson, someone who identified himself as Bill Brady had called on Saturday morning and asked to talk with Lisa. Overhearing Lisa's end of the phone call, Mrs. Sorenson understood that the girls were going to meet Bill at the pavilion for the championship game. It was her impression that Brady was, or had been, a student at Central Valley.

Lisa and Gail were members of the CV Pep Club, and had access to the cheering section near courtside. Both girls wore their distinctive blue Pep Club jumpers, which would get them into the preferred seating. Bill Brady would not be allowed into that section, so upon reflection, it struck Mrs. Sorenson as odd that Lisa had arranged to meet him before the game.

In any case, she felt that Lisa was safe as long as she was accompanied by Gail. There's no better chaperone than a little sister. Following the game, the girls had gone to a pizza parlor with some of the other kids, but Mrs. Sorenson did not know who. She assumed it was other kids from Central Valley.

The girls got back to the Sorenson home a couple of hours after the end of the game. They slept late on Sunday, and Justine Sorenson had served a late breakfast for the girls before they started their six-hour drive back to Spokane. Before leaving, Lisa asked her aunt how to find Highway 2, which seemed to Justine like a strange way to get to US-10. A more direct and faster route would be to go straight south, through Bellevue.

Lisa acknowledged that, but said they were going the other way in order to link-up with Bill Brady, who had asked if the girls could follow him on the way to Spokane, because he'd been having some kind of car trouble. It seemed to be a reasonable thing to do, and going that way would not add more than fifteen or twenty minutes to the trip. Justine understood that the girls were to meet Brady at a Shell gas station on Highway 2 in Woodinville and proceed home from there.

Lisa phoned her mother just before leaving Bothell, and said she expected to be home before dark—around 6:00 p.m. A receipt found in Lisa's car showed that she'd filled her gas tank at a Shell station in Woodinville at 12:55. An attendant at the gas station remembered the girls in the new Falcon, but had not seen them with anyone else.

Another receipt found in the car showed that at 3:45 Lisa bought 12.6 gallons of regular at an Enco gas station outside Moses Lake. When contacted several days later, nobody at the station could recall having pumped the gas.

Forty-five minutes later, around 4:30, the girls were seen at Hand's Café, at the junction of US-10 and US-395. Sandra Hutchins, a waitress at the café, identified Gail and Lisa as the two girls who sat at a table next to the front windows and ordered burger baskets with soft drinks. She also said that a young man "with greasy hair" had briefly joined the girls at their table.

Sandra said that she'd overheard him saying something about "engine trouble." This, when taken together with what Lisa had told her aunt, led investigators to speculate that the young man with the greasy hair might be Bill Brady.

The girls left the café around 5:00, and were never seen again. When they hadn't made it home by 6:30, their parents became concerned, and at 9:30 they raised the alarm. A statewide all-points-bulletin was issued for Lisa's light blue Ford Falcon, which had been an early graduation gift from her parents, just a month earlier.

At 5:30 the next morning, the breakfast cook at Hand's Café noticed the light blue Falcon at the far end of the parking lot. At 10:40, a Ritzville police officer spotted the Falcon and identified it as the subject of the APB. Its doors were unlocked, but suitcases, overnight bags, and other personal items were left, apparently undisturbed, on the backseat.

Keys to the car were found in the ashtray. It seemed apparent that whatever happened to Lisa and Gail had happened at Hand's Café. Investigators reasoned that upon leaving the café, the girls must have encountered someone before they got to Lisa's Falcon.

Later in the day, after reading that the girls had disappeared from Hand's Café, Chet Winston called Ritzville Police to report that he'd been at the café around the same time as the girls, though he hadn't noticed them. But as he was getting into his car to leave, he noted a young man with the hood raised on a dark green Chevrolet fastback from 1949 or 1950. He said that the man had "slicked-back" long hair.

Considering the waitress's statement that the greasy-haired young man who had been at the girls' table and mentioned having engine trouble, investigators believed that both witnesses may have seen the same man. Once they made this connection, and believing that the girls must have known the young man, Bill Brady became the first suspect in the case, and a new APB was issued for a dark green 1949 or 1950 Chevrolet Fleetline.

The working theory was that Lisa and Gail joined Brady in the parking lot outside the café, and for some reason went with him in the old Chevy, leaving Lisa's new Falcon behind. Whatever happened after that was open to speculation, but none of the options boded well for the girls. Finding Bill Brady became the number one focus for the police.

The case was being handled jointly by the Ritzville City Police and the Adams County Sheriff's Office. When they learned that Bill Brady might be a current or former student at Central Valley High School in Spokane, they contacted the school office. But nobody by that name was or had ever been enrolled at Central Valley.

The principal sent out a memo to all home-room teachers, directing them to ask any students who had seen Lisa or Gail Draper at the basketball tournament to report to the school office. About two dozen students responded, mostly girls in the Pep Club. None remembered seeing either of the girls with anyone they didn't know.

Fingerprint technicians dusted Lisa's car, but it would take weeks or months to identify the prints found. The job was made especially difficult because neither of the girls had ever been fingerprinted. Their prints would naturally be expected in the car, but separating them from any prints left by a suspect would be nearly impossible. That didn't especially bother the police, since they had no reason to believe that Brady, or whoever the greasy-haired kid was, had ever been in Lisa's car.

One odd thing that investigators noted was that Lisa's gas tank was nearly empty. It should have had over twelve gallons still in it after the fill-up at Moses Lake. The best explanation for that was that maybe someone had syphoned the gas out during the night.

* * * * * *

By 1960, I believed I was qualified and capable of solving any crime, including the murder of Candy Rogers and the disappearance of the Draper sisters. All I needed was for someone to hire me for the job, so I kept myself prepared for that eventuality by collecting and absorbing every shred of information that came to me regarding these and several other prominent cases.

In the scant information available on the Draper case, several things stood out. The first was about Bill Brady. He'd apparently lied about having gone to school at Central Valley. Either that, or his name wasn't actually Bill Brady. An innocent explanation might be that Justine Sorenson had gotten the name wrong. A more ominous explanation was that he had lied about his name.

Few people lie about their names unless they're hiding something, or planning something that they don't want to be connected with. If Bill Brady had any kind of sinister intentions, it is entirely probable that he'd have used a false name. This would leave the question unanswered as to whether he did or did not attend school at Central Valley. But if he was putting the hustle on Gail or Lisa, saying that he had gone to their high school would be a way to break the ice.

My next question had to do with Brady's car. If the car really had a mechanical problem so significant that he wanted the girls to follow him, why was he even *thinking* about driving it clear across the state? Was it simply youthful recklessness, or was the "car trouble" just a ploy to lure the girls into a position where he could do something?

And on that point, let's not tiptoe around the obvious. This was almost certainly a sexually-motivated crime, though the newspapers had carefully avoided saying so. I felt that from the very first interaction between the Draper girls and Bill Brady, he had been trying to get them into a position where he could take advantage of them, either by seduction or by force. The tale about car trouble was a key part of his plan.

Brady's car was identified as a green Chevrolet Fleetline. I recalled something that Spokane Police Sergeant Jeff Warden had told me once when we were discussing the Candy Rogers case. There was a witness who saw a bright green car driving very slowly toward Candy at about the time it was believed the abduction had taken place.

Among the evidence gathered from the area where Candy's body was found, there was a green seat cover from a car. I knew that police had even questioned the owner of a green car, but apparently that was a dead end. Or was it? Now we had two more girls abducted, and multiple witnesses had seen a green car at the scene.

Perhaps the biggest question was why the girls had left Hand's Café in Brady's apparently broken-down Chevy instead of Lisa's new Falcon. I cannot think of anything that Brady could have told the girls that would motivate them to do that. It would almost certainly have taken some kind of physical force or tangible threat. Yet, I have a difficult time imagining Brady doing that in such a highly visible place and time.

The question of fingerprints in Lisa's car is probably irrelevant. For fifty years, fingerprints have been touted as the best forensic evidence you can have. But that's true only if you have the fingerprints of a suspect, to compare with latent prints from the crime scene. No prints from the Falcon could help identify a suspect unless his prints were already on file.

The empty gas tank was a much more important thing. Knowing that the tank was filled at Moses Lake meant that the absence of at least twelve gallons of gas had to be explained. There were only three possible explanations: leakage, driving, or theft. Since the police were saying that theft was the best explanation, I have to think that they checked for leaks and found none. Since the car had been parked all night at the café, theft was the only thing left. But there was no physical evidence to show that anyone had syphoned gas out of the tank.

Those were my thoughts on the case at that time, pending the discovery of the girls—and at this point, I had no illusions that they'd be found alive. Like everyone else in Spokane, a year earlier I'd held onto hope for Candy Rogers right up to the day when her body was found. That case shattered a lot of illusions. And the killer of Candy Rogers was still out there.

※ ※ ※ ※ ※ ※

"What is happening to Spokane?" Dale asked. "Things like this don't happen here."

"Apparently, they do," I said.

"But it doesn't even feel safe to let kids go outside anymore."

"No, I guess it doesn't. If *we* had a girl, what would we do to protect her?" I asked.

"Do we have to figure that out before we make one?" she asked.

"Are you hinting at something?"

"Well, look at us. You're almost thirty years old, and I'm close behind. If we're ever going to have a family, we should get down to business, don't you think?"

I said, "I thought we got down to business the day we got married."

"But you never actually mentioned trying to have children," she said.

"I never mentioned trying *not* to," I countered.

"Well, that's interesting…"

"Are you saying that you thought I *didn't* want to?"

She paused to think about that. And then she gave me an odd smile.

"It was something your mom said."

"My mom? What on earth did she say?"

"A few days before we got married, she sat me down for a serious talk about pregnancy, and shared all of the ways to avoid it. I thought she was speaking for you."

I laughed, and quickly apologized, "I'm sorry. I don't mean to take this as a joke. It's the Catholic thing, that's all. Mom was just telling you what all good Catholic women do if they don't want to have traditional large families."

That made Dale laugh. "It never occurred to me… I mean, well, I'll be!"

Chapter Eleven

A Break in the Draper Case
April 16, 1960

The first real break in the Draper case came on April 16th, four weeks after the girls disappeared. Two boys picking up pop bottles along the road looked under the bridge that crosses Crab Creek, ten miles south of the little town of Harrington and seventeen miles from Hand's Café. There were no bottles there, but they found a large black plastic bag tucked into a nook at the top of the embankment under the bridge.

The first thought that the twelve-year-old boys had was that maybe there were body parts in the bag, and that was an irresistible lure. One of the boys tentatively tugged the bag from its hiding place, while the other pinched his nose—just in case. The bag was clean, and appeared to be fairly new, and there were no objectionable odors. The more adventuresome of the pair used his pocket knife to cut the twine that held the bag closed, and looked inside.

"Ahh!" he screamed, "Holy crap!"

He tossed the bag into the lap of the other boy, who let out a scream and frantically crab-walked away from it.

"Jesus Christ! What's in there?" he demanded, while his friend broke out laughing.

"Man, like you should've seen your face. I thought you were going to shit!"

"You asshole! So, what's in the bag, anyway?"

"Just some clothes and stuff. But, oh man, I got you good!"

Still laughing, the boys took a more careful look inside the bag. As soon as they realized what they'd discovered, they put the bag back where they found it, and rode their bikes to the nearest farmhouse, to call the sheriff. When the boys talked to the Lincoln County deputy who responded to their call, they reported that, in addition to clothing, the bag held two purses containing driver's licenses and I.D. cards belonging to Lisa and Gail Draper.

Neither of the boys mentioned the prank. The more complete version of the story came out in the locker room at the boys' school two days later, and the gym coach shared it with others members of the faculty, including an English teacher who moonlighted as a stringer for the local newspaper. A photo of the boys and a sanitized version of prank made it into the newspaper, along with details about the contents of the bag, thus compromising the authorities' ability to use that knowledge to screen suspects.

That detailed inventory of the bag's contents included everything that both girls were believed to have been wearing when last seen. All of the clothing had been folded and placed in the bag almost as if someone had been packing a suitcase. Nothing was torn or stained in any way that would suggest that it had been removed from the girls by force.

Eventually, everything was turned over to the Adams County and Ritzville authorities who were handling the Draper investigation. But by then, everything in the bag had been handled by at least ten different people, and photographed by reporters from Spokane. If there had been any trace evidence present, it was rendered useless by all of the careless handling.

While the media had a feeding frenzy talking about how the bag was found and what was in it, I was trying to figure out what the discovery meant. The first issue was the bag itself. It was described as "new," and had been secured by twine. Since plastic bags and twine would not be routinely carried around in a car, it follows that their use in the disposal of the girls' clothes and purses suggests that the crime was premeditated.

That bolsters the theory that Bill Brady's story about car trouble was a ploy to set the stage for the abduction. If he did that, then it makes sense that he'd bring bags for disposal of evidence.

I found it interesting that the kidnapper had placed the bag in a protected location, where discovery was at least possible, if not probable. Why would he do that? He could have burned it, buried it, or distributed it in dumpsters and trash cans. It was as though he *wanted* it to be found; or maybe he intended to retrieve it at some later time, for some unknown reason.

And why was it hidden at Crab Creek? It was eight miles off the highway to Spokane, on a secondary road that led to the little town of Harrington. If Bill Brady had actually been a student at Central Valley, and lived in Spokane valley, why was he on the road to Harrington?

His choice of the Crab Creek bridge implies that the kidnapper, whether Bill Brady or someone else, was familiar with the area. He almost certainly knew in advance that there was a hiding place under that particular bridge, and that suggests that he lived nearby, rather than in Spokane valley.

But the strangest thing in the whole discovery was the condition of the clothes. Nothing about them indicated that there had been a struggle. Apparently, the girls had somehow been persuaded to strip naked without the use of physical force. By all accounts, the girls had no history of promiscuity, so the logical deduction is that the kidnapper had used some kind of coercion—perhaps involving a weapon and its threatened use. So, maybe that's how he got the girls into his car in the first place.

The temperature in Ritzville that night was in the thirties. A sexual assault is the most likely reason the girls' clothes were taken, but it's fairy unusual for a sex crime to be committed outdoors, or even in a car, when it's that cold. What's more, it would be very difficult for a lone kidnapper to deal with two victims in the confined space in a car. For these reasons, I considered it likely that the assault took place in a building, rather than in the car or outdoors.

This again supports the conclusion that the kidnapper lived in or was very familiar with the immediate area. Thus, my interpretation of the known facts was that the girls were taken to a house or other heated building, either by ruse or coercion, A reasonable inference is that the evidence—the bag of clothing and personal effects—was removed from the scene of the assault because it was a place that might be visited by other people.

But the greatest question of all was still unanswered. Where were Lisa and Gail? I tried to imagine a scenario to support the hope that they might still be alive. Maybe the kidnapper took their clothing as a means of control. Escape in the cold weather would be almost suicidal without clothes. I guess some desperately optimistic people could cling to that.

I couldn't. I was almost certain that the girls had been killed—probably within twenty-four hours of their abduction. Authorities had organized search parties who worked on foot and horseback to scour the area within a twenty-mile radius of Hand's Café, but nothing was found, and it was becoming increasingly difficult to find volunteers.

Meanwhile, the search continued for the green Chevrolet that witnesses saw at Hand's Café. The identification of it as a Fleetline model helped narrow the search, as it had been a less popular style, but it was still a huge task. News reporters encouraged everyone to call police if they saw such a car, resulting in hundreds of leads, all requiring investigative follow-up.

There was a cluster of reports in Spokane valley, one of which came from the owner of a green 1949 Fleetline. He told a detective from the Spokane County Sheriff's Office that he was being harassed everywhere he went, and wanted to clear his name. But when Frank Stearman revealed that he was a 1958 graduate of Central Valley High School, his voluntary statement backfired. He was taken to an interview room at the sheriff's office and grilled for several hours by detectives from both the Adams County and Spokane County sheriff's offices.

The key question was whether Stearman had been in Seattle for the basketball tournament, something that he emphatically denied. His employer backed him up, stating that Stearman had been at work until 4:00 p.m. on March 18th, the Friday before the Draper girls disappeared. And on Sunday evening, Stearman had been cited for speeding on the Spokane valley freeway near Sullivan Road. A Washington State Patrol officer confirmed that he had written the ticket at 6:45 p.m., and stated that Stearman was alone in the car.

This left a very tight window of opportunity for Stearman to be the person known as "Bill Brady." Since Stearman was unable to produce a verifiable alibi for the time between 4:00 p.m. on Friday and 6:45 p.m. on Sunday, authorities did not completely dismiss him as a suspect. However, because there was no hard evidence, Stearman could not be held in custody.

The newspapers went overboard, publishing Stearman's year book photo and pictures of his car, which had been impounded and was being carefully examined by detectives. The fact that his name was nothing like Bill Brady was easily dismissed. Obviously, someone intent on committing a major crime would use an alias.

As for Stearman's alibi, reporters were quick to point out that he could have driven straight to Seattle after work on Friday and arrived in time to encounter the girls after CV's evening game. Then, on Sunday, he had at least an hour and forty-five minutes to do whatever he'd done to the girls. The drive from Ritzville to the location of the traffic stop was only 55 miles, and could easily be done in ninety minutes. That left at least fifteen minutes unaccounted for.

Reporters reminded us that the witnesses who saw the Draper girls leave Hand's Café had said that it was approximately 5:00. Defining "approximately" as plus-or-minus fifteen minutes, they gave Stearman half an hour—maybe more, given his documented tendency to exceed speed limits.

For the next two weeks, authorities and reporters dug into every detail of Frank Stearman's life. They got his high school records and determined that he had a below-average academic record, and had been disciplined for multiple infractions. Classmates from Central Valley described him as a "rod," a term applied to hotrodders and members of teenage gangs. They were guys who commonly wore blue jeans and t-shirts, smoked cigarettes, and sported "DA" haircuts.

The duck-ass haircut was commonly associated with juvenile delinquency and rock-and-roll music. Like many boys in the late 1950s, Stearman had tried to emulate Elvis Presley, thus giving him the slicked-back, greasy hair described by witnesses at Hand's Café, though none of that showed in his yearbook photo. One enterprising newspaper illustrator took an enlarged print of the yearbook photo and added the DA haircut with pen and ink. The doctored photo became the most commonly-used picture of Stearman in subsequent news reports.

Adams County authorities, however, refrained from charging Stearman with abducting the girls, and when reporters demanded to know why, the sheriff's spokesman would say only that they were "evaluating" the evidence. I wanted to know what evidence they had, but the authorities were keeping that to themselves.

In my mind, the location where the girls' clothing was found all but excluded Stearman as a suspect. The extra time needed to get to and from the Crab Creek bridge, force the girls to strip, and then conceal their clothes exceeded even the thirty-minute window of time generously given him by the reporters.

The furor gradually died down without resolution, even though many people were convinced that Frank Stearman had abducted and killed the Draper girls. On May 2, 1960, Frank Stearman was found in his apartment on East Valley Way, dead from a self-inflicted gunshot wound.

Chapter Twelve

The Arson Case

Early in June, a man came in through the "C.R. Pratt Investigations" door and rang the bell on the vacant reception desk.

I loudly said, "I'm in the darkroom. I'll be with you in a second. I just need to finish rinsing this film."

After hanging the freshly developed film to dry, I grabbed a paper towel and went up front. The man who had rung the bell was probably in his fifties. His slumped shoulders hinted that he had some kind of back problem. I took his business card and motioned for him to have a seat.

Victor Piquet, President
Inland Empire Entertainment Group
Dishman, Washington

"Name's Vic," he said. "Last name is pronounced P-K."

"I'm Connie Pratt. What can I do for you?"

I finished drying my hands and tossed the paper towel into the empty waste basket.

"My company owns—I should say, owned—the roller-skating rink that burned down last month. Are you familiar with it?"

"Certainly. Last I heard, they were saying it was an arson fire."

"Indeed. And that's the problem. Our insurance company is resisting a pay-out until the person who set the fire is arrested. They say that's the only way they can be sure that we didn't do it ourselves."

I said, "I'm no attorney, but that doesn't sound right."

He sighed, "And you're correct. Our attorney says we'll win in court unless they can prove that we set the fire or hired someone to do it, which they can't, because we didn't. But we'd like to avoid getting into a legal battle."

"Last I heard, the police were still investigating the fire."

"They told me, 'off the record,' that they know who did it. They just don't have enough evidence to make an arrest. I think they've put it aside, to work on bigger cases."

"I can take a look at it," I said. "At the very least, I'll be able to confirm whether or not the police actually have a suspect."

"Fair enough. I heard what you did with that car theft ring. I hope you can do as well for us."

After Piquet left, I went to the file cabinet in the store office and got the phone number for a TV repair customer who was a medic for the Spokane Valley Rural Fire Department.

"Yeah. The alarm came in at 4:00 in the morning. We were called to the scene in case someone got hurt," he confirmed. "That was one hell-of-a-fire. The building was fully-involved when we got there. Never was any hope of saving it."

"I read the early news reports. They said it was suspected arson."

"Yeah, when the first unit made the scene, they saw a car peel-out of the parking lot and make tracks up Sprague."

"Could anyone describe the car?"

"They only saw it from behind, but one guy said it was an Edsel."

"Did they see the driver?"

"Not in any detail. But they did say that there were other people in the car—three, plus the driver."

"Which way did it go?"

"Nobody saw where it went—only that it turned east. We were all too concerned about the fire."

"Besides the car that took off, were there any other indications that the fire was deliberately set?"

"Plenty. The fire started *outside* the building, and we could smell gasoline around the southwest corner of the building, where the fire started. Within five minutes of the Skateland alarm, there were two apparent diversions. One was another fire, straight across Sprague Avenue, at Union Sash and Door. Our guys got that one knocked-down pretty quick. The other diversion was four phone calls from people claiming that there was a fire at the Mormon Church up on Argonne Road. That turned out to be a false alarm, but it pulled two units away from Skateland."

"Anybody get hurt?"

"Nothing that took anything more than a Band-Aid. Mostly, there was nothing to do but stand back and pour water in from outside. All of that waxed hardwood went up like tinder. Nobody could get inside. The place burned to the ground before sunrise."

After I wrapped-up that call, I drove down to the scene. All that remained of Skateland was two rows of blackened concrete columns, and the skeletal remains of a bus in the eastern end of the wreckage. Two apparently undamaged Skateland busses were parked off to the side. Workers were scooping ash and charcoal into a couple of dump trucks.

I walked around to the corner where the bus garage had been, and on the driveway slab next to it, I could see black marks where someone had spun the tires and burned rubber into the concrete. I shot a roll of film as I walked the full perimeter of the site.

Across the street, the freshly painted rear garage door was the only sign of the fire at Union Sash and Door. Just to get a feel for what the arsonists had done that night, I drove over to Argonne

Road, and up to the LDS Church at Boone Avenue. As I looked around the parking lot, I noticed a pair of parallel J-shaped skid marks on the asphalt.

I'd been seeing similar marks on roads around the valley for several months. Thirty-Second Avenue seemed to be a favorite place for whoever was doing it. Curious now, I contemplated how the marks were made. The guy most likely to know the answer was Maxey, at the Texaco station where I'd inspected the Crown Victoria that I was now driving.

"Push-button automatic," Maxey said. They get going as fast as they dare in reverse, then punch neutral and stomp on the gas. As the engine revs, they punch it into low gear. Tires break loose and start spinning forward while the car is still moving backward. They keep burning rubber until the backward momentum is used up and the car starts forward. At some point, they let off the gas before the engine blows up."

"Push-button transmission, huh. So, that means a Chrysler product," I surmised.

"Or a Packard. They had it first. And now Edsels have it, too."

"So, you know how it's done. Do you know who's doing it?"

"Not specifically. But I can think of maybe a couple dozen hoodlums who might do things like that. Mostly high school punks or dropouts. Loudmouth greasers wearing their jeans at half-mast. You know the kind."

"Push-button transmissions haven't been around very long. I can't see the kids you're describing being able to buy a new car."

Maxey shrugged. "Who knows? Maybe they steal 'em and take 'em out for a joy ride—and they don't give a shit if they tear up the tires and transmission."

* * * * * *

It was late in the afternoon when I returned to my office. I made a few phone calls before turning off the lights and switching my phone to the answering service. Dale was just finishing her day in the store, so we decided to go try a new restaurant a couple of miles toward town on Sprague.

As we drove past the site where Skateland had been, I pointed-out the remains of the 16,000 square-foot building.

"The owner of that place came in today. He's grown impatient with the police. He doesn't think they're putting enough effort into it, and hired me to find out what happened."

"So, was it arson?"

"Looks like it to me—and that's what the fire department says."

"Any idea who did it?"

"Not yet, but I have some ideas where to start looking. I talked to a fireman who was there. He said someone saw a car speed away from the place when the first truck arrived. I'm trying to find out what kind of car it was."

"I guess that's a start," she said.

"Yeah, I know it doesn't sound like much. But the cops have connected this thing to a string of fire alarm calls at the Mormon church up on Argonne. I went up there, mostly to see how long it would take to drive to it from Skateland—only a couple of minutes. But I noticed some very distinctive skid marks in the church parking lot that might help."

"Skid marks? How does that help?"

"Have you noticed J-shaped double skid marks down on Thirty-Second?"

Dale shook her head. "I haven't been down there lately."

"The thing is, they're just like what I found in the church parking lot. Maxey, out at the Texaco station, told me how those skid marks are made. Turns out that they're done by a car with a push-button automatic transmission. That limits it to only a few models—and they can't be more than a couple of years old. Next, I need to talk to someone at the high school, and see if any students there have access to a car like that."

"You lost me. What makes you think it's a high school kid?"

"The skid marks. That's something that grown-ups just don't do," I said.

"So, what's next?"

"Pizza," I said as we arrived at Shakey's. "Everything I know about pizza came from Dean Martin."

Dale looked surprised. "Your mom is Italian, and you're telling me you've never had pizza?"

"Mom was thoroughly Americanized. I doubt that *she's* ever eaten pizza."

Looking around, it struck me as odd that the Italian restaurant was designed entirely around an old English pub theme, down to the lettering on their menu. I had to rely on the waiter's recommendation when I placed my order for "Shakey's Special." And now I'm hooked.

* * * * * *

After my service calls the next day, I drove out to see the principal at Central Valley High. It was not the same school I'd attended, which had been built in the 1920s. The new school was on Sullivan Road and had opened in 1957.

The building was different, but the name on the principal's door was the same as it had been eleven years before, and it somehow conjured a trace of the dread that accompanied any visit to the principal's office when I was a kid. Not that I had that many…

"Well, Connie! It's nice to see you again. What's it been? Ten years?"

"Yes, sir. Eleven, to be exact."

"Oh yes. Class of forty-nine. Well, you've done all right for yourself. I saw that article in the newspaper a while back. Now, what ever became of your dad's radio shop? I always figured you'd end up owing it."

"You figured right. I own it, and my wife runs it. You might remember her—Dale Jeffries."

He smiled broadly. "I most certainly do. What a lovely girl. I remember when her parents died. A real tragedy. I'm happy to hear that she's doing well. So, what brings you here today, Connie?"

"Well, Mr. Aronson, I wanted to ask…"

He interrupted, "Call me Brad. Please."

I nodded and continued, "A case I'm investigating involves—or at least I think it does—some high school-aged boys."

"Can you tell me their names?"

"I don't know their names. That's what I'm hoping you can help with."

He nodded, so I continued, "Maybe you've noticed some unusual skid marks on the roads around here—pairs of parallel J-shaped skid marks."

"Well, now that you mention it, I *have* seen some of those. There was a pair right out front a couple of weeks ago."

"The marks can be made only by a late-model car with a push-button automatic transmission—probably a car built by Chrysler or Edsel. So, I'm looking for a rebellious or unruly boy who has access to a car like that."

Aronson rubbed his chin and gazed at the ceiling. He finally said, "You aren't looking for him because he leaves skid marks on the road."

"No. The skid marks are just his signature. I'm looking for him in connection with a criminal matter. And right now, the skid marks are my best lead."

He pressed the button on the intercom box that sat on his desk and said, "Miss Ryerson, can you bring me the file on student parking permits, please?"

"Yes sir. It'll be just a minute."

The list contained about fifty names, and the newest car on it was a '57 Chevrolet. No Edsels at all, and no Chryslers, Dodges or Plymouths newer than 1954. But there was a small stack of notes paper-clipped to the file folder.

"When a student comes to school with a car that isn't on our parking list, he's supposed to fill-out one of these."

Aronson thumbed through the pink note slips. He pulled one slip free from the stack.

"Matt Balmer," he said. "He fits the description of the kind of kid you're looking for, and this says that he came to school once last fall in his mother's car—a 1958 Edsel."

"What can you tell me about the kid?"

"He's been a bit of a trouble-maker. Nothing terrible, but lots of minor things. He's a sophomore, but he ought to be a junior. Held back for academic reasons when he was in junior high."

"Do you know who he hangs around with?"

"He's kind of a loner, but there are a few boys who've gotten in trouble with him."

Aronson thought about it for a few minutes, writing down names as he thought of them. He came up with five: Lance Warfield, Jerry Lorenzo, Carl Emery, Steven Drum, and George Reser, I didn't know any of them, but some of the family names were familiar. He gave the list to the secretary and asked her to add addresses and parents' names.

* * * * * *

My strategy to get information from Matt Balmer and his friends hinged on the fact that I, as a private investigator, was not obligated to get parental permission to question minors, as were police detectives. Any private citizen can have a conversation with any other private citizen.

A greater question was what I could do with anything I learned in those conversations. If I learned something that would potentially be useful in a future prosecution, it would be rendered useless in court by the fact that my testimony would be hearsay and thus not admissible. On the other hand, an audio recording of the conversation *would* be admissible evidence.

And at this point in my thought process, I remembered the old Russian wire recorder. It was designed for concealment and portability. The recorder itself was about the size of a modern transistor radio, and could be carried in a jacket pocket. It was powered by batteries carried in pouches on a leather belt worn inside the spy's shirt. If I could make it work, the device would be useful in this and future investigations.

The first thing I discovered when I pulled it from the drawer where it had been for more than a decade was that the batteries had split open and leaked their corrosive ammonium chloride electrolyte into the pouches on the belt, destroying the wiring and eradicating any identifying marks on the batteries.

But the shape and size of three of the batteries coincided with D-cell 1.5-volt American batteries. Based on how they had been arranged in the belt, two in one pouch and the third in a separate pouch, I surmised that the paired batteries would power a 3-volt motor to drive the wire recorder, while the solo battery would power the filaments in the two miniature vacuum tubes.

The fourth battery had to be the "B-battery" that provided anode or plate voltage to the tubes. In most American-made portable radios, before the introduction of transistors, the B-battery would be an 80-volt dry cell. We stocked some of these in the store, so I picked the most compact one, along with three heavy-duty D-cell batteries.

I connected them to the recorder in what I guessed to be the proper configuration, and flipped the tiny toggle that I assumed to be the on-off switch. There were four push-buttons that I figured were play, stop, rewind, and record. When I pressed the first button, I was pleased to see that the motor ran and turned the spools containing the magnetic recording wire.

With a few seconds of experimentation, I figured out which of the other buttons did what. I could see what appeared to be a tiny built-in microphone on the side of the metal case, and below it, a miniature phone jack. This, I figured, was the audio output connection.

In our parts supply, I found a plug that fit, and with that, I made a jumper cable that let me plug into the phonograph input on a high-fi amplifier. When I pressed the play button, I heard a garbled sound dominated by raspy static. I cleaned the recording head and magnetic wire and tried again.

It worked. I found myself listening to the voice of someone repeating "testing, testing, testing, one-two-three, testing." Next, I tried the record button and spoke the same mantra. On playback, I recognized my own voice.

I experimented with various audio-level adjustments, and tuned the device for maximum sensitivity and best audio quality. Then I went to work making something to carry the battery pack. Instead of a belt, I used an old shoulder holster for the .38 revolver that I never carried anyway.

* * * * * *

George Reser was the first of the kids I tracked-down. I approached him at Ron's Drive-In, which was a popular gathering place for Central Valley students. He was outside, sitting at a picnic table, smoking a cigarette.

"George Reser?" I said, as I approached.

"Who wants to know?" he asked.

"My name's Pratt. I want to talk to you. It's important."

He gave an indifferent shrug. "So, talk."

"Are you aware that when you call the fire department to report a fire, the call is recorded on a tape recorder?"

I saw a tiny reaction to that question that belied his noncommittal response. "So?"

"Did you know that four false alarms were phoned-in during a five-minute period around 4:00 a.m. on May 8th?"

"What about it?"

"I've been told that you were one of the ones who called. You know, you can get in a lot of trouble for that."

"Whoever told you that was lying. I never made any calls like that."

I said, "There's one way to find out. All I have to do is call you on the phone, with a recorder running. As soon as you talk, I'll have you on tape."

He stood up and said, "Get your kicks however you want. I'm cutting-out."

I hadn't been so optimistic as to believe that he'd make any kind of confession. But, guilty or innocent, if he knew anything at all about the false alarm calls, he'd be telling his friends all about our conversation.

Half an hour later, I staked-out Frank Lorenzo's house on Valley Way, near the library. When Jerry Lorenzo drove up in his old Mercury, I switched on my wire recorder and intercepted him before he got to the house.

I said, "Your friend George says maybe you like to call-in false fire alarms. Do you know that the fire department keeps tape recordings of all alarm calls?"

"Reser's a lying fink! He don't know from nothing."

"Then, maybe you can set me straight. Who made the calls?"

"I ain't ratting-out nobody, so stop bugging me." He turned to leave.

I said, "You were seen with Matt Balmer in his mom's Edsel, hot-rodding around in the LDS church parking lot."

"So what? That don't mean I made any false alarms!"

I found Lance Warfield pumping gas at the Phillips 66 station on Pines at Mission. While he filled my tank, I switched on my wire.

As I handed him a five to pay for the gas, I asked, "Is this where you, Lorenzo, and Balmer got the gas to start the Skateland fire?"

His jaw dropped and he stared at me. "Did Balmer tell you that?"

"Well, what do *you* think?"

"Listen. I'm giving you the straight skinny, okay? This is just between you and me. So, if this gets to the fuzz, I'll deny it all. It'll be your word against mine."

"Fair enough. Now, what about the gas?"

"I didn't know what Balmer wanted the gas for. I just filled the cans, and nobody can prove anything else."

"Yeah? And I suppose you didn't light the match, either."

"You're damn right, I didn't."

"So, the whole thing was Balmer's doing," I said.

He ignored my sarcastic tone. "You know it, man! It was all him!"

"And you were just an innocent spectator."

"I was there, okay? But that's it. I never got out of the car."

"What about the fire across the street?"

"That was Fletcher. We had nothing to do with that."

"Fletcher? Who's Fletcher."

"Donny Fletcher. He's a West Valley puke. He and Balmer are neighbors, over on Herald Road. They figured out the whole thing—start two fires at the same time, and watch the show. After he lit his fire, he ran across the street and jumped into the car with us. By then, the fire engines were rolling in, so we split."

"And went up to the Mormon church on Argonne?"

He looked surprised. "That's right. Balmer turned a brodie in the parking lot, and then cut out."

"Where did you call-in the fire alarms?"

He sighed. "Looks like you know the whole story. There's a phone booth at the gas station up at Mission and Argonne."

"So, it was you, Balmer, Lorenzo, and Fletcher."

"Yeah, but except for the false alarms, Lorenzo and me didn't do nothing. Just sat in the backseat and watched."

* * * * * *

Before going home, I drove over to Herald Road and found Balmer's house. There were two cars on the driveway—Matt's beat-up 1940 Chevrolet Sedan and his mother's two-door Edsel Citation. The fact that it was a two-door supported Warfield's statement that he and Lorenzo never got out of the car, something that would be difficult to do if the front seat was occupied.

I knew what had taken place on May 8th, and I had my wire recordings to prove what the perpetrators had said. My job was done. All I had to do was turn-over the recordings to the sheriff's office detectives and let them finish it.

The next day, I called my friend, Jeff Warden, to report what I'd found out. He didn't know right off who was in charge of the Skateland case, but promised to find out and let me know. Two hours later, he gave me a name and phone number.

"Deputy Dunsmuir, I understand that you are in charge of the investigation of the Skateland fire," I said.

"That's correct. And you are…"

"I'm Connie Pratt, private investigator. I have some information regarding the fire."

In a voice filled with boredom, Dunsmuir said, "I'm sure that anything you can tell us will be helpful."

"I have audio recordings of two of the boys involved in setting the fire. They've told me everything that happened."

"How did you get this recording?" asked Dunsmuir.

Somewhat proudly, I said, "I have a miniature wire recorder from a Russian spy. It's very small, and I had it running in my pocket while I talked with some of those involved."

"So, you had a concealed recording device?"

"Right. And I can give you the names of the four individuals who were seen in a car at Skateland at the time of the fire."

He said, "Matt Balmer, Donald Fletcher, Jerry Lorenzo, and Lance Warfield."

I was taken aback. "You already knew that?"

"Sure. We had that information a week after the fire."

Trying to cover my disappointment, I said, "But nobody has been charged."

"Knowing who did it is one thing. Convincing the district attorney to prosecute is a whole other thing. The DA won't take a case without hard evidence, which we don't have."

I proudly said, "Well, my recordings ought to take care of that!"

"Don't bet on it. The DA's office sees this as a matter for juvenile court. Even if they have a prosecutable case, they aren't going to fight for adult charges against juvenile offenders. And since the most they could get on a conviction in juvenile court is a couple of years in Chehalis, they don't think it's worth their time."

"That's ridiculous! They burned a quarter-million dollar building to the ground, and could've killed the people who were in it. It was only be sheer luck that those folks got out."

"Yeah, but the DA sees it as a teenage prank that got out of control. He won't send kids to Walla Walla for that."

When I told Dale that the Skateland arsonists would never be charged, she said, "But that's so unfair! The owners deserve at least the satisfaction of seeing the criminals go to prison."

"Someone should tell that to the district attorney."

"So, nobody will ever know that you solved the case?"

I said, "I guess my correspondence course left out that bit of reality."

No arrests were ever made in connection with the Skateland fire.

Chapter Thirteen

No News is...No News
September 3, 1960

Breaking the Skateland case should have been big news. Instead, it became invisible—so much so that I didn't get the bonus that Victor Piquet had promised for solving the case. And I didn't get the wave of new business that would have followed a favorable front-page news story.

Throughout the summer of 1960, I repaired a lot of radios and television sets and investigated several unfaithful spouses and a case involving employee theft. And throughout all of it, I watched carefully for any developments in Spokane's big unsolved cases—Candy Rogers and the Draper girls.

Few people paid any attention to a page-11 article in the morning newspaper on Saturday, September 3, 1960.

Bones on Reservation

Human remains discovered on the Spokane Indian Reservation near Wellpinit are thought to be those of an Indian. A pheasant hunter found the scattered bones near the Ford-Wellpinit Road, four miles west of Ford last week, and reported the find to tribal authorities. The hunter reported that the remains appeared to have been scattered by animals, but some straight black hair was present at the scene.

The article was inconspicuous, low on the page, next to the Steve Roper comic strip. It was of no greater interest than the article above it talking about preparations for an upcoming policeman's ball the following weekend. And nobody, it seemed, was curious about the bones of a dead Indian.

If it had been anything important, it would have garnered more than a single paragraph on page 11. And surely, if anyone had any reason to believe that it was connected to either of Spokane's big open cases, it would have been front-page news. I don't remember why I tore out the page and put it into my unsolved crime file.

Many people considered the Draper case solved. I didn't. There was no evidence whatsoever to support the accepted theory that Frank Stearman had abducted the girls. Indeed, I'd seen no evidence that he'd done anything at all, beyond possibly using too much hair oil.

Sometime around the end of September, I got wind of another suspect in the case, while having a beer with Jeff Warden.

"You've always been interested in the thing about the missing cheerleaders," Warden said. "The word around our office is that they've identified a pretty solid suspect."

"Cheerleaders? You mean the Draper girls?" I asked.

"Yeah. That's the name. Anyway, one of the detectives here has a contact in the Adams County sheriff's office who says that almost from the beginning, they've been looking pretty hard at an unemployed carpenter from Ritzville. He matches the witness descriptions of the guy seen with the girls just before they vanished. And apparently, he had the same kind of car."

"Why do you say 'apparently?'"

"As I understand it, the car burned, so the color hasn't been verified."

"It must've been the right make and model," I speculated.

"Yeah. A '49 Chevy fastback sedan. I don't know any details about the suspect, though."

"Why hasn't it hit the news up here?"

"My guess is that they're still building their case against him. Without bodies or any other physical evidence, they'll probably need a confession before they can charge him."

"You said that his car burned. How did that happen?"

"The deputy didn't say. But they do have some good circumstantial. A few months before the girls disappeared, this guy had been working for a contractor, building a barn out of town—out on Klein Road, not too far from Crab Creek, where the girls' clothes were found."

"Does he have a name?"

"No doubt. But that's under wraps. Meanwhile, the detectives are spending most of their time tracking down leads generated by witnesses who claim to have seen the girls alive in various towns all over the state."

September 27, 1960

Blanche. E. Boggs was a 69-year-old widow living on an old-age pension at 807 East Euclid Avenue on Spokane's north side. On September 27, 1960 she was found in her bed with multiple injuries from a blunt object. Police said the weapon was "something like a hammer, wrench, or gun butt," but no weapon was found at the scene.

The attacker apparently entered through an unlocked window sometime during the night. The victim's purse was found open, and no cash was found in it, leading police to speculate that robbery was the motive behind the attack.

I didn't miss the similarities between this and the still un-solved murder of Gloria Brie, ten months earlier. But the big difference in the ages of the victims argued against any connection. Autopsy results released a few days later indicated that Mrs. Boggs was the victim of an attempted rape.

October 26, 1960

A month later, another attack made front-page headlines. Beverly K. Myers had been struck in the head three times during the early hours of October 26, 1960. The 23-year-old woman was listed in "fair" condition, and was conscious following surgery to repair a nearly-severed ear.

The attacker is believed to have entered Miss Myers's apartment building through a basement workshop, where a door was left unlocked. Police said that the weapon used was a plumber's pipe-threading tool, which was left in the apartment, along with a 12-inch Crescent wrench. Both tools had come from the basement workshop.

Beverly Myers recovered from her injuries. By this time, I was convinced that this attack may well have been the work of the same man who had murdered Gloria Brie and Blanche Boggs. All were viciously beaten in their beds in the middle of the night, by a prowler actively looking for unlocked doors or windows. But none of these attacks seemed connected with the Draper sisters or Candy Rogers.

Chapter Fourteen

Headline News

November 28, 1960

The Spokane Daily Chronicle of November 28, 1960 had two front page articles that grabbed my attention. One told of the latest twist in the Candy Rogers case.

Factual Link Said Lacking in Idaho Man's Confession

In Sandpoint, Idaho, a 24-year-old man confessed to the murder of Candy Rogers. Donald Dean Stokes was being held without bond in the Bonner County jail. Several people notified police that Stokes had talked extensively about the case and bragged about committing the crime. At least two polygraph tests were administered, but the results from both were inconclusive or ambiguous.

Spokane County Prosecuting Attorney John Lally and Sheriff William Reilly said in a joint statement that they had no factual basis for believing Stokes's confession. They said that Stokes had given no information that wasn't readily available through news reports.

After extensive interrogation of the suspect, some of it conducted under hypnosis, police reached the conclusion that his confessions were fabricated, and that Stokes had nothing to do with Rogers's rape and murder.

The other front-page article fell beneath the banner headline:

WSU Co-Ed Missing; Friend Slain

Beverly Allan was missing, and Larry Peyton was dead, found in his 1949 Ford coupe on a secluded dirt road in Portland's Forest Park. He had been beaten and stabbed multiple times. nineteen-year-old Beverly was a student at Washington State University in Pullman, and had gone to Portland to spend the Thanksgiving weekend with her boyfriend at his parent's home.

Larry Peyton was a student at Portland State University. During the evening of November 26, 1960, the couple had been in downtown Portland. At 9:30 p.m. the next day, a Multnomah County deputy was making a routine check of the twisting lane when he spotted the blue Ford. Peyton lay dead in the front seat, covered with mud and soaked in his own blood. There was no sign of Beverly Allan.

All around the car police found evidence of a protracted fight. There was a bullet hole through the passenger side of the windshield, and a small pocket knife was found near the car. Peyton had 14 stab wounds in his chest and nine in his back. His skull was fractured, but he had no bullet injury. The bullet that went through the windshield had been fired from inside the car.

Beneath Peyton's body, police found a piece of cloth torn from Beverly Allan's blouse, and on the ground next to the passenger side of the car, they found her blood-spattered jacket. A few feet away, they found her glasses with one lens smashed.

Witnesses came forward in the days following the initial news reports, including a former high school friend of Larry Peyton, who reported seeing the Ford cruising downtown in the area around Portland State, between 11:00 and 11:30.

Another witness was the attendant at a Flying-A service station on Southwest Barbur Boulevard, who said that around 1:00 or 1:30 a.m., he had pumped gas into a Ford coupe that he described in very specific details that matched Larry Peyton's car.

One of Larry's friends said that Peyton had once shown him a small pistol that he carried in the glove compartment of his car. No such weapon was found at the crime scene.

December 9, 1960

On December 9, Portland police arrested a 28-year-old ex-con named Edward Wayne Edwards, when he was caught setting-off fire alarms in a residential neighborhood. Upon questioning, he admitted to having made multiple false alarms over the past two months. When he was being interviewed, he was found to have a partially healed gunshot wound in his upper left arm, which he claimed resulted from mishandling a gun while cleaning it.

A detective recognized the distinctive name, and went back through his case notes. A police officer who was guarding the Forest Park crime scene the day after Larry Peyton's body was found had seen two men snooping around the area. The officer took their names and told them to move on. They were 22-year-old Wayne Berggren and 28-year-old Edward Edwards.

The detective put that together with the fire-alarm puller's week-old bullet wound and the bullet hole in the windshield of Peyton's car, so Edward Edwards became an early suspect in the Peyton-Allan case. He was booked into Rocky Butte Jail on Friday, and jailers were instructed to hold him through the weekend for questioning by Peyton-Allan detectives on Monday.

But before that could happen, Edwards arranged to have a friend phone the jail, posing as Edwards's parole officer. He "ordered" that the prisoner be released, and so he was. Edward Edwards simply walked away, and the Peyton-Allan team did not follow-up.

When I read about that, I was frankly dumbfounded. How could the Portland police fail to follow-up on such a promising suspect? Over the ensuing weeks, I would note other lapses in police performance that were bound to impair future prosecution of the killer or killers.

On January 9, 1961, six weeks after her abduction, Beverly Allan was found dead on a steep slope off Highway 26 in

Washington County, 38 miles from where Larry Peyton was killed. She had died of strangulation, and there were signs of a possible sexual assault. She had been bound using olive green nylon parachute cord. She had no bullet wound.

The fact that Beverly Allan had been forcefully abducted, of course, made me look for similarities with Spokane's Draper case. I'd already concluded that some kind of force or threat of force had been used to get Gail and Lisa to abandon their car and get into the old green Chevy, so that was a logical connection.

For the price of a couple of beers, Jeff Warden got me a copy of the arrest record of Edward Wayne Edwards:

1951   Auto theft in Florida

1952   Impersonating a police officer in Pennsylvania. Sent to Chillicothe Prison, released 1953

1955   Breaking and entering in Texas
Escape in Ohio
Armed robbery in Oakland and Sacramento, California

1956   Robbery conviction in Great Falls, Montana, Sent to Deer Lodge Prison, released 1959

1960   Escape and impersonating an officer in Portland, Oregon

Edward Edwards could have gone just about anywhere between his 1959 release from prison in Montana and his 1960 arrest in Portland. But the highway between Deer Lodge and Portland goes straight through Spokane and Ritzville.

* * * * * *

Dale came into my investigator's office and handed me a cup of coffee. When she saw my notes raising the possibility that a criminal from Montana had come through Spokane in 1959 or 1960, she asked the question that I'd been pondering since hearing about Edward Edwards.

"Do you think one man could be responsible for all of these murders?"

"These and maybe even more," I said.

"If he was committing crimes in Great Falls, maybe Penny knows something about him," Dale suggested.

My cousin Penny moved from Great Falls to Spokane in 1955. I followed Dale back into the store, where Penny was finishing the sale of Brenda Lee's new hit, *Rockin' Around the Christmas Tree*.

"When you were in Great Falls, did you ever hear a criminal named Edward Edwards?" I asked.

She shrugged. "The name isn't familiar."

"His name came up in connection with the Larry Peyton and Beverly Allan murders in Portland last November."

Penny said, "You know, I remember hearing about something very similar to the Peyton-Allan thing, that happened in Great Falls a few months after I moved to Spokane. A pair of unsolved murders—at least, they were still unsolved last I heard."

"Tell me about that," I said, with genuine interest.

"A young couple was making-out in his car. He was murdered, and his girlfriend was taken away. Her body was found the next day, eight miles away."

That got my attention. I went back to my office and made a long-distance call to the publisher of the Great Falls Tribune, and asked about an unsolved double murder there in 1956.

"You bet," he said. "Duane Bogle and Patricia Kalitzke. He was an Air Force enlisted man stationed at Malmstrom Air Force Base. She was a high school girl. It happened the day after New Year's Day. They went down to a place called Pete's Drive-In and got vanilla Cokes. Some of Patty's friends were there, so they socialized for maybe an hour. From there, they went to Wadsworth Park—that's where kids around here go to make out."

I asked, "Have you read about the thing in Oregon? It sounds a lot like this."

"Don't I know it! At first, Patty's parents thought that maybe the couple had eloped. But in the morning, Bogle was found lying next to his car with his hands tied behind his back. He'd been shot through the head. Twice. A day later, they found Patty, shot in the back of the head. There was no indication that she'd been raped. Maybe she resisted. Who knows?"

"Are you familiar with the name Edward Wayne Edwards?" I asked.

"Doesn't ring a bell right off hand," he said.

"He was arrested in Great Falls on March 6, 1956 for sticking-up a gas station. He was sent up to Deer Lodge for five-years on an armed robbery beef."

"I remember something about that. He faked a suicide attempt and tried to escape."

"Well, here's something for you to chew on. Edwards was in Portland, Oregon last November. In fact, his name was on a list of people who were snooping around the Peyton-Allan crime scene the day after they found Peyton. Edwards was arrested about ten days later on some petty charge, but he had a partially healed gunshot wound in his arm. Police knew that a bullet had been shot through the windshield of Peyton's car, but Edwards managed to escape from the city jail before he could be questioned about Larry Payton's murder."

"Is this for real?" he asked.

"Sounds real to me…"

Chapter Fifteen

Sad Reality

April 10, 1961

I was in my office on a Monday afternoon in April, 1961, when Jeff Warden called to say, "There's something brewing in the Draper case—something big. An official on the Spokane Indian Reservation notified the Spokane County Sheriff's Office this morning that the remains of the Draper girls may have been found."

"*May* have been found?" I repeated. "What does that mean."

"There hasn't been positive identification. The remains are being transferred to the Spokane County Coroner's office today."

"So, the remains must have been found on the reservation," I surmised.

"Yeah. The original discovery was last September. But someone thought they were Indian bones, so they were put in storage on the reservation."

"How in hell could that happen?"

"There's no great mystery here. First off, the remains had been scattered around by scavengers. At the time, they believed they all came from one person. And the remains *looked* Indian. Remember, the Draper girls had dark brown hair—almost black. There wasn't much tissue left, and whatever skin *had* remained was mummified and had turned mahogany brown. The remains were found on the reservation, so under the circumstances, it was a reasonable identification.

"Then, last week, while studying the bones, they realized that there were *three* humerus bones. So, they sent a search team out to where the bones were found, to make a more thorough search. That's when they found the second skull, and that's what started them looking at possible connections with the Draper case."

"Well, why didn't they properly search the area when the first bones were found?"

"They thought they did. But the bones they found were on the surface. They didn't see any signs of a burial, and they could hardly dig-up the whole area. This time out, they expanded the search area and found a pit covered with branches and pine needles."

"Okay, I get it," I conceded. "How long will it take to make a positive identification?"

"I can't say. It depends on exactly what they have. If there's teeth, maybe they can get a match to the girls' dental records. Without that, it might be impossible to make a positive I.D. So far, they haven't even determined the sex of the victims."

All of that sounded pretty vague. But how many pairs of missing people were there? I didn't know of *any*, other than the Draper girls. One thing that jumped out at me was that these bodies had been concealed in exactly the same way as the body of Candy Rogers.

I had only a vague idea where Ford was located, so I got out a map and found the little town about 20 miles north of Reardon, a dot on the map only slightly larger than Ford. The remains had been found four miles west of Ford. The route between there and where the girls' clothes were found was anything but direct. It was nearly 50 miles away, via four different highways.

If these actually were the Draper girls, it exonerated Frank Stearman, because his window of opportunity was extremely tight, even without the extra time it would have taken for him to get to the disposal site, and *utterly impossible* with it. Anyone who still believed that Stearman had committed suicide out of guilt would now have to acknowledge that he did it because of the hounding by reporters and the treatment he was receiving around town.

Two days later, on April 12th, a press release confirmed what Warden had told me, emphasizing that positive identification might take several weeks. But the big news that day was that a Soviet air force pilot named Yuri Gagarin had become the first man in space. His 108-minute orbital flight underscored the Soviet advantage in what was being called "the space race," and the news about the Draper girls failed to make the front page of the afternoon newspaper. I couldn't do anything about the space race, but I had some definite opinions about the Draper case.

Ritzville Police could see the same thing I did. If the bones on the reservation belonged to Lisa and Gail Draper, Frank Stearman couldn't have been the killer. So, investigators announced that they were going to take a second look at their other suspect, the unemployed carpenter.

Gordon Permann's name was leaked to the press, apparently by someone inside the investigation, along with details on how the 22-year-old man had come to the attention of police. A few days after Lisa and Gail disappeared, the Adams County Fire Department responded to a garage fire northeast of Ritzville, on Danekas Road.

The garage had burned to the ground before the firefighters could even get any water on it. But they recognized in the middle of the smoldering rubble the burned-out hulk of a 1949 Chevrolet Fleetline—the same model identified in the statewide APB three days after the girls disappeared.

Nobody was home at the time of the fire, so police tracked-down the property owner through county tax records. The owner said that the garage and the house next to it were rented by Gordon and Rachael Permann. There was no phone number listed on the rent agreement, so all the police could do was leave a note on the door, asking Permann to contact them.

A day or two later, Permann appeared at the Ritzville police station and said that the reason he hadn't notified police sooner was that he didn't have a phone or a car. During the subsequent interrogation, Permann speculated that the fire may have been started by a work light. He explained that he had been working under the hood, and the only light he had was a bare bulb in a socket plugged into the end of an extension cord.

When asked about the car, he insisted that his car was blue, not green, and when asked where he had been at the time of the fire, he said that he had been in town shooting pool with a friend. He gave the name of a witness who could corroborate that alibi—an Adams County maintenance worker named Leon Stark.

The detective tracked-down Stark, and asked how he knew Permann. Stark said that they both had attended high school in Pasco. Stark graduated a year ahead of Permann and got a job in Ritzville. A couple of years later, Permann came to Ritzville and briefly lived with Stark, until he got a job. Since then, they'd remained friends and done things together, including hunting, drinking, and shooting pool.

When detectives asked Stark where he had been on the evening of Permann's garage fire, he confirmed that he'd been shooting pool with Permann. But the alibi wasn't conclusive. It left a window of opportunity—albeit a tight one—when the suspect might have had time to start the fire.

Also in that interview, Stark told police the name of Permann's employer, Carl Stearns Construction, who subsequently confirmed that Permann worked for him, but had been laid-off since November. The last job he'd worked on was a barn on Klein Road, northeast of Ritzville.

But once it was determined that Permann's car was the wrong color, further investigation was put on hold. Then, when Frank Stearman appeared as a suspect, Permann's file was set aside and forgotten—until it was revealed that the bones from the Indian reservation might belong to Lisa and Gail Draper, and the timeline on the case against Stearman collapsed.

At that point, police brought Leon Stark back for a second interview, and he revealed that Permann had had a few brushes with the law while in high school. Checking into that, the detective found that most of Permann's short criminal history was petty crime, but he *had* been convicted of battery involving his girlfriend. While attempting to coax her to "prove her love," he'd twisted her arm until a bone snapped. For that offense, he should have served two years in prison, but the judge gave him two years on probation, because it was his first offence.

The name of the victim in that case was not on file, because she was underage at the time of the fight. But among the minor offenses for which Permann had *not* been prosecuted was a case where he'd set a field on fire, and another where he started a fire in a dumpster at his school. These things reinforced the idea that maybe he *had* started the garage fire that brought him to the attention of the police in the first place.

Permann was then brought in for another interview, which started with questions about the two fires he'd started when he was a kid in Pasco. Permann said that the dumpster fire was caused by a cigarette that he'd hastily thrown away to keep from getting caught smoking, and the fire in the field was started by a candle in a fort that he and a friend had built of straw bales.

Police again questioned him about color of his Chevy, and he repeated that it was dark blue. People he'd worked with had seen the car, he said, and they'd back him up on its color.

At this point, the city cop told Permann that he was going to be held in custody pending charges relating to the garage fire. But the real reason for detaining him was so that he could be questioned by the Adams County detective in charge of the Draper case.

Attempting to bolster their case, police obtained a copy of the registration for Permann's Chevrolet Fleetline, which turned out to be a 1951 model, not 1949, and was trophy blue, not fathom green. A fire department arson investigator confirmed that the serial number on the car matched the registration. But they had no way to determine what color the car had been before the fire. Police were hoping to find someone to say it was dark green.

That led to another call to Carl Stearns. Unable to get him to say Permann's car was green, they switched topics, and focused on specific projects where Permann had worked before being laid-off. Stearns mentioned a barn construction project that was located only a mile from the Crab Creek bridge, where the Draper girls' clothes had been found.

The Adams County Sheriff presented the case to the District Attorney, who ordered him to turn up the heat on Permann regarding the murders of the Draper girls. Permann said what you'd expect him to say. He didn't know the Draper girls and had never met them. He had no idea what had become of them. He had not attended the basketball tournament. He did not go to Hand's Café on March 20th.

These were the things an innocent man would say, but they were also what a guilty man would say. The interrogation was long, thorough, and intense. The lead interrogator tried every trick he knew, in his attempt to get a confession from Permann, but was unable to do it.

Eventually, they had no choice but to release him. The sheriff was sure that they had their guy, but until the bodies found on the reservation were identified, they couldn't charge him with killing the girls, because they couldn't prove that the girls were dead.

On May 7th, the Spokane County medical examiner confirmed the identity of the remains found on the Indian reservation. The Draper girls had been found. Deputies went to arrest Permann, but found the house vacant. He'd blown town. A statewide manhunt got underway.

With his photo on the front page of every newspaper in the Northwest, it was impossible for Permann to hide for very long. The search ended in Madras, Oregon, where an off-duty deputy sheriff spotted him trying to hitch a ride to California. Permann was returned to Ritzville and charged with two counts of first-degree murder and kidnapping.

I had lost my chance to solve the great mystery.

Chapter Sixteen

The Trial

They say that the "wheels of justice" turn slowly. But not in this case. Gordon Permann received the speedy trial guaranteed by the Constitution. Jury selection was begun at the Adams County Courthouse in Ritzville, on July 19, 1961, and the trial began on Friday July 21st.

Nearly 80 years old, Jacob Novak had been the county prosecutor since 1928. He had prosecuted cases involving bootlegging, murder, robbery, and everything in between. He publicly announced that he would retire upon conclusion of this trial.

In his opening statement, Novak promised the jury that it was an open-and-shut case. He then told his version of the events that culminated with the arrest of Gordon Permann. It all started at Hand's Café, where Permann encountered unspecified engine trouble with his car. While he was working on his car, he encountered Lisa and Gail Draper. He had his car repaired by the time the girls left the restaurant, and he enticed them to accompany him on a test drive.

"Exactly how he did that is unknown," Novak said, "but he may have asked the girls to get in and press the starter button while he watched the carburetor. Once they were in the car, he closed the hood and climbed into the driver's seat, blocking the girls from getting out, having already removed the inside door handle from the passenger door."

He went on to tell how Permann had driven to the barn he had helped to build, where he killed the girls—most likely during a sexual assault. He then put their clothes into a plastic bag, which he concealed beneath the Crab Creek bridge a short distance from the barn. He transported the bodies to the Spokane Indian Reservation and concealed them in a pit near the road.

"And he might have gotten away with it," Novak said, with a dramatic gesture, "but for witnesses who had seen him at Hand's Café, who provided authorities with detailed descriptions of Permann and his car."

With the fervor of a gospel preacher, he told how Permann had panicked when he heard his car described in a news report, and had attempted to destroy it by setting fire to his garage.

"Ultimately, that was his undoing," Novak concluded.

Permann was represented by Thomas Weingart, a 28-year-old court-appointed attorney who had never represented a client accused of a capital crime. He did not make an opening statement, other than assuring the jury that Permann was completely innocent.

Testimony started the following Monday. Novak brought in the Ritzville police officer who had responded to a call from the morning cook at Hand's Café. The cook reported that a car parked outside the café matched the description of the one he'd heard about on the radio—the car belonging to the missing girls.

The officer described the car, what was found inside it, and what condition it was in. He told how he'd had the car towed to the police station for a more thorough investigation.

Next, Novak brought in two witness who testified that they had seen Permann at Hand's Café in the afternoon of March 20, 1960. Sandra Hutchins, the waitress who had served Gail and Lisa, told how she'd seen a "greasy-haired man" talking to the girls. She identified Gordon Permann as that man. Chet Winston described how he had seen a man working under the hood of a car in the parking lot. He too identified Permann.

In his cross-examination of the witnesses, Weingart attempted to weaken their testimony by pointing out discrepancies between their original statements and their testimony in court: The man had said the car was green, and Permann's car was blue. The waitress said the man inside wore jeans and t-shirt, while the man outside said he wore gray coveralls.

On re-direct, Novak offered the witnesses logical reasons for the discrepancies—it was late in the day, and a person could easily mistake the dark blue for dark green in the light of the setting sun, and certainly the suspect could have taken the coveralls off before going inside.

Then, Novak called Permann's employer, Carl Stearns, who testified about the project near Crab Creek where Permann had helped build a barn six months before the girls were abducted. Sterns pointed-out on a poster-sized map how the barn was only a mile from the Crab Creek bridge.

Novak brought in one of the boys who'd found the bag of clothing under the Crab Creek bridge, and then told the jury how Permann had taken the girls to the barn he had helped build, and once there, he'd made them strip and had done "god knows what" to them, before hiding the clothes under the bridge and taking their bodies to the Indian reservation.

Weingart allowed all of that to stand without objection, even though Novak had presented no evidence to support his version of events.

The next witness was an independent arson investigator who testified that the fire that destroyed Permann's Chevrolet Fleetline "could easily have been" deliberately set. In his description of the burned-out car, he said specifically that there was no inside handle on the passenger-side door. His testimony was accompanied by photos of the burned car and garage.

On cross-examination, Weingart got the witness to admit that he had no official connection with the Adams County Rural Fire

Department and had not worked in their behalf. On re-direct, Novak clarified that the arson investigator was an "expert" hired by the prosecutor's office.

The district attorney wrapped up his case with a surprise witness. Leon Stark, Permann's old high school friend. Neither the prosecution nor the defense had previously mentioned him except as Permann's alibi witness.

"Mr. Stark, how are you acquainted with the defendant?" asked Jacob Novak.

"We went to high school together in Pasco. After graduation, I got a job up here, doing maintenance work for Adams County. Then later, there was an opening, so I told 'Soup' about it."

Novak interrupted. "Soup?"

"Yeah. That's what everyone calls Gordon. You know, Soup Permann—*Su*perman."

The judge had to call for order to stop the laughing.

"Anyway, Soup didn't get the job, but he hung around at my place for a few days, because he was having trouble with his ol' lady."

"How long did he stay with you?"

"A week. Maybe two. He went around applying for jobs. Ended up getting hired by that construction company. Then his ol' lady came up and they rented the place out off Danekas Road."

"Did you and the defendant stay in touch after that?"

"Yeah. We'd sometimes meet-up and shoot pool on Friday nights."

"Anything else?"

"We went pheasant hunting a couple of times."

Novak finally got to the point. "Did you ever go to Crab Creek with the defendant?"

Stark said, "We went that way once, hunting pheasants. When we struck out on that, Soup said we could go down to the creek and catch crawdads to cook up."

"And what happened at the creek?"

"We were wading around, catching a few crawdads, when a black cloud rolled in and it started to hail, real hard. We ran up and hid under the bridge until it blew through."

"That would be the bridge on the Harrington Road?"

"That's right."

"The exact place where the Draper girls' clothes were found?"

Stark said, "I don't know anything about that."

With that, Novak rested his case, without ever mentioning the basketball tournament in Seattle, the Draper girls' encounter with Bill Brady, or their having linked-up with him for their drive back to Spokane on March 20th.

The judge declared recess until morning.

On Tuesday July 25th, it was Weingart's turn to speak. He entered a motion for dismissal based on the assertion that the prosecution had failed to show evidence that Permann had committed a crime. The judge denied the motion and told Weingart to proceed.

He called his only witness—Gordon Permann. Permann said the same things he'd said when he was first questioned: He didn't know the Draper girls and had never met them. He had no idea what had become of them. He did not go to Hand's Café on March 20th and had never owned a green car of any brand. Nor had he set fire to his garage.

Novak's cross examination consisted of a mocking repeat of Permann's words, making them sound too ridiculous to even challenge.

The defense rested, and the court recessed for lunch.

Closing statements and the judge's instructions to the jury took about two hours, and then the jury was escorted out to begin deliberation. They were back with a verdict twenty minutes later. Gordon "Soup" Permann was guilty on all charges. The judge sentenced him to die on the gallows on October 10, 1961.

News hacks and comedians had a field day with the conviction of "Superman," recommending that the executioner be armed with kryptonite.

July 25, 1961

"That really surprises me," I said to Dale over dinner that evening. "I really expected the prosecution to show some kind of evidence."

"Well, the two witnesses identified Permann as the guy they saw at the café," Dale pointed out.

"Yeah, but eye-witness testimony is notoriously unreliable. You'll never hear a witness on the stand say the defendant was *not* the person he saw. It doesn't happen. The fact that he is sitting at the defendant's table means that he *had to be* who the prosecutor says he is."

"Wait. Are you saying that you think Permann is innocent?"

"I'm saying I don't think the prosecutor proved he isn't. He built a story around flimsy circumstantial evidence and called it a case."

"He proved that Permann had been under that bridge," Dale said.

I had to admit, "That was the strongest thing he had. But that was six months before the crime, and nothing found under the bridge connected Permann to the bag of clothes."

"So, you think they're going to hang an innocent man?"

"It sure wouldn't be the first time," I said.

"Ouch!" Dale exclaimed. "Your baby just kicked me."

She rested her hands on top of her bulging belly.

I said, "Give him a break. It's his first exposure to the injustice in our justice system."

"Well, he certainly knows how to lodge an objection."

"Objection sustained. But the fact remains..."

August 10, 1961

Nancy Ellen Pratt was born on August 10th. On the international scale of adorability, which I just made up, she scored a perfect ten out of ten We spent hours identifying which of her features belonged to which parent, but the reality was that she seriously favored her mother, which was a singular stroke of good fortune for her.

On the trip home from the hospital two days later, we stopped by the store and introduced her to her Grandma Aletta and Aunt Penny, who wasn't actually her aunt, but I could never quite sort out all of the variations on cousinship.

Some of the ladies in our neighborhood organized a dinner delivery from a different person on the block, every evening for a week. One of those dinners was delivered by Judy Hanson, the 19-year-old daughter of some friends from up the hill.

She said, "This might be the wrong time to ask, but I was wondering if you had any kind of work I could do in your store."

It was a question that I wasn't expecting. "What kind of work have you done?"

"I've done some secretarial work. Right now, I'm receptionist for a law firm downtown."

I paused, and for the first time, took a serious look at Judy. To me, she'd always been just one of the neighborhood kids. I'd seen her around, but never paid any particular attention. She was quite pretty, and I sensed some confidence and maturity in her manner.

"Why don't you come down to the store sometime, and we'll talk about it," I said.

"I could do that tomorrow—if you have time."

The upshot was that she talked her way into a job on the sales floor. It was something that Penny had been wanting for some time, and now that Dale was going to be out of the store for an uncertain period of time, Judy's timing was perfect.

"I like that girl," Penny told me. "She's young enough to be trainable, and old enough to not need too much of it. She can work the record counter right now, and work into product sales."

I said, "It was her poise that impressed me—first when she approached me about working here, and then even more so when she came in for her interview. When you talk to her, it's more like talking to a 30-year-old than a 19-year-old."

Penny nodded and asked, "Did you hear that the lawyer she used to work for is going to file an appeal for that Superman guy?"

"Yeah, I saw that in the newspaper last night. They cut it kind of close. He was scheduled to be executed about six weeks from now."

September 4, 1961

Labor Day was one of just six days during the year when our store remained closed. Our only plan for the day was to drive Mom to visit the old man's grave, but the existence of holidays didn't change my sleep patterns, so as long as I was awake, I decided to drive down to the shop and catch up on repair jobs.

I was pulling the chassis from a big console stereo when Penny came in.

"I think something is wrong," she said. "I knocked on your mom's door, but she doesn't answer."

We went upstairs to the apartment Penny had shared with Mom since she moved to Spokane five years earlier. I knocked on Mom's door and, as Penny had said, she didn't answer. Dreading what I feared I might find, I tentatively opened the door.

Mom lay on her back in bed, eyes closed, looking peacefully asleep.

"Mom?" I asked. "Mom, do you hear me?"

I touched her cheek, and her skin was cool.

"Is she…gone?" Penny asked.

"She must have died in her sleep," I said, as tears filled my eyes.

Aletta Pratt was buried next to Desmond Pratt, her husband of 25 years, in The Pines Cemetery, half a mile from our store, on September 9, 1961.

September 18, 1961

A series of events started unfolding in St. Paul, Minnesota that would soon shake-up major crime investigators all over the country. A man calling himself Darwin J. Corman had been phoning residents of an apartment building four blocks from the rooming house where he lived, attempting to identify unoccupied units that he could burglarize. One of those calls went to a 34-year-old social worker named Carol Ronan. "Corman" later admitted that he was aroused by Ronan's voice, so he went to her apartment on the night of September 18th, and entered through an unlocked door.

The next morning, Carol Ronan's body was found by co-workers who became concerned when she failed to show up for work. Carol had been severely beaten, raped, and strangled. Her skull had been fractured by a weapon that was determined to be a large padlock in a sock.

Shortly after this, in a seemingly unrelated event, a young woman reported to police that she had seen a man whose photo was on a wanted poster at the post office. Hugh Bion Morse was on the FBI's most wanted list in connection with the July 11, 1961 murder of Bobbi Ann Landini in Birmingham, Alabama. She had been raped and beaten to death with a pipe.

Following the tip, FBI agents tracked down Morse and arrested him on October 13th. His alias, D.J. Corman, broke down quickly, and his interrogation uncovered a string of assaults and murders across six states, going back to November, 1959.

Morse confessed that his first victim had been Gloria Brie in Spokane. He also confessed to the murder of Blanche Boggs and the assault of Beverly Myers. St. Paul police notified Spokane detectives, who immediately flew to Minnesota to interview

Morse about these cases, plus one more—Candy Rogers, who was murdered eight months before Gloria Brie.

Hugh Bion Morse had already admitted his guilt in the first three cases, but steadfastly denied having anything to do with the murder of Candy Rogers. Eventually, he would confess to five murders and seven non-fatal sexual assaults, including the rapes of three children.

Back in Spokane, a man named Dan Hite read a newspaper report about Hugh Morse, and recognized his photo. Hite had been a member of the Spokane Motorcycle Club when he met a "likable, clean-cut guy" who called himself "Chris."

Chris had been riding in Dan Hite's sidecar on a ride to an abandoned rock quarry around March 1st, 1959. They were marking the course for a motorcycle event called the Hare and Hound Rally. A week later, the body of Candy Rogers was dumped a hundred yards from that rock quarry.

Spokane detectives had one more thing to think about. While interrogating Morse in St. Paul, they noticed that he liked grape-flavored chewing gum. Wrappers and packages of Adams Grape chewing gum had been found in Morse's room at the time of his arrest. Grape gum had been found at the Brie, Boggs, and Myers crime scenes. And there had been purple-colored gum on the clothes Candy Rogers was wearing when she was found. These facts were not made public.

Even though the Candy Rogers case remained open, most of the detectives involved were convinced that Morse had done it, despite the fact that he had taken two polygraph tests indicating that he *was not* being deceitful when he stated his innocence.

Since Gordon "Soup" Permann had already been convicted in the Draper case, Morse was not considered as a suspect, even though he was known to have been in Spokane at the time. Then again, if Permann had been wrongfully convicted...

As for the Peyton-Allan case in Portland, it didn't seem to fit Morse's style. He was living in Spokane, so theoretically, he could have made a trip to Portland, but there was no evidence that he'd done it. Edward Edwards still seemed like the right guy for that, even though Portland authorities apparently had dropped him from their suspect list.

Hugh Morse was convicted and sentenced to life in the Minnesota State Penitentiary for the murder of Carol Ronan. He was later convicted in Spokane for the Gloria Brie and Blanche Boggs murders, but his concurrent life sentences would be served in Minnesota.

Chapter Seventeen

Soup Permann's Appeal

October 9, 1961

Several people were still watching the fifth game of the World Series on the TV in our showroom, even though the Yankee victory was inevitable. I'd already given up hope that the Cincinnati Reds might make a comeback, and the Yankees, with Mickey Mantle and Roger Maris, were cruising toward another championship. The ringing phone in my office gave me the opportunity to escape from witnessing the bitter end.

I immediately recognized the name of the attorney who called. He was a prominent criminal defense attorney in Spokane, and his name frequently appeared in news coverage of local criminal trials. And his name was on Judy Hanson's resumé.

"You hired-away my most promising employee," Brant Litton said.

"I hope you're not calling in hopes of getting her back," I said.

"No, as much as I'd like to do that, I have something else in mind. You probably already know that I notified the court of my intent to file an appeal of Gordon Permann's convictions, based on judicial error. I trust that you are familiar with the case?"

"As familiar as an outsider can be—I read in yesterday's newspaper that you got a stay of execution," I said, still not understanding the reason for his call.

"I'll need an investigator, and word around town is that you're pretty sharp. Interested?"

Trying hard to contain my excitement, I said, "Sure. I'm interested. Do you think you have grounds for a successful appeal?"

"Here's where we stand. My preliminary filing with the state supreme court got us the automatic stay of execution. They've agreed to consider my appeal and set the hearing for December 15th. That gives me ten weeks to get all of the facts and evidence together, and that's where you come in. I need a tireless, creative, determined investigator to collect everything related to the case and the trial."

* * * * * * *

I forced myself to wait for Dale to ask her daily question, "How was your day?"

"It was okay," I said. "The Yankees won the world series, and I got a call from Judy Hanson's former employer."

"The attorney? What did he want?"

"Oh, he was just wondering if I'd be interested in working with him on his appeal of the Gordon Permann conviction," I said.

"Oh my god! That's what you've been wishing for! This calls for a celebration."

Dale dug around in the back of the refrigerator and found a bottle cheap Champagne, and we celebrated until the bottle was empty. And then we celebrated some more.

The next day, I drove downtown to Litton's office to discuss how Gordon Permann's appeal would be handled and establish the terms of our working relationship. I was surprised to find Thomas Weingart there.

After introductions, Litton said, "Make no mistake. This is going to be an uphill fight."

"If I'd just done things differently, we wouldn't be in this position," Weingart lamented. "I was just so sure that the jury would see that there was no real evidence…"

"A reasonable belief, but you never know about juries," Litton said.

"Who's paying for the appeal?" I asked. I knew that Permann didn't have any financial resources—that's why he had been represented by the court-appointed attorney.

Litton said, "We'll be paid by Permann's family. His old man has money."

I looked at Weingart. "No offense intended, but why didn't the family offer to pay for his defense in the trial?"

"Weingart said, "Permann wouldn't allow it. There was some history there. So, I got paid by the court." He gazed vacantly out the window, and added, "The problem wasn't the money. It was my mistakes."

Litton said, "I have no intention of employing the 'ineffective counsel' appeal. I'll be looking first at possible misconduct by the prosecution, specifically in the area of discovery. I believe they knew things that they didn't share with defense counsel."

I asked, "What do we have to work with?"

"I've requested photocopies of the complete case files from the Adams County District Attorney's office but, so far, they haven't given me anything. The county just got one of those new $30,000 Xerox copying machines, and they've put off fulfilling my request pending installation. It's up and running now, and I intend to make them use it. I expect to find answers to the obvious questions about what was—and wasn't—presented by the prosecutor."

"How can Adams County afford to buy a $30,000 copier?" I wondered.

Litton said, "Oh, they didn't *buy* it. They *leased* it."

"I didn't know they could do that. Can you get two sets of copies? I could use one, too."

"I'll ask. They'll charge a nickel a sheet, times about 2,500 pages—$125 for the whole file."

"It's a bargain. The alternative is spending hundreds of hours on a microfiche reader and making notes by hand," I said.

"We won't have to do that. We'll get paper copies one way or another."

"That'll be a good starting point. And I want to talk with all of the prosecution witnesses."

October 16, 1961

While waiting for the case files, I still had TV repair work to do, so the next Monday, I was in the back shop engaged in the tedious process of an electronic re-alignment of a color TV, when Judy came in and said, "Connie, the Murphy kid is out front with an odd request."

"Can't you take care of it? I'm kind of busy here."

"I could if he was just buying parts like usual, but this a different situation." She lowered her voice and continued, "And besides, he has a terrible crush on me."

"Sounds like a personal problem," I said. "What's he want?"

"He'll have to explain it to you. It's a bit too technical for me."

I put down my oscilloscope probe and followed her out to the showroom.

"Miss Hanson says you have a technical question," I said to the kid.

"Uh, yeah, kind-of." He looked at the floor and said, "I'm working on a science fair project, see? And I want to make an electron beam welder out of an old TV."

I could see why Judy was stumped.

"An electron beam welder?" I asked.

"Well, not a real one. More like a working miniature," he said.

"Ah. I see. A *miniature* electron beam welder."

Completely missing my sarcasm, he explained, "Yeah. I want to demonstrate the principle—that a focused beam of electrons can melt metal."

I could understand the principle. I may have even read something about such a device. But I'd certainly never seen one, and I doubted that Kenny Murphy had either.

"So, what is your question for me?"

He shuffled his feet and said, "Well, a TV picture is made by an electron beam, right? So, what I have in mind is to set up the part of a picture tube that makes the electron beam and aim it at a positive-charged piece of metal—like a sheet of tin foil—and burn through it."

"Where did you get this idea?" I asked.

"Oh. Uh, my dad is a welding engineer at Kaiser, and he was talking about it, and said that it was just like a TV picture tube. So, that got me thinking, if I had an old TV set, I could take out the cathode and anode circuits, and make a working model of an EBW."

That actually made some sense to me. But I couldn't see how this kid could actually do it.

"The electron gun can't operate outside a vacuum. The filament would burn up in an instant."

"Oh, sure. I know where I can borrow a vacuum pump to use, and I already have a vacuum chamber."

"There are some pretty high voltages involved. It could be dangerous."

"Yeah, but the vacuum chamber is a glass cylinder with aluminum top and bottom plates, which will be grounded. All of the high voltage will be contained inside. If something happens and any part of the thing touches the aluminum, it'll blow a fuse, but it won't electrocute me."

He seemed to have thought this through, but I still couldn't encourage him to dabble with 20,000 volts. "You know, you can't just pull the electron gun out of a picture tube. It'll implode and blow pieces of glass all over the room."

"I thought I'd take it outside, cover it with a blanket, and shoot it with my .22," he said.

"Don't do that. It's way too dangerous."

"I'll get way far back."

"Don't do it. I'll tell you what. There's a place downtown that remanufactures burned-out picture tubes. I'll bet they'd sell you an electron gun. Heck, they might even give it to you—in the interest of education."

"Yeah? I'll have to check into that," he said without enthusiasm.

"The place is called Televac—on West Second. I can get you their phone number."

"Thanks. But the *first* thing I need is an old TV set. I was kind of hoping that you could help me find one. That's what I came here for. If I can't find one, I'll have to think up a different project."

Now I understood. But I needed to get back to work.

"I do have an old set that I can give you. A customer decided it wasn't worth fixing, and just left it here. You're welcome to it—providing you promise not to shoot the picture tube."

I took him into the back room and showed him an old Airline console TV with a 17-inch screen. When I switched it on, it made sound, but the screen remained black. The fact that the audio worked told me that the filament circuit was intact, so the old set would suit his purpose.

He made a phone call, and about twenty minutes later, Mrs. Murphy came in. Kenny and I loaded the heavy old beast into the back of the station wagon, and I was happy that it would be the last I'd ever hear of it. However, it wasn't.

A day later, Kenny came back into the store and asked to see me again.

"You know that TV set you gave me? Well, I got it working."

Surprised, I asked, "You already made your electron beam welder?"

"No. I mean, I fixed it—made it work as a TV."

"Yeah? How'd you do that?"

"After I took the back off, I plugged it in and switched it on. I saw a blue glow coming from the high-voltage box, so I guessed that the high-voltage rectifier tube was gassed. My folks weren't home, so I looked in their TV, and it used the same tube. I swapped tubes and that fixed it. So, I thought maybe you'd want to have the TV back, since it wasn't actually dead."

I held up my hands. "No, you keep it. A deal's a deal."

The truth was, that old Airline was one of the ugliest TV sets ever made, and nobody would ever buy it from me."

"Wow. Thanks. Uh. I don't suppose you have another TV you can give me. Now that it works, I don't want to tear this one apart."

"I think I can find something for you."

"That's great! Oh. And I need a new high-voltage rectifier tube—it's a 1B3. My mom got home before I could put the tube back in her TV, so I pretended to troubleshoot it, and put the good tube back in it. Now Mom thinks I'm some kind of genius and gave me ten bucks for the repair. The least I can do is give her the new tube and put the used one back in my set."

"To tell you the truth, I'm impressed that you knew the meaning of the blue glow in the first place."

He shrugged. "I saw it once before—at a friend's house. I have a couple of buddies—Bill and Art—and we fool around with electronic stuff quite a bit. Art's dad is a TV repairman—Gerry Wegner. He showed us the blue glow and told us what it was."

I'd known and liked Gerry Wegner for years. Small world.

October 23, 1961

A week later, a courier service finally delivered a cardboard carton to my office. It contained a complete copy of everything in the Adams County Prosecutor's file. My first impression as I leafed through the pages was that it was very disorganized. Either things got shuffled during the photocopying, or Adams County had a really poor filing system.

So, one way or another, I had to straighten it out in order to make sense of it. The stack of paper, which Litton had estimated to be 2,500 sheets, was over a foot tall. I could think of two ways to sort them: by subject or by date. Either way, for the files to be of any use, I'd need a cross-referenced index. At this point in my thought process, I recognized the need for help.

"You know, before Nancy was born, I thought that I'd go right back to work in the store," Dale said. "But I don't think I can do that. I simply can't imagine leaving her with a babysitter every day."

"We hired Judy so that you wouldn't have to," I said. "And that's working out just fine so far."

"Then, what are we talking about?"

"I have a clerical project that's too big for me to do alone. I need a couple of weeks help organizing the Adams County DA's files."

"I'm sure I could work on it at home while Nancy's napping. It'd be hit-and-miss, though."

"No, we'll need to work on this together. And I really need to be in my office—not just because I have to be there for phone calls and walk-in business, but also to be there if Judy and Penny need help in the store."

"Okay, I can tell that you have something in mind. So, what's your idea?" Dale asked.

"I can convert the old storeroom into a baby room. It's just been a 'catch-all' for years. Probably two-thirds of what's in there belongs in a dumpster."

"Okay, but what'll you do with the rest?"

"I was looking at that a few days ago. I managed to give a couple of the customer-abandoned TV sets to Kenny Murphy."

"I always figured that you'd never be able to part with your treasures," Dale commented.

I think she was mocking me, but I continued, "In most cases, the customer has given us permission to dispose of things that aren't worth repairing, and I just haven't gotten around to it.

"So, do you think you'll actually be able to get rid of all of them?" she asked.

"Well, the ones that have already been stripped for parts will go straight to the dump. But there's a few where the customer simply vanished. I'll have to check the law regarding what we can do with those.

"Meanwhile, I'll stash them in the garage out back. I'll do the same with about a dozen other old sets don't work but still have some value. Maybe we'll have a rummage sale."

"Seems like a lot of effort for just two week's work," Dale said. "Why not just get a Kelly Girl?"

"Two reasons. First, I doubt that this will be the only time you'll want to bring Nancy down here, and more importantly, I enjoy having you around. What do you think?"

"Since you put it that way, I think we can make that work. It might be nice to work together again. Or, it might be a complete disaster. But I'll risk it if you will."

I cleaned-out the storeroom, and installed a new counter with a baby-sized sink. I cut door and window openings through to my office, to provide natural light to the formerly windowless room. I patched-up the old plaster and painted the walls pale pink, and I rolled-out carpet over the old linoleum floor. Some new light fixtures, furniture, and a load of baby supplies completed the job.

It was Saturday before all of that was done, and I had just finished moving the last few customer-abandoned TV sets to the garage out behind the shop, when Kenny Murphy showed up with his friend Bill.

"You said you might have some more TV sets to give away," he reminded me.

I escorted them to the garage out behind the shop, where I'd stacked over a dozen sets along the wall, next to my old Ford coupe.

Kenny exclaimed, "A 1940 Deluxe coupe! Oh man, I've been trying to find one of these. Would you consider selling that to me?"

I said, "That's my first car. I haven't driven it in a couple of years, but it's not for sale. I'm going to restore it someday."

"Oh. Well, if you ever change your mind…"

"That won't happen. You can have your choice of the TV sets, but the coupe stays here."

Shaking his head sadly, Kenny focused his attention on the television sets. He and Bill picked a couple of table models that would fit in the backseat and trunk of Bill's car and promised to come back for more, if they were able to make those work.

Despite the necessity of the renovation project, I was annoyed with myself for having neglected my primary job. With humble apologies to Brant Litton, I set to work. A lot of the material in the file consisted of multi-page documents that had to be stapled together. But a troubling number of the pages had gotten shuffled somewhere in the process, and I kept finding them randomly mixed with unrelated sheets.

Before long, I had my desk completely covered with short stacks of paper, so I went to a rental store and picked-up a couple of folding tables. Soon, I had so many piles that I had to bring in a box of rocks to use as paperweights.

Dale brought Nancy down the next day and installed her in her new crib. I brought in a handful of electronic components from our parts bin and explained to Nancy how to tell the difference between a resister and a capacitor.

After the baby settled down from all that excitement, Dale joined me in my office.

"I hope we don't have a gust of wind in here," she said.

"This is turning into a job for one of those UNIVAC data processors."

"That's pretty grandiose. I doubt that even the FBI has one of those. Besides, it would take up the entire office. You'll just have to get by with me."

"Wait until they transistorize data processors. You know how they took radios the size of a bread box and shrank them down to the size of a cigarette pack? They'll do that to data processors, and reduce them to the size of a washing machine. Wait and see," I predicted.

"Sounds like science fiction."

"Not really. UNIVAC uses 5,000 vacuum tubes. When you consider all of the circuitry needed to power them, plus all of the space required to cool them, it makes for a very bulky piece of equipment. A transistor is the size of a pea, operates on very low current, and generates far less heat than a vacuum tube. A six-transistor radio is the size of a pack of cigarettes. Using that unit of measure, a 5,000-transistor device would be the size of 833 packs, or about 42 cartons of cigarettes."

"Great. Let's get one."

"Unfortunately, it won't happen in time to help with this."

Dale paused to ask a serious question. "This is a disorganized mess. Do you think that this is how the files are organized in the Adams County DA's office?"

"I can't imagine that they would be. The scrambling most likely happened during the copying process."

"To me, it looks almost like they were deliberately scrambled to make it hard for us."

"I won't say that's impossible, but I'm not going to jump to any conclusions."

"There's a name that I'm seeing on a lot of the internal memos—Doreen Fraiser, or her initials, DF. Do you have any idea who she is?"

I flipped through my notes. "Doreen Fraiser is an administrative assistant at the Ritzville Police Department."

"Administrative assistant? Not a police officer?"

"No, she's not a police officer. And I agree that her name or initials are on many of the key documents—especially the ones that are difficult to read."

"If this is an example of how well she does her job, I think she needs to find a new line of work."

"It's probably like in the army. The low man on the totem pole gets the job that nobody else wants. And the output ends up somewhere in the lower regions of barely tolerable."

* * * * * *

Our new file organization started with assigning a number to each document, based on the date and time each document was originally created. Not every document had a date and time written on it, so we had to estimate when some were created based on content and context. The process wasn't perfect, but it would be a vast improvement over what we started with.

We searched each document for people's names, and made an index that would let us easily find every document that contained any person's name. We did the same with references to places, events, and things—pieces of physical evidence. The job took ten days.

When we were done, we put all of the documents into a filing cabinet drawer, with dated file tabs that allowed us to quickly retrieve any document we wanted to see. A looseleaf binder containing the cross-reference index sat on top of the file cabinet.

Chapter Eighteen

The Heart of the Matter
November 6, 1961

On Monday, with the organization and indexing of the files complete, I telephoned Brant Litton and gave him a report. He said that he'd send an intern to our office with his set of documents, to duplicate our filing system.

I said, "While organizing the documents, I've run across one glaring problem. A surprising number of them are such crappy copies that they aren't readable."

Litton said, "That's a long-standing problem in my business. I'm sure you know that Thermofax copies don't age well. The images are made by heat, and are very vulnerable to degradation, even when stored in the dark. They're no good for long-term storage. Until now, photography has been the only way to preserve documents—microfiche slides or rolls of microfilm."

"I understand that. But when you make prints from microfilm readers, they're produced in the same way as the Thermofax copies and have the same limited shelf life."

"Completely true. But the Xerographic process offers hope for the future. Xerox prints can theoretically last for centuries with proper storage."

I said, "I didn't mean to get into a technical discussion. I'm just concerned about the practical reality of the prints we have.

At least ten percent of the documents in our files are useless. All of the material generated outside the Adams County DA's Office consists of second-, third-, or fourth-generation copies. And a lot of it consists of typewritten transcriptions of telephone conversations and typed replicas of Thermofax copies of the originals."

"No surprise there. The only way around that is to figure out where the original documents are stored and go get fresh copies."

"Yeah, I already figured that out. I just wanted to make sure the budget for this case can tolerate what that's going to cost. Evidence has come from at least half a dozen jurisdictions—Ritzville city police, Lincoln County, Spokane County, Stevens County, and the Spokane Indian Reservation. It'll take some time to track-down and make copies of the originals."

"Can you estimate what that's going to cost?" Litton asked.

"In going through the copies from Adams County, I marked over 200 documents that are so bad that I can't read them. By the time you add up my travel time and expenses, it could easily come to three thousand dollars—maybe as much as five."

Without hesitation, he said, "I'll run it past Permann, but his old man seemed prepared to spend whatever it takes to keep Gordon from meeting the hangman."

"I'll add one more complication. There's a lot of type-written stuff—transcriptions of tape-recorded statements, typed copies of hand-written notes, and apparently of bad Thermofax copies. They're loaded with typographical errors, indicating that they were hastily and perhaps carelessly done, and apparently were never subjected to proofreading."

"You're preaching to the choir. So, what's your plan for dealing with that?"

"While I'm making the rounds, I'll have to watch for the source material for the typewritten documents. I doubt that I'll get access to any of the tape recordings, though."

"You may be right. but if it's the only way to be sure that our reference material is complete and accurate, I can subpoena the tapes and get copies made."

I said, "Fair enough. I'll start in Ritzville this afternoon and work outward."

Litton said, "Good. And keep your eyes open for anything relating to how evidence against Permann was found. If the authorities proceeded without probable cause, we might get some evidence tossed out and a new trial ordered."

* * * * * *

I drove to Ritzville and walked into the police department at 11:00 a.m., armed with a notarized letter from Brant Litton, endorsed by a district court judge, designating me as an officer of the court. That allowed me to have legal access to documents relevant to Litton's case.

I told the sergeant at the front counter who I was, and that I needed to make fresh copies of the documents for the Draper case.

"I can't authorize that. You'll have to talk to Chief Donnelly," the sergeant said.

He stood there just looking at me. I looked at the name badge above his shirt pocket.

"Well, Sergeant Sherman, will you please get Chief Donnelly?" I asked pointedly.

The chief appeared, having apparently overheard the entire exchange.

"Private investigator, huh?" he said, looking at my officer of the court document.

"I am representing the attorney who is handling the Gordon Permann appeal," I explained.

"What I don't get is why would anybody want to get that scum out of jail," said the chief.

I gave a theatrical shrug. "Yeah, I hear ya. The jury says he's guilty, that's good enough for me. And hell, that's probably where it'll end. But what do I know, right? Attorney asks for documents, my job is to get them."

That probably didn't get me onto the chief's Christmas card list, but it did seem to at least get me off of his shit list. He led me to the evidence room and instructed the clerk to give me what I needed. I gave her a full list of the documents that were unreadable or of questionable accuracy.

The clerk gave me an apologetic smile and said, "I'll have to charge you for any copies." She gestured toward an old 3M Thermofax copier on the counter—same old problem.

My immediate impression was that she was intelligent, competent, and helpful. She appeared to be in her thirties, plain but not unattractive. Her engraved name badge said *Doreen Fraiser*—the very person that Dale and I been talking about. Maintaining my notoriously bad poker face, I just nodded.

I would have to deal with more Thermofax copies, so even though these copies would be fresh, I'd still need to find someone with a plain paper copier to make permanent copies before these Thermofax copies started to fade.

Copier technology would be a recurring theme throughout this investigation. I could only hope that a day would come when everyone could afford to have a plain-paper copier, unlikely though that seemed.

I spent all afternoon with Doreen, identifying and copying the original documents that had either been retyped when they were entered into the Adams County case file, or were unreadable due to poor copying. All told, the bill came to $17.60 for the 352 Thermofax copies. The documents included witness statements, crime scene reports, police officers' notes, original telecon summaries, and assorted scraps of paper. I gave Doreen a twenty and told her to keep the change, anticipating that I'd need more help from her as the investigation continued.

On my way back through Spokane, I stopped at Standard Blue Print on West Sprague, because I knew that they had one of the new Xerox machines. I asked them to copy all of the fresh Thermofax copies I'd picked-up in Ritzville. This may not have been strictly necessary, but I didn't know how long it might take to solve this case, so I wanted stable copies in my files.

"How long will this take?" I asked.

"It'll take some time," the clerk said apologetically. "We'll have to manually place each sheet on the glass, but I think we can have your copies ready by 10:00 tomorrow morning."

I picked them up on my way back to Ritzville the next day, and then I set out to learn about Permann's garage fire, since that apparently was what called attention to Gordon Permann in the first place, after a firefighter reported to Ritzville Police that a car destroyed in the fire matched the description of the one sought in reference to the disappearance of the Draper girls.

Before going to the fire station, I stopped at a little bakery and bought a tray of still-warm cinnamon rolls. At the fire station, I showed my Officer of the Court credentials and offered the cinnamon rolls to the men on duty.

"I'm sure you remember the garage fire out on Danekas Road back in March last year. Is there anyone here who knows what happened there?" I asked the station chief.

"We have two units at this station. The rescue unit and the engine company. Both responded to the call, so except for our new rookie, *everyone* here was on that call."

I opened my briefcase and showed the chief my new battery-powered portable tape recorder, and asked if it was okay to tape our conversation.

"I hate to rely solely on my memory," I explained.

"No problem. Go ahead," he said.

"What can you tell me about the Danekas Road garage fire?"

"It was a rip-roaring mess. We could see the fire from half a mile away. By the time we got the hoses rigged and the water turned-on, the roof had collapsed and the walls were burning through. Our main job at that point was to keep the house from going up too, so we cooled that down first. Then, when we put water on the garage, it just fell into a pile of steaming charcoal."

"There was a car in there," I led.

"That's correct. It helped fuel the fire. When the cops interviewed the car's owner, he said that it had half a tank of gas in it."

"There's a note in the police files saying that a firefighter reported that the car in the garage might be the one that the state cops were looking for."

"I doubt that," he said. "We don't allow just anyone to communicate with other agencies. That's my job, and I never made that call."

Surprised, I showed the chief a copy of the typewritten phone call note. "This is what's in the file. The firefighter identified himself as Fireman Thomas Parker."

"I'm sure it's some kind of misunderstanding," the chief said. "Whoever wrote that note must have been mistaken about who the caller was, because there is nobody here named Parker."

Changing the subject, I said, "I read that arson was suspected."

"I think 'suspected' is too strong a word. Of course, arson is always a possibility where no obvious cause is visible, but an old garage like that is a natural place for an accidental fire. As far as I know, it was a newspaper reporter who first asked the question. I told her that there wasn't enough left of the garage for us to determine the source or cause of the fire. Fact is, there was so much combustible material in that garage, *anything* could have started it on fire."

"An arson investigator testified in the trial," I said. "He said it was probably intentionally set."

Looking like he'd just swallowed a stink bug, the chief said, "Gerald McQueen. He's not an arson investigator. He's a charlatan—a professional witness. He testifies to whatever he's paid for."

"He has credentials," I said.

"Of course he does. But he's still a whore. Nobody hires him to investigate fires. They hire him to say what they want to hear."

"I think there was some uncertainty as to the car's paint color."

"Uncertainty? There was no paint *left*. Everything was burnt to bare metal. Our guys searched through the ashes after the fire was out, looking for remains, in case someone had been in the garage. We found nothing."

The chief went to a cabinet and pulled out a file containing an envelope full of eight-by-ten photos of the fire scene.

"That's all that was left of the car," he said.

I looked through the photos, and stopped at one that showed the inside of the passenger-side door. It clearly showed that the door handle was gone. I called the chief's attention to that.

"They talked about the missing door handle during the trial," I said.

"It doesn't mean a thing. There's no window crank either. They're made of chrome-plated pot metal. They melted away and vaporized in the fire."

"Do you know who called-in the alarm?"

"It was a neighbor across the street who saw the fire and called it in."

"What about the people who lived in the house?"

"They weren't around at the time of the fire. The cops tracked down the property owners, and they said that they'd rented the property to a couple who'd recently moved to the area from Tri-Cities. The tenants didn't have a phone, so the officer left a note. The guy showed up a few days after the fire. He claimed that he had been in town shooting pool at the time of the fire."

"Was anyone able to corroborate that claim?"

"You ought to be talking to the Ritzville Police about that. Of course, you know that the renter is the guy who killed those two girls last year. Some people thought that he burnt the car to get rid of evidence."

So, the logic there starts with the *belief* that Permann was guilty of abducting the girls. Burning the car would destroy the evidence, therefore he must have started the fire. And starting the fire to destroy evidence proves that he was guilty. This is how the prosecutor, Jack Novak, presented the garage fire to the jury, but the logic is a perfect illustration of the fallacy of circular argument. The conclusion is based on the premise, which is based on the conclusion.

In reality, the garage fire proved nothing, unless it could first be proven to have been deliberately started, and the fire chief just told me that there *was* no proof of arson. The lynchpin of the case against Permann was invalid.

And what about the color of the car? The registration said it came out of the factory with dark blue paint. Permann insisted that it had never been re-painted, and the prosecutor had produced no evidence or witness to indicate otherwise. Our justice system is supposed to give preference to the defendant. If Permann said the car was blue, it was blue unless the prosecution proved it wasn't. Novak had not done so.

That left only two possibilities. Either the people who saw the car at Hand's Café were mistaken about the color, or the car they saw was not Gordon Permann's. In court, Novak dealt with that by merely saying that it "could have been" repainted at some point. He led the witness, a 29-year-old grocery store clerk named Chet Winston, through his testimony focusing on his identification of Permann as the man he saw working on the car in the parking lot outside of Hand's Café.

* * * * * *

I went to the IGA supermarket where Winston worked, and introduced myself to the store manager, showing him my Officer of the Court document.

"Does Chet Winston work here?" I asked.

He pointed at a man at the checkout counter. "That's Winston."

"If you don't mind, I'd like to ask him a few questions."

The manager glanced at his watch. "He has a break coming up in a couple of minutes. You can talk to him then."

In the parking lot, Winston leaned against a Dodge hardtop and lit a cigarette. "What do you want to talk about?"

"You testified in the trial of Gordon Permann," I said. "Is that correct?"

"That's right. I was at Hand's Café right around the time when the Draper girls were last seen."

"If it's okay with you, I'd like to record this." I showed him my recorder and he nodded.

"Can you tell me what you saw?" I asked

"I already told the cops, three days after the girls were reported missing. And I told it all over again in court," Winston said.

"I know. I'd just like to hear it myself."

He sighed. "I was just leaving the café. As I got to my car, I saw this guy with the hood up on his car. I asked if he was having engine trouble, and he said it was nothing serious."

I interrupted, "Where were you parked?"

"I was in front of the café. Off toward the left side."

"And the green car was there as well?"

"That's right. Then, after the guy said he didn't need any help, I drove away. Couple of days later, I heard that the girls disappeared right about that same time, and a waitress said that she'd overheard them talking to a guy who said he was having car trouble. I put two and two together and went to the police station, where I told the cops what I saw."

"Can you give me some details about that? What did the man you saw look like?"

"He was maybe around 20 years old. About five-nine, one-sixty. Long hair, combed back like some kind of a juvenile delinquent."

"How was he dressed?"

"Well, you know. Like a greaser."

"I think you said he was wearing coveralls? So, when you say 'greaser,' are you talking about a mechanic?"

"Yeah, that's right."

"If you thought he was a mechanic, why did you ask if he needed help?"

Winston shrugged. "Just being neighborly. And maybe he *wasn't* wearing coveralls. It was just an impression that I had."

"In court, you identified Gordon Permann as the man you saw."

"That's right."

"And you're sure about that?"

I saw a moment of hesitation. "Yeah. He looked kind of like the guy. I mean, in court, he was all cleaned up and had his hair cut, but he was the one the cops said did it."

I switched topics. "What about the car?"

"It was a General Motors car from around 1950—one of those cars that's supposed to look streamlined."

"The 'fastback' style?" I clarified.

"Yeah, that's right."

"So, a Chevrolet Fleetline, then."

"That's what the newspaper said, but I never said that. I said it was a GM car. It wasn't a Cadillac, but it could've been a Pontiac or Olds. That's what I told the cops. I wasn't really paying much attention, but if it'd been a Chevy, I would've recognized it, because I used to have one."

"What color was it?"

"It was dark green. I'm sure of that. In court, someone said Permann's car was blue, but he must have painted it or something, because it was green when I saw it."

Winston took a last drag on his cigarette before dropping it and grinding it out under his shoe. He turned toward the store and said, "I gotta get back to work."

From the earliest news reports, the car had always been referred to as a 1949 or 1950 Chevrolet. Yet the key witness just told me that he had never identified it as such. In fact, he said specifically that it was *not* a Chevy. So, where did that come from?

And as for Winston's identification of Permann, he had demonstrated the automatic bias that eyewitnesses have when asked to finger the suspect. If the cops believed that Permann was the guy, then who was he to say otherwise?

* * * * * *

My next stop was at the Adams County maintenance shop, where Novak's surprise witness, Leon Stark, worked.

I introduced myself and got permission to record our conversation.

I then said, "I understand that you testified in court that you knew Gordon Permann before the Draper girls were killed."

"Yeah, that's right. We went to the same school in Pasco. I was a year ahead of him."

"And you helped him find work here in Ritzville?"

"Not exactly. There was an opening here, and I told him about it. But he didn't get the job. He went off on his own and found work with a construction company."

"When was that?"

"It was in the summer of 1958. Soup was out of work, and about out of luck. His old lady moved back in with her folks when he couldn't pay the rent. So, I let him crash at my place until he got paid and rented a place of his own. Then Rebecca joined him and, for a while, things were okay. He had pretty steady work until the early part of 1960. He got laid-off, and things went downhill again."

"Are you married?" I asked.

"Me? Heck no. I thought Soup was crazy getting married when he did—before he could even pay his *own* way, let along support a wife."

"In court, you said that you and Permann used to go hunting together."

"A few times. I mean, it wasn't serious hunting—just an excuse to drink a few beers and take a few shots at birds or ground squirrels."

"And what took the two of you to Crab Creek?" I asked.

"We didn't set out to go there. It was just where we found a little turn-out to park the car. When we didn't find anything to shoot, Soup thought we might be able to catch some crawdads in the creek. But the ones we found were too small to bother with."

"I understood that Permann was familiar with Crab Creek—maybe from when he was working on a barn up near there."

"I don't think so. I mean, he never said anything about it. Only reason we stopped there was because of the parking space."

"So, what about that barn he was building?"

"Soup never said anything about it. I didn't know he worked there until the prosecutor told me about it."

"You testified that you took shelter under the bridge when there was a hailstorm."

"Well, that's what the prosecutor wanted me to call it. It really wasn't much—didn't last more than a minute or two, and the hail was more like BB-sized balls of snow."

"Why would Novak want you to exaggerate the hailstorm?"

"How should I know? The whole thing never made much sense to me. I mean, we ducked under there and didn't stay for more than a minute."

"When did this happen?"

"It was during the summer of 1959. Probably August or early September. The wheat fields had been cut, and that's why we thought we might get some pheasants out in the stubble."

"What do you remember about Permann's car?" I asked.

"He got that car right around the time he graduated from high school."

"And what color was it?"

"It was blue. Some people said it was green, but it was blue. They must've seen it in the dark."

"Did you know Permann at the time he got in trouble for starting fires—while he was in school?"

"That was a load of crap. He never set any fires—not on purpose, anyway. I think he flipped a cigarette into a trash bin that caught on fire."

"What about the alleged assault and battery?"

"It was nothing. The girl's arm got broke when she was trying to hit him. But her old man insisted that Soup was beating *her* up, and he made the charges stick. But the girl herself said it was just an accident."

"The name of the girl was kept confidential because of her age. Do you know who she was?"

Stark laughed. "It was Rebecca—the girl he married."

"Why didn't you say any of this in court?" I asked.

"Before the trial, when the prosecutor interviewed me, I tried to tell him how it was, but he told me not to say anything in court except what he asked for. He was real firm about that."

"So, Novak knew that Permann's car was blue, that he never deliberately set fires, and that the girl he was convicted of assaulting disputed the charges? Is that what you're telling me?"

"Yep. Novak and me talked about all of those things before the trial."

I thanked Stark for his time and he went back to work.

* * * * * *

It was past lunch time, so I went down by the highway and found Hand's Café. I took a seat at a small table near the dining counter and ordered a burger basket and iced tea.

"Is Sandra working today—Sandra Hutchins?" I asked.

"Not right now. She'll be coming in for the evening shift, starting at 4:00."

While waiting for my lunch, I leafed through the copies I'd gotten from the Ritzville police, and I found a hand-written witness contact form from the officer who interviewed Chet Winston. The notes confirmed what Winston had told me. He never said the car was a Chevrolet. He called it "an air-flow style Pontiac or Oldsmobile."

Yet, I distinctly remembered that the official transcription of the tape-recorded interview identified the car as a '49 or '50 Chevrolet Fleetline," and that was the description that was used in the all-points bulletin and every news report right up through Permann's trial. If the car Winston saw wasn't a Chevrolet, everything about Permann's car showed that he wasn't involved.

With nowhere else to go until Sandra Hutchins got to work, I stayed at the café, drinking iced tea and going through the witness interview forms. I was surprised to find two more witnesses who saw a green car parked at Hand's Café.[1]

---

[1] Just for fun, search the Internet for "Hand's Café, Ritzville WA" and take a look at the color image that comes up on flickr.com. Is this a monumental coincidence, or did this whole story actually happen?

Neither of these witnesses had been called to testify in Permann's trial. What's more, neither had said the car was a Chevy. One said it was a "two-door fastback sedan," and the other said simply that it was a big old green car.

The "two-door fastback" witness said he'd seen it "maybe around 5:30." Both Sandra Hutchins and Chet Winston had said that the girls left the café at 5:00, so 5:30 might be a stretch. The "big green car" witness said that she'd seen it there at 7:15, at least two hours after Lisa and Gail left the café, so this was presumed to be a different car, irrelevant to the case.

The time discrepancies probably were the reason that these statements were discounted and ignored. My overall impression was that it underscored just how thin the case against Permann had been.

Sandra Hutchins appeared to be in her forties and had her hair tucked tightly into a hair net. Her white cap was pinned in place, and she had a white apron tied around the waist of her pale blue dress. She had the look of a professional waitress—by that I mean she'd been doing it for a long time.

I introduced myself and switched-on my tape recorder.

I asked, "Do you have a minute to talk?"

"Well, Hon, I can give you just about exactly that—a minute."

"I'm interviewing witnesses to the Draper kidnapping," I said.

"I thought that was all over."

"Can you tell me what you saw?"

She pointed to a booth next to the front window. "The girls came in and took that table, right over there. They ordered baskets and cherry Cokes."

I interrupted. "Did you note the time?"

"It was a couple of minutes after 4:30. Anyway, while they were waiting for their order, a guy came in and talked to them. I heard him say something about having trouble with his car. Then he went back outside."

"Can you describe him?"

"He seemed like a kid, maybe the same age as the girls. He was wearing blue jeans and a white t-shirt. He had his hair combed back the way those rock-and-roll singers do."

"Did you get a good look at his face?" I asked.

"Well, mostly he had his back to me. But I saw his face through the front window after he went back outside. And later, he came in and went to the restroom. At least, I *think* it was him."

"You identified him in court," I reminded her.

"Sure. He was all cleaned up and wore a suit, but he was the same guy as in the pictures the police showed me, no doubt about that."

"Are you saying you identified him based on photos?"

"Well, not *just* that. I mean, he *did* look like the guy who was here."

"What time did the girls leave?"

"It was 5:00. Maybe five after."

"Did you see them get into a car?"

"Nope. They went out the door, turned left, and walked out of sight."

"What about the guy? Did you see him around that time?"

"Nope. Never saw him after he went to the restroom."

And then something occurred to me. I flipped back to the notes I'd taken while talking with Chet Winston.

"The first time the guy went outside, which way did he go?" I asked.

"Um, he turned right. That's when I saw his face."

That corroborated what Winston said about where the green car was parked, but Sandra had just said that the girls turned to the *left* when they left the café.

"Did you ever see the car that belonged to Lisa Draper—the blue Falcon?"

"No. It was parked in the side lot, around the corner of the building—at least that's what everyone said."

"So, the girls walked toward Lisa's car when they left."

Sandra nodded. But if the girls had left Ritzville in the green car, they must have walked back across the front parking area.

I asked, "Did you see them walk back in front of the café after that?"

"No. But I wasn't watching them. I was waiting tables, you know?"

Maybe those witnesses who said they saw the green car at the café long after it was believed to have left were *not* mistaken about the time. In other words, maybe the girls never got into the green car, but rather left the café in Lisa's car.

Chapter Nineteen

Errors and Omissions

Guilt or innocence has nothing to do with what goes on in the appeal of a conviction. It is all about the process. The question is not about whether the convicted party actually committed the crime, but rather is about whether those involved in the trial process followed the rules.

My conversations with witnesses in Ritzville had revealed some significant discrepancies with what was presented in court. So, the question at hand was whether or not those discrepancies represented violations of Gordon Permann's rights. I was almost one-hundred percent sure that Permann was not guilty, but that was an issue that could not be addressed head-on. Brant Litton had to prove to the Washington Supreme Court that either the prosecution or the judge had violated the law to such a degree that it could have affected the jury's decision in the case. My job was to provide proof of those violations.

November 8, 1961

I got into my office early Wednesday morning and started updating my 2,500-page master file, removing each of the typewritten transcriptions and replacing it with a photocopy of Ritzville PD's corresponding original document. Next, I stapled each of the transcribed documents to the Thermofax copy of the original, so that Litton and I could compare them to one another.

With a lot of help from Dale, and a minimal amount of distraction from Nancy, I had the master file updated by the end of the day. I phoned Litton and asked if he could spare some time to meet with me.

"Are you saying that you've already collected all of the documents you were after?" he asked.

"No. I've been to the Ritzville Police Department, and I've talked with half a dozen witnesses. I still have a long way to go, but I've found some things that I think you should see."

We arranged to meet at his office Thursday afternoon and go over what I had collected so far. That left me all morning to go out on a string of service calls.

I ran short on time and ended up going straight from my last service call to Litton's office, still wearing my Pratt's Electronics shirt and driving the old Ford panel truck. Having anticipated the possibility that this might happen, I'd had the foresight to take along the folder containing everything I'd gotten in Ritzville.

Litton's first question was, "Have you found anything that I can use in the appeal?"

"It appears that the prosecutor had knowledge of exculpatory evidence that he did not share with defense counsel or present in court," I told him.

I showed him Chet Winston's statement from the official case file, and then played the recording of my conversation with Winston, where he specifically stated that the car he saw at Hand's Café was either a Pontiac or an Oldsmobile. So, either Winston is mistaken about what he said when he was questioned by Police, or someone screwed it up when typing it. We need to find out which, because the Washington State Patrol used the information from the typewritten statement when they issued their APB on the suspect vehicle.

"Now, the typed statement was probably copied by someone at Richland P.D. from hand-written notes made during the questioning of Winston. If so, the original notes should have been in the Richland P.D. files. But they weren't."

Litton suggested, "So maybe the original interview was tape recorded, and the statement on file is a transcription of that recording."

"In that case," I said, "the tapes are probably stored at the police station. Either way, we need to verify that the car actually *was* a Chevrolet Fleetline, because that had a huge effect on the investigation, from the very beginning. There are far more Chevys of that era and body style than Pontiacs and Oldsmobiles combined. So, it's possible that not only were authorities looking for the wrong car, they were also looking in a far larger universe of possibilities."

Litton said, "All of that is true, and it might prove that the document given to the prosecution was inaccurate, but in order for me to use that in our appeal, we have to prove that Novak *knew* that it was inaccurate."

In frustration, I repeated, "What Winston told me was that the car he saw was a Pontiac or Oldsmobile, not a Chevrolet. But when his statement was typed, the car was misidentified as a Chevy Fleetline. In court, Novak carefully avoided asking Winston about the make and model of the car he saw. To me, it suggests that he knew that the answer would favor the defense. In other words, he knew that Winston had *not* seen Gordon Permann's car."

"Correction," Litton said. "It *implies* that he knew it, but it doesn't *prove* it."

I shook my head. "Well then, there's the whole question of the color of the car. Winston and two other witnesses said the car at Hand's Café was green. Permann's car was blue. Novak said that Permann could have painted it green, but offered absolutely no proof that he had. In fact, Leon Stark told me that Novak *knew* that Permann's car was not green, and had coached him to avoid mentioning the color of the car when he testified in court."

"That's a pretty strong argument, but it doesn't negate the possibility that Chet Winston had been mistaken about the color of the car he saw," Litton said. "And as for the other two witnesses, Novak will say that he dismissed their statements as irrelevant, since they were at Hand's Café after the Draper girls left."

"Come on! You can't believe that."

"I'm just telling you what the other side will say when I present this to the state supreme court."

I took a deep breath before speaking. "Well, what about the fire that brought Gordon Permann to the attention of Ritzville PD in the first place? Novak presented it to the court as having been an arson fire, but the fire chief told me that there was no evidence to support that. Doesn't that show prosecutorial misconduct?"

"Only if we can prove that Novak *knew* that the fire wasn't arson-caused. Since the chief was not able to determine the cause of the fire, we can't prove it was accidental. Certainly, Tom Weingart should have challenged the credentials of that arson investigator. If he's a phony, Weingart should have exposed him in court. At the very least he should have pressed him on how he reached the conclusion that the fire was deliberately set. But without that challenge, there's no procedural issue to appeal."

I could only shake my head. "Novak deliberately tied the garage fire to the two fires that Permann was accused of setting when he was a kid—the cigarette tossed into a dumpster, and the kid's fort in the hay field. Even though he was not charged with any kind of crime, those two incidents were presented by Novak as proof that Permann had a history of arson. Those accusations should have never been presented as evidence."

"True. I've petitioned Franklin County to give us all of their files on Gordon. That includes everything about his conviction for beating his girlfriend."

"Are you aware that the girl Permann was convicted of beating denied that he did it?"

"That's what he says."

"And that the girl later married him?"

"Of course. He told me that too. He also told me that he never mentioned these things to Weingart, because he didn't know that Novak was going to bring them up. So, there may be a discovery issue there if Novak really did spring this on them by surprise. When I get the court records, I'll figure out where I can go with this."

"You don't sound optimistic about Permann's chances," I said.

Litton said, "It's an appeal. Appeals are always tough. But stay on it. There's still more to learn."

I had a hollow feeling inside as I drove back to my office. I'd thought that what I found in Ritzville would get Permann off the hook. The one inescapable truth was that ultimately, the best way to prove your client didn't do the crime is to find the person who did.

My outlook on life improved when I found Nancy in her office nursery and Dale sitting at my desk reading a book about parenting.

"Doctor Spock says that spanking a child for misbehaving will leave psychological scars for life," she said.

"Since our child is perfect, that's something we'll never have to worry about."

"I'm serious. We have to think about things like this."

"Did your parents ever spank you?" I asked.

"Once, when they caught me with a pocket full of penny candy that I snitched from the dime store. Then they took me back to the store and made me pay for the candy out of a silver dollar that my grandma gave me for Christmas. That hurt more than the spanking."

"What does Spock say about that kind of punishment?"

"He seems to be against *any* kind of punishment," she said. "Personally, I think that 'permissive parenting' is not parenting at all."

"Yeah, I think it'll lead to a generation of lawless hooligans," I said.

* * * * * *

The next name on my list of people who had testified against Permann was his former employer, Carl Stearns. It was Stearns who helped Novac solidify the connection between Permann and the site where the Draper girls' clothes were found.

When I tried to phone Stearns, I found myself talking to an answering service, who told me that he was out of the office. She said that all she could do was leave a message for Stearns, because his schedule was unpredictable.

"May I ask the nature of your business with Mr. Stearns?"

I almost told the truth, but caught myself. "It is in regards to a new construction project."

I gave her my name and home phone number and added, "It's very important that I speak with Mr. Stearns as soon as possible."

I called Dale and told her to expect a call from Carl Stearns.

"Don't give him my office number. Just say that I can't come to the phone, but I'll call him right back in a minute. Then, call me."

"That sounds mysterious," she said.

"I think he'll be more likely to meet me if he thinks it's about his business, rather than mine."

My phone rang about an hour later. Dale read the number that Stearns had given her. It was not his office number, so I guessed that he was at a job site.

I called and introduced myself, thanking him for getting back to me.

"My secretary said that you want to talk about a new construction project," he said.

I corrected him. "Oh… It's not a *new* project. It's a *recently completed* project that I want to talk about. I guess I wasn't clear when I spoke to her."

"So, what is it that you want to talk about?"

There was a trace of impatience there, so I got straight to the point.

"I need to talk with you about the job out on Klein Road—the one you testified about in the Gordon Permann trial."

He exhaled. "What's your interest in that?"

"I'm working for Brant Litton, the attorney representing Gordon Permann."

"I thought that was a done deal," he said.

"I need about five minutes of your time. All I want to do is clarify what Permann did when he worked for you on that job."

"Look. I'm really busy here right now. If you want to talk, be at my office at 7:00 tomorrow morning. I'll give you five minutes."

November 10, 1961

It was still dark Friday morning when I parked next to a company truck in front of the Carl Stearns Construction Company office. The lights were on, so I tried the door.

"You Connie Pratt?" the man at the desk demanded.

"That's right."

"I'll give you points for punctuality. Being on time is *everything* in this business."

"How about Gordon Permann? Was he punctual?"

"He was a good worker, if that's what you want to know. And yeah, he got to work when he was supposed to."

"What was his job?"

"He was a carpenter. No credentials—we're a non-union shop—but he knew how to work a hammer and saw."

"Tell me about the Klein Road job."

Stearns opened a drawer and pulled out a folder, from which he pulled an envelope—the kind you get when you send film in to be processed. He flipped through the prints and tossed a couple of them across the desk to me.

"That's the project. We finished it about this time last year."

I looked at the photos and asked, "Is this a cattle barn?"

"Of course. A feeding barn, to be exact. What did you expect on a dairy farm?"

"I guess I just assumed that it was a wheat farm. I expected to see tractors or combines."

"Well, there you go. You got cows instead of combines. But you're here to talk about Permann. The only thing I said in court was that the job site was nine-tenths of a mile from the Crab Creek bridge."

"The prosecutor used that to speculate that the girls may have been assaulted in that barn."

Stearns laughed. "I almost busted a gut when he said that. Have you ever smelled a dairy barn in the wintertime? I don't care who you are, you aren't going to go into a cattle barn for sex."

I admitted, "I guess I never thought about that. Was there some other place nearby where a kidnapper might have taken the girls?"

"None that I know of. Certainly, none that I had anything to do with—or Permann either, as far as I know."

"Do you mind if I borrow these photos? They tell a story that someone needs to hear."

"If you want the whole story, you have to go there and smell it. I'm proud of my work, but I have to tell you, that place stinks!"

Before heading back to Spokane, I stopped for breakfast at Hand's Café—bacon, eggs, hashbrowns, and toast for $1.50. A nickel more for coffee, and a 20-cent tip. Then, I drove out Danecas Road, past the site of the garage fire. Every trace of the fire had been cleared, and the gravel driveway ended at a bare patch of burnt ground.

A short way further, I turned left onto Sage Road. When I got to the Crab Creek bridge, I parked in the little turn-out where Leon Stark and Gordon Permann had parked to go pheasant hunting. I worked my way down the slippery embankment to get a look under the bridge at the place where the bag of clothing had been stashed. My immediate impression was that it was a really poor place to hide evidence of a major crime. Someone was bound to find it there. So, what was the point?

I back-tracked down Sage Road and found Klein Road. I turned left, and less than half a mile further, I saw—and smelled—the dairy farm. I understood what Stearns had said. This was *definitely* not a place anyone would go for sex, under any circumstances.

Chapter Twenty

Going Back to the Beginning

In less than two weeks, it would be Thanksgiving, and everything would slow down for the rest of the year. Too many people would be thinking about and doing things related to the holiday season, so it would be tough to do my job.

Talking with Dale, I said, "Litton has petitioned the supreme court to delay Permann's hearing to compensate for the long time it took Adams County to get us the files, plus the time it took us to make them legible. But so far, they haven't responded."

"Meanwhile, a man who may be completely innocent sits on death row," she said.

"The more I see, the more I'm convinced that Permann had nothing to do with these murders. It aggravates me that we can't go directly at the question of guilt or innocence. In sports, it is the lousy coaches who always say, 'What matters is not whether you win or lose. It's how you play the game.' But that's what our legal system says as a matter of law."

"So, if the prosecutor *did* play the game wrong, the verdict will be tossed out," Dale said.

"Maybe. And then they'll get a do-over, with no guarantee of a fair outcome."

"You're being awfully cynical. You think Permann has any chance at all?"

"Honestly, I think his only chance lies in our ability to find out what really happened."

"As you've said before," Dale reminded me.

"You're right, of course. What I need to do is go back and take a fresh look at the entire case, starting with the girls' trip to Seattle. That's where this thing started."

Just saying those words brought my gameplan into focus. I opened my phone book and found the number for Earl and Evelyn Draper. I hesitated before dialing. I could easily imagine what their emotional state must be. This was not a call to be taken lightly. But it was the necessary starting point.

I'd read somewhere in the press coverage of the case that Earl Draper worked in the insurance business. With a few phone calls, I came up with a number for the Washington State Insurance Commission office in Olympia. Insurance licenses are public records, so I had no trouble finding that Draper worked at a Safeco agency on East Sprague in Greenacres.

On the theory that Earl would be better able to handle the topic of the murders than his wife, I called his office and introduced myself.

"You're the TV repair guy, right?" He continued, "You've been to our house and worked on our TV set."

"That's right. But that's not the reason for the call. You may have heard that I also do investigative work."

"Oh yeah. You broke up a big car theft ring, or something like that," he said.

"Mr. Draper, this is very hard for me to say. I need to talk with you about your daughters. I've been hired by Brant Litton. He's..."

Draper interrupted, "I know who he is. He's the shyster who's trying to get my daughters' killer out of jail!"

"Please, Mr. Draper, hear me out. I will never knowingly work to set a guilty man free. *Never.* I took this case for one reason only—to guarantee that the person who committed this crime gets the punishment he deserves."

"So why..."

"I've been on this case for less than a month, and I don't have all the answers—not even close. But I've seen some things that don't make sense. Things that make me question, in my own mind, whether they got the right guy."

"That's ridiculous! I don't want to listen to this crap. He was tried and convicted. Why can't you just let the system follow-through?" I heard the words catch in his throat.

"Listen. All I'm asking for is half an hour. I'll show you what I have. After that, if you tell me to, I'll withdraw from the case. On the other hand, if I can convince you that Gordon Permann may be innocent, I promise you that I'll work on this until I find your daughters' killer."

The long silence that followed told me that some part of Earl Draper was willing to consider the possibility that someone other than Permann had committed the crime.

"I don't want my wife involved in this. And I don't want you to get the idea that I believe you now, or that I will believe anything you tell me. But I'll give you half an hour."

"I can meet you at your office," I suggested.

"No. Are you familiar with a dive called Sid's Tavern in Greenacres?"

"I'll find it. What time?"

"Make it 5:30. Buy me a beer, and when my glass is empty, we're done."

My case would have to be convincing and concise. I wrote down what I felt were the key parts of the case against Permann, and then rounded-up the evidence I had found to refute each point. I walked into Sid's at 5:25 carrying a cardboard box. I recognized Earl Draper from photos that had been in the news.

Introductions were quick and awkward. Earl signaled for the bartender to bring a couple of beers. The clock was running.

I showed Earl my list of the six most damning things in the case against Gordon Permann.

"These are the key things that I believe led the jury to their verdict. I'll take them in order."

Earl scanned my list and nodded.

At the top of the list was the assertion that Permann owned the car that witnesses saw at Hand's Café at the time the girls were last seen.

"The first evidence released to the public about this case was the State Patrol's APB for a car that police believed was connected to the case—a dark green 1949 or 1950 Chevrolet Fleetline."

I showed Earl a copy of the actual APB Teletype message that had been read on police radios all over the state and repeated in hundreds of news reports.

Next, I showed him a copy of the registration certificate identifying Permann's car as a 1951 Chevrolet Fleetline. Its color was shown as Trophy Blue.

"They covered that in the trial," Earl said tiredly. "The car was repainted."

I corrected him. "They said that the car *could have been* repainted. They offered no proof that it had been.

"People paint cars all the time."

"You remember Leon Stark? Permann's old high school friend?"

Earl nodded, so I punched the PLAY button on my tape recorder.

Stark's voice said, "It was blue. Some people said it was green, but it was blue."

"So, the witness at the café was mistaken about the color. It was late in the day," Earl said.

"Here's what that witness told me about the car he saw."

I again pressed PLAY. Chet Winston's voice said, "It was dark green. I'm sure of that. In court, someone said Permann's car was blue, but he must have painted it or something, because it was green when I saw it."

I said, "Winston is very clear about what he saw. And there's more."

I once again showed the registration certificate.

"Permann's car was a 1951 Chevrolet. Let's hear what the witness reported."

I resumed playing the tape. My voice said, "So a Chevrolet Fleetline, then."

Winston's voice responded, "I never said that. I said it was a GM car. It wasn't a Cadillac, but it could've been a Pontiac or Olds. That's what I told the cops. I wasn't really paying much attention, but if it'd been a Chevy, I would've recognized it, because I used to have one."

"But they *always* said it was a Chevy," Earl protested. "From the very beginning, everyone said it was a Chevy Fleetline!"

"Everybody who read the APB said that. But the APB was based on erroneous information."

"Then why did Permann think he had to burn it? If the car they were after was a Pontiac or Oldsmobile, he wouldn't have needed to set fire to it."

"Your logic is impeccable. And, in fact, the prosecution presented no evidence that Permann set that fire."

Earl argued, "They certainly did! They brought in the arson investigator, and he said it was arson!"

"Maybe it was, maybe it wasn't. But they presented no evidence to connect the fire to Permann. And here's what the fire chief had to say about the prosecution's arson investigator."

The voice on tape said, "Gerald McQueen. He's not an arson investigator. He's a charlatan, a professional witness. He testifies to whatever he's paid for."

"And on the question of arson, the chief himself wouldn't say one way or another," I said.

"Okay, so maybe they can't prove that," Earl conceded. "But they still have the two eyewitnesses who identified Permann as the man they saw at Hand's Café. There's no getting around that."

I said, "The witnesses are Chet Winston and Sandra Hutchins."

On tape, I said, "In court, you identified Gordon Permann as the man you saw."

Winston said, "That's right."

I said, "Are you sure about that?"

Winston's answer was, "Yeah. He looked kind of like the guy. I mean, in court, he was all cleaned up and had his hair cut, but he was the one the cops said did it."

Earl started to speak, but I held up my hand and played what Sandra Hutchins had told me.

"Mostly, he had his back to me. But I saw his face through the front window after he went back outside. And later, he came in and went to the restroom. At least, I *think* it was him."

My voice said, "You identified him in court."

She said, "Sure. He was all cleaned up and wore a suit, but he was the same guy as in the pictures the police showed me, no doubt about it."

I said, "Are you saying you identified him based on photos?"

Her answer: "Well, not *just* that. I mean, he *did* look like the guy who was here."

I pressed STOP and looked at Earl.

"You've already said that Winston must have been mistaken about something as simple as the color of the car he saw. How confident can you be in the rest of his testimony? Personally, I believe that he *did* see a green car, and that it was *not* a Chevrolet. Those things are easy and basic. But he impeached his own testimony about the identity of the man he saw. He fingered Permann, simply because the cops said he was the guy.

"As for Sandra Hutchins, she's a nice lady with the best of intentions. But she herself admitted that she never got a good look at the face of the man she identified as Permann—only that Permann looked like the man in the photos the police showed her. And of course, they showed her Permann's photo."

"You're pretty good at picking at little things…"

"Those aren't little things. They're the heart of the case," I said quietly.

"But Permann had a record! Assault *and* arson."

"The prosecution's source for that was Leon Stark, but they never offered any evidence to support it. But here's what Stark told me.

I played the tape, starting with my question, "Did you know Permann at the time he got in trouble for starting fires—while he was in school?"

Stark said, "That was a load of crap. He never set any fires—not on purpose, anyway. I think he flipped a cigarette into a trash can that caught fire."

My voice again: "What about the alleged assault and battery?"

Stark said, "It was nothing. The girl's arm got broke when she was trying to hit him. But her old man insisted that Soup was beating *her* up, and he made the charges stick. But the girl herself said it was just an accident."

My voice again: "The name of the girl was kept confidential because of her age. Do you know who she was?"

Stark: "It was Rebecca—the girl he married."

"I think it's safe to say that Permann's alleged criminal history is irrelevant and should have never been brought up in court."

"Apparently the prosecutor has a different opinion," Earl said.

Moving forward, I showed Earl the photos that the fire chief had given to me.

"These show what was left of Permann's car after the fire. Remember what the prosecutor said in his opening statement regarding his theory about how the crime happened?"

"He said what everyone already knew—that Permann somehow got Lisa and Gail into his car, and then…" he choked on his mention of the girls' names.

I continued for him. "He said that Permann had removed the inside door handle on the passenger side of the car, so that the girls couldn't get out."

"I remember that," he said whispered.

"And he showed this photo as proof."

Earl looked at the photo. "So? There's no door handle, just like he said."

"Do you notice anything else?"

"Just tell me what you're getting at," he said impatiently.

"There are no window cranks either," I said.

I showed him a different photo, which showed the driver's door."

"No door handle there, either. And no window cranks. They melted away in the fire. The lack of a door handle on the passenger door means nothing. And if the prosecutor studied the photo hard enough to see that the door handle was gone, he almost certainly knew that the window cranks were gone too. Earl, he made the whole thing up!"

Our glasses were empty, and had been for several minutes. But Earl let me continue.

"And then there's the question of where your girls actually died. The prosecutor used two things to create his hypothetical crime scene—the fact that Permann had helped build a barn near

Crab Creek, where the girls' clothes were found, and the fact that Permann was known to have been at that site before the crime."

"I'd say that's pretty important," Earl said.

I showed him a photo of the barn that Permann had helped build.

"This was taken right around the time of the crime. What do you see?"

He shrugged. "A bunch of cows. So what?"

"Earl, it's a feeding barn. It's where the dairy cows go when there's no grass on the ground. It's hardly a place where anyone would take girls—for any reason. And the girl's clothes were perfectly clean. Do you think it would be possible to come out of there with clean clothes? I don't know where the crime took place, but it certainly wasn't in this barn!"

Earl was shaking his head. "So, all of this... What am I supposed to believe?"

"That's the question I've been asking myself. "I believe that the case against Permann was fabricated—that the testimony of witness was suborned, and that evidence was manipulated. I'll stop short of saying that Permann didn't do the crime, because right now I can't prove that. But I do believe that he was railroaded."

"But if he did it..."

"Here's where I am, Earl. I feel like I need to start at the very beginning—the girls' trip to Seattle for the basketball tournament. I think that whatever happened started there. But I feel like I need your approval before I talk to this case's first witness, your sister, Justine Sorenson."

"All I *really* want is for none of this to have ever happened. I want my girls back. But since that can't happen, I just want all of this to be over. It just drags on and on."

"I can't make it go away. Nobody can. I can promise only two things. I will do nothing to help a guilty man go free, and I will stay on the case until I know who did it."

Earl looked me in the eye and said, "Then do what you have to do."

Chapter Twenty-One

Road Trip

Dale asked, "Why couldn't you just call Justine Sorenson and talk with her on the phone?" You have no idea whether or not you'll learn anything from her that you don't already know."

"Sometimes the smallest bit of information is all that is needed to give new direction to a difficult investigation," I said.

"Still, it seems like a long way to go, just to talk."

"It isn't just that. One of my reasons for going to Seattle is to experience first-hand the things that Lisa and Gail Draper had seen and done in the last days of their lives, culminating with their stop at Hand's Café in Ritzville."

I anticipated that my drive across the state would take six hours, following the same route that the girls had taken on their way to the state basketball tournament. Like their trip in March, my November trip was right on the periphery of the winter driving season in Washington.

The girls had been fortunate, and had nice weather and clear roads. I had decent conditions all morning, but once I started climbing toward Snoqualmie Pass, the misty rain turned to light snow, and near the summit, the road became very unpredictable, with many patches of ice.

By starting the drive at 6:00 a.m. on Monday the 13th, I'd hoped to get to Seattle around noon. But when I realized I was going to be late, I stopped at a phone booth in Rockdale and let Justine know that I'd be late for the lunch she'd offered—over my objections—to prepare.

It ended up being mid-afternoon when I finally arrived at the Sorenson home in Bothell. Justine welcomed me into the living room, where a plate of sandwich quarters sat on the coffee table.

"Would you like a cup of tea or coffee, Mr. Pratt?"

"Coffee would be great—black. And please, call me Connie."

"My husband was hoping to meet you, but he had to get back to work. But really, he didn't actually see much of the girls while they were here."

"So, tell me about their visit," I prompted.

"They drove over on a Wednesday in March—the 16th, I believe. The tournament started that morning, but their game was the last of the day, starting at 9:30 in the evening. Lisa and Gail were so excited! It was the first time in years that their school had made it to the state tournament."

I said, "You know, I went to the same school—Central Valley. And I graduated the year of their most recent trip to the state tournament prior to 1960. So, I too was happy to see them go again."

"They were so keyed-up they could hardly eat. Then, after dinner they drove in to the UW campus, where the tournament was held. I think it was after midnight when they got back, thrilled because their team had won a close game that went into overtime.

"The girls slept late on Thursday, because once again, theirs was one of the late games. They went into town early, to meet some of the other girls in the Pep Club for pizza before the game. Central Valley won, but I guess it was another nail-biter. Both girls had lost their voices from cheering but, oh my, they were happier than I'd ever seen them.

"Now, I know you're here to talk about that guy, Bill. I can't be sure, but I think they met him that night. I heard Gail say something to Lisa about a boy, but I didn't catch a name. It was just a comment—something about him being too proud of himself, or something like that."

"What makes you think it was him?" I asked.

"Actually, I didn't think anything about it at the time. It wasn't until after—well, everything—that I remembered Gail's comment and thought that it fit with things she said about 'Bill' on Friday."

"Tell me about that," I said.

"We had an early dinner on Friday, because the CV game was at 7:30, and Lisa said something to Gail—I don't know what, but it was about Bill. Then, Gail said, 'I don't know why he's still hanging around.' It was pretty clear to me that she didn't *want* him hanging around."

"That almost sounds like maybe Lisa and Bill had had some kind of falling out."

Justine said, "I don't know. I mean, they were still talking to each other the next day—Saturday. And then on Sunday Lisa was willing to go out of her way to caravan home with him. So, if they'd had any kind of falling out, they got over it pretty quick.

"Anyway, Friday's game was a cake-walk for Central Valley—a nice break from the tension of the first two. Then the girls stayed to watch the next game, because the winner of that one would be Central Valley's opponent for the state championship. It turned out to be Renton. But the thing is, Bill was with them, watching that game."

"You're sure of that?" I asked.

"Definitely. Over breakfast on Saturday, Gail complained about how her ears were still ringing from Bill's loud whistling. And there was some friction going on between her and Lisa. At one point, Gail suggested that she take a pack of breath mints for Bill, and Lisa told her to shut up."

"Sibling rivalry?"

"Maybe. Then, that afternoon, I answered the phone, and the caller introduced himself as Bill Brady and asked to talk with Lisa. I think that was the first time I heard his last name. It might've been the only time—I'm not sure. Overhearing Lisa's side of the conversation, I gleaned that Bill was going to meet the girls at the pavilion before the game.

"Thinking about it afterwards, I wondered what was the point of that, since the girls would be in the Pep Club section and Bill wouldn't be allowed there."

I commented, "The game was on TV in Spokane. I watched it—at least until it was obvious that CV couldn't win. I probably saw the girls in some of the crowd shots during the game. But of course, I wasn't looking for them."

Justine continued, "After it was over, some of the kids went to a restaurant of some kind. I'm pretty sure that Bill was there, but I can't put my finger on what gives me that impression—undoubtedly something one of the girls said.

"So, the next morning, Sunday, we had a late breakfast, interrupted by another call from Bill. Lisa went into the other room, so I didn't hear any of the conversation. Later, while I was helping the girls load their suitcases into the trunk of Lisa's car, she asked how to get onto Highway 2.

"That seemed odd, because it wasn't the fastest way to get to US-10. But she explained that she was going that way to link-up with Bill. He'd asked her if she could follow him on the drive to Spokane, because he was having trouble with his car. It would add a few minutes to the trip, but it didn't seem like an unreasonable thing to do."

I asked, "Didn't you wonder why Bill would attempt a cross-state drive with a car that wasn't running right?"

"Not really. It hasn't been so long since I was young and invincible. Didn't we all have the ability to forestall calamity through the power of determination?"

"I guess we *thought* we did," I conceded.

"I wish I'd insisted that she go the shorter way and forget about linking up with Bill."

"Hindsight will make you crazy. There was nothing wrong with your decision."

She sighed. "No. Except for the result."

I changed the subject. "There was a report that Bill might have been a former student at Central Valley."

"I may have speculated about that once. I mean, he seemed to be around for all of their games, and he apparently lived in Spokane."

"Central Valley wasn't the only Spokane school in the Tournament. Shadle Park was there too."

"I suppose it's possible that he went to Shadle, but I never heard anything to support it."

"I was thinking about Gail's comment on Friday, when she said she didn't understand why Bill was still hanging around. Shadle Park was eliminated from the tournament in the first game on Friday."

"I hadn't thought of that. But it sure makes sense."

"When I get back home, I'll check the enrollment records at Shadle Park. Maybe we'll find Brady there, as a current or past student."

"I guess the police tried to find him through the Department of Licensing."

"Yeah. They found drivers licenses for several William Bradys, but none could be the guy we're talking about—they are all too old."

"Maybe Bill is a middle name," she suggested.

"Yeah, I tried that too, and still came up dry."

"Do you think it's a fake name, then?"

"It's a distinct possibility," I said.

✶ ✶ ✶ ✶ ✶ ✶

Not wishing to drive six hours in the dark, I decided to spend the night at a motel in Woodinville. While there, I stopped at the Shell station where Lisa had bought gas, and where she was believed to have linked-up with Bill Brady. I talked to all of the people working at the station, but none had been there in March of 1960.

There remained the question of where Brady was staying while he was attending the tournament. Justine had no information, other than that it must have been somewhere around Woodinville, since that's where he chose to link-up with Lisa. I checked the phone book, but it listed nobody named Brady.

The drive home took me right back through Ritzville. While waiting for a broasted chicken dinner at Hand's Café, I gazed out the window toward the intersection of US-10 and US-395. The café sat at the hub of this case. From where I was sitting, highways went to all of the places connected with the case. My eyes stopped at a sign pointing south that said *Richland 85*.

Richland. I pulled out my notepad and flipped through the pages. Richland High School had also played in the 1960 basketball tournament. Brady could have been heading there, just as easily as Spokane. And Richland had also bombed out of the tournament on Friday.

Something else to check out.

Chapter Twenty-Two

Turkey, Football, and Unanswered Questions

I got home Tuesday afternoon, in time to phone the office at Shadle Park High School. The principal said that he couldn't recall having had a student there named Brady, but he promised to check the records and call me back.

Next, I placed a call to Richland High and asked to speak with the principal.

"This is Cheryl Leland. What can I do for you?"

"Mrs. Leland, my name is Connie Pratt, calling from Spokane. I'm involved in an investigation that might involve a current or former student from Richland. The name is Bill, or William, Brady."

Mrs. Leland said, "This is my first year as principal here, so I can't say whether anybody by that name has attended this school in the past, but I'm pretty sure he's not here now."

"I hate to impose on your time, but could you or someone else check on that—maybe go back five years—and see if you've had a student named Brady?"

"That's no trouble at all, Mr. Pratt. Give me your number, and I'll have someone call you back with that information."

From there, I started working my way through my list of evidence sources outside Adams County. Fortunately, I was able to do most of it by phone, starting with a call to Pasco regarding Gordon Permann's alleged criminal activity.

"I'm following-up on a request by Brant Litton for Franklin County's criminal files on our client, Gordon Permann," I told the clerk who took the call.

"We have no record of any criminal activity by that individual," she said.

"There was testimony given in his trial that he was accused of arson, and actually was convicted on some kind of assault charge," I said. "Could it be that these things were handled in juvenile court?"

"If they were, those records are either sealed or expunged. Either way, even if they exist, I don't have access to them."

That was a dead end, so I called the sheriff's office in Lincoln County, where the girls' clothes were found under the Crab Creek bridge.

I said, "Regarding your interview with the boys who found the Draper girls' clothes, the copies of your notes that I got from Adams County are not legible. Can you make fresh copies and mail them to me?"

"No problem. We'll have to charge for that, though."

"That's fine. Just include an invoice with the documents."

Two days later, when the documents arrived, I found nothing that contributed to Permann's appeal. Meanwhile, I made several local calls to Spokane County officials regarding their involvement in the identification of the remains found on the Indian reservation. Here too, I found nothing of value to us.

I called Jeff Warden, the Spokane Police sergeant who first tipped me off that the Draper girls' bodies had been found. It had been weeks—well, months actually—since I'd talked to him.

"Hey, Connie," he said. "I've been expecting a call ever since I heard that you were working with that attorney on the Permann appeal."

"What can you tell me about the investigation of Frank Stearman?"

"There was nothing to investigate," he said. "Stearman came to us, because he drove a car that matched the APB put out right after the girls went missing, and he wanted to clear himself."

I reminded Jeff that someone had gone to the trouble of calculating a timeline that showed that Stearman theoretically could have been in Ritzville when the girls were last seen."

"Yeah, that was someone in the Sheriff's office. But it didn't come to anything."

"That's not what was in the news," I said.

Come on, Connie. You know better than to believe anything in the news. They'll print anything, if they think it'll sell a few papers. Nobody in law enforcement actually believed that Stearman did anything wrong."

By Wednesday, November 22, I had run out of calls to make, and I'd received calls from Shadle Park and Richland high schools. Nobody named Brady had attended Shadle Park. At Richland High, there *had* been a student named Brady, in the class of 1957. Laura Brady had been an honors student, and was currently a pre-med major at the University of Oregon.

That left me with the same two questions: Who was Bill Brady, and why was Gail surprised that he hadn't left the tournament before Friday night. And nobody was going to answer those questions on Thanksgiving Day.

Our Thanksgiving observance was always a low-key affair. Between us, Dale and I had only one extended family member—my cousin Penny. We watched Macy's Thanksgiving parade in color on a new RCA console that we took home because so many people had commented on our lack of television. How could we own a TV store and not have television at home?

The traditional Thanksgiving dinner was far too extravagant to prepare for just the three of us, but it was a pleasant afternoon.

"What ever became of that Edwards guy?" Penny asked after dinner. "Did they ever catch him?"

I said, "Not that I know of. The police in Portland must have cleared him as a suspect."

Other than that, we avoided discussing the unhappy cases that dominated my work.

On Friday, November 24th, I said to Dale, "I need to shake something up, starting with the description of Brady's car. Chet Winston is adamant that he saw a Pontiac or Oldsmobile. And I believe him. But the official record says it was a Chevrolet."

"So, how can you pin that down?"

"The witness statement on record is a typed copy of something—either hand-written interview notes, or more likely, a tape recording of the interview."

"If it was from hand-written notes, shouldn't those have been in the stuff you got from the Richland police?"

"Should have been, but they weren't, so maybe there's a tape recording."

I picked up the phone and made a person-to-person call to Doreen Fraiser at the Richland Police Department.

"This is Doreen Fraiser. Who's calling, please?"

"It's Connie Pratt. You helped me copy some files a couple of weeks ago."

"Sure. What can I do for you?"

"I have a question about the statements from some of the eye-witnesses," I said.

There was a brief pause, and then Doreen asked, "What about them?"

"They're typed. They couldn't have been typed while the interviews were taking place, so how were they made?"

"I think they were transcribed from tape recordings," she said, "probably by the officer who conducted the interview."

"In that case, I'd like to get copies of the tapes," I said, "just to confirm the accuracy of the transcriptions."

"I'm not sure we can do that. There are problems with some of the recordings."

"What kind of problems?" I asked.

"They told me that while the tape was being played, the take-up reel stopped, but the tape kept rolling. It piled-up and got sucked down inside the recorder, until it finally jammed up and stalled. By then, 50 feet of tape was wound around everything inside the recorder. They got it untangled and wound back onto the reel, but it's all creased and crinkled, and nobody wants to risk playing it."

"But listening to the tapes is the only way to validate the official record."

"I know, but if we try it and the tape falls apart, we'll never get a second chance. We might be able to find an audio specialist somewhere with a recorder built to play fragile tapes like that one, but once it's fallen apart, there'll be no chance of ever hearing it."

"Hmm. I guess for now, we'll have to go with what we have."

I hung up the phone and looked at Dale.

"I've never heard of audiotape getting damaged in a way that would make it *fall apart* if played. I mean, if it was going to fall apart, it would've happened while winding it back onto its reel. I've spent my whole life fixing electronic things. Why have I never heard of anything like this?"

It was something I'd have to look into. In the meantime, I'd have to move forward believing what Chet Winston had told me in person, rather than what the unverified transcriptions said.

"Is there anything else we can do?" Dale asked.

"I've been trying to put myself in the killer's shoes, wondering what I'd do in that spot."

"What are the things that he would find most threatening?"

I said, "That's easy: the eye witnesses who saw him, and the description of his car. Fortunately for the killer, the car probably was misidentified right out of the gate, and both of the witnesses who saw Brady at Hand's Café have already identified Gordon Permann."

"But if Litton wins Permann's appeal, won't the witnesses have to reconsider what they saw?"

"Maybe, but where's their credibility? If they were wrong about Permann, how can you believe them if they finger someone else?"

"Still, it ought to make Brady nervous that people are looking for him again."

"So, what would he *do* about it?" I pressed.

"Let's look at what we know—or *think* we know—about him," Dale suggested. "We think that he went to school in Spokane, or somewhere else in Eastern Washington. But if he went to Central Valley, Shadle Park, or Richland High, it was under some name other than Brady. So, either he was using an alias or he went to school somewhere else."

"The one thing we're pretty sure about is the car. It was a dark green Pontiac or Oldsmobile fastback from about 1950. So far, the mistaken report that it was a Chevy has protected Brady. But what happens once everyone learns that we're out looking for a Pontiac or Oldsmobile. That might make him feel vulnerable."

Dale asked, "You think he'd ditch the car? Would he be able to get rid of it in a way that wouldn't lead right back to him? We know what happened to Permann when *his* car got destroyed."

"I think you're onto something. If I were in Brady's spot, I'd hurry up and paint that car. If he's smart, he probably did it right after the crime. Dale, let's start calling car painters, and asking if anyone remembers painting a green GM fastback in the last year and a half. Maybe we'll get lucky."

I got out the Yellow Pages and counted 59 listings for car painters in Spokane.

"That's a manageable number," I said. "I'll start at the top and work down, and you start at the bottom and work up."

I used the phone in my office, and Dale worked from home, using our personal line. I started each call by introducing myself and asking to speak with someone who would know about paint jobs they'd done in the last 20 months.

"Specifically, I'm looking for someone who remembers doing a color change on a dark green 1949 or 1950 GM fastback—probably a Pontiac or Oldsmobile." After a few rounds, the words flowed out automatically.

It usually took several minutes to get the right person on the phone, and then I'd have to repeat the introduction and question. Some shops had a work log of some kind, but most had to leaf through invoices. In the high-volume shops, it could take a couple of hours or a couple of days to do that, so in most cases, that meant they'd have to call back. For back-calls, we gave them the answering service number, so that we could continue using our own lines.

Being the day after Thanksgiving, a few shops and many employees took the day off, so the job carried over into Monday, and then Tuesday. Dale and I were both approaching the middle of the Yellow Pages listings, and my hopes of success were rapidly fading. But I knew from the start that it was a long shot.

I dialed the number for Jackson's Auto Painting, and introduced myself to the man who answered the phone. I recited my reason for calling, and explained what I was looking for.

"Yeah, ya know, we did a job like that last year. It was a young fella. He wanted it done quick and cheap—and that's our specialty. Like the sign out front says, *'Car Painting as low as $39.95.'* Of course, most people want more than just the basic job, but not this kid. He didn't want me to paint the door jams, under the hood, or inside the trunk. He didn't even care about fixing the scratches. All he wanted was a light sanding and a coat of paint."

"And what kind of car was it?"

"It was just like what you're looking for—a dark green GM fastback. At the time, it struck me as funny, because the paint wasn't in bad shape at all. But the kid wanted it black."

"Do you have the customer's name and address?"

"I'll have to check back through my old paperwork. Might take 'til tomorrow, though."

When he called back, he said, "Well, I found the invoice for that paint job. It was a 1950 Oldsmobile Futuramic two-door. Basic paint job, no extras. Brought it in on April 3rd, 1960. Picked it up on April 5th."

"What was the customer's name?"

"Well, it was a cash job, so there's no name on the invoice."

"How about a phone number? Or the car's license number?"

"Sorry. There's no law says we have to keep track of that stuff."

Of the 59 auto painters we contacted, Jackson's was the only shop in Spokane that had repainted a dark green GM fastback in the last two years. The car was right, and the timing was right, just two weeks after Gail and Lisa Draper were reported missing. But did it tell us anything?

If it really was Brady's car, we now knew three things: that it was a 1950 Olds Futuramic two-door, it was now black, and since it was painted in Spokane, it reinforced the belief that Brady lived in this area.

Those were good pieces of circumstantial information, but they were totally predicated upon the big "if." If the car belonged to someone other than Brady, then none of it meant anything at all. So, what were the odds?

To find out, I phoned my friend, at the Department of Licensing office in Olympia, and asked if it would be possible to find out how many Ivy Green 1950 Oldsmobiles were registered in Washington State.

"That's a pretty tall order," she said. "We have data cards for vehicle registrations, but they include only the information that law enforcement needs—license number, owner, owner's address, and serial number."

From my Crown Victoria investigation, I knew that vehicle serial numbers include codes for body style, engine, and other variables, including paint color.

"Would you be able to sort the data cards by serial number and then read the data codes?"

"In theory, yes. But first, I'd need to have a document showing what the codes mean. They're different for every manufacturer and model year."

"I think I can get you that. If so, can you do it?"

"Yes, but only if I can get access to the IBM machine."

"I'm not trying to get you into trouble," I said.

"I wouldn't do it if I thought it would. People here run specialized data sorts all the time, but we need to schedule it and have a good reason."

"So, what constitutes a good reason?"

"The best reason is a request by law enforcement."

"I'll see what I can do, and get back to you," I concluded.

November 28, 1961

I was still past due for a social visit with Jeff Warden.

"Second call this month? To what do I owe the honor?"

"What, I can't just call to wish you happy holidays?" I protested.

"Is that what you're doing?"

"No. I'm offering to buy you a beer and a chance to catch up on things."

My need for a serial number search fell under that umbrella. His watch ended at 4:00, so I met him in the lounge at the

Stockyards Inn at 4:30. We covered a lot of recent events over our first two rounds of beer, and that included what I'd been doing on the Draper case.

"I've found some document discrepancies, and maybe some discovery issues. It'll be up to Litton to determine what he can use in the appeal."

"Connie, I know you. You're too much of a Boy Scout to work for someone who you think is guilty."

I signaled the girl to bring another pair of beers.

"Last round," I said. "I'm already late for dinner. And you're right. The deeper I get into the facts of the Draper case, the more it looks like Permann got the shit end of the stick."

"There's been some talk around the department," Warden said. "Not that anybody's going to come out and say anything in Permann's defense—cops don't do that. But some of the guys expected more from the prosecution."

"One of the key things that they got wrong was the witness statement about the car that the suspect was driving. The prosecutor said the car was a Chevrolet. The witness *actually* said it was *not* a Chevy, but rather was an Oldsmobile or Pontiac. I've done some work that points at a 1950 Oldsmobile Futuramic."

"I heard all along that it was a Chevy," Warden said. "That's what was in the official bulletin."

"That's right. I don't know how it happened, but the initial report to the State Patrol said it was a Chevrolet Fleetline. And the fact that Permann had owned one is what led to his arrest."

"But if the suspect car was an Oldsmobile…"

"Yeah." I paused for effect. "That's why even a Boy Scout like me can stay on this case."

"Well, good luck getting your guy off."

I couldn't tell if that was sarcasm or sincere.

"I need more than luck. I need a list from the Department of Licensing, of all the 1950 Oldsmobile Futuramic two-doors with Ivy Green paint."

Warden didn't blink. "I knew you were going to ask for a favor, and I was fully prepared to refuse to play along in your crazy game. But I have to say, you make a pretty good case."

I let out the breath I'd been holding.

"Does that mean you'll make the request?"

"I will. But it's not a favor for you. It's for the girls."

"So, who's the Boy Scout now?"

November 29, 1961

The next day, I went to Barton Oldsmobile downtown and got a copy of the data code sheet, which I took to Standard Blue Print. They sent it by Telefax to Fran Meldrum in Olympia.

On December 5th, Jeff Warden called to say that he had the information I'd asked for. "It may surprise you to know that a total of 4,582 1950 Oldsmobiles are registered in Washington state. Of those, 768 are Futuramic two-doors, and 77 are Ivy Green."

"We've got him," I said. "I'm betting that our suspect is somewhere on that list of 77."

"*Your* suspect," he corrected. "This is as far as I can go with it until something happens with Permann's appeal."

"In that case, if you're going to be in the station, I'd like to drive in and pick up the list."

"No. Don't come here," Warden said. "Meet me at the lunch counter in Woolworths."

"I'll be there in thirty minutes," I said.

I got there first, and ordered a ham sandwich and a cup of coffee. When Warden arrived, we made momentary eye-contact. He paused just inside the door and slowly scanned the store.

"I'd prefer that nobody from the department see me here with you," he said, placing a manilla folder on the counter.

I said, "Thanks. I…"

But he was already walking toward the door. The folder contained an eight-page copy of a print-out from the IBM machine at the Department of Licensing headquarters. It listed the 77 registrations for Oldsmobiles matching the description of the suspect car, including the names and addresses of the owners.

After leaving Woolworth's, I stopped at a Shell station and picked up a new map of Washington. In my office, I spread the map on my desk and put a pen mark on the location of Jackson's Auto Painting. Using a drafting compass and the Scale of Miles in the corner of the map, I drew a circle with a ten-mile radius from Jackson's Auto Painting. Next, I drew additional circles at twenty-mile intervals out to 150 miles.

The logic behind that was the theory that people who lived closest to Jackson's Auto Painting were more likely to go there. The further they were from there, the less likely they were to be the owners of the car I was looking for. That prioritized my search.

There were three cars on my list registered at addresses within ten miles of Jackson's. I was able to locate all three owners in the Spokane telephone directory. I wrote down the phone numbers, but refrained from calling, because I didn't want to tip-off the guy I was looking for.

Over the next two days, I made the rounds, looking for the Oldsmobile at each of the addresses, to see if it was still green. If it was black, I'd have my suspect. At two of the three addresses, the car was not visible, so I had to just park and wait. Eventually, I had seen all three cars, and they were still Ivy Green.

I repeated the process for registrations at addresses between ten and thirty miles from Jackson's, with the same result. The larger my circles were, the more time it took to visit each location, and by the time I was working on the 70-mile radius, the job had become untenable. In eleven days, I'd looked at thirteen cars, all of which were still their original color.

December 8, 1961

We were rapidly running out of time. Despite Litton's multiple requests for a continuance on the appeal, the supreme court stood fast on the December 15th hearing date, which was only a week away. Dale worked all weekend, calling directory assistance for the 74 names with addresses not in the Spokane phone book. She finally raised the question that had been bothering me.

"How far would a person drive to get his car painted? I mean, we have cars registered all over the western part of the state, as far away as Long Beach, out at the coast."

"There's always the possibility that someone is living or working away from his home address—like a college student or military man. I'd say that anyone beyond the 150-mile radius would have to be in that category."

Dale said, "Or that the car Jackson painted has nothing to do with the case, and this whole exercise is a bust, meaning that we're right back where we started—not knowing the specific make, model, and year of the car at Hand's Café."

"Welcome to the glamorous world of criminal investigation. On balance, most of what we do amounts to chasing wild geese. That's how it is, but it needs to be done. We still have 61 registrations to check out. We'll just have to do it by phone."

"Yeah," she said. "The question is how do we do it?"

I picked up some notes I'd been writing while we talked.

"Maybe we can call and say something like, *'I represent a client who is offering a reward to anyone who can provide information about an accident that you may have witnessed. Do you own a green Oldsmobile two-door?'* What do you think?"

"It might work, providing that they answer your question before asking details about the accident."

"If they don't answer my question, I'll just repeat it. First things first. Then, if someone says he *does* have a green Oldsmobile, our follow-up question would be, *'Were you in the area of the post office last Tuesday?*' The answer to that will almost certainly be no, and that will be the end of it. But if someone says he *does not* own a green Oldsmobile, he could be our guy."

Litton called on Monday, December 11th and asked, "Have you come up with anything solid on your search for the painted car?"

"We're still working on it, but we have nothing so far," I said.

"Okay. The hearing is Friday. I'll write it up with what we have. But stay on it."

"Yeah. I'll keep you posted."

Thursday morning, I had to tell Litton that we still hadn't found the car. He took the train to Olympia and presented his appeal to the Washington State Supreme Court. The case focused on discovery issues associated with what the prosecution knew about Permann's burnt car, but hadn't shared with the defense.

He also alleged prosecutorial misconduct in regards to his questioning of Chet Winston, after having coached him not to mention the color of Permann's car, as well as the claim he made about the missing door handle being proof that Permann intended to trap the girls in the car.

The court promised a ruling before the end of the year.

Dale and I had spent most of the last two weeks making the phone calls. More often than not, we got no answer and had to try again later. We made the last call on Saturday, two days before Christmas. Of the 61 registered owners, we had managed to talk with 55.

Only three said no, they did not have a green Olds two-door. A man in Aberdeen had traded-in his Olds on a newer model a week before, and a lady in Everett said hers had rolled off the Puget Sound ferry and sunk. The day after Christmas, a man in Camas said that he had a 1950 Oldsmobile two-door, but it was black, not green. His name was Charles Winterhalter.

Chapter Twenty-Three

Zeroing In

I needed to get a photo of Charles Winterhalter, to show to Luke Jackson. If Jackson identified Winterhalter as the man whose car he painted, it would make him a legitimate suspect. In some states, driver's licenses have photos. But Washington was not one of them.

"There has to be a better way to get a picture of him than driving clear across the state in wintertime," Dale said.

"I'm open to ideas. I guess I could fly to Portland and rent a car. But I'm not sure it would save any time."

"Could you find a private detective in that area to take a picture and send you the film?"

"I'm sure I could," I said, "but we simply can't afford the mailing time."

To avoid having to drive over White Pass or Satus Pass in winter conditions, I drove to Pasco, and then followed the Columbia River to Portland on the new Interstate 80N. From there, I crossed the river on the US-99 Interstate Bridge and then drove 30 miles east to Camas.

Camas was a mill town, dominated by the Crown-Zellerbach paper mill—the largest toilet paper factory in the world. The sulfurous emissions from the plant could be smelled as far away as Vancouver, and could be suffocating in Camas. It was a misty, dismal afternoon when I arrived there two days after Christmas.

In the waning daylight, I located the address on Charles Winterhalter's vehicle registration. It was a bungalow from about 1920 in a low-lying area near the Washougal River. The picket fence around the front yard was missing many boards and had only the faintest remnants of white paint. The unmowed front yard was cluttered with car parts, old appliances, and overflowing trash cans.

I waited around until it was too dark to take pictures. Finally, as I was preparing to leave, the black Oldsmobile rolled up and parked next to the fence. In the darkness, I couldn't get a good look at the man who got out of the car and went into the house. But since his arrival coincided with the shift change at the mill, I concluded that my best chance to get his picture would be in the morning, when he left for work.

After a mac and cheese dinner at a dingy restaurant on Third Avenue, I got a cabin in a tourist court out by the highway to Vancouver. The cabins were arranged around a circular drive, with a shared toilet and shower building in the middle. I was pleased to get one of the few cabins that actually had its own bathroom.

At 7:00 the next morning, I paused across from Winterhalter's black Oldsmobile. What I saw was disappointing. The rain had stopped during the night, and a gentle east wind had dried-off the car, so I could see the flat finish of spray-can primer. There was no way that this was done by Jackson's Auto Painting. Still, as long as I was there, I parked and slouched down behind the steering wheel, with my camera ready. I didn't have to wait long. Winterhalter came out at 7:30, carrying a steaming cup of what I assumed to be coffee. I snapped three quick photos, using a 200mm telephoto lens.

The man appeared to be about 30, but he did fit the description of a "greaser," or hot-rodder. When he started the Oldsmobile's engine, it made the throaty rumble of glass-packs or straight pipes. I followed him to the gate at the paper mill, and drove on by when he pulled into the employee parking lot.

I went back the restaurant where I'd had dinner, and got a quick breakfast. With a full stomach and a full tank of gas, I got on Highway 14 heading east. The long drive back home gave me plenty of time to contemplate my next move. I considered it extremely unlikely that Winterhalter was the guy. He was too old, the paint on the car wasn't right, and nobody at Hand's Café on the afternoon of the abduction had mentioned noisy exhaust.

Before I got out of range of the Portland radio stations, I heard on the news that the supreme court had rejected Permann's appeal and set a new execution date—Wednesday, February 7th.

With a renewed sense of urgency, I contemplated my last hope of developing a lead from Luke Jackson's paint job. I had to somehow make contact with those last five registered owners we had been unable to reach by phone. Short of driving all over the state and trying to find them in person, my only remaining option was to contact them by mail. I started mentally composing a note.

December 29, 1961

In my office on Friday, I typed the message on the back of a post card from Pratt's Television & Radio. I made a card to each of the five Oldsmobile owners, and delivered them to the post office.

```
Dear J.T. Dunne,

    I have $20 for you. All you need to do is make
a two-minute phone call.

    The call is free. Simply ask the operator for
Zenith 18800. We will ask two questions to
determine if you are eligible to receive a reward
of up to $2,500.

    This is not a trick, and we won't try to sell
you anything. A $20 check already has your name
on it. Call by midnight, January 5, 1962.

C.R. Pratt
```

The toll-free Zenith number connected to my answering service, who would first confirm the name and address of the caller. If it matched one of the five cards I sent out, our receptionist would read the following script:

"Thank you for calling. Your $20 check will be in the mail tomorrow. The reason we asked you to call is that you are the registered owner of a green 1950 Oldsmobile two-door. Is that information correct?"

If the caller confirmed ownership, our receptionist would say, *"We are offering a reward of up to $2,500 to anyone who can provide information about an incident that occurred on December 1, 1961 at the post office in _____."* She would insert the name of the town from the caller's address, and continue, *"Were you there on that day?"*

The answer would almost certainly be no, and that would be the end of it. The receptionist would thank the caller and repeat that the $20 check was on its way—which it would be. I guess there was a small chance that someone would claim to have been at the post office that day and try to scam us out of the big reward, but if that had happened, the call would have been directed to me, and I'd have taken care of it.

But it was the *first* question that really counted. If the person denied owning a 1950 Oldsmobile, he would be an automatic suspect. And if he said that his was black, not green, his car would be suspected of being the one painted by Jackson, thus making its owner a suspect in the crime.

The second caller was James T. Dunne in Toppenish, Washington. He answered the first question with a correction. His car was black.

As promised, each of the five people who responded to the post card, including Dunne, was sent a $20 check.

Chapter Twenty-Four

Another Road Trip
January 5, 1962

The day after Dunne's phone call, I drove to Toppenish and found the address in a little subdivision with houses of the kind built by the thousands all over the country in the mid-50s, especially for Korean war veterans to buy on the G.I. Bill.

There was no car on the driveway, so I parked a hundred yards away and hunkered down to see if Dunne would show up. The shiny black Oldsmobile drove past me at 5:20, and turned into Dunne's driveway. Watching with binoculars, I got a brief glimpse of Dunne when he walked from the car to the house.

I knew right away that he wasn't our suspect, even though the car was exactly right. Dunne looked like he was 60 years old, and nobody would mistake him for a teen-age rock-and-roller. His gray hair was sparse on top and cut short. On the other hand, he might be the suspect's father, or possibly even grandfather.

So, I waited around to see if anyone else showed up. By 9:00, I was cold and drowsy. There was no point hanging around if I was just going to fall asleep, so I found the only motel in town and checked in.

The next day was Saturday, so I didn't see the need to get over to Dunne's place early. I got breakfast in a diner, and then went back to where I'd parked the evening before. Once again, I settled-in to watch the house and the car.

A tap on my window startled the daylights out of me.

"Can I help you with something?" the man asked loudly.

I lowered my window a crack and said, "No thanks. I've just been waiting for someone."

"You were here last night too, weren't you?"

"Yes, I was." I handed him a business card.

"Private investigator, huh? Who are you investigating?" he asked.

I said, "Not who. What. I'm investigating a car."

He looked up the street. "Which one?"

I had to tell him something, and the truth worked as well as anything I could have made up.

"The black Oldsmobile. You know the owner?"

"Sure. Jim Dunne. We've been neighbors here for close to ten years."

"How long's he had that car?"

"It's not stolen or something is it?"

"No, nothing like that," I said. "So, how long's he had it?"

"A year. No, he got it in the springtime, so it must be more like a year-and-a-half now."

Dunne wasn't our guy. He'd bought the car after it was repainted, weeks after the Draper girls were abducted and killed.

"Well, that eliminates any other questions I might've had," I said, even though it didn't.

I needed to know who sold the car to him. I could get that information from the Department of Licensing, but a much quicker way was to simply ask Dunne. I thanked the neighbor, and then drove down and parked in front of Dunne's house. When he answered the doorbell, I gave him my card.

"Connie Pratt. Say, aren't you the guy who sent me that post card?"

"That's right. I was interested in your car," I said, gesturing toward the Oldsmobile.

"I don't understand. I thought you were looking for a green one," he said.

"I believe this one originally *was* green."

"Yeah, it used to be. Still was, when I bought it—in the trunk and under the hood. But how did you know?"

"The serial number code. It says it was green when it left the factory."

"It was black when I bought it," he said, and added, "The paint job was so fresh I could smell it—and there wasn't a scratch on it."

"Where did you buy it?" I asked.

"Bought it from an old lady from Yakima."

"Do you know her name?"

"Not right off. I found the car in the want-ads, and paid cash for it. She signed-off the title and gave me a bill of sale. But I turned those in when I transferred the title," Dunne said.

"Can you tell me where she lived?"

"Nope. I never went there. She drove the car here. I took it for a test drive, and gave her the money. I offered to give her a ride home, but she used my phone to call some other old lady to come and pick her up."

"That seems a little bit odd, doesn't it?" I mused.

Dunne shrugged. "I never thought about it. So, what's the deal? The car isn't stolen, is it? I mean, why did you want to find it so bad?"

"It's not stolen. But it may be connected with a case that I'm working on."

"What kind of case? Hit-and-run, or something?"

"I'm not at liberty to talk about the case. But it's not a hit-and-run."

"Has to be something pretty serious, or you wouldn't be going to all this trouble."

"Would you mind letting me look it over?" I asked.

"Not at all. There's nothing to find, though. It was very clean when I bought it, and I've always kept it that way."

Dunne was right—the car was impeccable. The speedometer showed 95,000 miles, but nothing about the car was visibly damaged or excessively worn.

"I couldn't stand looking at the green paint on door jams, and the insides of the hood and trunk," Dunne explained, "so I got some spray cans and finished the paint job myself."

"Did you ever find anything from the previous owner in the car?"

"Not a thing. Like I said, it was perfectly clean."

"If this does turn out to be the car I'm looking for, the police will probably want to take a good look at it."

"I'm beginning to get the picture."

"Let me know if you decide to do anything with the car, will you? Don't sell it without calling me, okay?"

"No problem."

This left me with multiple questions. If the car was owned by an old lady, who was the young man who took it to Jackson's Auto Painting? And if I was right about it being the car seen at Hand's Café, who was the "greaser" seen with it? In order to get answers, I needed to talk with the old lady who sold the car to Jim Dunne.

Chapter Twenty-Five

The Black Oldsmobile
January 8, 1962

Back in the office on Monday, I called Jeff Warden and gave him a full report on what I'd done with the information he'd given me.

"I'm pretty sure that this is the car that Luke Jackson painted a month after the girls disappeared. The current owner bought it a month after that. So, what I need now is the name of the prior owner. Can you get that for me?"

He sighed. "Yeah. No sweat."

"At what point do you want in on this case?"

"When you prove that a crime was committed in my jurisdiction."

"I don't think that's going to happen," I said.

"Then I don't want to know. See how that works?"

As soon as I got off the phone, I put on my coveralls and headed out to make a couple of service calls, both of which involved color sets that were a few years old. The first set was easily fixed by degaussing the picture tube, which had developed a magnetic field inside the envelope. The second set needed a new flyback transformer that I didn't carry in the truck. I'd have to get one downtown, and return to install it the next day.

Dale was in the store with Nancy when I got back. She was busy doing the annual inventory for the accountant.

I held up the bag from Northwest Electronics.

"I'm going to have to go back in the morning and install this. Any other work come in?"

"We got another call on a black-and-white set with no picture," she said.

"Those are starting to become a problem," I said. "Black-and-white sets are dropping in value, and it's becoming increasingly difficult to charge what it costs to make repairs."

"What can you do about that?"

"The best thing would be to sell them a new TV set, even if it's black-and-white. At least then, we wouldn't have to put our time and money into a set that's worth less than the repair cost."

Dale switched topics. "Get anything back from Sergeant Warden?"

"Not yet. It probably will take a day or two."

"Is there anything else you can do on the case?"

"I'm still thinking about the witness interview tape that Doreen Fraiser said had gotten tangled and was damaged too badly to play."

At that moment, I had an epiphany. Why not try to replicate the condition that Doreen had described, and see if anything could be done about it?

"Do we have any tapes that nobody's ever going to buy?"

"Sure. There're always a few stiffs lying around."

Dale dug out *Gene Autry's Christmas Album* on audio tape. We'd just finished the Christmas season, and nobody had bought it, so the chances of anyone buying at that point were nil.

I unrolled about fifty feet of tape into a pile on the table, and then I wadded it up, as if trying to make a snowball out of it. That didn't look bad enough, so I took the tape outside and put it behind the tire of my car. After driving back and forth over the unreeled pile of tape, it, looked unplayable.

While winding it back onto its reel, I wiped the tape clean with a dry cloth. When I tried to play the crinkled part of the tape, the sound was badly broken-up and words in the song Gene Autry was singing were difficult or impossible to understand.

I experimented with various ways of restoring the sound quality, first by "ironing" the tape. I mounted the tape on the recorder without threading it through the slot where the recording heads were. Instead, I wrapped it around a mug full of hot water. As I ran the tape slowly back and forth over the hot mug, the creases smoothed out a bit. It was far from perfect, but it helped.

Next, I tried increasing pressure on the pads that hold the tape against the playback head, hoping to press it flat as it played. But the amount of pressure needed to maintain full contact with the head was enough to cause the drive capstan to slip and drag down the playback speed, badly distorting the sound.

In the end, I found that playback speed was the answer. The tape was meant to be played at 7.5 inches per second. If I ran it at 3.75 inches per second, while moderately increasing the tape head pressure, the crinkled tape would mostly stay in contact with the playback head and produce nearly continuous audio. When the copy was played back at full speed, the audio quality was marginally acceptable.

My conclusion was that if the damage to the interview tape was similar to what I'd done to the Gene Autry tape, I could make a dub at half speed, and achieve acceptable sound quality when the copy was played back at standard speed.

All I'd have to do was convince Doreen to let me iron the interview tape as I'd done to the tape in my shop, and then play it on my modified tape recorder. I'd take *Gene Autry's Christmas Album* along, to demonstrate that what I wanted to do would not further damage the interview tape.

Tuesday morning, my first task was to finish the TV repair that I'd started the day before. With the new flyback transformer installed, the picture came up. I adjusted the convergence trimmers to refine the picture quality, to complete the job.

Back in the office, I was reaching for the phone to call Doreen Fraiser, when Jeff Warden called with the name and address of the old lady who sold her 1950 Oldsmobile to Jim Dunne. She was Margaret Tanner, and she lived in an apartment in Yakima. I was unable to get a phone number from directory assistance, so my only option was to go there and see her in person. This would be my third round-trip across the state in the last two weeks.

January 10, 1962

After the three-hour drive the next morning. I discovered that the apartment building at the address on Margaret Tanner's vehicle registration was actually a retirement home. I drove on past and found a flower shop, where I bought a bouquet of chrysanthemums in a white glass vase.

With flowers in hand, I approached the reception desk and asked, "Does Margaret Tanner live here?"

The receptionist looked suddenly sympathetic and said, "Oh dear, I'm so sorry. Mrs. Tanner passed away in November."

I guess that explained why she didn't have a phone number.

"Were you a relative?" the receptionist asked.

"A distant relative."

…of someone, somewhere.

"It was all so sudden and unexpected. She was very active for her age, and seemed quite well. And then she got sick one day and was gone the next. I'm surprised nobody in the family told you."

"I've been out of the country," I said.

That was true, as well. I had been half way around the world. Granted the Korean war was ten years back, but I assuredly had been out of the country.

"Can you tell me who was notified of her death?"

"I'm very sorry, but I don't have that information, and even if I did, I'd have to get their permission to release their names."

"Oh. Of course. I understand."

I'd have to figure out some other way to get the information I needed. I handed the flowers to the receptionist.

"I guess you might as well have these."

As I was walking toward the exit, I was intercepted by a slim blue-haired lady with a small dog on a leash.

"I heard you asking about Margaret Tanner. She never mentioned having a young, handsome relative."

I confessed, "We're not actually related. I just said that, hoping to get the name of a relative I could talk to."

I handed her my card.

"Connie Pratt, private investigator. Now, that's intriguing. Why would a private investigator come looking for Margaret?"

"I'm working for an attorney in Spokane. The case involves a car that Mrs. Tanner used to own."

"Oh, where are my manners? I haven't introduced myself," she said. "I'm Lilly Nash. Margaret was a long-time friend. Her apartment was right across the hall from mine."

"Well then, Miss Nash. Maybe you can help me."

"About the mystery car? I'd *love* to help. But please, call me Lilly. Would you care to join me for a cup of tea in our community room."

"That sounds great," I said.

Once we'd settled in, Lilly asked, "Now what's all this about a car?"

"Last summer, Mrs. Tanner sold a car that, as I said, may be connected to the case I'm working on."

"Margaret hasn't had a car since she moved here in 1958."

"It was registered in her name, at this address."

I showed her the copy of the registration form that Jeff Warden had given me."

"Oh, that's the Green Bomb! It wasn't Margaret's car. It belonged to her grandson. It was just registered in Margaret's name because his insurance, which she paid for, cost less that way."

"What can you tell me about him?" I asked.

"He broke her heart. She loved him so much, and all he ever did was cause trouble and take advantage of her. I guess some kids are just born bad."

"What do you mean?"

"Oh, I don't know all the details, of course, but Margaret used to tell me stories—like how Billy was too much for his mother to handle, even when he was a child."

"How old is Billy now?" I asked.

"He must be about 21 now—going to college. At least that's what Margaret said. Kind of hard to believe though."

"What do you mean?"

"It's like I said. Billy was always a troublemaker. He drove his mother crazy. I mean, literally crazy. He was a complete juvenile delinquent. He was always in trouble of some kind. Shoplifting, vandalism, theft, fighting—just about everything.

"His father died in Korea, and Clarise—his mother—was left with three kids to raise on whatever money she got from the government. By itself, that would've been a tough row to hoe, but when Billy started getting into more and more trouble, Clarise broke down. Her older son couldn't take it anymore and ran away. Clarise locked herself in a bedroom and wouldn't come out.

"After a week, one of the other kids told a teacher at school, and she called the police. They found Clarise sitting in a mess of feces, dehydrated and starving. She ended up in the mental hospital at Medical Lake. That's when Billy and his sister Rena went to live with Margaret in Wapato.

"The move to Wapato separated Billy from his delinquent friends, and he seemed to settle down some. I think Rena helped keep him in line—but then she got married, right after she graduated in about 1954. Margaret grew old riding herd on Billy. After he finally graduated, Margaret threw him out and came to live here."

I said, "So, Billy's name—is it Tanner? Where is he now?"

"Yeah, Billy—William, I guess—Tanner. I don't actually know where he is. Margaret said that he'd gotten into college, but I don't know where."

Billy Tanner. Bill Brady. Could be. It all depended on the car.

"So, about the car," I prompted.

"As soon as Billy turned 16, he badgered Margaret into buying him a car—the Green Bomb."

"The 1950 Oldsmobile."

Lilly nodded. "Margaret told me that the car gave Billy something to do, and I guess he took pretty good care of it—he even gave it a new paint job. Then, he came to her and said he wanted to buy a different car."

"Did he tell her why?"

"She didn't say. Anyway, she sold the Oldsmobile for him and gave him the money, but that wasn't enough. He conned her out of another $400, which was about two months' worth of Social Security. She had to cash-in some bonds to pay her rent."

"I don't suppose you have a picture of Billy…"

"Goodness no! That kid was no friend of mine."

I needed two things before I could offer-up Billy Tanner as a legitimate alternate suspect in the Draper case. I needed a photo to show the witnesses, and I needed to know where he was.

Chapter Twenty-Six

Billy Tanner

William Tanner had attended Wapato High School. It was a twenty-minute drive from the retirement home in Yakima to Wapato. I easily located the high school, and went into the principal's office.

I introduced myself the principal, whose name tag said Mr. Leach, and gave him my card.

"What can I do for you, Mr. Pratt?"

"Do you remember a student named William Tanner? I believe he was in the class of 1957."

"Yes, he was a student here."

"Did you know him personally?"

"I try to know all of my students, so yes, I knew Bill. What's your interest in him?"

"I'm gathering evidence for a Spokane attorney who is working on an appeal. The Tanner boy might be a witness in the case."

"And what would you like from me?" asked Leach.

"Just about anything you can tell me will help. I need to locate him as soon as possible."

"I'm afraid I can't be much help. I haven't seen him since graduation, almost four years ago."

"I've been told that he had disciplinary problems," I said.

"Let's just say that I knew Bill better than I knew most students."

"What kind of trouble did he get into?"

"Academically, he was an okay student, but he was implicated in some minor criminal activities."

"Implicated?"

"We knew he was involved, but couldn't prove it."

"What kind of things was he into?"

"I'm not at liberty to say. He was a juvenile, and it was a long time ago."

"Do you have any idea where he is now?"

"Nope. Like I said, I haven't seen him since graduation."

"What about friends? Did he have any friends who might be able to tell me how to find him?"

"It's funny. It seemed like Bill spent most of his time with a low crowd—the kids most likely to be found in detention on any random day. But his best friend was a great kid, who was a pretty good influence on him. Dave Shane was an excellent student, and he was on the basketball team—the best team we ever had."[2]

"Any idea where Shane went after graduating from Wapato?"

"He graduated from Central Washington State Collage last year, and then got married. He and his wife live in Lamont, where he works in his uncle's produce farming business. He should be pretty easy to find."

I thanked Mr. Leach and went out to my car, where I got my Polaroid camera. I took it to the school library and found a copy of the 1957 yearbook.

---

[2] The true-life star of the 1957 Wapato High School basketball team was Richard Skone, who passed away in 2003. The fictional character David Shane is loosely based on Richard Skone, whose name should be acknowledged and honored.

William Tanner's photo was on page 32. It was my first look at my suspect. He had the DA haircut exactly as Chet Winston and Sandra Hutchins had described. His belligerent sneer spoke volumes about his attitude. I got a good closeup photo of his picture, which I hoped would help negate the witness testimony against Gordon Permann.

I found photos of three other boys who had long hair combed back in the same way as Tanner's, and I shot pictures of them. This gave me a photo spread that I could put before the witnesses.

On my way back to my car, I passed a trophy case for the Wapato Wolves. Standing prominently in the center of the display was a trophy for third place in the 1957 state high school basketball tournament.

There was also a trophy for the 1960 Yakima Valley League championship, and that's what reminded me that Wapato had also played in the 1960 state tournament. Was Tanner the kind of fan who would take-off and go to Seattle to watch his old school play, three years after his graduation? Unquestionably, there were people who would do that.

I went back to the library and found the 1960 year book and turned to the sports section. The Wapato Wolves had gone into the tournament with an impressive 19 and 3 record, but were the first team eliminated, when they lost their first two games.

If Bill Tanner really was Bill Brady, and had attended the tournament, it made sense that Gail Draper had wondered why he was still around on Friday, the third day of tournament play.

January 11, 1962

In my motel room the next morning, I called directory assistance and got a number for David Shane in Lamont. Getting no answer, I figured that David must be at work. Mr. Leach had said that Shane worked in the family's produce business, so I called directory assistance again, and the operator found a listing for Shane and McCann Produce.

The receptionist there told me that David would not be in the office for the rest of the week, so I left a message asking him to call me when he could.

I checked out of the motel, but before leaving town, I went to the recorder's office in the Yakima County Courthouse. I was unable to find records of any kind for William Tanner. I tried looking for Clarise Tanner, hoping to find her maiden name, but lacking her husband's first name, it was a long task. In the end, I found no record of anyone named Tanner marrying a girl named Clarise.

Apparently, she was married outside Yakima County. I searched for birth certificates for Tanner babies born between 1930 and 1942, but did not find William or his sister Rena. My best guess was that the Tanner children had been born in the same county where Clarise had been married

By the time I gave up, I had a headache from the three hours I'd spent in front of the microfilm reader. The only thing I'd learned was that there was nothing more to learn in Yakima County. But as we investigators always remind ourselves, the fact that nothing is there is something learned.

My drive back to Spokane took me through Ritzville, so I stopped at Hand's Café. It was dinnertime, and Sandra Hutchins was waiting tables. She immediately recognized me when she came over to take my order.

"You're the private detective—Connie, right?" she asked.

"You have a good memory for names," I said.

"Well, are you ready to order?"

"I'll go for the broasted chicken dinner. It's hard to beat."

"Anything to drink with that?"

"Coffee, please."

She went behind the counter and clipped my order to the wire over the window to the kitchen. When she came back with my coffee, I spread out the pictures I'd taken from the yearbook.

Without hesitation, she put her finger on William Tanner's photo. "That's him. It's that Superman guy before he got all cleaned up for court. That's how he looked when he was here."

"Are you certain about that?" I asked.

"Absolutely. He looks younger, but this is him, for sure."

"What if I were to tell you that this is *not* Gordon Permann?"

"But it is. It's the guy who was talking to those poor girls," she said.

"I believe it is. But it is not Gordon Permann. His name is William Tanner."

"But the police said… I mean, Permann was convicted in court. It *had* to be him."

I said, "If this is the man you saw, Permann was wrongfully convicted."

Someone at a nearby table waved, and Sandra had to cut-off our conversation right there. While waiting for my order, I went to the pay phone by the restrooms and dialed Chet Winston's number. He answered on the third ring.

After introducing myself, I asked, "Do you have a couple of minutes. I have some photos for you to look at."

"Yeah. I guess I can do that."

"Great. Listen, I'm having dinner right now at Hand's Café. I can meet you afterwards."

He agreed to that and gave me his address. Half an hour later, I knocked on his door. He welcomed me in and offered me a beer, which I declined.

"So, what do you have to show me?" he asked.

I spread my four Polaroids on the table.

"Does anyone here look familiar?"

He pointed at Tanner. "Yeah, sure. That's the guy who killed those girls. He doesn't look so wholesome without his haircut and

Sunday suit on. But see that look in his eyes? Who could ever forget that?"

I asked Chet the same question I asked Sandra, "What if I tell you that this is *not* the man who was convicted of killing the Draper girls?"

"That's crazy talk. I just told you it's him."

"It's not Gordon Permann. It's William Tanner."

I pointed to the name under the photo.

"I don't get it. Who the hell is William Tanner?"

"He's the guy you saw in front of Hand's Café. You just said so," I said.

"Yeah. He's the guy. He must have changed his name or something."

"No, you remember from the trial how they had Permann's high school record from Richland? This photo came from the Wapato High School yearbook."

"But everyone said Permann did it," he protested.

"Yeah. Makes you wonder, doesn't it?"

January 12, 1962 - Morning

On Friday morning, I took my Polaroid photo spread to Jackson's Auto Painting. Luke Jackson was in the spray booth painting a car, so I had to wait around until he was finished. While he was cleaning his spray gun, I told him how I'd tracked-down the car that I thought he'd painted.

I said, "The current owner bought the car in May, 1960—when the paint was so fresh, he could smell it."

Jackson shrugged. "Yeah? So, all you need to do is find out who sold it to him, right?"

I laid down the four Polaroid photos.

"Do you see the person who brought the car to you?"

"That's him, right there." He put his finger on the photo of William Tanner.

"You're sure about that?" I asked.

"Absolutely, positively, no question about it."

Next, I went to Brant Litton's office and reported everything that I'd found:

- Chet Winston told me that the car he saw at Hand' Cafe was a Pontiac or Oldsmobile, not a Chevrolet. The APB was incorrect.
- An Ivy Green 1950 Oldsmobile Futuramic two-door was painted black by Jackson's Auto Painting in April 1960, less than a month after the Draper girls vanished.
- The Department of Licensing provided a list of all cars registered in the state that match that description—77 cars in all.
- Two of those cars had been re-painted in black.
- One of those is currently owned by James Dunne in Toppenish. He purchased it a few weeks after Luke Jackson painted it.
- The former owner was Margaret Tanner, now deceased.
- The Oldsmobile had belonged to William Tanner, but was registered to his grandmother, Margaret Tanner.
- The car painter picked William Tanner from a photo spread, and identified him as the man who had the Oldsmobile painted.
- William Tanner, age 21, was a 1957 graduate of Wapato High School.
- Wapato HS played in the 1960 state basketball tournament.
- Sandra Hutchins and Chet Winston both identified William Tanner from his yearbook photo as being the man they saw at Hand's Café.

I added, "Permann became a suspect *only* because he owned a 1951 Chevrolet Fleetline, as described in the original APB on the suspect vehicle. The APB was wrong. The car was an Oldsmobile. Permann never owned an Oldsmobile. Tanner is the guy. We've got him cold."

"Got him *where*? Where is he?"

"I'm still working on that. I'm expecting a call from Tanner's high school best friend. I'm hoping that he can shed some light on Tanner's present location."

"What about that APB? How did the State Patrol get the car wrong?"

"Their information came directly from the Ritzville Police Department's witness statement summary. That appears to be the source of the error."

"How did you determine that it is an error."

"Originally from my interview with Chet Winston. He said emphatically that the car he saw was not a Chevrolet, and that it most likely was a Pontiac or Oldsmobile. I found the car painter by following a hunch that the suspect would want to get rid of the car or get it painted. The painter's records say that it was a 1950 Oldsmobile."

"So, how did the witness statement get it wrong?"

"I'm working on that. The statement summary on record is actually transcribed from a tape recording of the witness interview. The clerk at Ritzville PD says that the tapes are damaged and cannot be played without risk of completely ruining them."

Litton shook his head. "That's going to be hard to work around. The fact that the witness now says something different from what's on record may not impress the appeals court. It is a well-established fact that witnesses sometimes change their minds when they're uncomfortable with the consequences of their testimony."

"Winston is not saying this out of remorse for Gordon sitting on death row."

"Prove it."

"Actually, I might be able to do just that. The police department clerk told me that the tape recordings had been damaged somehow. In my shop, I tried to replicate the kind of damage she described, and then find a way to restore and play the tape. It took some doing, but I was able to successfully dub a copy of my intentionally damaged tape. The sound quality is far from perfect, but it is clear enough. And my original tape incurred no additional damage in the process of making the copy."

"Will they let you try to copy the interview tapes?"

I shook my head. "The clerk turned me down the first time I asked. But that was before I did the experiment in my shop. She's been pretty helpful throughout this whole thing, so I'm hoping that after I demonstrate to her that I can play my damaged tape without destroying it, maybe she'll let me try playing their tape."

"Maybe I should try to get a court order," Litton Suggested.

"It may come to that. But like I said, the lady has gone out of her way to help, so I'd rather not antagonize her or the police department down there by storming in with a court order."

"So, when are you going to go down there?"

"I'll give her a call this afternoon and try to set something up for next week."

"Okay, but we're running out of time. The court is still refusing to grant a stay of execution unless and until we can prove what you're saying. If that clerk balks at letting you dub the tapes, I'll bury the Ritzville P.D. in subpoenas."

* * * * * *

On my way back to my office, still thinking about ways I might track down William Tanner, it occurred to me that there was a question that I had neglected to ask Principal Leach when I was at Wapato High School.

In my office, I called Mr. Leach and asked if Tanner had ever requested a copy of his academic records, something that he would need when applying for admission to college.

"I can't say right off," he said. "Requests for transcripts are quite routine, and they're handled by the office staff."

"Do they keep a record of transcripts they send out?"

"Not specifically, but we do have a file containing copies of all correspondence with former students. So, if Tanner mailed us a request for a transcript, that letter and our response should be in the file."

"How hard would it be to determine if such an exchange took place?"

"The correspondence is filed by date, so unless a copy was left in the student's folder, we'd have to go through them all, looking for his name."

"How long would it take to do that?"

"Since I already know that there's nothing like that in Tanner's file, it could take several hours to leaf through the correspondence file. We can do that, if you like, but it may be a day or two before we can get to it. We're down to the last week of our semester, and everyone's pretty busy."

Next, I called the Ritzville Police Department and asked for Doreen Fraiser.

"She's not in the office today. Can someone else help you?"

I stifled a wave of desperation, bordering on panic.

"Do you know when Mrs. Fraiser will be in?"

"She'll be here on Monday. Would you like to leave a message for her?"

I couldn't think of any kind of message that could convince Doreen to let me try copying the tapes. It would he hard enough to do in a phone call.

"No, thanks. I'll call her Monday," I said.

I dug back through all of my notes on the case looking for anything else that I could do while waiting for back-calls from Dave Shane and Wapato High School.

Dale asked, "Could you go to Ritzville PD and make your case to whoever's there?"

"I think it's too much of a gamble. Some of the cops there resent my tampering in what they consider to be *their* case. Doreen is the only one who's been willing to listen."

Chapter Twenty-Seven

The Big Freeze
January 12, 1962 - Afternoon

All across the country, extreme weather was creating havoc. Frost in the deep south was destroying crops, blizzards in Montana closed schools, and the entire mid-west was paralyzed by sub-zero weather. In Washington, rivers west of the Cascades were flooding, while Spokane received a couple of inches of snow Friday night.

With no fresh ideas, I decided to take another look through the big file. While reading the incident report from the officer who was first on the scene when Lisa's car was found, I was reminded of something that Justine Sorenson had said to me when I interviewed her in Bothell.

She recalled that while loading the girls' luggage into the trunk of the car, Lisa had asked about the route to Woodinville, where she'd meet-up with Bill Brady. I'd paid attention to only the second part of Justine's statement. But in looking at the police officer's description of the car when he found it, a discrepancy jumped out at me.

The girls' luggage was found "undisturbed on the backseat," not in the trunk, where Justine said it was.

I had to have another talk with Earl Draper. I left a message with his answering service, and in the middle of the afternoon, he called me back, and we agreed to meet again at Sid's Tavern.

"I assume you have news. Is it good or bad?" he asked bluntly.

"Both. I haven't quite closed the loop on the question of the suspect's car, but I'm getting close."

"Close only counts in horseshoes and hand grenades."

"That was the bad news. The good news is that I have a very solid suspect. Three key witnesses picked him from a photo line-up. I know his name, and have connected him to the car."

"So, who is the son-of-a-bitch?"

"I can't reveal his name until he's in handcuffs. The second he thinks we're onto him, he's likely to take off."

Then, why did you want to talk to me?"

"When we talked before, I didn't ask anything about Lisa's car. I understand that it was released back to you."

"That's right."

"What was in the car when you got it back?"

"Everything that was in it when they found it, except for the gas receipts. They kept those for evidence."

"The Ritzville police reports say that there was a receipt for a fill-up at Moses Lake shortly before the girls got to the café in Ritzville."

"That's right. A month later, we got her credit card bill showing the fill-up."

"And yet the Police said the gas tank had only a gallon and a half of gas in it."

"Yeah, they said that someone probably syphoned the gas out that night," Earl said.

"I'm looking for a better explanation," I said.

"Other than the empty tank?"

Sarcasm. That was a good sign. He was tracking what I was saying.

"Did the Falcon get pretty good gas mileage?" I asked.

"Around town, about 15 miles a gallon. On the highway, closer to 20."

"So, two and a half gallons to get from Moses Lake to Ritzville. That means close to twelve gallons still in the tank, leaving ten gallons unaccounted for."

"What are you getting at?"

"How far could the car go on ten gallons of gas?" I asked.

"Simple math. 150 to 200 miles. What's your point?"

"Just a theory. Do you know how far it is from Ritzville to the place where the girls were found?" I didn't wait for an answer. "It's 75 miles."

"Hold on. Are you saying…"

"That car was almost new. How many miles were on it at the time of the crime?"

"It showed just under 1,600 when we got it back."

"Did you see the mileage before the girls went to Seattle?"

"No, but Lisa kept… Wait a minute! Lisa's mileage log wasn't in the car. I gave her a special notebook to keep track of her mileage and expenses. It should have been there."

"I found no mention of a mileage log in any of the evidence files," I said. "Is there any way to estimate what the mileage was when they left?"

"The car had 600 miles on it when I bought it. The dealer had used it as a demo car, and I got a really good deal on it. That was two weeks before the state tournament."

"My trip to your sister's place and back was 650 miles. The girls did some local driving. Let's say 50 miles. So, their trip was around 700 miles. That leaves 300 miles. Did Lisa put 300 miles on the car before going to Seattle?"

"Impossible. It couldn't have been more than a hundred," Earl said.

"The mileage log would clear it up."

"I think you're telling me that the girls took the killer away from Hand's Café in Lisa's car."

"It would explain why no witnesses saw her car there overnight. And it would explain why two witnesses saw the suspect's car at the café after the girls left."

"Still, Permann could have done it, just as well as anyone else."

"Except that both witnesses who saw the old car there after the girls were gone said the car was green. The prosecutor didn't want the jury to hear that, after having to concede that Permann's car was blue. They might get away with saying one witness got it wrong, but not all three."

"…and if the mileage log showed that Lisa's car was driven 200 extra miles after the fill-up at Moses Lake, the perp's car probably was left behind," Earl finished for me.

"Exactly. And there's something else. When I was talking with Justine, she mentioned that she had helped the girls load their luggage into the trunk of Lisa's car."

"So?"

"The cop who found the car said that the luggage was on the backseat."

The color drained from Earl's face. "The girls weren't killed where they were found, were they?" It was more a statement than a question.

"Probably not."

"That would mean that their dead bodies were transported in the trunk of the Falcon."

"Very likely," I said. "That's why the luggage was in the backseat."

Earl groaned. "Knowing that, I can't use it anymore. I'll never get in that car again."

January 14, 1962

Light snow continued to fall intermittently, and by midday on Sunday we had accumulated three or four inches—just enough to bring out the kids with their sleds, toboggans, inner tubes and "flying saucer" discs.

The Murphy kids brought out their antique eleven-foot long Flexible Flyer six-passenger sled, a relic from their dad's childhood. On the Union Street hill, this sled could achieve terrifying speeds, often forcing kids on slower snowcraft to dive out of the way of the careening behemoth.

"Can you actually control that beast?" I once asked Kenny Murphy.

"Control is a relative word," he said philosophically. "It steers like an ocean liner. It'll turn, but it takes some real estate."

"How do you keep from running over the slower sleds?"

"We shout a lot. It's up to them to stay out of our way. Mostly, they do."

"Mostly?"

"Well, one time Dennis Johnson let his sled get in our way, and we blew it to pieces."

"So, what happened to him?" I asked.

"Oh, nothing. He wasn't on it—he just kind of flipped into our path, hoping to see us execute some kind of radical maneuver. He found out that we were much better at destruction than maneuvering."

I laughed and changed the subject. "How's the science fair project coming?"

"I tore apart that old Emerson TV and took everything I need—the power supply, video output and flyback circuits. Except for the tubes, most of the rest went into the trash. I'm using an old radio chassis as a platform for my project. I have it just about wired."

"How'd you do on getting the electron gun?"

"You were right about Televac. They gave me one—donated it—and gave me a plug to match the picture tube socket from the old Emerson. I have the one that I got from the original tube, too."

"Didn't you promise that you weren't going to do that?" I reminded him.

"That was for the *first* set you gave me, not this one. Besides, I was careful about it. We took it over to the sand pit, wrapped it in an old blanket, and shot it with my .22 from a hundred feet back. Boy, did it make a noise!"

"There are some things I don't want to know about."

"My biggest trouble has been with the vacuum chamber. The original one was a glass cylinder from an old-fashioned gas pump. But when I tried to pump it down, the glass started to crack We dove to the floor and yanked the vacuum pump plug out of the wall. We stayed down until we couldn't hear the air hissing in through the crack. Without a vacuum chamber, I didn't have a project, so, my dad is building one out of aluminum, with a thick glass porthole."

"When is the science fair?" I asked.

"The CV Science Fair is in the last week of February. Then the Inland Empire Science Fair will be in the second week of April."

"Well, good luck. Hope you can make it work."

The snow flurries continued on and off through the entire weekend, but the road crews had been able to stay out in front of it, so the main roads were mostly clear, and Monday morning, I was optimistic about making the drive to Ritzville.

January 15, 1962

The first thing I did on Monday was call Doreen Fraiser.

"The last time we spoke, you explained what happened to the witness interview tapes in the Draper case," I said.

"Yeah, so..." she began.

"Since then, I've looked into ways of retrieving content from damaged tapes, and I'm 99 percent sure that I know how to play the damaged tape without doing any further damage."

"It could be pretty risky. Shouldn't a job like that be left to a professional?"

"That's exactly what I'm getting at. In addition to being a private investigator, I own Pratt TV and Radio. I have worked as an electronics technician since I was ten years old. I *am* the professional who can play that tape."

There was a long pause.

"Uh, have you done anything like this before?"

"Over the years, I've worked on many tape recorders, and some of them were brought in because they ate the tapes. And I've worked at attempting to restore damaged tapes."

"Yeah, but the stakes are pretty high here, don't you think?"

"That's my point. Gordon Permann will be hanged in three weeks unless I can find proof that he's not guilty."

"I get that, but..."

"Listen, I don't want to get you in trouble here. Maybe I should talk to your Chief."

"No," she said quickly. "You don't have to do that. I can authorize it."

"I want you to be sure of this. I'll bring along a demonstration tape to show exactly what my plan is, before we do anything with the interview tape. Will you be comfortable with that?"

"I guess that sounds like the best way to go," she conceded. "It's too late to do it today, and I have a training session all day tomorrow. How about Wednesday afternoon?"

"If that's the soonest you can do it, that's when it'll have to be. But sooner would be better."

"That's it, then. I'll see you Wednesday."

Chapter Twenty-Eight

An Anonymous Tip

The massive low-pressure system had settled-in over eastern Alberta and western Saskatchewan, 200 miles north of the Canadian border, and the counter-clockwise rotation of the atmosphere around it brought arctic air directly into eastern Washington.

January 16, 1962

On Tuesday, the temperature at the airport had been around twenty degrees in the morning, but by noon it was down to ten and still dropping. Overnight, the light snow in the weather forecast turned into a blizzard that shut down nearly all of the schools in Spokane the next day.

The kids in the neighborhood loved it, but the snow forced me to postpone my planned trip to Ritzville for my appointment with Doreen Fraiser. By Thursday morning, most of the major roads in Spokane were clear, and the school busses were running, so I phoned Doreen and she said she could spare some time for me in the afternoon.

I worked on some TV repairs in the shop until 1:00, and then made a final check on road conditions in Ritzville. I was pleased to hear that Ritzville had gotten only an inch of snow, most of which had simply blown away in the ten to fifteen mile an hour wind. But the temperature was dropping fast toward a predicted low well below zero.

As I drove toward Ritzville, I tuned my radio to the Moses Lake station to get a local weather forecast. They said that there was a possibility of more snow, so when I got to the police station, I backed into a parking space at the side of the building. It was a precaution intended to make it easier when it was time to leave.

I gathered the tape recorder that I'd modified to play my intentionally damaged tape, along with two fresh reels of tape and a new Wollensak 1500 that I'd borrowed from our showroom. Inside the station, the air was warm, and it felt good, so I peeled-off my hooded sweatshirt. But the lack of humidity quickly made my breathing passages go dry, and the air felt stifling and uncomfortable.

"How were the roads getting here?" Doreen asked.

"There's still packed snow on the Sunset Hill, but it's been sanded, and it wasn't too bad. Once I got past Cheney, the highway was clear. But it's getting damn cold out there," I said.

"So, what's all this?" She gestured toward the tape recorders.

"Well, like I said on the phone, I know how to get a copy of those interview tapes."

"Okay, but I warned you that the tapes are damaged, and playing them might destroy them."

"Can I at least look at them? That can't hurt anything," I said.

"I guess there's no harm in that."

Doreen went into the back room and returned with an evidence box containing, among other things, two boxed reels of Scotch 111 recording tape, the same brand I'd taken along. One had Chet Winston's name written on the label, and through the transparent plastic of the reel, I could see the part of the tape that had been damaged, about a third of the way into the reel.

I got out my Gene Autry tape and let Doreen compare the damage with the Winston tape. After studying it, she agreed that the damage looked about the same. I played the Gene Autry tape as it was, and then played my copy of it, to demonstrate that I could get a usable copy of a damaged tape.

"That's all well and good for *Rudolf the Red-Nosed Reindeer*, but are you really sure that you want to take a chance on our interview tape?" Doreen asked.

"If you're reluctant to let me do it, I could get a court order," I said, "but I'd prefer to get it done today."

Maybe it was just my imagination, but it seemed like Doreen's demeanor shifted slightly in response to my pressure. It was subtle, but she seemed less enthusiastic about helping me. She glanced at the large wall clock.

"How long's all this going to take? I'd like to get out of here before it gets too late."

The only other person in the office was the sergeant at the front counter. He was reading a news magazine and smoking a cigarette. "Yeah, you and me both," he said.

Doreen held up her hands in surrender. "Can you give me a minute to make a phone call?"

I nodded, and she disappeared into one of the small offices. A few minutes later, she returned, carrying a fresh cup of coffee. "You want one?" she asked.

"No, thanks." I knew from past experience that the police station coffee was awful. "But I *would* like a mug of hot water. The hotter the better."

She gave me a strange look, but went and got what I'd requested.

"So, where do we start?" she asked.

"First, we'll wind the tape forward to the damaged part. I'll wipe it down with a tape-cleaning solution that contains a lubricant for the recording heads. That'll protect the tape while I iron out the crinkles as much as possible."

Looking nervous, she nodded. "If this goes all wrong, just remember that I didn't want to do it."

After carefully cleaning the tape, I showed Doreen how to hold the tape against the mug of hot water while I slowly wound the tape through the damaged area. It was slow going, and the length of the damaged tape was about double what I'd dealt with on the Gene Autry tape.

At 5:00, the sergeant stood up and stretched. "Okay, that's it for me. Turn off the lights when you leave."

"Will do," Doreen said.

Ten minutes later, there was a tap on the glass, and we looked up to see a man at the front door, all bundled-up in a hooded parka, with a scarf over his face. He carried a bundle wrapped in brown paper.

"It looks like the linen service," Doreen said.

We paused what we were doing, and she went out front and unlocked the door, letting the linen service man in.

He said, "Boy, it's colder than a grave digger's ass out there!"

Doreen said, "You're not the regular deliveryman."

"No. The regular guy is out today. I wish I was, too"

Doreen took the package and signed the invoice, and the man jammed his hands into his pockets and went back outside. Doreen locked the door behind him. We'd just started back to work when there was another tap on the front door. The linen delivery guy was back.

"Does one of you own the yellow and black Ford?" he shouted through the closed door.

My heart sank, thinking he'd somehow run into it.

"What's the problem?" I asked loudly.

"Can you give me a jump? My damned old truck won't start!"

"Oh. Uh, sorry, I don't have any jumper cables," I said.

"I have jumpers. I just need something to hook them to."

Doreen and I looked at one another, all four of our hands occupied with ironing the tape.

She said, "Well, maybe it's time to call it quits for the day."

"No, we're almost done with this part," I protested. "And I need to get this done."

The linen guy said, "Hey, it's no problem. I can manage by myself, if that's okay with you."

I looked back and forth between Doreen and the linen guy. If I went outside to help the guy, Doreen was going to close-up shop. Litton was counting on me getting this tape so that he could file a brief requesting a stay of execution.

"Go ahead. Just don't short-out my battery," I said.

We continued the task, winding the tape across the hot mug, and a few minutes later I heard the laundry truck's engine start, followed by the sound of hoods and doors closing. The laundry guy honked his horn and waved as he drove away.

At 5:45, we finished ironing the tape, and I set up the two recorders to dub the copy. At 3.75 inches per second, it would take an hour to make the copy. We were watching the reels turn on the two recorders at about 6:30, when the phone rang.

"Ritzville Police," Doreen said into the phone.

I heard only her end of the conversation.

"Yes, I'm familiar with the case."

"Uh huh. What is your name, please?"

"I see. Okay, Mr. Jones, what can I do for you?"

Doreen grabbed a notepad and started writing things down.

"How do you know that?"

"A green Buick?"

"Yeah? Is he someone you know?"

"Okay, where is this place?"

Doreen scribbled furiously as the caller continued talking.

"Is he there now?"

"Right. When did you last see him there?"

"So, he could be anywhere now."

"Why not?"

"Yeah? I understand. Can you give me your number so a detective can call you back?"

"Hello? Hello…"

Doreen pressed the receiver button, then dialed a number from memory.

"Captain? This is Doreen. Yeah, I'm still at the office. A call just came in from somebody who claims that he knows who killed the Draper girls."

"Yeah, I know the case is closed, but the caller said we got the wrong guy."

"He said his name is Jones. I don't believe it. But he sure sounded like he knew what he was talking about."

"Okay. He says that he knows a guy who lives in an abandoned wrecking yard two miles from the place where the bodies were found, and he drives a green Buick fastback."

"I know, but apparently the guy talks about the case when he's had a lot to drink. He said that one of the girls was wearing a ring, but he couldn't get it off her finger. I don't think that was ever made public."

"No. Jones hung up when I asked for his phone number."

"That's all I know, Captain. Yeah. Okay, I'll see you in the morning. Sorry to bother you."

As she hung up the phone, she exhaled loudly and turned her eyes toward the ceiling. Then, she apparently remembered that I was there. Turning to me, she tossed the note pad onto the counter and shrugged.

"Was that for real?" I asked.

"Who knows. Captain doesn't think so," she said. "Anyway, where were we?"

"It looks like we're about finished."

Doreen said, "That's good. It's been a long day, and I want to get out of here."

As we wrapped things up, Doreen packed the original interview tapes back into the evidence box, while I put on the sweatshirt that I'd taken off right after I arrived at the police station. While I closed-up the tape recorders, she carried the evidence box back into the storeroom.

As soon as Doreen was out of sight, I grabbed her note pad from the counter and pocketed it. I put my copy of the witness interview tape into its box, and slipped it into the hand-warmer pocket in the front of my sweatshirt, to keep my hands free to carry the recorders.

I put my car coat on over my sweatshirt and pulled on my gloves. I was picking up the tape recorders when Doreen came back from the storeroom.

"I'll get those tapes for you," she said, picking up my demonstration tape and the original Gene Autry tape. She unlocked the door and followed me outside.

I can always tell when the temperature is below zero, because I can feel the moisture in my nose freeze when I inhale. That's the first thing I noticed when I stepped outside. I hurried to my car, and put the two tape recorders in the backseat. Doreen tossed the tapes in behind them, said a quick goodbye and hurried back inside the station.

I got behind the wheel, hoping for some vestige of warmth, but it was as cold inside as it was outside. When I turned the key, the starter growled, and for a second, I feared that the linen guy had run my battery dead. But the engine cranked over a couple of times and fired. I let it sit at fast idle for a couple of minutes, until the engine generated enough heat to open the automatic choke.

By then, my breathing had fogged the windshield, so I switched on the defroster.

I tried to wipe the fog from the windshield, only to find it had frozen into a frosty layer of ice. Gradually, the defroster managed to blow a pair of clear spots at the bottom of the windshield, and when they were large enough, I put the transmission in gear and pulled out of the parking space, congratulating myself on having had the foresight to back in.

The tires made little squeaking sounds in the fresh layer of dry snow that had fallen. There was a momentary crunching sound from somewhere, and I took my foot off the gas. Listening for anything that might give a clue as to what the noise was, I shifted into Neutral and revved the engine a couple of times. There were no more strange sounds, and nothing on the dashboard hinted at a problem.

Chapter Twenty-Nine

Fire and Ice

Hand's Café was only a couple of blocks from the police station. I drove there and stopped in front. Leaving the engine running, I went inside and ordered a ham and cheese sandwich and a cup of coffee to go. When I got back into my car, the windshield was defrosted and warm air was blowing from the heater.

I pulled Doreen's notepad from my pocket, and read her scribbled note from Mr. Jones's phone call:

> **Old wrecking yard**
> **A Mile and three-quarters west of bodies**
> **Green Buick, Bread truck**

While eating my sandwich I flipped through my case notes. The girls' bodies had been found four miles west of Ford—probably not an exact measurement. I figured that I should find the wrecking yard about five or six miles west of the tiny town of Ford. I looked in my glove compartment for a state map, and found several—but none for the state of Washington.

That was okay. I knew the general directions: Go to Davenport, turn right and look for the secondary highway to Ford. There were very few other cars on the road as I drove out of Ritzville, heading toward the road to Harrington. There was snow on the road, but it wasn't excessively slick, due to the extremely low temperature. I had decent snow tires on the car, and I never slipped or spun a tire.

It was 9:45 when I got to Ford. Nothing was open, and there were almost no car tracks in the snow. There were a few lights on in houses, but no other signs that anyone was awake on this bitterly cold night. I found the road leading to Wellpinit and noted my odometer reading.

Three miles past that junction, I started scanning the roadside for anything that would suggest a crime scene. Three-and-a-half miles, then four, and four-and-a-half. Nothing. At five miles, I started looking for an old wrecking yard. At 5.75 miles, there was nothing. I drove another mile, and started to look for a place to turn back, thinking I must have missed the wrecking yard.

Or maybe there was no wrecking yard. Maybe Mr. Jones was just another crank wanting to insert himself into an investigation. *But he knew about the ring*, I reminded myself. I crept forward at about ten miles an hour, until I spotted a snow-covered driveway on the right. I carefully pulled into it, intending to back out and head back toward Ford.

But as my headlights swept through the pine trees, I spotted a row of snow-covered old cars. I continued up the driveway until I reached a two or three-acre clearing littered with wrecked or abandoned cars. When I found room enough, I looped around and stopped the car. I'd have to finish this on foot.

I knew that I was ill prepared for the cold weather. I had nothing to cover my ears except for the hood on my old sweatshirt. I zipped up my medium-weight car coat, and put on a pair of fur-lined driving gloves. I got a flashlight from the glove compartment, switched off the engine and opened the door.

The air outside was paralyzingly cold, and tiny snowflakes swirled around in the breeze. I switched on the flashlight and turned off the headlights—this would be a bad time to run-down the battery. The beam from the flashlight was feeble. I walked quickly around the clearing, shining my light at each car, hoping to find a green Buick. Back in a far corner of the clearing there was an old bread truck that appeared to have been converted into a camper.

I'd been outside for no more than ten minutes, but already the cold was driving frozen knives through my clothes. I hurried over to the bread truck and pounded on the side, dislodging some snow, but raising no sign of life from within. I tried shining my light inside, but the beam was so dim that I could see nothing, so I tried the door.

It was not locked. Tentatively, I stepped inside and found a light switch. Nothing. I could see only that someone had been living in the truck—no clue as to his identity or how long it had been since anyone was there. As I turned to leave, I spotted a Popular Mechanics magazine on the counter. It was dated August 1959. This whole stupid adventure was a bust.

I hurried back to my car, and once inside savored the residual warmth from my long drive to get there. My hand was shaking when I reached for the key and gave it a twist. Nothing happened. I tried again. Still nothing. I tried the headlights, and they burned bright. The battery was not dead. And yet, there wasn't a sound when I turned the key.

I told myself not to panic. Just think it through. If my starter had gone bad, I could still start the engine if I could somehow get the car up to about 25 miles an hour. But I quickly gave up that idea, because the ground was nearly flat. The car didn't roll at all when I shifted into Neutral and released the parking brake.

Something was wrong under the hood. Bad starter? Loose wire? I got out and opened the hood. In the dim orange glow from the dying flashlight, I couldn't see anything out of place. I did about the only thing I could do. I got back into the car. I sat for five minutes vigorously rubbing my legs and arms to restore circulation. My breathing caused frost to form on the insides of the windows, and within a matter of minutes I couldn't see out.

Fire. If I could find something to burn, I could start a fire. I *had to* start a fire. I went back outside to look for firewood. There were some dry sticks and branches from some of the pine trees poking through the snow. I hastily gathered them into a pile in a wind-sheltered spot next to an old car that was lying on its side. I tore the pages out of Doreen's little note pad, wadded them up for kindling, and arranged twigs and sticks over and around them.

My fingers and feet were getting numb, and I fumbled with the cigarette lighter in my car. I managed to get a piece of paper to smolder, but couldn't make it break out in flames. I needed better tinder. I scraped some dry moss off of one of the tree branches I'd gathered, and pushed the lighter back into its socket. When it popped out, I placed the moss on the red-hot element. It started to smoke, and I blew gently on the glowing ember.

I blew harder. Too hard! I put out the ember. On my second try, I got the moss to flash into a small flame, and I managed to light a twist of paper. I took it out to my kindling pile and lit the wads of paper under the sticks. There was a quiet crackle as a twig caught fire. I hastily broke more twigs and laid them over the tiny fire.

I was shivering badly and found it very difficult to perform the delicate task of coaxing the fire to take hold. Too many twigs! I smothered the flame. I desperately blew on the embers and got the flame to flare up again. A stick at a time, I got a fire just big enough so that I could warm my fingers. But the little pile of sticks I'd gathered was nearly gone.

I rushed around, kicking at the snow in search of more firewood, breaking dead branches from small pine trees, periodically going back to feed the little fire. It was a losing fight. I couldn't stop gathering wood long enough to get warm or I'd run out of fuel for the fire. So, even as the fire got bigger, I was getting colder, because the bigger fire needed more wood.

In a last desperate attempt to save myself, I scooped my little fire into a wheel cover from one of the old cars, and carried it into the bread truck camper. The fire was flickering out by the time I got there, but pages from the old magazine quickly brought it back. I dumped the fire into a pile of old vinyl upholstery, which melted and caught fire. And the fire grew and spread.

I grabbed a musty old quilt from a bed at the back of the truck. I shook the dust off and wrapped it around my shoulders. It stunk, but it helped. I backed out of the truck and propped the door open so the fire would get air. It went from a crackle to a roar as the thin plywood paneling caught fire. A window broke and flames burst through, and the warmth on my face felt wonderful. But as the fire grew, I had to back away. The thin aluminum skin on the truck body burned through and flames burst toward the sky.

If somebody was in a position to see the fire surely, they'd get someone up there to see what was happening. I turned myself around and around like a chicken on a spit, absorbing as much heat as I could. Half an hour later, the fire was burning itself out. The truck box had collapsed and soon only the tires were left burning.

I suppose I could have carried embers around to other vehicles in the clearing, setting fire to them one at a time until morning. Then, someone was bound to see the smoke and come to investigate. But I was beat. And I was again getting cold.

Taking shelter back in my car, I soon realized that staying there would kill me. When I stopped moving, my circulation would slow, and the cold would take over. I had to get moving. I no longer had the coordination to gather fuel to keep a fire going. About all I could do was walk.

Back out at the road, I contemplated which way to go. I remembered having seen a sign as I was leaving Ford indicating that it was ten miles to Wellpinit. I'd driven nearly seven miles, so Wellpinit was the closest town. I had no idea how big the town was, but I knew that it was the reservation headquarters for the Spokane Indian Tribe. I started walking.

My leather oxfords had taken a beating. They were scuffed, scorched, and wet inside from sweat and melted snow. But that was changing. My system was unable to create enough heat to ward off the penetrating cold, and my feet ached as I plodded along the shoulder of the highway.

I checked my watch. A quarter to two. I had neglected to call Dale before running off on this ill-conceived goose chase. She'd be awake, wondering where I was. I kept stumbling ahead. Normally, I could easily cover three miles in an hour, but my pace was slow. Why didn't someone come driving up the road? There had to be *someone* out, even on a night like this. I checked my watch again. Five minutes to two.

I hit a slippery spot and lost my balance, falling hard on my left arm. Struggling to my numb feet, I wondered if my arm was broken. Odd. I couldn't feel it. My nose and cheeks felt frozen, so I pulled the stinking quilt up over my head and clutched it tightly, leaving a small hole to see through. When I paused to look back at my tracks, I saw that I was just shuffling along, no longer actually taking steps. Ten after two. Time was running out.

I stumbled and lost my balance. When I tried to catch myself, nothing worked, and I went to the ground, rolling down the embankment into a snowdrift. I rolled over and pushed myself up onto my knees. I struggled to crawl back up the steep embankment…

January 19, 1962

…there were bright flashes in the distance, where the KORCOMS were launching mortars into the American lines. I wanted to get my hands on a weapon—any weapon—and jump into the fight. But I had to fix the radar that would warn of incoming enemy aircraft. I was the only one who could do it. God, it was cold! I swear, the radar signals themselves must have frozen. If I could just find the right adjustment to fine-tune the radar set, everything would be okay.

A Korean soldier brought me a cup of warm tomato soup. I clutched it with my frozen fingers, trying to stop my teeth from chattering. The soup dribbled down my chin, because I couldn't feel my lips. It was like the time the dentist gave me a shot of Novocain, and I couldn't tell that I was slobbering all over myself.

"Take it easy. Don't try to gulp it down all at once. Just take it slow—a little sip at a time." The soldier spoke perfect English with no trace of an accent.

"I have to get the radar fixed," I said. My words were all slurred because of my numb lips.

"You can let that go for a while. It'll keep, okay?"

A Korean lady brought a pan of warm water and placed it at my feet.

"I'm going to take off your shoes and try to warm your feet."

It stung ferociously when she lowered my feet into the water.

"I don't know anything about treating frostbite, but I've heard that warming too fast isn't good," the lady explained. She too spoke in perfect English.

That made me wonder if they were North Korean intelligence agents. I couldn't remember ever hearing a South Korean soldier speak English without a heavy accent. But the man and woman weren't dressed like the KORCOMS. They *must be* on our side.

"What were you doing out there on the road?"

"I was tuning the radar set for Major Thomas. He's going to have my ass."

"Just close your eyes and relax. Another fifteen minutes out there, I think you'd be dead."

I guess I dozed off, because when I opened my eyes, the room was filled with daylight. I checked the time. It was a quarter after two. Twelve hours had passed. I wasn't in an olive-colored canvas tent in Korea. I was in somebody's living room, lying on a sofa in front of a fireplace. I held my hands in front of my face and wiggled my fingers. They were bright red, but they worked.

"So, you have returned from your spirit world," the Korean lady said.

Only she wasn't Korean. She was Indian. I'd made it to a house on the reservation.

"I need to call my wife," I said urgently.

"I talked to her this morning. She knows you're okay," the lady said. "I found your phone number in your billfold."

"What is your name"" I asked.

"Melody Denton. Also, Autumn Flower."

"How did I get here?"

"I do not know. My husband heard sounds in the night and found you on our porch. You were very close to death, I think."

"Where is he—your husband? I'd like to thank him for helping me."

"He's working today. He drives a tow truck. He's been out helping start cars all day."

"My car wouldn't start."

"Is that why you were out there last night? It was twenty degrees below zero."

"No, I was…I was looking for the man who killed the girls."

Melody looked startled. "What girls? Who was killed?"

"The girls who were found last year, down the road toward Ford."

"Those white girls from Spokane? Isn't the man who killed them in prison?"

"Yeah. No. He didn't kill them. Someone else did."

"Would you like something to eat? Maybe some soup?"

I realized that nothing I'd said was making any sense to her.

"That would be wonderful. Whatever you have would be great. I don't want to put you to any more trouble than I already have."

"You've been no trouble at all."

Chapter Thirty

Sabotage

January 20, 1962

I ended up spending another night with the Dentons. Melody washed everything that I'd been wearing, while out in the snow. She'd removed my copy of the witness tape from my sweatshirt before putting it into the laundry, and it was stacked on top of my folded clothing when I woke up.

I carried it with me on Saturday morning, when Melody's husband—who simply went by Denton—drove me in his tow truck back to my car. The temperature was still way below freezing, and the deep ache in my feet and fingers made any kind of movement difficult. As we turned off the highway at the wrecking yard, I noticed immediately that someone else had been there.

When I'd walked out, the only tracks in the snow were my own—just one set of tracks going in toward the clearing. That was very clear in my memory, because I'd been careful to walk in the car tracks so as to minimize the amount of snow I'd get in my shoes. But as Denton drove his tow truck toward the meadow, I could clearly see car tracks over the top of mine.

Someone had driven in and out of there after I walked out. As we approached my car, Denton said nothing about the freshly burned remains of the bread truck camper. Nor did we talk about the extra car tracks. I looked around for any clue as to why someone had driven in there.

I could see the tracks where the car had made a three-point turn, and apparently had stopped, as evidenced by footprints that appeared in the snow where the driver's door would have been. The footprints led toward my car and merged with my own tracks, so it was impossible to see what the visitor had done before returning to his own car.

When Denton stopped next to my car, I got out and walked once around it. Nothing appeared to have been disturbed, and when I tossed my tape recording into the backseat, I noted that the two tape recorders were still there, apparently undisturbed. My keys were still hanging from the ignition switch.

Concerned about someone having snooped in and around my car, I found a piece of sheet metal and placed it over the clearest of the footprints in the snow. In theory, it could have been made by a curious passer-by, but my instincts told me otherwise.

Denton raised the hood and looked around the engine compartment.

"Let's see what's going on here," he said. "Try to crank it over."

I turned the key, and just like Thursday night, there wasn't a sound.

"I should have at least heard the starter relay," he commented. "Try your headlights."

I pulled the headlight switch, and Denton said, "Okay, the battery's not dead. Shut 'em off and let's see what the trouble is."

Poking his head further under the hood, he said, "Well, that's not right. Let me try something."

He went to his truck and poked around in his tool box. He returned carrying a remote starter button, something mechanics use so that they don't have to keep getting in and out of the car while they're working under the hood. He clipped one wire from the starter button to the positive terminal on the battery and the other somewhere deep under the hood on the passenger side.

"Pump the gas twice and switch on the key," he said.

He pressed the button and the engine cranked over and started.

"Okay, that'll get us back to the service station. Then we'll see why you're missing the wire that's supposed to go from the ignition switch to the starter relay. People usually don't lose them."

In the warm service bay at the gas station in Wellpinit, Denton rigged a work light over the engine compartment, and we got our first good look at what was wrong.

"Look at that," he said. "The terminal is still attached to the relay, but the wire has been broken loose."

"How could that happen?" I asked.

"Metal fatigue, maybe. If the wire wiggled back and forth over a long period of time, the strands might break."

"That's a theory, but can it actually happen?"

"I've never seen it. But if the wire was attached somewhere on the engine, I guess the engine vibration could eventually break the wire."

"I don't see the wire," I said. "Can you see it?"

Denton moved the work light and searched around the rear of the engine. He poked around with a long screwdriver and managed to drag a tape-wrapped pair of wires up from somewhere in the transmission tunnel. The terminals on both wires were gone, and there were areas where the insulation had melted.

Seeing that, I asked, "Did a short circuit melt that insulation?"

"I don't think so. Looks to me like it got up against the exhaust pipe."

He pulled the wire up to where he could study the broken ends.

"Funny. I don't see any sign of metal fatigue. In fact, it looks like the wires were stretched and manually ripped loose."

"What'll it take to fix it?"

"I'll just need to replace the wires from the point where the insulation is melted over to the starter relay. Won't take more than half an hour."

While Denton worked on that, I contemplated what he'd told me. The wires had been yanked loose. The starter had worked fine when I left the police station in Ritzville. So, when and how had the wires been torn loose?

My first idea was that someone must have done it while I was poking around the old wrecking yard, or maybe while I was inside the old bread truck camper. But I hadn't noticed any footprints in the snow, and I would certainly have heard if someone had closed the hood—there was no way to do that quietly. So, that meant that the wires must have been torn loose while I was getting my sandwich at Hand's Café. Either that, or it had happened while I was driving.

That's when I remembered that odd "ka-chunk" sound when I first pulled out of the parking lot at the police station. Could that have been the sound of the wires being torn loose?

While Denton was at his workbench installing terminals on the ends of the new wires, I took a closer look under the hood. The engine compartment was fairly clean, but the car was over six years old, and I hadn't ever tried to keep it looking new under the hood. Generally, there was a film of ordinary dirt on the firewall and inner fenders. I rubbed a spot on the firewall, and the dirt wiped off easily. Over on the passenger side inner fender, there were several spots where the dirt had been rubbed off—beneath the heater box, where the starter relay was located, and a couple of other places between there and the front corner of the car, where the battery was located.

It was easy to believe that Denton had done that while connecting his remote starter button. These were precisely the areas where he'd have been working. Looking closer, I spotted a half-inch hole punched in the inner fender. I had no idea what it was for, but it appeared to have been done at the factory. Cars of all makes have unused holes in body panels for various accessories or simply for manufacturing convenience.

But the way the dirt was rubbed away in a fan-shaped pattern from the hole a couple of inches back in the direction of the starter relay made me take a closer look. There was something else there. At first, I thought it was a bit of moss, similar to what I'd used when starting my fire. But how could it have gotten there?

"Do you have something like a pair of tweezers?" I asked

He pointed toward his tool box. "Top drawer, right-hand side. There's some forceps—for when I drop parts where I can't reach."

I found the forceps and used them to pick up the greenish fibers. There were four short strands, thinner than a hair and less than half an inch long. All of the fibers were frayed, as if they'd been scraped from a piece of cord. That's when I figured it out.

A piece of green-colored cord had been tied around the wires leading to the starter relay, with the other end fed through the hole in the inner fender. It would have dangled directly in front of the tire. As I left the parking space, I ran over the loose end of the cord, pinning it to the ground. With the car moving forward, the cord would be pulled down through the hole until it ran out of slack. The cord was stronger than the wires, so the weaker thing broke.

I strained my imagination trying to think of some other scenario that might explain the evidence I'd found, which admittedly, wasn't much. But I couldn't come up with any other possible explanation for the broken wires. Somebody had deliberately sabotaged my car.

That theory led to a cascade of inferences. Whoever did it must have had a purpose in mind. He wanted me to be able to start my engine one time—in the police station parking lot—but then be unable to start it thereafter. That implied that he might have known that I was going someplace where there would be no help. And he'd have known that the sub-zero weather that night would be deadly.

I immediately thought of the linen delivery guy. I'd actually given him permission to get under the hood of my car. If he'd planned all of it in advance, he could have easily done the job in the time it would have taken to jump-start his truck. In fact, it was so simple that he might have even been able to do it right in front of me, if I'd gone out to help him.

So, who was he, why did he want me dead, and how did he know where I'd be going? At the time he was supposedly jump-starting his truck, even I didn't know that I'd be going anywhere other than home.

Jones! The linen man had to have made the call to Doreen, claiming to be Mr. Jones.

That thought raised a whole array of secondary questions. How did he know about Lisa's ring? How did he know exactly where the bodies were found? How did he know that the green car was not a Chevrolet Fleetline, as all of the news reports had stated? Could he have known that I'd talked to the witness who had seen the car? How did he know about the old wrecking yard?

One answer covered all of the questions. Mr. Jones, whether he was the linen guy or not, was the killer of Lisa and Gail Draper. And I would bet dollars to donuts that he was William Tanner. And if Tanner was the linen guy, he ought to be easy to track down through the linen service company.

The one thing I needed to do first was to validate my theory about how the cord was rigged to disable my starter. When Denton was finished repairing the wiring, I expressed my extreme gratitude and forced him to take a fifty-dollar tip on top of the bill for the rescue and repair of my car.

"Buy something nice for Melody," I said. "I'll never forget what the two of you did for me."

I stopped at the Wellpinit General Store and bought a small bag of plaster of Paris, a cheap plastic bowl, a couple of Mason jars, and a spatula. I filled the jars with water, and then drove back to the wrecking yard to make a cast of the footprint next to where my car had been.

The road conditions made driving difficult. In some places the pavement was bare, and in other places, there were drifts two-feet deep. Sometimes I'd lose visibility in brief white-out conditions created by the drifting snow. So, my drive back to Ritzville took nearly three very painful hours. I parked at Hand's Café and looked in the gravel where I'd parked when I got my sandwich. I found nothing to hint that my car had been rigged there—but I hadn't really expected to.

I drove the short distance over to the police station. Careful to avoid letting anyone inside see my very distinctive Crown Victoria, I parked around the corner and walked over to where I'd been parked two nights before.

The thing I was looking for was right there in the gravel.

The snow had blown thin, and the olive-green parachute cord was in plain sight. I picked it up and studied it. Its color matched the fibers I'd picked from under the hood. It was about 48 inches long, and had a small overhand loop tied in one end. It was exactly the thing that my theory of the sabotage would have required.

I took the cord and drove home. Unless they had seen me while I was in Ritzville, the people who rigged my car would have every reason to believe that I was dead. If I'd frozen to death in my car in the abandoned wrecking yard, it might have been months before anyone found me.

Chapter Thirty-One

The Interview Tape

It was late in the afternoon when I finally got back to Spokane. It seemed like weeks had passed since I left for Ritzville, but it actually had been three days. I pulled up in front of the store, and Dale came out before I shut off the engine. When I got out of the car, I nearly fell because of the pain in my feet.

"My god, I was so scared," she said, wrapping her arms around me.

We kissed, right out there on the sidewalk.

"Me too," I said.

"What the hell happened? Why were you in Wellpinit?"

"I'll tell you all about it later. Right now, I just need to get this stuff inside."

Dale said, "I'll get it. You go inside and sit down."

She put the tapes and my notes on my desk, and the two tape recorders on the floor next to it.

"Were you able to get a copy of that interview tape?"

"Yeah. I think so, but I haven't listened to it yet." I gestured toward the three tapes that she had put on my desk."

The Gene Autry tape was there, in its original box. The other two boxes were for the Scotch 111 tapes I'd taken along, one containing my copy of the interview tape, and the other containing the test copy of the restored Gene Autry tape.

I urgently needed to listen to the witness statements. But as I looked at the tape boxes, I became confused. One of them was in new condition, and the other was water-stained and crushed along one side.

I had dubbed the witness interviews onto a new blank tape, so I first opened the undamaged box and saw the original transparent Scotch reel. That wasn't right! We'd been in a hurry that night, and I hadn't rewound the tape back onto its original reel when I finished recording. It should be on an off-brand reel!

The level of pain in my frostbitten fingers and feet spiked as panic took over my brain. Someone had taken my tape and put this one in its place. My fingers were painful and stiff as I fumbled to set up the Wollensak recorder.

"What are you *doing*?" Dale demanded.

"I have to listen to this!" I said in desperation.

"No! You need to go home."

I ignored her and mounted up the tape. I pressed PLAY and waited breathlessly as the tape rolled across the playback head. My heart sank when the leader ran out and I heard only the quiet hiss of a blank tape.

No, wait! This must be the other tape.

I forced myself to focus as I fumbled to open the crushed, water-stained box.

Yes. I remember! This was the one that I'd had with me in the snow.

The tape I found in the damaged box was on the take-up reel that came with the new Wollensak recorder. It had to be my copy of the witness tape.

But something still wasn't right. The tape in the undamaged box shouldn't be blank. It should have contained the recording that I made in the store from the restored Gene Autry tape. How did I end up with a new blank tape?

"You shouldn't be doing this now," Dale insisted. "You belong at home, in bed."

I shook my head. "No, I won't be able to rest until I know what we have here."

Dale said something under her breath and rewound the blank tape. She mounted-up the tape that was on the Wollensak reel from the damaged box. After rewinding the tape, she flipped the reels and rethreaded the recorder. I held my breath as she pressed PLAY. Ten seconds of leader was followed by a series of pops and clicks, and then the words of a police officer.

"It is March 22nd, 1960. I am Sergeant Adam Massy. Please state your name."

"Chet Winston."

I exhaled. I didn't mind that I'd lost the Gene Autry dub, but Gordon Permann's life might depend on what was on *this* tape. I pressed PAUSE and limped over to the file to get my copy of the official transcription of Winston's statement.

"Okay, Mr. Winston. Tell me why you're here today."

"I saw something on TV about the girls who disappeared from Hand's Café Sunday afternoon."

"Do you know something about that?"

"I was there at about the time they said the girls were last seen."

"You were at Hand's Café?"

"Right. I was there around 4:00 to 4:30. Maybe a bit later."

"Did you see the Draper girls?"

"I saw a couple of girls come in and take a table by the front windows. I didn't pay any attention, because they were nobody I recognized."

"Would you be able to identify them if we show you the girls' photos?"

"Maybe. Like I said, I didn't pay much attention."

"Did you see anything else?"

"There was a young guy. He didn't sit down with the girls, but he talked with them for a minute or two."

"Did you get a good look at him?"

"Not right then. But maybe ten minutes later, when I was leaving, I saw the same guy in the parking lot doing something under the hood of a car."

"Can you describe him?"

"Well, he looked like a greaser, ya know. He was about eighteen to twenty years old, five-eight, one-fifty. He had long hair, all slicked back."

"Do you think you could identify him if you saw him again."

"Yeah, probably."

It was at this point that the damage on the original tape started, and the audio quality of the recording immediately deteriorated. But as I'd hoped, it was still intelligible. Pretty quickly, however, I started to hear words that were missing from the transcription. I started penciling-in the missing words, which are underlined here:

"You said he was working on a car. Can you describe it?"

"Yeah, sure. It was dark green, and it was a GM car from 1949 or 1950—it was a two-door coupe, <u>kind of</u> like a car I used to have. <u>That was</u> a Chevrolet Fleetline.

"A Chevrolet Fleetline?"

"Yeah, that's what <u>I had. Only that's not what</u> the kid was working on. I'm just saying it was the same body style. You know, that teardrop style?"

"You mean a fastback?".

"Yeah, <u>only it was a Pontiac or Olds</u>. <u>I wasn't paying much attention, but I'd have</u> recognized it right off, <u>if it'd been</u> a Chevy, because like I said, I used to have one."

At the end of the interview, I re-read the transcription. The words that had been omitted from the official transcription completely changed what Winston had actually said. And there was no way that it could have been accidental. It was clear to me that someone had deliberately edited the transcription, and then vandalized the tape to conceal the crime.

I allowed the tape to continue playing past the end of Chet Winston's interview, and found interviews with the other two witnesses who saw a green car parked at Hand's Café. I stopped the tape and retrieved the interview transcriptions that I'd first run across while I was at Hand's Café, waiting to talk with Sandra Hutchins.

At the time, the thing that caught my eye was that both witnesses saw the green car when it was too late to have been Bill Brady's, based on when Hutchins had seen the Draper girls leave. I had dismissed these statements as irrelevant on that basis and, presumably, the prosecution had done the same. It implied that there may have been two different green cars at the café that evening.

Still, the statements were possibly relevant in some other way, so I rolled the tape. Time discrepancies notwithstanding, these statements could underscore just how thin the case against Permann had been.

"State your name and occupation please."

"Roger Sanford. I'm a truck driver."

"Where were you on the afternoon of March 20th, 1960?"

"I was hauling a load of aluminum from Spokane to Richland. I stopped at a café at the junction of Highway 10 and Highway 395 in Ritzville."

"Hand's Café?"

"Yes."

"What time was that?"

"It was around <u>6:00, maybe</u> 5:30"

I paused the recording, and on the typewritten transcription, I penciled-in the missing words.

"Do you recall seeing cars parked at the café?"

"There were four or five cars parked in front, and some more on the side."

"Was anything unusual going on around the cars?"

"No. Nothing in particular. But when I heard about the car that police were looking for, I remembered seeing a car like it."

"Okay. Can you describe that car?"

"Sure. It was dark green. A two-door fastback. <u>I think it was a Buick or Oldsmobile</u>."

As with the Winston interview, the pattern of the deletions was conspicuous.

"Did you notice a blue Ford Falcon?"

"There could've been one there, but it didn't stand out. The green fastback stood out because it was right out front. Otherwise, I probably wouldn't remember seeing it."

The next witness was named Heather Fields.

You were at Hand's Café on March 20th, 1960. Is that correct?"

"Yes."

"Do you recall the time of day?"

"Not specifically, but it was after dark. Maybe around 7:30."

"Did you see other cars there?"

"Sure. There were some."

"Did you notice a light blue Ford Falcon?"

"No, not that I recall."

"How about an older dark green car?"

"I saw a big green car parked in front of the café. I didn't pay much attention to it, <u>but I'm pretty sure it was an Oldsmobile</u>."

So again, a selective deletion obfuscated the witness's clear description of the car.

Dale rewound the tape and made a copy for Brant Litton. Nothing could more clearly prove that the prosecution of Gordon Permann was deliberately rigged against him. I called a courier service to deliver the tape and copies of the marked-up transcriptions to Litton's office downtown.

At Dale's insistence, we went home, where she made a nest for me on the sofa. Only then did I stop to really think about when, how, and why the demonstration tape had been swapped. There were only two places where the exchange could have happened. The switch took place either at the police station, or at the old wrecking yard after I took off on my death march.

I couldn't specifically recall having put the tape back in its box after playing it for Doreen. It's possible that when we were packing-up to leave, she simply put the wrong tape in the box. But the more sinister possibility was that the tapes had been switched by the person who had gotten into my car at the wrecking yard.

I knew from the tracks in the snow that someone had been there. What he was doing there had to be deduced from a few assumptions. He had to have known that I had copied the witness tape that night, and he had to know that the tape was a threat—as was I.

The sabotage of my car was a desperate effort to eliminate both threats. I would die in the sub-zero weather, and he would get the incriminating tape recording. But why did he feel the need to plant a substitute for the tape?

To my knowledge, three other people knew that I was making a copy of the interview tape: Doreen Fraiser, the sergeant on duty that afternoon, and the linen delivery man. But only the linen guy had access to the engine compartment of my car.

That meant that the linen guy knew ahead of time that I was a threat, figured out how to rig my car to leave me stranded in the cold, and used the need for a jump-start as an excuse to get under the hood of my car. But could he have known what was on the tape recording? He'd been inside for only a couple of minutes, while we were still ironing the original tape.

That meant he had to have had an inside accomplice—the person who made the bogus transcriptions and damaged the original interview tape. It seemed very unlikely that Doreen would have helped me make the copy of the tape if she was the linen guy's accomplice, so it must have been the sergeant.

Leaving the blank tape in place of what he believed was my copy of the interview recordings would have been necessary to answer questions from Doreen. Since we hadn't replayed the tape, she wouldn't have known what was on it. A blank tape would simply mean that our recording process had failed, whereas a missing tape might have raised red flags.

Everything pointed toward the desk sergeant—the same officer I'd encountered on my first visit to the station. I couldn't recall his name, but I could get it from the duty roster at the police station in Ritzville.

Chapter Thirty-Two

Recovering

As we lay together in the dark that night, Dale asked, "Just exactly what the hell happened out there?"

"The car wouldn't start," I said. "I turned the key, but nothing happened. I started a fire, but couldn't gather firewood fast enough to keep it going. I got so desperate that I started an old camper on fire, hoping someone would see it. It kept me from freezing for a while, but nobody came."

"How did you end up at the Dentons' house?"

"I don't know. I started walking toward Wellpinit. I started having hallucinations, and I thought I was back in Korea. When I first realized that I wasn't dead, I thought Denton was a North Korean intelligence officer of some kind."

Dale said, "I was so scared. I didn't know where you were or even who I could call. God, I was relieved when Melody Denton called!"

"I'm really sorry about that. I was so obsessed with pursuing the big lead, I didn't take time to think. And it was all a trap."

"A trap? What do you mean, a trap?"

"He sabotaged my car, and then he called the station claiming to know where the Draper girls' killer was—out there near where the bodies were found. He knew that if I took the bait, I'd be stranded out there to die in the cold."

"He? Who are you talking about?"

"I think it had to be Bill Tanner."

Dale interrupted. "But if Tanner was the linen delivery man, why didn't you recognize him from the yearbook photo?"

"I never got a good look at him. He was wearing a hooded parka, and had a scarf over most of his face. But it *had to be* him. He told Doreen things that were never made public. But somehow, he had to have known what I was doing there—copying that tape. And he must have known that the falsified interview transcription would be revealed."

"But how could he have known that?"

"Only one way. Whoever doctored the transcription told him, and it had to be someone inside the Ritzville Police Department—someone who knew I was there and what I was doing. There was a sergeant there that afternoon, and he easily could have overheard me talking with Doreen."

"Then he must be the one who messed with the transcriptions, too."

"Yeah, and if Tanner had an accomplice inside the police department, they could have worked together to manipulate the investigation from the very beginning."

"So, if the accomplice was so active in covering-up Tanner's guilt, he must have had some part in the abduction and murders."

"That is the part I don't understand. Both of our witnesses said that Tanner was alone. My best theory is that Tanner took the girls to a place where his accomplice was—maybe somebody's house."

"Where do you go from here?"

"I need to get the name of the sergeant who was on duty Thursday afternoon, and then find out who he really is. Meanwhile, I still need to track-down Bill Tanner."

January 21, 1962

The burning sensation in my feet and hands prevented me from getting much sleep that night. It was very hard to lie still and, at some point during the night, I moved back to the sofa in the living room. Sunday morning, Dale called our doctor, because ominous purple spots were forming on my toes and fingers.

"You belong in the hospital. This is more serious than I can handle here."

Without waiting for any discussion, he asked to use our phone. He first called for an ambulance, and then called Sacred Heart Hospital. An hour later, I was in the emergency room being examined by a team of doctors and medical technicians, who started connecting tubes and wires to me.

They gave me something that blurred my senses. It didn't take away the pain, but rather made it so that I didn't care that it hurt. I lay in a sedated stupor for the rest of the day. When I woke up, I was in a private room, enclosed in an oxygen tent.

My hands and feet ached to the bone, and were completely wrapped in bandages. There was a call button on a cord lying at my side, but I couldn't do anything with it, because of the thick bandages.

"Hello," I called. "Anybody hear me?"

A very young lady in a red-and-white pin-striped dress came into the room.

"Good morning," she said cheerfully. "How are you feeling today?"

I held up my hands. "Helpless," I said.

"Would you like me to call a nurse for you?"

Hmm. I thought *she* was a nurse. "Please."

The real nurses' uniforms were all white. The first girl, I learned, was a "candy-striper," a volunteer hospital helper with aspirations of becoming a nurse in the future. The nurse wore a plastic tag saying Mary Elizabeth Hartley, RN.

"Well, how are you feeling this morning, Mr. Pratt?"

"I've had better times," I said.

"Your surgery went well, and it doesn't look like you're going to lose any of your extremities."

"Surgery?"

"Yes. There was some necrotic tissue that had to be trimmed away, and then they did some tissue grafts."

"I guess that explains why my butt hurts."

"Well yes, that might be the case. Do you feel like you need anything for the pain?"

I did, but I said, "No. I think I'd rather try to get along without taking anything."

"Very well. But if you change your mind, feel free to ask, okay?"

"This is kind of embarrassing, but when I wake up in the morning, the first thing I need to do is pee. Like right now," I said.

Nurse Mary Elizabeth signaled to the candy-striper, who retrieved a bed pan from a roll-around cabinet. This isn't how I wanted to start my day.

"The alternative would be a catheter, if you'd rather go that route."

"Uh. No. That doesn't sound like fun."

After the humbling experience of having two ladies help me pee, I dared to mention that I hadn't had anything to eat since Saturday evening.

"Well, we'll have to take care of that," Nurse Mary Elizabeth said. "We'll keep you on a liquid-only diet for a day or two. Our private chef has an excellent selection of broths and juices for you to choose from."

"In that case, I'll take the roast beef broth, medium rare, with a cranberry juice cocktail."

"Excellent choice."

"Doctor Highland will check-in on you later, and maybe see about streamlining some of your bandages to give you a little bit of mobility."

Dale came in with a card signed by everyone in the store and a large bouquet of flowers.

"Brant Litton called to say that he got the tape recording and transcriptions. He's working on a brief to present to the supreme court asking for another stay, pending a new appeal."

I slept on and off through Monday and Tuesday. On Wednesday, Dr. Highland came in and carefully unwrapped my fingers. Satisfied with what he found, he carefully re-bandaged them, but in a way that gave me some limited use of my hands—enough so that I could work the call button.

After the doctor changed the bandages on my feet, Nurse Mary Elizabeth helped me get out of bed and shuffle to a wheelchair. That ended the tyranny of the bed pan and greatly improved my general outlook on life.

There was a phone in my room, and I found that I could hold a pencil between my thumb and the side of my hand, and use the eraser end to turn the dial. I called Dale and asked her to bring my case notes when she came to visit.

"I need your help finding out who is the inside-man at the Ritzville Police Department," I said. "Someone there tipped-off Tanner about what I was doing there that night, prompting him to rig my car."

It had to have been the officer who had been on duty while Doreen and I were working on the tape recording, but I needed his name. I didn't want to make the call myself, in case the accomplice in the police department was still unaware that I'd survived his attempt on my life.

I gave Dale the number for the Ritzville P.D. and she called the operator to place the station-to-station long-distance call, with third-party billing to my office number. By making the call early in the day, I hoped that the phone would be answered by someone other than the sergeant who was on duty Thursday evening. Dale held the receiver away from her ear, so that I could hear both ends of the call.

"Ritzville Police, Officer Raney speaking."

Dale said, "Oh, hi. My name is Sue Cornell. Are you the officer who was there last Thursday afternoon?"

"No, ma'am. I believe that was Sergeant Sherman. Is there something I can help you with?"

"Oh. Uh, I don't think… Uh, can you tell me Sergeant Sherman's first name? I want to send him a thank-you card."

Raney laughed. "His name is Terry, but everyone calls him Tec."

"Tek? T-E-K?

"Actually, it's T-E-C, short for Tecumseh."

"Oh, thank you, Officer Raney. Can I ask one favor?"

"Of course."

"Don't tell him I called. I want to surprise him."

When the call ended, I said, "Well done. You ought to do this for a living."

"No thank you. I have a store to run and a baby to raise."

Chapter Thirty-Three

Back to Business

After Dale left, I used my pencil eraser to dial my answering service and check for messages. There was a message from Brant Litton, mostly checking on my status, but also letting me know that he was going to make another trip to Olympia at the end of the week.

My next call was to long-distance directory assistance, where I got a phone number and address for Terrence Sherman in Ritzville. I made a few more calls and found a store that had maps for counties and small cities in the state. I called Dale and asked her to go there and buy a map of Ritzville and bring it in next time she came to visit.

"You'd better hurry-up and get well, because this is going to become tiresome," she said.

That afternoon, I got a message to call the office at Wapato High School. Once again, I had to use third-party billing to make the long-distance call.

"Principal Leach asked me to check our files for any transcript requests from former student William Tanner."

I confirmed, "Yes. That is what I need."

"Well, we did find three requests. In June, 1957, we sent a transcript to the registrar's office at Washington State College in

Pullman. Then in 1959, we sent one to Eastern Washington College of Education in Cheney. The most recent request was in May of 1961. That went to Fresno State College."

Following the theory that Tanner was the linen service delivery man, the only one of these schools that he could possibly be attending was Eastern. But even that was a stretch, because it was nearly 50 miles from Ritzville. Still, I had to follow through.

The registrar's office at Eastern said that they had no student named William Tanner. I called the other two schools, with the same result. William Tanner was not enrolled in any of the schools that had received copies of his high school transcript.

That probably meant that Tanner was using a different name. To test that theory, I called the Standard Linen Service in Ritzville. Without introducing myself, I asked the lady who answered the phone if she could tell me who had made the delivery to the police department last Thursday.

"Phil Kincaid does all of our deliveries. But you must be mistaken about the day, because we do our pick-up and delivery on Mondays."

I recalled Doreen saying that it wasn't the regular delivery guy, so I said, "I think it was a substitute driver. He was at the police station Thursday afternoon, around 5:15."

"Last Thursday, our truck was in the shop for service. I'm sure you're mistaken. Who did you say you are?"

I ignored the question and said, "I guess you're right. It must have been someone else's truck."

Indeed, I'd gotten only a glimpse of the truck and hadn't actually seen the linen service name on it. And Doreen hadn't recognized the delivery man. From that, I concluded that the whole linen deliver had been a set-up, undoubtedly orchestrated by Sergeant Sherman.

When Dale came in on Thursday with the Adams County and Ritzville maps, we found Sergeant Sherman's Kanzler Road address a couple of miles northwest of town, in a sparsely populated area. On paper, it looked like a good place to do bad things. The only way I could know for sure would be to go there and see it for myself.

January 26, 1962

On Friday, when Dr. Highland came in, he asked if I felt well enough to go home. It was the closest I have ever come to kissing a man.

"You're not going to feel much like walking around for the next week or so, but I don't think you're going to need that wheelchair. You'll still need to be very careful about exposing yourself to cold or hot conditions, because you'll be very sensitive to high and low temperatures."

"So, no sledding?" I quipped.

"I'm serious about this. There was a lot of tissue injury here, and you need to give it plenty of time to heal. And the process is not going to be without pain. Aspirin may help, but in case it becomes too much, I'm giving you a prescription for Darvon. It's a very strong pain reliever, so be careful with it. It's serious stuff."

Dale picked me up later in the day and drove me home. On the way, she brought me up to date on the latest from Brant Litton. The supreme court had been unable to find time for him until the following Wednesday, which would be just one week from Permann's execution date.

Under strict orders, I took it easy at home through the weekend, but on Monday morning I simply had to get back to work. Under protest, Dale drove me down to the store, where I awkwardly worked on a couple of TV sets with my bandaged fingers.

Chapter Thirty-Four

Ambush

January 30, 1962

As of Tuesday morning, Litton was finally on his way to Olympia to present his new brief to the supreme court, requesting another stay of execution, based on the proof of evidence-tampering that I'd given him. Meanwhile, with my search for Tanner stalled, the best thing I had was his suspected accomplice, Tec Sherman.

"I'll be fine," I assured Dale. "I'll just shoot a few pictures. I won't even get out of the car."

"Constantine Pratt, you are about the most stubborn individual I have ever met! The least you can do is wait a few more days. I never should've let you checkout of the hospital."

"And I'd have happily stayed there," I lied. "But I don't have time to make myself comfortable. A week from now they'll be giving Gordon Permann his last meal."

Dale took a deep breath. "I know, but... Just be careful, okay?"

I'd have preferred to take Dale's car on this trip, but it was in the shop with some kind of transmission problem. I probably should have rented a car, but I was still trying to economize wherever I could on the Permann case, because I knew that his family wasn't wealthy. And that's why I ignored Dale's last words of advice, and drove my own car.

I certainly didn't want anyone in Ritzville to notice me, and my yellow and black Crown Victoria was hardly the ideal car for keeping a low profile. On the other hand, as far as I knew, the only person who'd actually *seen* my car was Doreen, when she helped me carry my things out of the station after dubbing the witness tape. As long as I stayed away from the police station, I'd be pretty safe.

I found Sherman's house outside of town and snapped a series of pictures using my telephoto lens. There was nothing remarkable about the place, and nothing about it suggested that it had been the scene of a double murder. But it did possess some attributes that would make it a good place to carry one out. There were no neighbors close enough to hear anything, and it would be easy to get in and out without anybody seeing.

At some point, I'd have to reveal myself and try to find the connection between Tanner and Tec Sherman. But I wanted to talk with Tanner's old high school friend first. So, having accomplished my mission for the day, I drove back through town to Highway 10, and headed back toward Spokane.

It was well past lunch time as I approached Cheney, so I was looking for a place to stop and get something to eat. Half a mile south of town, the speed limit dropped to 30, and just ahead I spotted a truck-stop café on the right.

I was slowing down to pull into the gravel parking lot, when there was a loud crack, and I was showered in particles of glass. Instinctively, I stomped the gas pedal to the floor. The transmission dropped into second gear, and the car accelerated quickly to 70 miles an hour. In ten seconds, I found myself racing into the Cheney business district, and I slowed down, hoping to see a cop car. But as the old saying goes, they're never there when you want them.

I pulled up in front of the service bay at a Texaco station, got out, and took off my jacket. As I shook off the slivers of glass, I looked at the hole in the rear side window. The bullet had passed through the car and exited through the side glass on the other side.

"What can I do for you?" I turned to see a man wearing a dark green Texaco uniform, with the familiar star on his hat and shirt.

"Can you call the police? Someone just put a bullet through my car," I said.

He leaned in to take a look at the hole in the left side window. "Big bullet. Maybe .30 caliber. There shouldn't be anyone out hunting this time of year."

"I don't think this was a stray shot. Can you call the cops?"

Five minutes later, a Spokane County Sheriff's car wheeled into the station and pulled up alongside my Crown Vic.

"You reported a shooting?" asked the deputy.

I pointed at the bullet hole. "Missed me by about eighteen inches."

The deputy took down all of the information, and then went to his radio and requested an investigation unit to search the area where I estimated the shot had originated.

"I'll need you to show me the place," he said.

I held up my still-bandaged hands. "Frostbite. Hurts like hell. I *really* need to get someplace warm."

He let me climb into the backseat of his metallic green Fairlane Interceptor. He drove me back out of town, slowing to a crawl when we approached the diner where the incident took place. We went past the area and then circled back.

"It had to be right along here," I said. "I was slowing down to stop at the cafe. The shot came from my left."

I pointed toward an area of basalt outcroppings and open forest on the other side of the highway.

He pulled to the shoulder and stopped. "You want to stay here?" he asked.

"Yeah. I wish I could get out and help, but I just can't tolerate the cold."

The deputy walked slowly along the edge of the highway, stopping at one point to study something on the ground. He looked across the highway to the north. The investigation unit arrived and the deputies talked for several minutes. They started searching the area north of the highway, where the shot had probably originated.

When the first deputy finally came back to where I was, he said, "There are fresh footprints in the snow up there. The investigation unit will get some people out here to look for evidence."

I was taken back to the Texaco station, where I asked the attendant if he could vacuum the glass off the seats in my car. The deputy took pictures of the bullet holes in the windows before letting the Texaco man put Scotch tape over them.

"You have any idea who might want to take a shot at you?"

I was expecting that question and had thought about how to answer it. "I'm a private investigator, and I'm working for the attorney who is appealing Gordon Permann's conviction. This is connected to that."

"You mean Superman? Isn't he about out of time?"

"I hope not. The attorney is in Olympia right now trying to delay the execution."

"You think someone doesn't like you because you're trying to get a killer set free? Imagine that."

"It could be that, but I think it's far more likely that it's someone who is feeling the heat from my investigation."

"Are you saying that you've actually found something that points at someone else?"

"Exactly"

"Then, you need to tell us about that."

"It isn't my place to do that. Like I said, it is being presented to the supreme court right now. I could compromise our case by jumping the gun."

"If you are withholding evidence, you can be charged as an accessory."

"Not while someone already stands convicted in the case," I reminded him.

"I'm going to have to take this to higher-ups," the deputy said.

"Please do." We exchanged cards, and I said, "Now we know how to get in touch with each other. But right now, all I care about is getting warm."

* * * * * *

Not wanting Dale to see the bullet holes in my car, I stopped at McCollum Ford on my way back home, to see about getting the windows replaced. The bodyshop manager said it would be a few days before they'd be able to get the replacement glass and work the job into their schedule.

"Can you get me a loaner?" I asked.

"I'll have to check with the boss on that."

I said, "Take your time. I'm going to go up front."

I limped my way to the new car showroom, where I found a gold-colored Thunderbird coupe that had every available option. I looked at the window sticker, hyperventilated briefly, and mentally subtracted fifteen percent from the price.

The salesman was already on me. "She's a real beauty, isn't she?"

"I have a '56 Crown Victoria in the bodyshop for some new glass. Other than that, it's in great shape. That's my trade-in. My offer is $4,700 plus my trade. Write it up however you want, as long as it ends up at that number." I smiled, making myself look harmless.

"You're serious?" he asked.

"Easiest sale you'll ever make," I said.

I phoned Dale to let her know that I had stopped at the Ford dealer for some minor car repairs, and would go straight home from there. The sales manager got the parts runner to give me a ride to my bank to pick up a cashier's check for $5,000, which also covered the sales tax, title, and license.

"When you get a car fixed, you really do it right," Dale said, as she admired the T-Bird.

"Are you sure you like it?" I asked. "Maybe we should take it out for a spin around town."

"Wow, this is really living in luxury! Even power windows!" she said as she got in.

"Power *everything*," I corrected.

Over a steak dinner at the Stockyard Inn, Dale asked, "So, what went wrong with your old car?"

"Windows developed leaks."

"Huh? You never mentioned that the windows were leaking."

"The leaks came up kind of quickly."

She gave me her squinty-eyed look. "Just how big are these leaks?"

"About .30 caliber, I'd guess."

"Someone took a shot at you?" she exclaimed.

"I'm starting to think that someone doesn't like what I'm doing. And he knows that I'm getting close. That shot was an act of desperation."

"You could have been killed!"

"It's not as easy as you think to hit someone in a car going 30 or 40 miles an hour."

"Well, it's a good thing he isn't a good shot!"

What I knew, but wasn't about to say, was that this guy was a pretty damn *good* shot. The only thing he did wrong was aiming at where I was, rather than where I was going to be when the bullet got there. In the few milliseconds it took for the bullet to get from the rifle to the car, I'd moved about eighteen inches, and that's how much he missed by.

"I located Tec Sherman's house and took some pictures. I don't know where I was spotted, or by whom. But the ambush was set up just outside Cheney. You see what that means?"

"It means I was right. You should not have gone there," she said without a hint of a smile.

I ignored the jab. "It means that Bill Tanner is probably a student at Eastern, but is registered under a different name. Someone in Ritzville phoned and told him that I'd be driving through Cheney. All he had to do is sit and wait."

Dale sighed. "I hope you're still alive when this is all over."

"I called the answering service while I was waiting around at the Ford dealer. There were no messages from Brant Litton, so I guess that means he didn't get a summary decision on the stay."

"There's been nothing in the news about it, either."

"Actually, it'll probably take the court a few days to digest everything about the car and understand how that exonerates Permann. And at the same time, they'll be considering whether or not the witness interview tape shows that there was prosecutorial misconduct."

"But shouldn't they grant the stay of execution while they go through the evidence?"

"I find it hard to understand why they haven't already done it," I agreed.

Chapter Thirty-Five

David Shane

January 31, 1962

I was in my office early on Wednesday. I figured that there was no need to call Brant Litton. When he had something to report, he'd call me. In the meantime, I'd continue my search for William Tanner—while staying away from Ritzville, if at all possible. Two weeks earlier, while in Yakima, Lilly Nash had told me the story of how Billy Tanner came to live with his grandmother Margaret.

It was because Margaret's daughter-in-law, Clarise Tanner, had suffered a breakdown and was sent to the state mental hospital at Medical Lake. I tried briefly to track her down, but couldn't get past the patient confidentiality barrier. Nobody at the state-owned mental hospital at Medical Lake would even confirm that Clarise was there.

But if she was there, it might make sense that Bill decided to attend college at Eastern, just ten miles from Medical Lake. I made a note to ask Litton if there was a way to use the law to compel the hospitals to tell us if Clarise Tanner was being treated there.

When I answered my ringing phone, the long-distance operator asked if I would accept a collect call from David Shane, in Lamont, Washington.

"Yes, I will accept that call," I said.

"Hello, is this Connie Pratt?"

"Yes. Thank you for calling, Mr. Shane. I am a private investigator, working on behalf of an attorney in Spokane. We are working on a case that requires us to locate someone you knew in high school."

"Please, just call me Dave. Who is it you are trying to find?"

"William Tanner," I said. "Principal Leach said that you and he were friends. For what it's worth, he said that you were a good influence on him."

"Wild Bill… He had a hard time making friends. He was always kind of an outsider. I don't think he actually had any close friends."

"Wild Bill? Why do you call him that?"

"Irony. He was just the opposite. He was quiet—a loner, maybe a little bit sullen. He seemed to be attracted to the kids on the bottom-rung of the social ladder. I think that's where he saw himself."

"So, how did it happen that he was your friend?"

"He showed up at Wapato in our freshman year. Most everyone else in our class had grown up and gone through grade-school together, so right-off, he was an outsider. Word got around that Bill was an orphan, which made him kind of an object of interest—something that he hated. But alphabetical seating in the classes we shared kind of put us together—Shane and Tanner.

"Our lockers were side-by-side, too, so we'd see each other half a dozen times a day, without any reason. When we talked about things, we found that we had some common interests. He liked to talk about current affairs and sports."

"Principal Leach also said you were the star of the basketball team."

"I was on the team. I don't know about being a star."

"You're being modest. I read your stats in the 1957 yearbook. I'd have to agree with Mr. Leach," I said.

"Yeah well, we were talking about Bill Tanner, not me. I know that some kids thought Bill was a dunce because he wouldn't talk much in class, but he was actually pretty smart. We talked about sports and lots of other things—cars, airplanes, politics. He knew a bunch about history."

"Did he ever talk about what happened to his family?"

"Not much. I knew that he was living with his grandmother. There were stories around school that his mother had committed suicide and his dad was in prison. He blew up once when a kid said that in the cafeteria during lunch. He climbed over tables to get to the kid and pounded the daylights out of him. Got in some trouble over that, and got himself a reputation.

"A few days after that, he told me that his dad had actually been killed in the war, and his mother worked herself into a breakdown trying to raise three kids—he had a brother and sister, both older than him. Anyway, they took her to a hospital to be treated for exhaustion, and sent the kids to live with their grandmother. So, he wasn't actually an orphan."

"Did you stay in touch with him after high school?"

"Barely. After graduation, I spent the summer working in my uncle's produce business, and then in the fall I started school at Central Washington State in Ellensburg. As for Bill, I heard that he had some kind of a blow-up with his grandma, and went to live with his sister."

"Do you know the sister's name, or where she lived?"

"His sister was named Rena. She was married, and I think she lived in Richland. Or somewhere around there—I'm not sure."

"Do you know her married name?"

"No. I've probably heard it, but I don't remember it."

"When's the last time you saw Bill?"

"Actually, I haven't seen him since graduation. But we exchanged phone numbers at the time. Of course, we were both moving around, so it was hard to keep in touch, other than a Christmas card every year. Last I heard, he was taking classes at Eastern."

"EWSC?" I asked.

"Right. He had some kind of a full-time job at a nursing home or something, and was taking a half-time class load at Eastern."

"So, when was the last time you actually talked with him?"

"It was almost two years ago. I was in the middle of my junior year at Central, and out of the clear blue, Bill called and wanted me to go to the high school basketball state tournament with him. Wapato was back in the tournament, and he thought it'd be fun to go."

"You're talking about the 1960 tournament?"

"Yeah. It probably would've been fun, but the tournament didn't coincide with my spring break, and I couldn't skip classes for three days, so that was it."

"Do you know where he was planning to stay while he was in Seattle for the tournament?"

"He said his brother had a place somewhere nearby. That was where he was going to stay, and he was pretty sure that I could too."

I said, "I'm fairly sure that Bill ended up going. Did he ever say anything about that?"

"Nope. That was the last time we talked. Last year, I wanted to send him an invitation to my wedding, but I didn't have an address for him."

"Any idea how I might catch up with him?"

"It'd have to be through the school or his work, I suppose."

"I contacted the registrar, but there's nobody by his name enrolled there."

"Which name?" Dave asked.

That puzzled me. "What do you mean, *which name?*"

"He doesn't use Tanner anymore. He started using his father's name after high school—Grady. That's actually his real name. He went by Tanner just to avoid the whole stigma of having a different name from what was on the mailbox."

"Grady? His name is Bill *Grady?*" I gasped.

"Well, yeah. I figured you knew that."

* * * * * *

As soon as I hung up the phone from that call, I phoned Jeff Warden.

"I'm hoping you can get me a driver's license for an individual, along with registration data for any vehicles he owns."

"Come on, Connie. You're taking advantage of me. You know that I'm not supposed to do this kind of thing for civilians. Especially for civilians trying to free a convicted felon."

"Well, this isn't about Gordon Permann. It's about a guy who took a shot at me yesterday as I was driving through Cheney."

"That was *you?* I heard something about that on the squawk box."

"I think a guy named William Grady is the gunman. I need his license and vehicle data to confirm it."

"That's the sheriff's business."

"Of course. And I'll be meeting with them tomorrow. I just want to be prepared when I go in."

"You need to make more friends, Connie. Then you'll be able to spread the favors around."

"So, you'll get me the info?" I asked.

"Yes, dammit. This time, but for god's sake, don't ask for anything else."

An hour later, I had William Grady's address, on West 4th Ave. in the town of Four Lakes, midway between Cheney and Medical Lake. And he owned a 1955 Oldsmobile Super Eighty-Eight, license number CDB 643.

When Dale got a call saying that her car was repaired and ready for pick-up, I drove her down to Appleway Chevrolet. The transmission problem turned out to be nothing more serious than a leaking vacuum hose. I continued on through Spokane and up the Sunset Hill on Highway 10.

At Four Lakes, I turned west off the highway, and at the end of West 4th, I found a trailer park at the address listed on Grady's driver's license. He lived in a 40-foot New Moon trailer house sitting on blocks next to the unpaved driveway. There was no car in the parking area next to the trailer, so I figured he wasn't home.

I didn't feel much like walking, so I paused only long enough to snap a few photos of the trailer, which seemed unremarkable in every way. Since Grady's accomplice had been able to phone him to set up the ambush, I knew that he had a telephone, so I stopped at a phone booth out by the highway and looked him up. I copied his number into my notebook.

Next, I drove on down through Cheney to take another look at the site of the ambush. The patch of pine trees where the gunman had hidden was on a strip of land bounded on the south by Highway 10, and on the north by West Cameron Road. I parked at the truck stop and walked gingerly down the shoulder to the spot where splinters of glass sparkled on the ground.

Directly opposite that spot, there was a gap in the thin forest. From the eastern side of that clearing, the gunman had a clear view of cars coming up the highway from Ritzville, while the trees and rock outcroppings provided cover.

I crossed the highway and limped a hundred yards up a path in the clear space that may have once been a driveway. This was the same path that the crime scene investigators had taken in search of the sniper's shooting position. One spot in particular was well-trampled, about midway between the highway and Cameron Road.

This probably was where Grady sat, waiting to see a yellow and black Crown Victoria coming up the highway. I watched passing cars and counted-off the seconds from the time they first came into view and when they reached the point where the bullet hit my car. Grady had six seconds to acquire the target, aim, and squeeze-off a shot.

He was a damn good marksman, but not an experienced sniper. His best chance of a hit would have been from head-on, through the windshield. A trained sniper would have known that and picked his ambush site accordingly. It was my good fortune that he didn't.

Chapter Thirty-Six

The Big Picture

February 1, 1962

Litton called early Thursday morning, so I brought him up to speed. "Yesterday, I learned the name of our suspect. He's William Grady, a student at EWSC, and he lives in a trailer house in Four Lakes."

"How did you come by all of this?"

"I got a call from a guy who knew William Tanner in high school. Turns out, his father's name was Grady. When he went to live with his grandmother, Margaret Tanner, he took her name. Then, after high school, he went back to using his father's name—Grady."

"I'm very glad to see you're still making progress. I don't know if my latest brief impressed the court, so we need to keep moving."

"I'll be calling the EWSC registrar this morning. I expect to confirm that he's a student there, and with some luck, I'll find out where he works. His friend also told me that Grady has a job in a nursing home. I think it actually might be one of the hospitals at Medical Lake, possibly the one where his mother is."

"Okay. I don't want this to drag into the weekend. I want to save that time in case the court denies the stay. If it comes to that, I'll need to go straight to the governor."

"There's one other thing. Someone took a shot at me Tuesday, while I was driving through Cheney. At the time of the shooting, I didn't know Grady's name, but I'm pretty sure he's the guy who did it. The sheriff's office is involved in the investigation, and they're pressing for information about our case."

"What do they know?"

"Bare minimum. When they asked if I had any idea who would want me dead, I told them that I was working for you on the Permann appeal, and that it was likely that the shooting was done by someone who is unhappy with our investigation.

"I got the impression that the deputy was among those unhappy with our investigation. He wanted me to tell him what I knew, and threatened to charge me for withholding evidence. The sheriff's investigators want to talk with me this afternoon."

Litton said, "Now, as long as Permann stands convicted of the Draper murders, Grady can't be named as a suspect, so his connections to the case can't be used as probable cause for warrants in connection with the shooting."

"That's what I figured. Still, I'd feel a whole lot better if he was off the streets. And a warrant to search his trailer house might help us. I'd like to see if Grady has boots that match the plaster cast I made up where my car was stranded in the snow."

"I think I should be there when you're questioned, just to make sure that nobody's rights get walked on."

* * * * * *

After wrapping up that call, I direct-dialed the registrar's office at EWSC.

"My name is Pratt. I'm an investigator working with the Spokane County Sheriff's Office."

It was fair to stay that, since I had the appointment to meet with them later in the day. That constitutes "working with them."

"What can we do for you, Officer Pratt?"

I never claimed to be an officer. She jumped to that all by herself. Sort of.

"We are attempting to locate a potential witness who may be a student at Eastern. His name is William Grady," I explained.

"I'll see if we have a file for that individual. Will you hold, please?"

"Certainly. Thanks." That was further than I'd gotten before.

A few minutes later, she came back on the line. "Yes, it looks like we do have a person by that name enrolled here. What would you like to know?"

"Just some basic information—enrollment history, address, phone number, and information about any financial assistance he may be receiving."

"Well, let's see. He enrolled here for the second term in 1958. In 1959, he reduced his class load, and he's been a half-time student since then. Currently, he is listed as a first term junior."

She then read-off Grady's address and phone number, confirming what I already knew. "As far as financial assistance goes, he is not receiving any. It looks like he is employed and able to pay his own way."

"Do you have information about his employment?"

"It appears that he is employed by the state, at the Eastern State Hospital in Medical Lake. He works in facility maintenance. Employed there since 1959."

I said, "Thank you very much. You've been very helpful."

"You're very welcome, Officer Pratt."

I met Brant Litton in the lobby at the sheriff's office downtown headquarters, and recapped what I'd learned from the college. A deputy came out and ushered us into an interview room, where we were introduced to Wayne Evans, the deputy in charge of the shooting investigation.

Evans said, "Why don't we start with your description of the shooting."

"I was on my way from Ritzville to Spokane and, just outside of Cheney, I was slowing down to make the turn into the truck stop café. I heard a loud noise and was showered in bits of glass. I floored the gas pedal and got out of there as quickly as I could. When I stopped at the Texaco station, I found the bullet holes through the quarter-window glass on both sides of the car."

"Did you see the person who fired the shot?"

"No. I didn't look around. I just got the hell away."

"The first deputy on scene wrote in his report that you had an idea who may have fired at you."

"That is correct. I believe that it is someone who doesn't like what I'm working on."

"The report says you're trying to overturn the conviction of Gordon Permann."

Litton interrupted. "Mr. Pratt is working for me. I represent Gordon Permann, and I have an appeal in process, pending a stay of execution order by the state supreme court."

Evans said, "I'm not here to adjudicate Permann's case. I'm concerned only about the shooting, so if Mr. Pratt knows, or thinks he knows, who pulled the trigger, he needs to tell me."

"Since the suspected gunman's motive is connected to Mr. Pratt's investigation into the crime for which my client stands convicted, revealing his name for this case would prematurely show our hand in the larger investigation," Litton explained.

"I understand your position," Evans said, "but it seems to me that you'd want the guy locked up."

"The evidence that connects our suspect to the shooting is the proof that he committed the crime for which my client was convicted. We need to get that conviction vacated before our suspect can be charged in the case, and until that happens you can't use his possible guilt in our case as probable cause for an arrest in the shooting."

"Well, that's a conundrum. Help me find a way through this. I know you want to see the gunman held accountable. Can we share what we know and work together on it?" Evans asked.

I asked, "Were your people able to collect any physical evidence at the scene?"

"They found the gunman's nest. It looked like he was there for some time—maybe thirty, forty-five minutes—so obviously, he was waiting for a specific target. In other words, he knew you were coming up the highway, and he knew what you were driving. It is my understanding that this is not a drive that you make regularly, or on any kind of a schedule. Is that correct?"

"That's right. I believe that someone in Ritzville phoned the suspect and told him when to watch for me coming into Cheney."

"So, he had an accomplice, presumably with a shared motive to see you dead."

"That is what I believe."

"And you know who it is?"

"I have a pretty good suspect, but it's not something I can prove yet."

"But you think you *can* prove the gunman's motive?"

"I'm sure of it," I said.

"Okay. We'll come back to that. At the gunman's nest, investigators collected some evidence, including a cellophane wrapper from a package of Hostess cupcakes. We hope to lift fingerprints from that. We also took casts of some footprints in the snow leading to and from the nest."

I nodded. I had seen the plaster residue when I visited the site.

"There's more. Down on the other side of the highway, our guys dug a bullet out of a pine tree. It appears to have been in a straight line from the gunman's nest, through the windows of your car. The preliminary observation is that it is a .30-06 round with full jacket—possibly selected because of the need to penetrate the glass window before hitting the intended target."

"Will there be ballistic evidence?"

"Definitely. We'll just need to find a weapon to compare it with. Now, what do you have?"

I looked to Litton, and he nodded.

"This was not his first attempt on my life. Two weeks ago, he disabled my car and left me stranded through that night when it was twenty below zero. That's how this happened."

I held up my frostbitten hands.

"I made a cast of a footprint from that scene. It appeared to be from a work shoe, size ten."

"You have a cast? Let's compare it with ours, and tie the two events together."

"It's in my car. I'll bring it in when we're finished talking."

"So, we have footprint casts, a bullet, and a cupcake wrapper that might have fingerprints. That's good stuff that could potentially get a conviction—if we can get something to compare them with. If the mutt has fingerprints on file, we'll be able to get a search warrant to look for his rifle and shoes."

"When will you get the lab report on the cupcake wrapper?"

"Day or two, maybe. Then, if there are prints, it could take weeks to see if we have a match in our system. Of course, that could be cut short if we knew whose prints to look at."

I said, "Based on what I know about my suspect, I doubt that he's ever been printed by law enforcement. I haven't been able to find any criminal history for him. Is there any way to get his prints without a warrant?"

Litton said, "You would need to find his prints on an object *and* have good reason to believe that *he alone* handled the object."

"So, if you follow him into a bar and watch him handle a glass, and then get the glass before anyone else touches it, you could use prints from the glass?"

Evans said, "Not good enough. The fingerprint evidence might not be allowed, because following him into the bar for the purpose of gaining evidence against him requires us to have probable cause. And your word won't do."

"Okay, how about this: I'll find out what day his trash is collected. I'll get there ahead of the garbage truck and take all of his trash. Just about everything in there should have his prints."

Litton said, "The courts are about 50-50 on that. Some say that once you put your trash out for pickup, you relinquish all rights to it, and anyone is free to take it. Others say that it's still yours until the authorized trash collector takes it away. It'll have to go to the supreme court to get everyone on the same page."

I said, "I'm guessing that you don't want this to be the test case for that."

"We're spinning our wheels here," Evans said. "Let's see what the lab can develop from the footprint casts. With some luck, there'll be enough detail to identify the brand of shoe. And with some more luck, maybe it'll be something uncommon. Then we could try to track sales and connect the shoes to the suspect."

"How about watching him go out to the street to pick up his mail? If he's wearing the same shoes, we could try to get a cast to compare with the ones we have," I suggested.

"There's a lot of speculation there. You're assuming that there's going to be mud or snow to take a footprint, and that it will be in the public right-of-way, and finally, that you can spend half an hour making a cast without him seeing you," Evans said. "But in theory, it could be done."

Litton slapped his hand on the table. "You're talking about things that might take weeks or months. Gordon Permann has six days. That's what we have to focus on."

He looked squarely at Deputy Evans and continued, "Now, we can give you a mountain of proof that this suspect killed the Draper girls, but Adams County won't charge him for it, because someone else has already been convicted."

Evans started to speak, but Litton waved him off and continued, "However, if you will take the time to review and understand the evidence we have, I believe that it will give you the probable cause you need to get an arrest warrant for our suspect."

"I can't guarantee that I'll reach the same conclusion that you apparently have. I'll look at the evidence and draw my own conclusions—as I always do."

"I don't expect you to guarantee the outcome. But I am completely confident in what it will be," Litton concluded.

"I'll look at what you have. That's all I can promise."

Litton looked at me and asked, "How long will it take you to gather everything you've found in your investigation and get it down here?"

"It's already gathered, and it's in my car, along with that footprint cast. The only thing we'll need is a tape recorder," I said.

Evans agreed to Litton's proposal, and while I went out to my car, he rounded up a tape recorder. Ten minutes later, we reconvened around the conference table, and were joined by two more deputies and a stenographer named Roberta Cole. I started by showing some of the hundreds of unreadable documents that were given to us by the Adams County D.A.

"These are worthless, as you can plainly see," I said. "So, I went to Ritzville and started making the rounds, going to the original sources for the information contained in each of the unreadable documents. This did not start out as an investigation. It was simply a quest to get the complete case file used in the prosecution of Gordon Permann."

I recapped my first visit to the Ritzville Police Department, and walked through the process of making fresh Thermofax copies, and then making stable plain-paper copies of them.

"The point here is that it's quite possible that the district attorney may have been working with an incomplete case file, simply because of the limitations of the old fashioned Thermofax copying process," I explained.

Moving on to my second trip to Ritzville, I explained how I had contacted the key witnesses—the Ritzville fire chief, Chet Winston, Leon Stark, and Sandra Hutchins. I played the tape recordings of my interviews, and compared their statements to me with what was presented in court.

Several times, Litton interrupted me to underscore specific violations of Permann's rights and deviations from proper legal procedure that were being revealed. He emphasized the importance of the error in the identification of the vehicle described in the all-points bulletin.

This led directly into the discussion of the damaged interview tape and the process I'd used to make my copy of it, which I then played. I invited Evans to follow along on the official transcription of the interviews. At several key points, where critical words were omitted from the transcription, he asked me to rewind and replay parts of the recording. That was a good sign. He was paying attention.

Again, Litton explained how the misrepresentations of the witness statements completely negated the proof of Gordon Permann's innocence. "It isn't simply that the actual statements failed to prove that Permann was guilty. They actually proved that he *couldn't* have been guilty."

I played the tape of my interview with Carl Sterns contradicting what was said in court about Permann's employment and the construction project near the Crab Creek bridge, and showed photos of the cow barn where, according to the prosecutor, Permann had assaulted the girls.

"It was at this point that I became convinced that Permann was completely innocent," I said, "so this is when my work changed from documentation to investigation. The question was, since Permann *didn't* do it, who *did* do it? So, I went back to where the whole thing started."

I told about my trip to Seattle, and played the recording of my talk with Justine Sorenson. I paused the recording at key points to underscore the importance of specific things she said: (1) how "Bill" made multiple calls to Lisa; (2) how Gail Draper had wondered why he was still around on Friday and what that implied; (3) how "Bill Brady" was identified as a suspect; (4) how he had convinced Lisa to hook-up and follow him on the highway back toward Spokane; and (5) how Justine had helped load the girls' luggage into the trunk of her Falcon.

"As the police investigation focused more and more on Gordon Permann—largely because of the distortion of Chet Winston's testimony about the car he saw—the name 'Bill Brady' was largely forgotten."

Next, I described my search for the car Chet Winston had actually seen—the green Oldsmobile fastback. I explained my theory that the guilty person might want to do something about the appearance of the highly identifiable car he was driving, just in case the misidentification of it as a Chevrolet should break down.

"We contacted about sixty auto paint shops, and found only one that had painted a car like the one Winston saw. And it happened just a couple of weeks after the girls disappeared."

I detailed how I had tracked down the car and determined who owned it, who drove it, and who took it in to be re-painted—William Tanner. I played the tapes of my interviews with Jim Dunne, Lilly Nash, and Principal Leach.

I showed the Polaroid photos I'd shot from the 1957 Wapato High School yearbook, and played the tapes I'd made when I showed the photo spread to Sandra Hutchins, Chet Winston, and Luke Jackson, emphasizing that all three picked William Tanner's photo.

"So, that's how we arrived at our suspect," I said. "Now, regarding the shot fired at me in Cheney, as I said earlier, that was the *second* attempt on my life in two weeks."

I gave the full account of how I'd been lured to the abandoned wrecking yard on the Spokane Indian Reservation by a bogus call to Ritzville P.D. while I was there copying the witness interview recordings. I explained how my car had been sabotaged so that it wouldn't re-start after I got to the wrecking yard, and how close I'd come to death in the snow.

In building my argument that William Tanner was the one who rigged my car, I had to also explain that he had to have had an accomplice inside the Ritzville Police Department, probably Tec Sherman, though I had no hard proof of that.

Evans said, "See, now *that* part I can't buy. The kind of murder we see in the Draper case isn't a team sport. It's a one-man crime—the work of a loner. That's the way it always is."

Litton said, "And it may very well be that if Tec Sherman—or anybody else in Ritzville P.D.—was involved in this case, it was after the fact. So, for the purposes of the Permann appeal, it doesn't matter."

"But for the case of the ambush, your theory of William Tanner's involvement requires that someone tipped him off that Pratt was driving toward Cheney."

"Yes, that's true. But you don't need to know who that was to name Tanner as a suspect and seek search and arrest warrants."

"There's one more thing," I said. "William Tanner is not his real name. Tanner was his grandmother's name, and he started using it when he went to live with her. But after finishing high school, he went off to live on his own and went back to using his real name, William Grady."

Evans said, "Nice. Grady-Brady. I get it. That kind of closes the loop, doesn't it?"

I gave him Grady's phone number and address in Four Lakes, and concluded, "But the instant he thinks you're looking at him, he's probably going to bolt. He already knows that I'm on to him. If he finds out that we know his real name, he'll be gone in a heartbeat.

Chapter Thirty-Seven

Last Resort

February 2, 1962

Friday morning, I phoned my answering service from home before breakfast. There was a message from Brant Litton, urging me to call him immediately.

"These men must be the most dim-witted, thick-skulled, obtuse human beings on earth. How they can call themselves impartial jurists is a mystery for the ages. They have such unshakable faith in the criminal justice system that they refuse to consider the possibility that it might have gotten something wrong. We gave them everything! But did they look at it? Hell no!"

When he paused to inhale, I asked, "Are you telling me that the supreme court isn't granting the stay?"

"That's *exactly* what I'm telling you! They issued their decision without comment, meaning that they didn't even *look* at what I gave them. They rejected it out of hand, and wasted a week in the process."

"So, now it's up to the governor?" I asked.

"That's right. Pack your bags, Connie. You're going to make the same presentation to Governor Rosellini that you made yesterday to Deputy Evans."

"Wait! You want *me* to convince the governor to overrule the supreme court?"

"Listen, Connie, those three deputies all started out hating us for wanting to free a convicted killer. In ninety minutes, you completely turned them around. You boiled it down to bare bones, and convinced Evans and the others."

"Yeah, but this is a legal question. It's *your* field, not mine."

"One of the weaknesses in our legal system is that we tend to tangle facts with legalities. We take the simple and make it complex. I have already called the governor's office, asking for an hour of his time. Governor Rosellini is going to have to weigh the public resistance to overturning a conviction against the political consequences of allowing the execution of a possibly innocent man."

"So, what are our chances?"

"If he returns my call, he'll hear our case."

"Can he simply *ignore* your call?"

"No, but he *can* delegate it to a staffer, in which case we're screwed."

* * * * * *

In the middle of the morning, Litton called to tell me that the governor had agreed to hear our case. We were to meet at the Governor's office in Olympia, Sunday afternoon at 2:00, when there would be very few people around.

But I really was not well prepared to make a presentation to the governor. I hadn't even intended to make a presentation to Deputy Evans. I had gone into that meeting thinking that we were going to resist being forced to reveal our case.

The one thing I knew for certain was that the tape recordings were the heart of my show-and-tell. Going into the meeting at the sheriff's office, I had a box containing half a dozen reels of tape, most of them recorded on my little battery-powered portable tape recorder. As I went through the case for Deputy Evans, there was a constant shuffling of tapes, fast-forwarding, rewinding, and switching reels.

Turning that into an actual presentation meant dubbing each of the individual recordings onto a single tape, arranged in proper sequence, so that all I'd have to do is press the pause button between segments. The best equipment for this was the new Wollensak from the store, because it had a digital counter for indexing the tape.

As I dubbed the recordings, I wrote down the index numbers for each segment. I would always know when to pause the playback and what was coming up next. Then, I arranged all of the printed material that accompanied the tape recordings, so that there would be no paper-shuffling. My goal was to cut the total presentation time in half without sacrificing any content.

I spent all day Friday and half the night doing that, and writing an outline to follow, repeating the sequence I'd followed in my spontaneous presentation to the sheriff's deputies.

On Saturday, I made a couple of practice runs, first with Dale, and later with Brant Litton. By the time we boarded the DC-7 for the flight to SeaTac, I felt that I wouldn't embarrass myself. We rented a car for the drive to Olympia, which took longer than the flight across the state.

We checked into a hotel just north of the state capitol complex. Litton placed a call to Wayne Evans for an update on the status of the shooting investigation. Evans said that latent prints had been lifted from the cupcake wrapper, but the search for a match in the state police fingerprint file could take weeks. No matter what was the outcome of our meeting with the governor, we did not have weeks to find a fingerprint match.

On Sunday, a Washington State Patrol officer escorted us to the governor's office in the capitol building. Governor Rosellini stepped forward and shook Litton's hand.

"Nice to see you again, Governor," Litton said.

Until that moment, I was unaware the Litton was personally acquainted with the governor.

Litton turned toward me and said, "This is Connie Pratt, who has spearheaded our investigation into the Draper Case."

With introductions out of the way, Litton gave a summary of his two unsuccessful attempts to get the supreme court to hear an appeal of Gordon Permann's conviction.

The governor said, "We are all very, very reluctant to second-guess a jury verdict. Our entire system is built around our faith in the ability of a group of ordinary citizens to analyze the facts of a case and render a fair and impartial verdict."

Litton said, "I agree with everything you just said. The question I am raising is whether or not the jury actually heard the facts of this case. And that is why we're here."

"I agreed to meet you today, because I've always known you to be honest and scrupulously ethical. I do not think that you would bring this to me if you did not believe your client to be innocent. So, I'm giving you the opportunity to convince me."

"Mr. Pratt has spent the last two months assembling documentation of the events surrounding this case, and it is an ongoing process. New facts are still coming to light. But as of today, we can prove two things: Gordon Permann could not be the killer of the Draper girls, and the jury that convicted him did not get the facts of the case during the trial."

"That's a pretty serious indictment of the Adams County prosecutor, Brant."

"Let's hear what Mr. Pratt's investigation has discovered about what happened. Then we'll discuss *how* it happened and see who is indicted by the facts. But the key point is not who is at fault, but rather what was the outcome—the wrongful conviction of an innocent man."

"Go ahead," Rosellini said, nodding to me."

As with Deputy Evans, I started by showing a stack of documents from the official case file—hundreds of pages that were completely illegible.

"This is what the Adams County prosecutor had to work with."

Again, I explained the shortcomings of the Thermofax copying process, which was used by virtually everyone prior to the recent introduction of the Xerox plain-paper copier. In this way, I took everyone off the hook. It was the fault of the copiers, not the people. My objective was to disarm the defensive mentality of the supporters of the people involved in the prosecution.

The remainder of my presentation followed the same outline as before, walking through the evolution of my task from simple document collection to proactive investigation. My advanced preparations made the whole thing flow smoothly.

Occasionally, Rosellini interrupted me to ask questions or request that I re-play parts of the tape recording. He definitely was not sleeping through this. His interest was genuine, and the deeper we got into the facts of the case, the clearer it was that he saw what we saw.

I held back nothing, including the names of our main suspect, William Grady, and his possible accomplice, Ritzville police Sergeant Tec Sherman.

"You make a pretty strong case," the governor said when I wrapped up my presentation.

Litton said, "The substance of my appeal has evolved as we've gathered more facts. My new appeal will be built around the new evidence that neither the prosecution nor the jury had at the time of the trial. I will augment that point with proof that the prosecution withheld certain pieces of exculpatory evidence from the defense in their handling of the witnesses Chet Winston and Leon Stark. I'm not saying that it was done out of malice, but it was clearly done."

The governor asked, "Is your appeal ready to present to the supreme court?"

"It's evolving as we learn more facts, but yes. It is all typed and ready to submit. But as of three days ago, the court was not willing to hear the appeal or even grant a stay."

"I can't force the court to hear your appeal, but I can postpone the execution. You understand that there'll be a political price to be paid for doing that. The law-and-order lobby will be all over this, calling me soft on crime. So, I'll be counting on you to prove that I'm doing the right thing. Tomorrow, I'll announce a thirty-day stay of execution."

Litton said, "Thank you. And tomorrow morning, I will personally deliver my new appeal to the court."

"Good luck," Rosellini said, shaking Brant's hand.

Chapter Thirty-Eight

Hard Evidence

I took the train back to Spokane Sunday night, leaving Litton in Olympia to file the appeal. On Monday, I was in the shop working on my backlogged repair orders, when news of the governor's action came on the radio. This relieved me from having to concentrate on the case every minute of every day.

For two days, I was able to devote most of my time to making service calls and working in the back room. Dale brought six-month-old Nancy down to the store to brag that the baby had spoken her first word--Mama. But naturally, she wouldn't repeat the performance for me.

I got Nancy's attention and pointed at Dale. "Mama."

Then, I pointed at her and said, "Nancy."

And finally, I pointed at myself and said, "Old Man."

Over and over, I repeated the lesson, and finally got her to say "Mama." It would take a few more lessons, but eventually she said, "Omum" when I pointed to myself. Mission accomplished. After an appropriate period of gloating, I went back to troubleshooting a police radio—a job that came as a direct result of my improved relationship with the sheriff's office.

Later in the day, Kenny Murphy, who had recently turned sixteen, pulled up in front of the store, driving a three-wheeled

Vespa motor scooter. Its front wheel was steered with standard motor scooter handlebars, and the motor was under the seat in the enclosed cab. Behind the cab, was a small pick-up bed with a canvas canopy.

"Well, that looks like fun," I said when he came into the store.

"Yeah. Since you wouldn't sell me your old Ford coupe, I went out looking for something that would be cheap to drive around town, and this is what I found. And check this out."

He handed me a fresh-off-the-press copy of the Valley Herald, folded open to the classified ads. One ad had been circled:

> TV PICTURE TUBES $49.95
> including installation for most
> black-and-white sets. 1-year
> warranty. Evenings WA 6-9835

"Is that you?" I asked.

"Yeah. I guess you probably know that the wholesale price for a rebuilt picture tube from Televac is $19.95. And they sell their 'seconds' for only $10.95, with full warranty. So that leaves me a $39.00 margin. The imperfections are almost invisible, but if people don't want the factory second, it'll still be only $59.95.

"I bought a pretty good used tube tester from HCJ Electronics, so I can test the chassis tubes, and I'll carry a small inventory of common replacements. If their picture tube turns out to be okay and I can make the set work by replacing chassis tubes, I'll charge twenty bucks for labor, plus the retail price of the tubes."

While I was impressed by his initiative, I wondered how he couldn't see that he was turning himself into my competitor.

"What are you going to do if replacing tubes doesn't fix it?" I challenged.

"Well, the thing is, I know that I look like I'm about fourteen. Nobody's going to trust me to do anything beyond replacing tubes anyway, so I'll just put the old tubes back in and explain that it probably isn't worth what it would cost to troubleshoot it any further. If you give me some cards, I'll send them your way."

Dale had listened to the whole exchange, and she said, "Excuse me, Kenny. Connie, can I talk to you for a minute?"

In the back room, she said, "You remember when we were talking about the diminishing economics of servicing the old black-and-white sets?"

I said, "Sure, but this…"

"We can give Kenny cards offering a discount on any new TV set in the store. The discount will bring them in, and then we can do what we want to do—sell them a new set. We'll make more money than we would by doing that service call ourselves, because our only cost will be the discount we give."

She was right, of course, so I went back and told Kenny, "Come back next week and I'll have some cards for you to hand out."

But through all of this, the Draper case was never far from my thoughts. Despite the way the governor had reacted to our presentation, I still had little faith in the supreme court. Our best bet still lay in getting William Grady locked up.

The thing that was preventing an arrest of him for shooting at me was the lack of a fingerprint to compare with the one lifted off the cupcake wrapper found in the gunman's nest. It suddenly struck me that employees at the state mental hospital might be required to have their prints on file. It probably would be true of the medical staff, but what about a maintenance worker?

I dropped what I was doing, phoned Wayne Evans, and asked him the question.

"I don't know," he said. "It's worth checking, but we'll be right up against the probable cause issue if we go out soliciting a print card from Grady's employer—if there is one."

"Damn! Well, I guess it would still be useful to know."

"Sure. It'll bolster the case when we get there. Oh, and by the way, those footprint casts match—same tread, same size, and same wear patterns. So, you were right about that."

"Do you know what brand of shoe made the tracks?"

"We're still working on that. We've found a Redwing boot with the same tread, but we haven't determined if it is an exclusive."

February 7, 1962

Looking for anything that might move the case forward, I made the half-hour drive out to Medical Lake to visit the personnel office on the second floor of the three-story brick building at the Eastern State Hospital.

"My name is Connie Pratt, from eastern Washington state. A student, William Grady, put in an application for financial assistance. And he listed you as his employer. Can you confirm that, please?"

It is entirely true that I am from eastern Washington state—but I don't know how to speak in lower case letters. Apparently, the clerk thought I meant Eastern Washington State College, ten miles away. As for Grady's request for financial assistance, well, who doesn't want financial assistance? She went to a cabinet and pulled a file.

"Yes, William Grady is a current employee in good standing."

"Oh, great. Can you tell me what his work hours are?"

"He works the evening shift, from 4:00 p.m. to midnight, Friday through Tuesday, with Wednesday and Thursday off."

That explained how he was able to attend classes at EWSC. And it did not escape my attention that he would not have been scheduled to work on Thursday, January 18, when the linen service guy showed up at the police station in Ritzville.

I really wanted to ask if Grady took time off during the week of the 1960 state basketball tournament. But I couldn't think of any reason why a representative of EWSC would need to know that. It was something that would be a necessary part of a case against Grady, and probably would require a subpoena from the Spokane County Sheriff's Office.

So, I turned my thoughts to Grady's mother. I still hadn't been able to confirm that she was a patient at the hospital, even though it fit everything I'd heard from those who'd told me about Tanner/Grady.

And then something occurred to me. From the start, I'd believed that Clarise was Margaret Tanner's daughter-in-law, and that her husband was named Tanner.

But now I knew that William's father was named Grady. That meant that Margaret Tanner was Clarise's mother, not her mother-in-law. Would a war widow revert to using her maiden name? Probably not. I'd been looking for Clarise Tanner, when I should've been looking for Clarise Grady.

I went back down to the main floor reception desk and said I was in town from Columbus, Ohio and was wondering if I could visit my cousin, Clarise Grady.

"Mrs. Grady receives very few visitors. She resides in the Women's Psychiatric Unit, and regular visiting time is Sunday afternoon between 2:00 and 5:00. We serve a buffet meal in the dining hall, and welcome visitors to join the patients for dinner. That would be the best time for you to visit her, if you're still going to be in town then."

I said, "My plans are somewhat flexible. I'll see if I can work that out. I haven't seen Clarise in years."

"Well, just call ahead and let us know, so that we can have her dressed to receive a visitor."

"I'll do that. Thanks. I wonder if someone could give me a quick tour of the facility. You know, so that when I come back, I'll know where to go."

"Let me see if someone is available." She disappeared into a private office.

When she returned, she said, "An orderly will be here in a minute. He'll be able to show you around."

The tour took me to the gates at the entries to the men's and women's wings of the main building, and then out the rear through a corridor to the big dining hall. Out behind the dining hall, there were several smaller buildings. The orderly said that the buildings to our right were the bakery and the laundry, and the two-story brick building on our left was the "West Lodge," a dormitory occupied by the least-troubled of the patients at the facility.

Further away from the hospital complex were the hospital fire hall and two long Quonset huts that served as maintenance buildings. It was likely that one of them was where Grady worked. I noted that security gates blocked road access to the entire area behind the main building.

February 8, 1962

Thursday morning, I was leaning back in my chair, staring at the ceiling, pondering what I could do with the information I'd collected at the state hospital. But the ringing of my phone startled me out of my thoughts.

It was Deputy Evans, who said, "We may have a break in your shooting case."

"Can you give me details?" I asked.

"In their initial canvass, right after the shooting, deputies knocked on every door in the area around the shooting site. If there was no answer, they left a card requesting a call.

"This morning, we got a call from a homeowner out on Cameron Road, a hundred yards from the gunman's nest. When asked if he'd seen or heard anything unusual on the day of the shooting, he said that his wife had heard a gunshot, and when she looked out the window, she saw a car parked in the ditch along the road. She identified it as a blue and white sedan."

"That describes Grady's car," I said.

"It gets better," Evans said. "Thinking that it might belong to a poacher, she took a picture of it, because they'd had some recent trouble with poachers' apparent inability to distinguish the difference between game animals and cattle."

I exclaimed, "They have a picture of his car?"

Evans corrected me. "They *took* a picture. As to what it shows, we won't know that until the film is developed. A deputy is on his way to Cheney right now, to pick up the film. We should have prints within a couple of days."

"A photo showing William Grady's car in the area at the time of the ambush would certainly be enough to get a search warrant for his trailer," I said.

"That depends on a couple of things. If it shows a license number that we can trace to Grady, we're clear. Even if it just shows a car that matches what we know Grady owns, we can backtrack through the Department of Licensing records and get to him. It all depends on how good the picture is."

Chapter Thirty-Nine

Arrest Warrant

Late on Friday afternoon, I called Deputy Evans to find out if the film from the Cameron Road witness had been processed.

"We have the photo," Evans confirmed. "It clearly shows a blue and white 1955 Oldsmobile sedan. But only part of the license plate is readable. We have the Department of Licensing tracking the partial plate number against the description of the car."

"Any idea how long that'll take?"

"I can't even guess. I asked them to put a rush on it, but I have no idea what it takes to search their records that way."

The process wasn't very different from the search they'd done for Jeff Warden, and that had taken six days. But that search had no priority attached, so I hoped this one would go more quickly.

February 11, 1962

Early Sunday afternoon, I got a call from the sheriff's office stenographer who had been present during my presentation to Deputy Evans.

"This is Roberta Cole. I don't know if you remember me, but we met a couple of weeks ago."

"Sure, I remember. What's up? I asked.

"Well, I probably shouldn't be telling you this, but I guess you know about a photo of a car at the place where you got shot at? Well, I heard that the Department of Licensing has connected the car in the photo to the suspect in the shooting."

"William Grady?"

"I'm not sure about the name, but they got an arrest warrant. They're executing the warrant right now. I figured you'd be interested in knowing that."

She was right. I hastily grabbed a few things, including the Colt M-1911 that I'd brought home from Korea, and sped toward Four Lakes.

I arrived at Grady's trailer at 2:45 p.m. and found half a dozen Spokane County Sheriff's Office cars blocking the road and driveway. I threaded my way through a small crowd of spectators, and when a deputy challenged me, I asked to see Deputy Evans.

Looking around for Grady's car, I was disappointed to see that it wasn't there. Why had they decided to execute the warrant, when they could plainly see that Grady wasn't there? All it would do is put him on the run.

"We just missed him," Evans said. "A neighbor told us that Grady left just a couple of minutes before we arrived. I can't help wondering if somebody tipped him off."

My mind immediately went to the accomplice in the Ritzville P.D. Could he have somehow heard about the pending arrest? Did he have a contact in the Spokane County Sheriff's Office?

"We didn't find any firearms, but there's gun-cleaning supplies and a few boxes of ammunition of different kinds. And we didn't find any boots to compare with our footprint casts."

And then something occurred to me. "Maybe he went to see his mother. Visiting hours at Eastern State Hospital started at 2:00," I said.

"You sure of that?" Evans demanded.

"Sure, I'm sure," I said. "Her name is Clarise Grady. And whether he's visiting her or not, he's scheduled to start work there at 4:00."

"How do you know all of this?" Evans asked.

"I was there just a couple of days ago, following-up on some information I had about Grady."

"That's a big place. How much do you know about the layout of the facility?"

I shrugged. "I took a quick tour after confirming that Grady works there."

"Okay, you're coming along!" To the other deputies, he shouted, "Listen up. Secure this scene. We're heading to the Eastern State Hospital. No sirens. We'll stage in the parking lot in front of the main building."

Riding with Evans on the way to Medical Lake, I explained about the Sunday visiting time, the buffet, and Grady's work schedule. He drove through the town and around the north end of East Medical Lake, to the gate at Eastern State Hospital.

Evans showed his arrest warrant to the security guard, and said, "The subject is an employee here, and also is a relative of a long-term patient."

The guard asked, "Do you need assistance with the arrest?"

"I have a team of deputies enroute. They'll be here in a minute or two. But it would be very helpful to have one of your guys to get us into the building where we expect to find our guy. I'm going to establish a staging area in the parking lot. If you could have someone meet me there, that would be great."

Evans parked off to the right-hand side of the main entrance, where he wouldn't be immediately spotted by people inside. A security guard arrived as the other deputies came down the drive to the staging area.

"I can't let you take your firearms in there," the security guard told Evans.

"Let's be clear on who has authority here. This is an official law-enforcement action, and I will not put my men at risk by sending them unarmed into a probable confrontation with a suspected killer."

"I understand, but last time I checked, state authority supersedes county authority."

"Then, please contact your boss and get this thing cleared."

We waited impatiently for five minutes while the dispute was resolved—in favor of Evans. On the likelihood that Grady would be with his mother, Evans led the deputies inside. I showed him to the corridor leading to the dining hall.

"Okay, keep your weapons holstered and try to avoid drawing attention to yourselves."

He divided the deputies into two equal groups. They were to enter the dining hall, where one group would go left, and the other would go right. They'd position themselves at intervals along the back wall. A supervisor joined Evans and me, and would identify Grady and Clarise.

She scanned the crowd of several hundred patients and visitors as the deputies took their positions. The visitors, in their street clothes, were easily distinguished from the patients, all of whom wore pale blue hospital gowns.

She whispered to Evans, "There they are. He's the one with the Yankees baseball hat."

I turned my eyes in the direction she was indicating. There was a sudden shout, just as I spotted the man with the Yankee hat. He picked up a plastic bowl full of potato salad and hurled it into the face of a patient. Then, he picked up a tray full of food and flipped it toward a different group of people.

Some of those hit by the flying food reacted by picking up their own trays and slinging them at other people. Within seconds, the entire dining hall erupted in a massive food fight. I strained to keep my eye on Grady, but quickly lost him in the melee. Evans signaled for his deputies to fan out and block all exits.

Dodging the weaponized vegetables and desserts, Evans and I fought our way through the mob in the direction where we'd last seen Grady. A swarm of orderlies came into the dining hall, trying desperately to get control of the patients, while visitors tried to take cover under the tables.

There was a loud crash when somebody threw a bench through a window. The glass shattered, but the steel mesh prevented anybody from going out. So many people were shouting that it was impossible for Evans to communicate with his deputies. The double door to the kitchen, on the north side of the dining hall was torn down, and a surge of people flooded through.

"That way!" Evans shouted.

We headed toward the kitchen, but were blocked by a seething mass of humanity. The orderlies began collecting patients into small groups and leading them out toward the psychiatric wings. As the crowd was thinning out, order was gradually restored in the dining hall, but chaos continued in the kitchen, where pots, pans, plates, and cups were flying in all directions.

The hospital security staff pressed through the mob and started removing the most conspicuous rioters. By the time Evans and I got into the kitchen, things were quieting down, but the damage was catastrophic. Parts of the mob had gone clear through the kitchen into the receiving area, and outside through the loading docks.

About ten minutes had passed since the start of the riot. Small groups of patients were wandering around in the courtyard behind the dining hall. We scanned the area in search of the man with the Yankee hat. I looked beyond the patients toward the Quonset huts.

"I think Grady works in one of those buildings. If he got out of the dining hall, he might be heading in that direction," I said, on the theory that his car would probably be parked there.

Evans had the same thought. He said, "Let's block the exit, in case he tries to drive out."

We sprinted up the roadway to a gate in the security fence next to the laundry building. The guard there let us through, to the north driveway, where we turned left and headed toward the Quonset hut parking area. The blue and white Oldsmobile was at the near side of the lot. As we cautiously approached it, Evans pulled out a pocket knife and cut the valve stems, flattening the tires on the left side of the car.

"That'll at least slow him down," he said.

We made a quick search of the Quonset hut, finding no sign of Grady. But when we came back outside, Evans shouted, "There he is!"

Grady was sprinting away from his car, carrying a rifle and a hand gun of some kind. Apparently, he had gone to the car while we were searching the Quonset hut.

"Smart move, with the tires," I said. "He might've gotten away."

Two other deputies saw us and joined in chasing Grady, who ran to an employee gate in the security fence. He fumbled in his pocket and pulled out a ring full of keys. He was a maintenance worker. Of course, he'd have keys to the buildings and gates.

He got through the gate, but seeing more officers approaching from the other side, he left it open and bolted across the courtyard and toward the West Lodge. He ducked into an alcove at a service entrance and hurriedly unlocked the door.

He went inside and slammed the door. When we got there and tried the door, we found it locked. Evans ordered his deputies to surround the building and cover all of the exits, while the security staff cleared the patients from the surrounding area.

On orders from Evans, a deputy brought one of the Sheriff's interceptors around behind the main building. Evans got on the radio and asked for additional units, and for snipers to deal with the barricaded subject. There was a crash, as a second-story window shattered. I saw the rifle barrel and dived behind the car. A shot rang out and a slug clanked off the front wheel. I recalled my assessment of Grady's marksmanship skills. This time, I might not be a moving target.

More sheriff's cars were brought around, and as additional units arrived, a barricade of vehicles encircled the West Lodge. Grady was moving around, firing shots from different windows. The security chief approached Evans and told him that there were patients inside the building. That severely limited our options.

Someone brought Evans a bullhorn, and he started trying to talk Grady into surrendering. Grady answered with a shot that took the rotating red beacon light off the roof of one of the State Patrol cruisers. There was no return fire, because of the presence of patients in the building.

The standoff continued past sundown, and portable lighting was brought in to illuminate the exterior of the West Lodge. The state's new Special Assault unit was brought in, and they started formulating a plan to flush Grady out of the building. Meanwhile, Evans continued trying to talk him into at least letting the patients leave.

Every few minutes, Grady would fire a few rounds at the police vehicles, moving randomly from one window to another, preventing any of the snipers from getting a bead on him.

"We're going to have to smoke him out," the assault team leader insisted.

"What about my patients?" the hospital security chief asked.

"They'll cough a lot, and their eyes will water. But they'll be fine, as soon as they're outside," the armor-clad officer said.

Without waiting for an answer, he checked his wristwatch and raised a flare pistol.

"Ready in three, two, one, NOW!" he shouted.

He fired a red flare, and half a dozen of his men fired tear gas cannisters into the building. As the cannisters popped, white smoke started rising out through the broken windows. All of the officers had weapons trained on the exits, expecting Grady to burst through.

Minutes passed, and we could hear coughing and screaming from inside. There was gunfire around on the far side of the building, and I thought Grady must be making his break. Evans ran to his car and got on the radio, demanding a report from anyone who could see what was going on. But there was confusion all around. Conflicting reports had only one thing in common—that Grady was still inside.

"What the hell is that?" someone shouted.

The smoke from one of the ground-floor windows turned from white to black. It quickly turned into a billowing mass of dense smoke and sooty orange flame. Then, black smoke started coming from other windows, on both levels.

"He must be setting fire to the building. Take him down on sight," the assault commander shouted.

The panicked screaming from inside became increasingly urgent.

"I'm going to let some people out," someone, apparently Grady, shouted from inside.

The double door flew open and several shots rang out. A swarm of people stumbled out into the courtyard, with tears leaving streaks down their soot-blackened faces. They were gasping for air and choking. Some rolled on the ground, trying to extinguish their burning clothes.

"Stay under cover," the assault commander shouted repeatedly, when orderlies started toward the patients, who were running in all directions.

Many of them fell to their hands and knees, begging for help. Behind them, the fire broke into an ominous roar, apparently fueled by the air rushing in through the open doors. There was a loud crack, followed quickly by two more, causing the orderlies who were trying to get to the patients to dive for cover.

The hospital's on-site fire engine company started spraying water on the west wing of the main building, where windows were cracking from the heat of the fire. At that point, they were more concerned about keeping the fire contained to the West Lodge than they were about trying to put it out.

When they got a second hose working, they started pouring water into the West Lodge through the broken windows, but it had no apparent effect. Licks of flame started breaking through the roof, reaching toward the night sky. Sirens in the distance announced the approach of Medical Lake's two volunteer fire companies.

It was agonizing to watch how long it took for them to get their hoses unreeled, connected up, and pressurized, while the fire engulfed the entire building. The sound of gunfire continued to come from inside, even though it was difficult to imagine anybody still being alive in there. I figured it was the sound of Grady's ammunition cooking-off in the fire.

Everyone started moving the vehicles back, as the heat began to blister the paint and crack the glass. No longer worrying about gunfire, orderlies, deputies, and firemen ran out to drag the patients to safety. With a mighty roar, the roof collapsed, and a towering burst of sparks and fire burst upward in a massive mushroom cloud.

Only the brick exterior walls remained standing, and the fire shot eighty feet into the air. Water from six or seven two-inch fire hoses could not cool the fire.

I heard one of the firefighters say, "Looks like it's time to break out the hot dogs and marshmallows."

By then, there was nothing more for the sheriff's deputies to do. Evans gathered them together and asked, "Did anyone see our subject—or anyone in street clothes—come out of the building?"

When nobody spoke, he said, "Okay then. Let's back out of here and let the fire fighters and doctors take care of things. We'll all meet in the parking lot by the Quonset hut."

Evans ordered a thorough search of Grady's car and a canvass of Grady's coworkers in the Quonset hut. I watched the fire, as it consumed the last combustible material left inside the brick shell. I doubted that any remains of William Grady would be found in the ashes.

It was after 10:00 when Evans drove me back to Grady's trailer in Four Lakes, where my car was parked. Along the way, we talked, agreeing that there was no way Grady could have survived. He would never stand trial—not for shooting at me, and not for killing Gail and Lisa Draper.

I stopped at a phone booth out by the highway and called Dale, to let her know that I was on my way home.

Then, I called Brant Litton and told him what had happened.

"So much for clearing Gordon Permann's name. With nobody else to convict, there'll always be a group of people who'll insist that the Adams County jury got it right.

Someone inside the Ritzville Police Department, probably Sergeant Terrance Sherman, had assisted Grady in both attempts on my life. Whether or not he was involved in killing the Draper girls, I couldn't say, but he certainly had participated in the cover-up. I could not let that go.

Chapter Forty

Grady's Accomplice
February 12, 1962

Monday morning, I called Deputy Evans and asked if anything found in the search of Grady's trailer pointed at the identity of an accomplice.

"The case is closed, Pratt. William Grady is a handful of ash. Isn't that enough for you?"

"Gordon Permann is still sitting on death row. So, hell no, that's not enough! Someone in the Ritzville P.D. was helping Grady cover-up his involvement in the murder."

"Well, whatever happened in Ritzville, it isn't *our* case," Evans said.

My personal opinion was that Evans didn't want to follow-up on this because of his law-enforcement officer's institutional resistance to the idea that *any* cop could have been Grady's accomplice. Clearly, I was on my own.

I drove back to Four Lakes and parked next to Grady's trailer, which was still draped in yellow and black Police Evidence tape. I noted that the sheriff's seal on the front door remained unbroken—until I picked the lock and opened the door.

The deputies who conducted the search had shown no respect whatsoever for Grady's property. They'd torn the place up and dumped everything onto the floor. I got to my hands and knees and started pawing through the clothes, papers, magazines, food, dishes, and correspondence that covered the floor.

Not surprisingly, I found nothing of importance there, so I started looking for a hiding place where Grady could conceal his most coveted secrets. I looked in the backs of every built-in cabinet, in closets and cupboards, and in every piece of furniture. I pored over every square inch of the wall and ceiling paneling. I looked for a patch in the floor, anything that didn't match the trailer's original construction or décor.

In the bathroom, I noticed an electric space heater built into the wall. Its placement was odd—in a corner, where the adjacent wall would be exposed to radiant heat that could start a fire. I could not believe that the trailer manufacturer would put a heater there. And there was no sign of discoloration or scorching around the heater. I tried turning it on, but nothing happened.

I got a screwdriver and removed the heater from the wall. There was no electrical wiring. The cavity behind the heater contained two packages wrapped in brown paper from grocery bags, tied tightly with twine. I extracted the bundles from the wall and carried them to the kitchen counter.

The smaller package contained a bundle of letters and greeting cards secured by a couple of rubber bands. I flipped quickly through the letters and cards, but found nothing that fingered Tec Sherman as Grady's accomplice. I re-stacked the correspondence and put the rubber bands back on.

In the larger package, I found a photo scrapbook containing black-and-white photos from Grady's youth, a few picture post cards and some newspaper clippings. Among the clippings was a vital records column dated June 24, 1954, from the Yakima Herald, showing the marriage of Peter Fraiser to Doreen Grady. It didn't register immediately, and I had already put it aside, when I realized what I'd seen.

Doreen Grady? Peter Fraiser? *Holy shit!* Doreen Fraiser was William Grady's sister, Rena. That meant that *she* was Grady's accomplice in the Ritzville P.D. I could only imagine all of the ways she could have manipulated the evidence and misdirected the investigation.

I took the scrapbook and the rubber-banded packet of letters, and headed back to my car, locking the trailer door as I left. As I raced down the highway toward Ritzville, I wondered if Doreen had gotten the news about the fire at Medical Lake. And did she know that her brother's trailer had been searched?

At Ritzville, I rushed inside and told Sergeant Sherman that I had to see the chief right away.

"What do you want the chief for?" he asked.

"That's between him and me," I said, not wanting to say anything that Doreen might overhear that would reveal what I knew.

Chief Donnelly stepped out of his office and demanded, "What the hell do you want now, Pratt?"

"Can we talk in your office?" I asked.

"I'm busy here, so make it quick," Donnelly said, as he closed his door behind us.

"As you know, I've been working on the Gordon Permann appeal."

"Don't expect any help from me on that."

"Is Doreen Fraiser here today?" I asked.

He gave me a curious look. "As a matter of fact, she's two hours overdue, and she doesn't answer her phone. Do you know something about that?"

"Yes. I'm afraid I do," I said, wondering where to begin.

"Do you know where she is?"

"No. But she's on the run. You need to put out an APB on her," I said.

"Don't tell me what I need to do," he said. "Why would Doreen be on the run?"

I took a deep breath. "For three months, I've been building a case against an unknown suspect in the Draper murders. Last month, I finally got a name for him—William Tanner. We tracked him down using the description of the suspect's vehicle provided by the witness Chet Winston."

"So what? That's how we got Permann," the chief said.

"Not exactly. Permann was picked because he had owned a Chevy Fleetline. What Winston said he saw was an Oldsmobile. In fact, he specifically said that it was *not* a Chevrolet."

"You are mistaken. We've always known it was a Chevy, right from the original APB."

I said, "And that's where Doreen Fraiser comes in. She deliberately edited Winston's statement, and changed the suspect car from an Oldsmobile to a Chevrolet."

"I don't believe that," he said. But with less confidence than he'd had in the beginning.

"She deliberately damaged the tape recording of Winston's interview, to prevent anyone from comparing her transcription with what was actually said. But I was able to repair the tape enough to make a fairly clear copy. It proves what I'm telling you."

"Where is that tape?" he demanded.

"The original? After I was finished restoring the tape, Doreen put it back in the evidence file—or at least she said she did."

The chief pressed his intercom button. "Sergeant Sherman! Bring me the evidence file for the Draper case!"

"All of it?" Sherman asked.

"Yes, all of it. And make it fast."

A few minutes later, Sherman brought two boxes into the chief's office, and then he went back and brought two more. The chief was already digging through the boxes in search of the interview tape.

"It should be pretty easy to find," I said. "It's a seven-inch reel in a Scotch recording tape box."

"Well, I sure as hell don't see it here," the chief growled.

I shook my head. "That can only mean that she's gotten rid of it."

"And you can't prove a damned thing."

"Well, that's not exactly true. You see, in the process of restoring the tape, I made a copy of it."

"Okay, so where is that?"

"It's in my office in Spokane. But we need to act *now*. I played the tape for Spokane County Sheriff's Deputy Wayne Evans. He's heard it, and he's compared it with the written transcription. Get him on the phone, and he'll confirm what I'm telling you."

The conversation with Evans was brief and to the point. Yes, he'd heard the tape and was convinced that it was authentic. And yes, it proved that the transcription had been deliberately edited.

"Okay, so let's say that I believe all of this. How does that get Permann off the hook?" he asked.

"He owned a blue Chevy. Winston saw a green Oldsmobile."

"But Winston identified Permann himself in court. So did that waitress," Donnelly objected.

"I tracked the green Olds to a kid in Wapato. I shot Polaroids of his yearbook picture, along with those of three other guys who also matched the general descriptions given by the witnesses. When I showed them the photo spread, both witnesses picked my suspect."

"So, who the hell is he?"

I said, "When he was in school, he went by the name of William Tanner. But I found out last week that his real name was William Grady."

"William Grady? Wasn't he the guy in the big fire at the insane asylum last night?"

"Yes, he was," I said.

Then, I opened Grady's scrapbook to the newspaper clipping.

"Doreen Fraiser's maiden name was Grady. She is William Grady's sister."

The chief exhaled loudly. "Jesus Christ!"

He pressed the intercom button and said, "Sergeant Sherman! Get over to Doreen's place and see what the hell's going on. Break down the door if you have to. We'll call it a welfare check."

Ten minutes later, Sherman radioed-in that Doreen was not home, and it looked like she'd left in a hurry. Closets were open, and dresser drawers were emptied out.

I said to Donnelly, "I've been thinking about this all morning. It seems to me that if she's on the run, she probably got money from her bank. Can you find out about that?"

"Yeah. You want to come along?"

We met Sherman outside as he returned from Doreen's place. "We're going after her, Sergeant. We'll take my unmarked car. You're driving."

We made a stop at the Ritzville branch of the National Bank of Commerce. The chief knew that Doreen did her banking there, because he had deposited paychecks for her a couple of times.

"Funny you should ask, Chief," the teller said. "She was here about forty-five minutes ago. Closed her checking and savings accounts. Left with a little over $2,000 in cash. I asked why she was doing it, but she basically told me to mind my own business."

We went back out to the car, and the chief got on the radio and told the dispatcher to put out an APB on Doreen's red and white Plymouth Fury hardtop.

I said, "I don't think she went north. I'd have passed her on my way down here. So, she almost has to be going toward either Moses Lake or Tri-Cities."

The chief added that information to the APB. I unfolded a map and looked for the best way to get to Yakima or Wapato, on the theory that perhaps Doreen had in-laws or friends in that area.

"If I was going to Yakima, I think I'd start down US-395, and then cut west on Route 11A—and cross the Columbia on the ferry at Vernita."

"Sergeant, you heard the man. South on 395, code three. With the head start she got, she could already be on 11A."

Back on the radio, Donnelly requested a roadblock at the Vernita Ferry. Thirty minutes later, we were approaching Connell, where the turnoff to Route 11A was located, when the radio squawked. We were well out of range of Ritzville dispatch. This call was coming in on the State Patrol channel.

"Chief Donnelly, your APB calls for a 1958 Plymouth Fury hardtop, white over red. Is that correct?"

Donnelly said, "Affirmative. What's happening?"

"Our traffic unit was northbound on 395, near Eltopia. They reported a car matching that description heading south at a high rate of speed. By the time our guys got turned around, the car was too far ahead to catch up. They lost it in the traffic approaching Pasco."

"Stay on 395, Sergeant," the chief said, just as Sherman was slowing for the turn onto 11A.

"All right Pratt, since you're so good at predicting her route, which way's she going now?"

"If she's not going to Yakima, maybe she's heading for the new interstate in Oregon. I say that, only because it's the fastest highway around."

Ten or fifteen minutes later, as we were approaching Pasco, the chief asked for an update on the State Patrol checkpoint on 395 near Wallula.

"Nothing yet on that Plymouth Fury."

"Damn! If she's going that way, she should've gone past there by now. Sergeant, cross the bridge to Kennewick, and then take US-410 toward Prosser."

On the radio he told the State Patrol, "If she doesn't show up at Wallula in the next few minutes, we can assume that she went a different direction. We're heading west on 410."

While the chief was on the radio, I was thinking ahead as to where Doreen might be going. I remembered the bundle of letters in my jacket pocket, taken from Grady's trailer. I started leafing through them, looking at the return addresses on the envelopes.

I said to the chief, "Maybe there's something in here that'll tell us where she's going."

"Yeah, well read fast," Donnelly said.

And then, one caught my eye. "Here's something from Mabton, west of Prosser. It's a Christmas card from Don Strayhorn, postmarked December 4, 1958."

I opened the card and read aloud, "Merry Christmas from the Horse Heaven Hills. Donna and I are all settled into the new place, and it's sure great to be out of the city. Rena and Pete are coming for a visit between Christmas and New Years, so I'm extending the same invitation to you—a reunion of the old Wapato gang. Let me know if you can make it. Don."

The chief said, "Well, I don't know who Don is, and I don't know how to find his address. But right now, it's the best thing we have."

Ten minutes later, a WSP officer reported, "One of our cars is on Highway 3, approaching Prosser from Sunnyside. He reports no sighting of the subject vehicle."

Donnelly complained, "I wish to hell that somebody would see her. I hate to keep navigating by what they *don't* see."

Sherman said, "If she came this way, she had to have turned off at Prosser. That would mean either Highway 8, heading toward Patterson, or Highway 3A, heading toward Mabton."

I said, "I vote for Mabton."

Donnelly keyed the mic and said, "We're going to turn off at Prosser and head toward Mabton."

"It's like she knows exactly what we're doing at every step along the way, almost like she's here in the car listening to us," I commented.

Donnelly groaned. "Oh, shit. She *is* listening to us."

"Don't tell me…" I said.

"She has a police radio. Last year, when Motorola came out with the transistorized version of the Private Line transceiver, we upgraded and sold-off the old vacuum tube radios. The crystals were removed to prevent people from using our frequencies, but some of the radios went to members of the department, with the crystals still in them. Doreen bought one of them."

"Can we transmit something to mislead her?" I suggested.

"Good idea. But first, we need to find out where she's going. We need to see a postal delivery map of Mabton. Sherman, stop at the first gas station you see in Mabton and ask where the post office is."

As we approached Mabton, Donnelly keyed his mic and said, "WSP, please be advised that we are passing through Mabton, heading toward Toppenish."

It took us a frustrating five minutes to find the post office, and five more to study the map and write down directions to the Strayhorn address.

"Based on the rate that she's been moving, Doreen probably is already at the Strayhorn place," Donnelly said. "I hope she'll relax a bit, thinking that we're off her trail. We'll approach with no lights or siren."

A gravel road led to an area where the land had been divided into twenty-acre parcels, and sold as ranchettes. We found the Strayhorn driveway next to a sign advertising Strayhorn's Crop-Dusting Service. The driveway led to a tidy single-level house, a detached garage, and a small airplane hangar, set back about 200 feet from the road. Doreen's red and white Plymouth Fury was parked next to the garage.

"What's our plan?" Sherman asked.

The chief said, "Stop between her car and the house. You and I will approach the door, weapons ready. Pratt, you stay behind the car and keep us covered with that relic of yours."

Sherman hadn't even shut off the engine when the ranch house door opened, and a slim lady with long, blond hair and a cowboy hat stepped outside. She stood with her hands on her hips watching us.

"Okay. Don't show your weapon," Donnely told Sherman. "But be ready in case Doreen comes out behind her."

"Good afternoon, ma'am," the chief said. "We're with the Ritzville Police Department. We're looking for Doreen Fraiser."

The lady on the porch smiled, and said, "Oh, you just missed her. She left here about five minutes ago."

The chief pointed at the Plymouth. "Without her car?"

The lady laughed. "No, they borrowed our old pickup truck."

She extended her hand and said," I'm Donna Strayhorn."

"You said 'they.' Was someone with her?"

"Well, yeah. Her husband."

That was a surprise, since I understood that Doreen and Peter had been separated for several years.

"You mean Peter Fraiser?" Donnelly asked.

"Oh, heavens no. They split up three years ago. She has a new husband—Larry Carson."

Donnelly looked at Sherman. "Did you know about that?"

"This is the first I've heard about it."

Donna said, "Yeah, I didn't know about Larry either, until Rena called this morning and said they were coming here."

The chief frowned, and asked, "Do you know where they went when they left here?"

"They asked me for directions to Roosevelt—the Arlington Ferry. They're heading to his family's place in Condon, Oregon."

"Why did they want to borrow your pickup?"

"His parents are getting old, and they're moving into a retirement home. He and Rena are going to help them clean-out their house, so they can put it up for sale."

"Is your husband here?" Donnelly asked.

"No. He's in Yakima meeting with apple growers. Too bad, because I'm sure he'd have liked to see Rena. She and her brother went to school with Don. Hopefully, he'll be home when they come back next week"

"Would you mind if we take a quick look around?"

"Not at all. But like I said, nobody else is here."

"I believe you," Donnelly said, "but we still need to follow procedure."

Donnelly and Sherman went quickly through the house, garage, and hangar, confirming that Doreen wasn't there.

"You mentioned that they're coming back next week. Do you know exactly when?"

Donna said, "Larry said it would take two or three days to get everything done in Condon."

"Can you give me a description of the pickup?"

"It's a '54 Chevy three-quarter ton. Two-tone. Green and rust."

She gave Donnelly the license plate number and asked, "What's all this about? Rena isn't in some kind of trouble, is she?"

"That's what we're trying to find out, Donnelly said.

Chapter Forty-One

Race to the River

We had no time to waste. If Doreen got across the Columbia River ahead of us, she could go any direction and lose us permanently. And once we crossed the state line, we would have no authority and would have a difficult time getting any help from Oregon officials.

Bickleton Road, going out of Mabton, wound steeply up into the Horse Heaven Hills, and then turned southwest for eighteen miles to Bickleton. It was a paved two-lane road with no shoulders and lots of blind corners. Sherman drove as fast as he dared, but our average speed was probably under fifty.

When we turned south going out of Bickleton, we found ourselves on a winding road with long unpaved stretches of washboarded gravel. The last six-mile stretch was a steep downgrade with many blind curves and switchbacks. Even though it was paved, it was slow going.

"Well, *they* can't go any faster than we can," Sherman said.

"They had a fifteen-minute head start on us when we left Strayhorn's place. They've probably already reached the ferry landing. But there's a good chance that they got hung-up waiting for the ferry. There's only one boat, and it takes a long time to get across the river and back, so I'm hoping we'll catch up with them there," Donnelly said.

"If not, we're screwed," I said.

When the ferry landing came into view, we could see that the ferry was there, partially loaded, with nobody waiting in line. Sherman raced the last half-mile, and we arrived at the landing just as the landing guard was preparing to close the gate. One last car came down the hill behind us, and the guard let both of us through.

As soon as we were aboard the ferry, the cable barrier was stretched across behind us and the ramp was raised. Only then did I look around. The eight-car ferry was filled to capacity, with two rows of four cars each. We were at the back of the right-hand row. At the front of the left-hand row sat an old green Chevy pickup with two people visible inside.

The ferry was powered by a small tugboat secured to the right-hand, or downstream, side of the ferry. Hand-painted lettering on the side of the pilot house said Ben Flippin, Captain. The deck hand signaled the captain, and with a rumble, the ferry pulled away from shore.

It was a particularly blustery evening, so nobody was allowed to get out of the vehicles while the ferry was underway. Once we emerged from the sheltered cove onto the open water, the reason became apparent. A stiff wind blew upstream against the strong downstream current, and even though the ferry was staying on course toward Arlington, it was constantly being wrenched around by the conflicting forces.

Waves occasionally slapped against the side of the ferry, sending spray across the deck. This ferry was either a triumph of human engineering, or a monumentally reckless test of luck. I silently made my survival plan for the seemingly high probability of something going wrong.

As we approached the Oregon shore, we entered a nicely sheltered harbor, and suddenly found ourselves in calm water, free of current and somewhat sheltered from the wind.

Donnelly said, "We have to take them down before they get off the ferry. Sherman, you approach on the left. I'll take the right, and Pratt, you stay close. Be ready to go whichever way you need to, as the situation unfolds. Weapons ready."

We got out of the car, crouched down and crept forward, Sherman on the left, and Donnelly and I on the right.

"Hey, what are you guys doing?" the deck hand said loudly as we reached the midpoint on the ferry's deck.

Donnelly held up his badge and said, "Police action. Get back and stay down!"

I saw the silhouette of the driver as he turned to look in our direction. The pickup's brake lights came on, and I heard the engine start.

"Let's go," Donnelly said urgently.

We raised our weapons and rushed toward the pickup.

"Shut off the engine and show your hands. Do it!" Sherman demanded loudly.

I took position at the right rear corner of the pickup and drew a bead on the driver. The chief edged cautiously toward the passenger door.

Sherman again ordered the driver to shut off the engine.

As the ferry drew close to the landing, the tugboat's propeller was thrown into reverse, and the engine rumbled loudly. The ferry slowed to a crawl, twenty feet from the point where the roadway met the water's edge. Sherman tapped his weapon against the driver's window.

There was a sudden roar as the driver revved the engine and popped the clutch. The tire next to me spun and screeched as the pickup lunged forward, barely slowed by the cable barrier. The cable snapped and flailed wildly as the pickup blasted up the still-raised loading ramp.

If it was the driver's intention to jump the gap and land on the roadway, he misjudged badly. The pickup got halfway off the ramp, nosed-over, and plunged into the six-foot-deep water, landing upside down, the rear wheels protruding from the water about two yards from the river's edge.

The ferry stopped, and I worked my way forward to look off the end of the partially lowered ramp. The green water obscured most of the truck, and bubbles rose from the submerged, inverted cab.

"Damn!" Sherman exclaimed. He kicked off his shoes, stripped off his uniform jacket, and jumped feet-first into the ice-cold water, next to the driver's side door. I did the same on the passenger side.

The shock of the cold water took my breath away. My barely-healed frostbite protested painfully, making me feel light-headed and nauseous. I kicked myself into a surface dive and groped for the door handle. On my second try, I found it, but the door would not open. I dived over and over, trying to force the door open. Someone passed me a jack handle, which I used in a futile attempt to pry the door open.

Exhausted, freezing, and losing my ability to swim, I struggled to shore, and stumbled up the pavement to dry concrete. A lady from one of the cars waiting to board the ferry brought me a blanket, and I gratefully pulled it around my shoulders. Sherman was still trying to pry the driver's door open, with the help of the deck hand who'd jumped in.

Spectators cheered when Sherman came to the surface with the limp body of the driver. I shucked off my blanket and waded in to help him pull the unconscious man up onto dry land. His lips were blue and he was not breathing. He had a deep gash on the side of his head. I attempted artificial respiration as I'd been taught in army basic training, but lacked the strength and coordination to do it effectively.

A teenager who had been in another of the cars waiting to get on the ferry said he'd learned how to perform artificial respiration as a Boy Scout. He took over, and I huddled under my blanket trying to stop shaking. A fire engine arrived, and one of the firemen took over, using an oxygen ventilator. One of the other firemen called for an ambulance.

The deck hand who had been helping Sherman shouted something, and Sherman waded back into the water and helped drag the lifeless body of Doreen Fraiser up onto the pavement. A fireman checked her vital signs, and then covered her body with a yellow blanket.

"Does anybody know the identity of this man?" asked the fireman who had been forcing oxygen into the man's lungs.

I said, "I believe his name is Larry Carson. We were told that he has family in Condon."

"Do you know their names?"

I shrugged. "Carson, I assume."

By the time an ambulance arrived, Carson was breathing on his own, and his head injury had been bandaged up. But he remained unconscious.

"We'll have to take him to The Dalles," the ambulance driver said.

The fireman gave the driver the notes he had taken, including the name and location of Carson's family. By then, a big Holmes wrecker was on scene. They tossed a grappling hook out and snagged the pickup's rear axle.

There was a grinding noise as they dragged the pickup partway out of the water. While the tow-truck operator was re-rigging his cables to turn the pickup upright, a black coroner's hearse arrived. After documenting the death of Doreen Fraiser, the coroner loaded her into the hearse and drove away.

Once the pickup was back on its wheels, the tow-truck pulled it up and away from the ferry landing, making room for the ferry to finally pull-in and unload. Chief Donnelly drove his car over to where Sergeant Sherman and I were.

"Shall we see if there's a motel here, where you guys can get warm and dry your clothes?"

"That's the best idea I've heard all day," Sherman said.

I phoned Dale from my motel room and told her about our four-hour chase and Doreen's fatal splash into the river. I left out the details that I knew would not be well-received.

Chapter Forty-Two

Loose Ends

February 13, 1962

In the morning, we checked out of our motel and drove back to Ritzville. Along the way, I told the chief that he probably would have to testify about Doreen's actions with regard to the Draper case, and the circumstances of her death.

"With both Doreen and William Grady dead, there's nobody left to face charges in the Draper case. That could severely limit Brant Litton's options in Gordon Permann's appeal."

The chief said, "You've proved to me that Doreen manipulated the evidence, but I'm still not convinced that Permann didn't do it."

"I hope the supreme court sees it differently," I said.

I called Litton from the pay phone at Hand's Café.

"They're both dead," I told him. "We may never know exactly what happened to Gail and Lisa."

"Let's get together tomorrow and figure out where to go from here."

In my office on Wednesday, before leaving for that meeting, I got a call from Chief Donnelly.

"There's something going on in Oregon. The guy Sherman pulled out of the truck regained consciousness overnight. Based on what you told the firemen at the ferry landing, he was registered in the hospital as Larry Carson. But there's something hinky about that, starting with the fact that he can't prove it."

I said, "Well, I know that they didn't find any I.D. on him when they were loading him into the ambulance. I assume he lost it in his crash."

"The thing is, when he first woke up, the doctor addressed him as Mr. Carson, but he seemed to be confused about that."

"Well, he did have a head injury," I said.

"Yeah, and that's what they figured was responsible for his confusion. Then, they told him that his wife had drowned in the crash. He started to say that he wasn't married, and—according to the doctor—seemed to remember something that suddenly cleared up his confusion."

"Is that so unusual?" I asked.

"I don't know. But when the hospital staff started trying to fill-in his paperwork, he couldn't remember his address, his employer, or his insurance company. When they pressed him to say how he planned to pay for the ambulance ride and the hospital bill, he said that there was $2,000 cash in his wife's purse."

"That would be the money Doreen withdrew from the bank."

"Right. And her purse was found in the pickup, with the cash still in it. But Arlington Police won't give it to Carson until he proves that he's married to Doreen—and I don't believe that he is."

"What about Carson's parents in Condon? They should be able to say, one way or the other."

Donnelly agreed, "Yeah, except Arlington P.D. checked, and there's nobody named Carson living in Condon."

I said, "Maybe his old man died or split, and his mother re-married. They'd be living under the step-father's name."

"Well, this is where the Oregon State Police got involved. They want to know what happened on the ferry that led to Doreen's drowning. When they asked him about his parents in Condon, he said that his parents had been dead for years, and he didn't know anybody in Condon."

"At Strayhorn's place, they knew they were hot as long as they kept driving Doreen's car, so they had to come up with a plausible excuse for borrowing the old pickup. That's when they invented Carson's parents in Condon."

"When you look at the individual parts of this, you can explain them. But when you put them all together, the big picture just doesn't make sense."

"So, what's your theory?" I asked.

"His name isn't Larry Carson, and he was never married to Doreen Fraiser."

I sighed. "Yeah, that thought has been crowding its way into my mind, ever since Donna Strayhorn told us about him."

"So, who is he?"

"He has to be someone connected with this case. I saw William Grady incinerated in the hospital fire, so there must've been another accomplice."

"Yeah, but who?"

"The guy in the hospital in The Dalles."

"You just went in a circle."

"I know. But try this on: Doreen had *two* brothers, William and an older brother, who lived somewhere around Woodinville."

Donnelly said, "And you think he might be Larry Carson?"

"It's the only idea I have at this point."

* * * * * *

I had just put down the receiver from that call, when my phone rang again.

"This is Wayne Evans. Fasten your seatbelt, Pratt. Our guys have been processing everything they found in Grady's trailer. Looks like you were right about him."

"What have they found?" I asked.

"For starters, fingerprints were lifted from all over the trailer, and we found a match for the one on the cupcake wrapper from the nest of the gunman who took the shot at you."

"That's good, but the photo of his car at the scene already connected him with that."

"Fingerprints are not the only things our guys found in the trailer. There was also a receipt from an auto parts store for a fuel filter and fuel pump for a 1950 Oldsmobile. It was dated March 14, 1960—just two days before the start of the state tournament.

I said, "That confirms that he had been having car troubles before he drove to Seattle.

"Right. So—just speculating here—maybe he replaced the filter and thought the problem was fixed. But then while he was in Seattle, the problem came back. Now, suppose he hadn't taken the fuel pump along. Rather than buy another, he decided to take the chance and drive home.

"And he hedged his bet by getting the girls to follow him." I speculated.

"Exactly. And by the time he got to Ritzville, the car was running so bad, he had to leave it, and ride with Lisa and Gail. When they arrived at his trailer, the girls went inside—maybe to use the bathroom, after drinking the cherry Cokes at Hand's Café. And that's when Billy Boy made his move."

"Was there evidence of an assault in the trailer?" I asked.

"Yeah. Our techs scraped a spot of blood off of the floor. It's Type AB. Less than four percent of the population have that. Lisa Draper had appendix surgery in 1958, and records show that she had Type AB.

I mused, "So, he gets them to strip, cuffs them, and at some point, he kills them. Moves the luggage from the trunk to the backseat of the Falcon, and puts the bodies in the trunk. Takes along the new fuel pump and maybe a few tools. Dumps the bodies on the reservation, then gets back to Ritzville in the middle of the night and gets his car running. Pretty long day for him"

"That's how it all adds up."

I said, "Well that's good circumstantial evidence, but…"

"Easy, Pratt. I'm just getting to the good stuff. In a drawer right next to his bed, we found a pair of Pep Club pins—Central Valley Pep Club pins."

"Holy shit!"

"We checked with Earl Draper. Lisa and Gail had Pep Club pins. They should have been on their jumpers, which were packed in their suitcases. When Lisa's car was released to the Drapers, they gave away a lot of the clothes. But they kept the Pep Club jumpers. Earl checked, and the pins aren't there."

I was jubilant. "With that, we just might get Permann out of prison."

Evans said, "I still haven't gotten to the best part. You know that guy you fished out of the Columbia?"

"Larry Carson?" I asked.

"Yeah, except his name's not Carson. I just got a call from the Oregon State Police. They found a wallet wedged behind the seat in wrecked pickup truck. It belongs to William Grady."

"So, you think…"

"No. We *know*. Remember when you speculated that Grady's fingerprints might be on file because of his job at Eastern State Hospital? Well, we never followed up on that, but Oregon State Police *did*, and the prints confirm that the man in the hospital in The Dalles is William Grady."

"So, he somehow got away from the fire…"

"Yeah, we figure he put on one of those hospital gowns and ran out with all of the patients. In all of the confusion, he shucked his gown and slipped away. He must've called his sister, who picked him up and took him to her place in Ritzville. The next day they went on the run."

"So, what's next for him?"

"OSP has charged Grady with reckless driving and negligent homicide in the death of Doreen Fraiser. He's chained to his bed, and he'll stay there until he's recovered sufficiently to be moved to jail. Meanwhile, since we now believe that the Draper girls were killed in his trailer, Spokane County is charging him with the double murder and a bucketful of related charges."

I was speechless.

"And there's one last thing that might interest you. In Grady's car at the Eastern State Hospital, we found a coil of olive-green parachute cord—just like what was used to rig your car."

I thought to myself, *Yeah, and just like what was found at the Peyton-Allan crime scene. Could it be…*

* * * * * *

I shared the news with Brant Litton, who immediately called the governor, provoking a flurry of activity in Olympia with regards to Gordon Permann. Spokane County issued a warrant for Grady's arrest for the kidnapping and murder of Lisa and Gail Draper, and sent an extradition request to Oregon.

"How many times did this case almost kill you?" Dale asked over dinner that evening.

"Horseshoes and hand grenades," I said.

"Yeah. And atom bombs," she said. "Close *does* count."

"What counts is that we got the guy who killed Lisa and Gail Draper, and saved an innocent man from execution."

"I'm not diminishing the outcome. What you accomplished is heroic. But you need to be more careful. That wasn't just about you. Your children might have been left without a father."

I almost missed it.

"Wait. You said 'children'…"

Dale smiled. "Yes, I did—due September third."

We spent the evening in front of the fireplace, with Nancy crawling all over and around us.

Over the next few days, we learned that William Grady had no resources to fight extradition to Washington, so he was transported to Spokane to be held without bail, pending trial. Additional charges were added, for the deaths of three patients in the fire at Eastern State Hospital.

The governor vacated Permann's conviction, and he was released from prison. He moved to Idaho and vowed to never again set foot in the state of Washington.

Disbarment proceedings were brought against Adams County Prosecutor Jacob Novak, but he died from a heart attack before his hearing.

So, *not everybody* lived happily ever after.

Epilogue

Subsequent Events

As of March, 1962, three major murder cases in the Northwest remained unsolved. By March 6th, three years after Candy Rogers was abducted and murdered, Police had compiled a list of likely suspects, including (among others) Alfred Graves, James Barnett, and Hugh Bion Morse.

Alfred Graves took his own life on the day Candy's body was found. He had lived just half a mile from her apartment, and died three-quarters of a mile from the place where Candy's Campfire mints were found. But dead men tell no tales, and detectives would never be able to conclusively determine whether he was or was not the killer.

In February 1960. James Barnett hanged himself in jail, four days after he was arrested on suspicion of having committed a sex crime against a child. And he had lived two blocks from the Rogers apartment. On the wall of his cell, he had written, "I have sinned against the Lord."

Upon being informed of his death, Barnett's wife said, "That bastard killed Candy Rogers, didn't he?"

So, like Graves, Barnett remained a suspect.

A number of other suspects had been investigated, but the one that stood out was Hugh Bion Morse. He was known to have attacked and killed women in several cities around the country, and he had confessed to two murders in Spokane around the time of the Candy Rogers killing.

Even though Morse confessed to numerous sexual assaults and murders, he adamantly denied having murdered Candy Rogers. But there was a witness who had been with him at the site where Candy's body was found, less than a week before she was killed.

And, more than anything else, the thing that interested police was Morse's taste for Adams grape-flavored chewing gum, because grape-smelling gum had been found on Candy's sweater and coat. Grape gum had also been found at the scenes of the two Spokane murders for which Morse had plead guilty.

Candy's parents were separated at the time of her murder. Her father, Carl Rogers shot and killed himself with a revolver in a hotel room in Walla Walla in June, 1963. Her mother, Elaine Rogers lived until 2006, never knowing who killed her daughter.

In the 1990s, when DNA science was being developed as an investigative tool, Spokane detectives took a fresh look at the evidence in the Rogers case, which had been carefully preserved. Spots of semen on Candy's clothing eventually yielded a DNA profile in 2001. That profile was compared with those of several suspects, including Hugh Morse. There was no match.

Morse died in prison in April of 2003. Some detectives refused to accept the DNA results as conclusive proof that Morse was innocent of the murder. For everyone else, the focus shifted back to Alfred Graves and James Barnett. But their DNA was unavailable, so they could neither be confirmed nor excluded as the killer.

In 2014, the Spokane Police Department's history committee published a series of books about the department's history. *Life Behind the Badge Volume IV*, included a summary of the unsolved Candy Rogers case as it stood at that time.

In the same book, ten pages after that discussion, there was an unrelated article about the department's acquisition of the new Identi-Kit, a tool for creating composite drawings of suspects with the help of eyewitnesses.

The article included a composite image created using Identi-Kit, next to the November 10, 1961 booking photos of their first arrest resulting from the use of this investigative tool. The suspect was John Reigh Hoff, who would be convicted of second-degree assault and spend six months in jail.

Then, in 2015, Cece Moore pioneered the use of genetic genealogy in solving cold cases. After her success in solving the Golden State Killer case made the news, Spokane detectives wondered if this technology might finally solve the Candy Rogers case.

On November 19, 2021, Spokane police announced that they had positively identified the man who abducted, raped, and murdered Candy Rogers. His name was John Reigh Hoff—the same man arrested in 1961 as a result of an Identi-Kit composite image. During the six months he spent in the Spokane County Jail, he was never suspected in the Candy Rogers Case.

John Reigh Hoff had been 19 years old at the time of Candy Rogers murder. He killed himself in 1970. It would be interesting to know if Hoff drove a bright green car in 1959, though it wouldn't change the certainty of his guilt. The Candy Rogers case is finally closed.

Rest in peace, Candice Elaine Rogers
July 18, 1949 – March 6, 1959.

* * * * * *

By 1966, the Peyton-Allan case had baffled Portland and Multnomah County investigators for nearly six years, during which time detectives interviewed 2,292 suspects, of whom only 453 were cleared. By October of 1966, the active file listed 47 suspects for the murders.

One suspect *not* on that list was Edward Wayne Edwards, nor was he among those cleared. He was seemingly just forgotten. Edwards was arrested for setting-off fire alarms in Portland, on

December 9, 1960, less than two weeks after Larry Peyton's body was found.

When Edwards was booked into the Rocky Butte jail, he was found to have a partially-healed bullet wound in his upper left arm. What's more, a police officer had talked with Edwards, who had been seen among spectators milling around at the crime scene the day after Peyton was found.

The bullet wound was of special interest, because there was a never-unexplained bullet hole in the windshield of Larry Peyton's car, so police wanted to question Edwards about the case. But before that happened, Edwards had a friend phone the jail. Posing as Edwards's parole officer, he asked that Edwards be released. Astoundingly, that is what happened. They simply let him walk out of jail.

On November 10, 1961, an article in the Oregon Journal featured a photo of Edwards, because he had just been placed on the FBI's Ten Most-Wanted List in connection with bank robberies in the eastern US. The article resurrected the humiliating story of how Edwards escaped from Rocky Butte, but apparently did not renew interest in him as a suspect in the Peyton-Allan murders.

Finally, late in October of 1966, Earl Son, chief homicide detective in the sheriff's office, received an anonymous letter placing blame for the Peyton-Allan murders on Eddie Jorgensen, his brother Carl, and Bob Brom.

All three had been previously questioned in the case, and all had prior brushes with the law. For the next two years, the Peyton-Allan investigation team focused on the Jorgensen brothers and Bob Brom, and finally, on August 19, 1968, the men were arrested and charged. All three plead not guilty.

The case against them was built entirely around the testimony of Nikki Sallak, a witness whose memory of the case had been "restored" through the use of hypnosis and psycho-active drugs. In court, the highly-questionable techniques used in these sessions were passed-off as routine and acceptable. And believing the testimony of that witness required ignoring the statements from several far more credible witnesses.

Raymond Ward, a service station attendant at the Flying A Truck Stop on Barbur Boulevard in southwest Portland, called police two days after Peyton's body was found. Ward said that at around 1:00 to 1:30 a.m. on November 26, he had pumped gas into a car matching the one described in news accounts of the murder scene. He gave accurate details of the car that had never been made public.

The problem for prosecutors was that Ward's timeline excluded the possibility of Brom and the Jorgensen brothers being responsible for the crime. So, they simply ignored his statement. Instead, they bolstered their case with testimony from a couple of jailhouse snitches who testified that the defendants had bragged of their guilt while in jail. In exchange for their testimony, they received favorable treatment in their own cases.

In the end, Carl Jorgensen, who was tried separately, was acquitted; but Eddie Jorgensen and Robert Brom were convicted, each receiving a sentence of life plus 25 years. Officially, that was the end of it. The case was closed and never re-opened.

Eddie Jorgensen served three years before being paroled. Bob Brom was paroled three years after that. Neither man ever admitted guilt or expressed contrition, things that are normally prerequisite to being eligible for parole. To the outside observer, it appears that the parole board either didn't consider the brutal double murder to be much of a crime, or they didn't believe that Jorgensen and Brom were actually guilty.

But following the convictions, whether right or wrong, most of the evidence was lost or destroyed. Cynics have speculated that this was done to protect those involved from ever being held accountable in what they knew was a wrongful prosecution. There will be no DNA, no genetic genealogy, and probably no definitive solution to this crime. Multnomah County authorities steadfastly insist that they got the right guys.

Edward Wayne Edwards, age 77, died in an Ohio prison on April 7, 2011. He was scheduled for execution on August 31 after convictions of five murders. Looking like Jabba the Hutt, this sweating mass of human filth was suspected in at least 15 additional murders, including those of Larry Peyton and Beverly Allan. Some people even credit Edward Edwards with having been the infamous Zodiac Killer, though that seems about as likely as his also being D.B. Cooper.

* * * * * *

Edward Edwards was also considered a prime suspect in the killings of Duane Bogle and Patricia Kalitzke in Great Falls, Montana on January 3, 1956. Another suspect was James "Whitey" Bulger, who had lived in the area at the time, and was known to have committed similar crimes, both before and after the Bogle-Kalitzke murders.

But as was the case in the Candy Rogers investigation, physical evidence had been carefully preserved, and would ultimately solve the murders. In 2001, a DNA profile was developed from a sperm cell in a rape kit from Patricia Kalitzke.

Sixty-five years after the crime, on June 19, 2021, genetic genealogy led to the identity of the killer. Kenneth Gould died in Oregon County, Missouri in 2007.

* * * * * *

And finally, for those who are wondering, Kenny Murphy (whose name is not Murphy) actually did successfully burn a hole through a piece of aluminum foil with his miniature electron beam welder before the filament in the electron gun failed, due to inadequate evacuation of air from the vacuum chamber.

He was thus unable to do a live demonstration for the judges in the Central Valley High School science fair, so his technical marvel was awarded a disappointing second-place trophy in the physical sciences division.

A year later, with the custom-built vacuum chamber repurposed as a model space capsule containing live animals and plants in a self-sustaining environment that demonstrated the feasibility of long-term survival in space without external life-support systems, Kenny won the Grand Prize.

His TV repair business was briefly successful, and he sold and installed an unknown number of picture tubes. However, the enterprise interfered too much with homework, and he had to reluctantly pull his ad out of the newspaper.

He never managed to buy a 1940 Ford coupe, but he did get a 1956 Ford Victoria hardtop, and a few years later, a gold 1962 Thunderbird.

He went to Vietnam as an aviation electronics technician in the U.S. Navy. He subsequently graduated from Washington State University and became a corporate advertising executive, a whitewater rafting outfitter/guide, and a real estate broker.

He currently writes mystery novels—including this one.

Also by Ken Baysinger
El Camino

The Mendelson-Devonshire case was legendary. It was also political dynamite. The disappearance of Jessie Devonshire and Randy Mendelson had been Portland's biggest news story of 1980. It remained the area's most notorious unsolved case. It couldn't even be properly called an unsolved crime, because it had never been proven that a crime had been committed. All that was known was that fifteen-year-old Jessie Devonshire had vanished without a trace and that Randy Mendelson, a twenty-year-old landscaper, had disappeared at the same time. Everyone had a theory, but nobody had an answer to the mystery. The one fact that everyone knew was that Jessie Devonshire was the stepdaughter of Wilson Landis Devonshire, who was an official in the Portland Mayor's office and a rising star among Oregon's political elite. The case that lands in the lap of a private investigator named Corrigan had been the biggest hot potato in Clackamas County law enforcement for at least ten years following the disappearances. At least three careers had ended because detectives had been unable to provide the answers that the politically powerful principals in the case demanded.

ISBN: 978-1-947491-98-4 © 2017

Yorkshire Publishing 392 pages $19.99

www.kenbaysinger.com

Also by Ken Baysinger
Deadly Gold

A tugboat captain salvaging logs from Oregon's Willamette River snags a roll of old carpet containing the skeletal remains of a long-missing young woman, weighted down by a cast iron anchor. The private investigator called Corrigan, having just solved the notorious Mendelson-Devonshire murders, once again finds himself trying to unravel the mystery of a murder victim whose body was pulled from the river many years after her death. The investigation takes Corrigan a hundred twenty-five years back in Oregon history.

In the afternoon of May 25, 1887, thirty-four gold miners lay dead on a gravel bar where Deadline Creek flowed into the Snake River in the depths of Hells Canyon. From the surrounding bluffs, a small gang of cattle rustlers had poured gunfire down on the defenseless miners, who had committed two cardinal sins: they were Chinese, and they had found gold.

In the course of his year-long investigation into the death of Tara Foster, Corrigan learns that there is no limit to the mayhem that is triggered by lust for the Deadly Gold.

ISBN: 978-1-947491-99-1 © 2017

Yorkshire Publishing 402 pages $19.99

www.kenbaysinger.com

Also by Ken Baysinger
Missing and Exploited

A car collector looking for a place to store his vintage Studebakers stumbles across a name carved in a wooden beam from a century-old building. Just a quarter-mile away, the skeletal remains of a young woman are found outside a homeless camp. The investigation that Corrigan starts as a favor to his old friend quickly becomes a nightmare beyond anything he could have imagined. As the body count rises, the mystery becomes ever deeper, until it takes on a life of its own.

For three decades children have been vanishing without a trace, until Corrigan uncovers the terrible truth. And nothing comes without a cost. Relationships are torn apart, and at times even nature works against Corrigan and his small team of investigators as they chase down obscure clues from the cold case files. Chasing leads across five states over six months, Corrigan faces the greatest challenges of his investigative career.

ISBN: 978-1-5245-5269-5 © 2016

Xlibris 390 pages $19.99

www.kenbaysinger.com

Also by Ken Baysinger
Confluence
Second Edition

Frustrated that their "people's revolution" never materialized, a cadre of geriatric radicals hatches a plot to blow up hydropower dams in the Pacific Northwest and replicate the great ice-age floods that carved the Columbia River Gorge.

They get support through an unexpected alliance with old-line communists, the new incarnation of Russia's KGB, the government of Iran, and a would-be terrorist in Key West who has possession of a cold war era hydrogen bomb.

Undetected by Homeland Security, the plot is uncovered by "Swede" Larsson, Town Marshal in Riggins, Idaho (population 406), while investigating the seemingly accidental drowning of a young man in the Salmon River. As the scope of the conspiracy becomes apparent, Swede is joined by his river guide friend Cassidy Pierce and former Vietnam combat pilot Terry Caldwell in a desperate race to prevent a cataclysmic flood.

ISBN: 979-8-21800-779-9 © 2022

Ingram Spark 670 pages $24.99

www.kenbaysinger.com

Also by Ken Baysinger
Identities

By the time he was 77 years old, David Adelman knew that his body was failing. When he read about a seminar that would explore the medical possibilities for getting a fresh chance at being young, David's curiosity was more than just academic. Despite his skepticism, he bought a $25,000 membership in the Human Transmigration Project.

A decade later, barely clinging to life, he learns that he holds the winning ticket in mankind's greatest lottery. And this isn't a simple game of chance. It is cutting-edge medical technology, and David becomes the subject of history's first human transmigration. But his new life holds a shocking surprise that forces him to question some of his life-long beliefs about human nature. Even as he makes the unexpectedly difficult transition into his new life, he finds himself in the center of a mystery that escalates into a desperate fight for the life of a girl he knows only through a strangely vivid recurring dream. And when questionable accidents start taking lives in the small college town of Arcata, California, evidence stacks up against one young man whose motives are as sinister as his actions are devious, leading to a deadly showdown.

ISBN: 979-8-218-01586-2 © 2022

Ingram Spark 360 pages $19.99

www.kenbaysinger.com

www.ingramcontent.com/pod-product-compliance
Lightning Source LLC
LaVergne TN
LVHW021755060526
838201LV00058B/3097